Then, the barest whisper. "Do you want me?"

The sound sent chills of fear through me. I clutched the covers to me. Wasn't this what I'd been wanting? Some physical manifestation of this phantom, this female being who'd come to me in a dream all those months ago?

I felt the faintest hint of a kiss against my neck. Nails light along my arm, then across my breasts. My body responded on its own, forgetting the pain, wanting only the pleasure. Her fingers traveled down, across my belly to the inside of my thighs. I couldn't help but raise my hips, urging her fingers to once again plunge into me.

Her fingers stopped their caress. "No," she said, laughing softly. "You have to tell me you want me."

Visit

Bella Books

at

BellaBooks.com


or call our toll-free number

1-800-729-4992

# CALL OF THE DARK

Erotic Lesbian Tales of the Supernatural

*Edited by Therese Szymanski*

Bella
BOOKS

2005

Printed in the United States of America on acid-free paper
First Edition

Editor: Therese Szymanski
Cover designer: Sandy Knowles


ISBN 1-59493-040-6

# Acknowledgments

*A work such as this is obviously the collected endeavors of many people. I would like to thank all the contributors for their hard work, and all those who submitted as well. And I'd like to thank my friends Barbara Johnson, Karin Kallmaker and Joy Parks for their help above and beyond.*

*Also, I'd like to thank Judy Eda and Pam Berard for their always excellent proofreading, and of course all of Bella's excellent staff who keep the machine going.*

*Oh, and of course Linda Hill and Terese Orban—the ones who really keep it going!*

*Therese Szymanski, March 20, 2005*
*Spring Equinox (aka Ostara)*

# Contents

# Introduction

Why is it lesbian, gay, bisexual and transgendered people seem to be so attracted to the supernatural? Could it be that because of the way we have been portrayed in mainstream culture—the 50's pulp evil-lesbian temptress with blood-red nails; the vampire-like predator seducing innocents; the monsters who hide in plain sight but are recognizable through intense scrutiny—we feel a certain kinship with these creatures? Is it their intrinsic *otherness* which makes us relate to their separation from the normal world? Is it because our culture's value on youth is so over-amplified that we exalt the immortal? Or are we fascinated with vampires, were-wolves, ghosts and succubae (oh my!) because of their speed, power, might and strength?

At times, that kind of invulnerability could come in handy. Honestly, who wouldn't want that added *oomph* to maul foes who seek to cage you like the wolf you become when the moon is full? Who couldn't use a little shape-shifting magic when a mob of angry villagers is at the door?

If this is the case, then how to explain the contradiction presented by the enormous gay fan base of shows like *Buffy the Vampire Slayer*? If we really do relate with or want to be like the creatures of the night—powerful, immortal vamps and demons—then why do we pop some corn and let the machine take our calls one hour each week so we can watch our otherworldly comrades end up dusty, bloody, beaten and dead? Is it because we know that even supernaturals can be good, and normal people can be evil? Or does it just mean we like beautiful people in really cool clothes (especially if said clothes are black and/or leather)?

Ψ

Shortly after having knee surgery, I was following my sister up a mountain in the lower Sierras with a fifty-pound pack on my back, trying to think about anything that would keep my mind off the pain, heat, bugs and sun, but mostly upcoming writing deadlines that had compelled me to drive across the country in the first place. All that avoidance must have stirred up an odd assortment of thoughts, because I looked at my straight sister, and said, without apparent provocation, "I really need to edit an anthology of sleazy lesbian supernatural stories."

She pretty much ignored me, even though she uttered a few interested-seeming words. She was being polite.

I know that feeling of otherness. I'm the only gay kid in a family of five. I'm the only writer in a household of engineers. But the truth is, most folks are *other* in some respect or another. And despite technologies and other developments that give us more ways to come together, we seem to go out of our way to find ever-more new things to distance ourselves from each other and create new categories of *otherness*. Want an example? Just look at the laundry list of self-identifiers in our own *community*.

Why we need to create these divisions is beyond my comprehension, since we've already got enough people willing to take a stand against us. It's why I focus on making women happy instead of writing political manifestos.

In fact, anyone who knows me will tell you I'm not really big on lofty sentiments, profound insights or deep thoughts. I live to give pleasure. And that's exactly what this collection is all about. Besides, ghosts, mummies, daemons and other beasties are severely overlooked in the realm of erotic lesbian fiction. I think it's time they had a chance at equality, starting here.

*Reese Szy*

# Lilith
## Karin Kallmaker

I don't get hung up on labels. Definitions can be so inadequate. For instance, most would call me a succubus. I am a female demon, yes, but it's not sleeping *men* I prefer to stalk in the long weary hours of night. My preference is now decidedly sleeping women, and that transition is part of my tale. But that preference would make me an incubus, were it not for my own decidedly female characteristics when I take human form. Not that I have been able to do that for years now—and that restriction is also part of my tale.

Regardless, succubus I am, and have always been.

I digress.

At issue, you must understand, is the fact that a demon is not meant to outlive her witch. I am not a being of intent, but one of power. It was my witch who thought up uses for me. Sometimes I was an affliction, and others a reward. When she was in a truly bad mood, I was both. It made no difference to me as long as I did what my witch had created me to do.

What was her intent? Like most witches she was part scientist and her goal was to create a new and improved succubus. The old model was often traced by priests or magicians and destroyed. That represented a waste of investment for witches, and she was determined to create an untraceable succubus. A kind of a

Succubus-Plus, you might say. If my witch could figure it all out, she'd have a line of Platinum-card-carrying adepts outside her laboratory door.

She had a good working idea of what she wanted. No actual physical form, which meant far easier arrivals and departures, and leaving no physical traces behind. Nothing for other bed partners to wake and find, and nothing for a wand-wielding do-gooder to sense. Instead of genitals, the new and improved succubus went directly to the primary sex organ in the human being—the brain, of course.

The first new model was untraceable, that's for sure. Disappeared so well my witch couldn't find her. The vict—er, test subject—showed no signs of arousal either.

The second try the witch included a tracking feature so that at least *she* could trace the demon. Succubus 2 found Succubus 1, and the two of them proceeded to redefine demonic sex. The witch, it seemed, had forgotten to include desire for humans in the mix.

Succubus-the-Millennium-Edition was hot for humans and the witch knew where she was at all times. In her invisible form, StheME craved contact with humans. Just one little problem: she found her exploration of the human sexual psyche completely absorbing. The witch's libido, long ignored in deference to scientific pursuits, was not as interesting as that of her test subjects. And so StheME would not come back, no matter how the witch called. Hard as it is to believe, StheME chose to be discontinued over loss of her human-spawned experiences. The highest achievement of the witch's art was a dismal failure.

She gave up.

You're probably wondering why I said that she gave up, because it's clear that she didn't or else I wouldn't be telling you my story. But she did give up, for a time. Then she thought of what might have persuaded StheME to phone home. Perhaps it was a dark and stormy night, all alone, when she considered what might have some allure. Her libido wasn't dead, as it turned out, it was just underemployed.

So she created me, and named me Lilith. I was everything that

StheME had been. I could enter the sleeping mind of any human and, drawing on my pre-loaded encyclopedic knowledge of humans and their sex play, plant fantasies there. I played them for the sleeper, wringing every last physical response. Mission accomplished, I would go home to my witch, after my subject was drained to incoherence, to claim the reward she offered for a job well done.

The reward? She would make me real for one night. For that night I would have fingers and breasts and a tongue—skin, I would have skin! I would be able to experience many of the physical pleasures with which I had tormented my subjects. Only my witch could make me real and so I must always return to her.

It was a good plan.

My first assignment was to bring a gentleman of leisure to the point of seeing reason. He owed my witch both money and respect. She allotted me one full turning of the moon to do as I liked. Then she would deliver a note explaining how he could get rid of the most pleasurable and distracting curse ever devised.

It all went well. He focused on sex the way a banker contemplated interest rates. Finding his libido was easy. He preferred women and so did I—a surprise to me as my design was to be pansexual. Perhaps some of my witch's bias crept into her spellmaking, given what she was contemplating as my eventual reward.

Whatever. I am what I am. Regardless, my inventive musings were to his liking. I created women of such wickedly wanton dispositions that his ego swelled (along with the rest of him) whenever I merely whispered his name seductively. "You're the king," I'd coo. "You're the master." He loved it.

That's no ego talking. Night one was over too soon for him, and night two he canceled a date to go to sleep, perchance to "dream" again. I guided him to my ever-expanding repertoire of willing, begging, insatiable women who assured king and master that only *he* could relieve their suffering. We played out the *hareem* scenario over and over. And over. And over. From the moment he slept, to the moment he woke. Within days he wanted to do nothing but sleep. I was all for that.

Night six was going along really well. Blondes tonight, just blondes. I have that mood sometimes. I dreamed up blondes that made me long to return to my witch (blonde) and have my reward. I knew all that I would do, all I would taste, caress, suckle. My dreams were his ruin.

Night six, however, there was some trouble with *his* dreams. Sleeping humans dream constantly. Oh, the drivel is endless. A cigar may be a cigar sometimes, but it is unfuckingbelievably boring all of the time, not to mention unpredictable.

As any demon will tell you, messing around on the dream plane is risky. Night six I took a wrong turn and was out of my dreams and into the percussive intensity of his. They were wild with music and color, rich with insatiable, inventive women as inspired as my own conjurings, and even more addictive was that his dreams were mighty oaks based on seeds of real experiences, laden with scent and sensation. They were as close to what I imagined my night of being in a skin of my own would be like.

I wanted more. Was this what StheME had discovered?

The woman of his dreams was cooing his name. Her swollen, red center opened to his gaze and taking. I wished his dream had lingered over the scent of her and the thick beauty of her wet. That was when I realized I had no way of controlling his focus as I did when using my own female-inspired material. Coos became caws, red flesh melted to goo. Presto, change-o—I was plopped nipples deep in parrots and persimmon pulp.


That's when I found something else floating free in his mind. Not a dream—a wish. Not even wishes, but imaginings. Positions impossible for a human male to achieve. Joinings that only looked interesting but gave little pleasure, but just looking was downright incendiary. Couplings that made his heart pound, blood flow.

I had found the secret, hidden world of *his* fantasies.

The witch had not told me about fantasies. Perhaps *they* were what StheME had found and I understood their appeal. Like dreams they were seeded by real experience, but unlike dreams they are ultimately safe because only the rare few fantasize about situations where they are truly not in control. Inherent in fantasy is the power of No and a multitude of safe but salacious Yeses. Persimmons appear only when they are truly wanted.

It did turn out he had a persimmon fetish, but that's beside the point.

Night after night I worked through his fantasies that I liked best. I would enjoy lusty hours of voyeuristic pleasures as he imagined spying on his *hareem* at play. He imagined the induction of a newcomer at the hands of his experienced, wickedly inventive wives and I drank in every moan. Even when he watched them together for hours, then impossibly satisfied all seventeen, one wife after another dropping to sleep with a "please, my king, I can take no more," I had a fine time. The witch had given me a full turning of the moon to complete my task. He was a shadow of his former self in ten days.

Lilith, my witch called me. I eschewed male couplings and brought ruin to their lives. I did so with relish. I enjoyed my work.

"Lilith, come to me," she would command softly.

I brought her the gifts of the fantasies I had gleaned. She made me real. She gave me skin. She gave me substance, form, scent and air in my lungs. I could feel my pounding heart and the exquisite pleasure of my taut, arched body responding to her touch. With her I revealed the fantasies I had experienced.

Her libido took off like the proverbial bat out of hell.

Demons are not supposed to outlive their witches. A succubus usually runs afoul of a local enchanter or priest. My methods, however, were so quick and painless that I escaped before my presence was even suspected.

Did my witch grow rich and powerful from the licensing of

Lilith 1.0? No, and therein lies the irony. She had created me to magnify—to make magnificent—sexual experience. After my first, wildly successful assignment I brought her fantasies and we lived them together.

Science yielded to sensuality. She made me flesh and skin and wet and *real*. I was in her mind, finding *her* fantasies, things she'd ignored or sequestered for years, showing her what she wanted, what would please her, and she was in my body, on my body, commanding my body.

And so she fell victim to her own curse. She kept me in her bed because I was exactly what she had made me to be. She did try to send me to a second haunting, but it was only four days before she recalled me to her.

"Lilith, come to me."

The next only two days.

"Lilith, come to me."

Then she would not let me go anywhere but to bed with her.

"Lilith, come to me. Come for me. Come with me. Come . . ."


I can only be what I was made to be. I knew I was fatal to her but could not make her care. Only at the very last did she try to change my nature. By then she was too far gone to effectively install the critical patch that would give me an OFF switch.

She went, utterly spent, to her next turn of the wheel and I became as insubstantial as her last breath. Floating, untraceable, unreal. There was no one to use my power. Some other succubus might bind herself to a new witch but that, for me, was a Catch-22. For me to find a new witch she had to be able to see me. And she couldn't see me unless I was bound to her. My witch checked out without giving anyone the password or source code for Lilith 1.0.

Wherever I drifted I listened for the one thing I knew I would never hear again: "Lilith, come to me."

There was no one to ask, freely and willingly, for me to come.

Ψ

A girl's gotta eat, even this one.

I continued to do as I had learned. Haunting men was easier because their fantasies were usually of women. I did not drain them—I was without malice toward them. I needed only to fill my own emptiness. If they were clever I might leave them tired, but the creativity of one man might span only several nights before I wearied of vastly unrealistic parades of their prowess.

King or peasant, when it came to fantasy, they were much the same. A pillowed bower or a warm, rustling haystack, the setting didn't matter to me. It was the women in their minds that I sought. Outlandish as a siren or as sweet as a first tumble, all I have wanted in the long, lonely night was to lose myself in fantasies of women. I hoped, in vain, that doing so might ease the emptiness in my existence.

I gathered ever more fantasies and yet had no witch with whom to share them. Truly, to have tales and no one to tell—is there anything sadder?

Oh sure, there are those who have said and will say I've got it easy. I have no mortgage, no credit card bills. I don't have to work out or worry that my cell is out of range of the tower. All I need is billions of men fantasizing about billions of women—what's so hard about that?

Well, think about it.

Few men linger appreciatively over the scent of a woman's wetness. Even fewer taste her and enjoy it with half the appreciation they might a glass of wine. They might thrill to the touch of a yielding body, but most never see how a woman's gentleness is also her strength. A hard nipple might delight, but only one in ten thousand would stop to enjoy the contrast between its hardness and the soft breast it graced. A strong, powerful woman might bring their blood to a boil, but it was her power, not her femaleness, that fascinated them.

That a woman could melt in passion is a gift rarely appreciated by a male rutting in his own fantasies. And they are *his* fantasies, after all, and what he needed. I was just along for the ride. And since I wasn't haunting them for my own rewards with my witch, why share with them *my* fantasies? It didn't seem like they deserved it, most of them.

I drifted from city to city, country to country. I found lesbians to haunt, don't get me wrong. *Look, look, look to the rainbow*, I like to sing. As a result, there are a number of very happy lesbians around the world now, relishing sex in new ways. I personally boosted the per capita spending on sex toys in Great Britain. Though I blush to brag of it, I was instrumental in putting the more interesting sex back in the, uh, city. But I always had to force myself to leave or they would get addicted. I wasn't real to them and that hurt in a way that did not bother me with men.

As I entered my seventh year, and was doubtless long past my planned obsolescence, my hunger to be real, to have a body and fingers and mouth, was so strong and so impossible that I began to think of end ways.

No one knows how long demons live. We don't outlive our witches, don't you see? I was the one wasting away now. Food all around me in the fantasies of men and not a morsel that would nourish me any longer.

I wanted the smile of a woman for me, the kind of smile my witch had given me, seeing me. I could no longer bear the smiles of women through the filter of men's eyes.

Demons have patience, even heartsick ones who wish to end.

A lesbian, again. I longed so much to be real that I felt the one in danger of addiction. My chaste Boston redhead fantasized about her next-door neighbor to the exclusion of any other pursuit. Life is too short, honey, I wished I could tell her. Instead, I broke into her nightly frustration—she wouldn't even touch herself—with images gleaned from a German photographer who had snapped pictures of over two thousand cunts. Photos so real I could almost smell the subjects. I wanted to taste and drown and my Boston redhead got no sleep for two nights.

On the third she asked her neighbor over for a glass of wine. They finished the bottle and once the first nipple was touched I couldn't get a word in edgewise, so to speak. The photo gallery had done the trick, however, and I was treated to a prolonged vicarious submersion into the wonders of the female body.

The redhead (and her new lover) were elated. I was more depressed than ever. I'm a succubus, you know, not a sex therapist.

Lesbian reality was too painful. Male perceptions of women too shallow. I wanted lips and eyes, a nose and legs. I needed a witch to make me real. I longed to be called to her bed. A voice in my ear crooning my name, loving what I am, what I give, what I take. Wanting me for exactly what I can be.

I took a ride on a train to I-didn't-care. I rifled through fantasies. Though I'd never been interested in anything not related to sex, I lingered for a month of crisscrossing journeys in old minds musing for bones that did not ache, and students picturing their first paycheck. Daughters who hungered for another hour with departed mothers. Mothers that wept on the inside, envisioning triumphs, graduations or grandchildren that would never be. Lonely hearts fantasizing of the moment they would look into the eyes of their one, true love.

If a demon could weep, I would. If a demon could end herself, I would end.

A gleaming city with rainbow flags snapping in the summer breeze greeted me when I left the trains. Raucous marching, furtive couplings, spirited dancing was all around me. I wanted to join the fun, spin in the sunlight, proclaim myself to be what I am.

I'm female, I love woman, can't I join your parade? I see that pets get to march, so you do include non-humans, don't you?

Slightly heartened by the sheer thrill of living that hundreds of thousands were sharing, I explored the mind of a creatively under-dressed brunette whose skin was thickly decorated with a variety of flowers, devils and creatures of prey. Her fantasy world was certainly rife with fodder. Drawing on a night I'd spent with an expert fetish worker, I gave her a zap of my own.

She didn't notice.

Perplexed more than anything else, I took her obviously cherished vision of two overly thin but wonderfully endowed brunettes and added a setting of a very real Irish dungeon.

Not one part of her reacted. She couldn't hear me! Was I losing my touch?

I tried another, this one in jeans and simple T-shirt towing a toddler by one hand. She'd never acted on her fantasy of a night with two very attentive lovers, but I gilded the lily of that fantasy for her and once again there was no reaction.

These lesbians not only couldn't see me, they couldn't perceive my fantasies. They were immune to Lilith 1.0!

I cast about for a witch. There must be a witch here, someone shielding all of them or controlling their minds. There was a woman speaking. I circled her mind—she was a writer, and most certainly no witch. She was blathering on about characters and sexual freedom and how important it was to allow for all kinds of expression. I thought, "Oh yeah? You want expression? Try this on for size, honey."

I was none too gentle slipping into the layer of her fantasies. Okay, she was inventive, I'll give her that. Biker daddies morphed into brown-clad delivery women who slipped into houses at the invitation of a robe-wrapped female and they ran upstairs together . . .

Except then they weren't on stairs, it was a hiking trail and they reached a summit with a beautiful, flat rock and their backpacks held endless supplies of blankets and toys and wine and chocolate and . . .

Painfully loud music thumped all around them as they ground together on a dance floor so crowded it was nearly impossible to tell whose hands were whose. Thighs split legs, shirts were torn open . . .

A voice from behind her fantasy self said, "You know you want this."

From in front of her, "Spread your legs for me."

All around her, a clamor of pleas. "Please, give it to me, I need it, do it, please . . . take me, suck me, fuck me, do it now . . ."

She groaned back to every demand a single, powerful, "Yes."

I was suspended in her fantasies, so rich and multi-layered, stunned to my core. I had never thought to find a mind that rivaled my own for fluidity, for the ability to tweak any factor any direction to turn up the heat.

I wasn't going to let some human one-up me. I was an expert in fantasy, after all.

Her ever-playing cineplex of fields and bars and—oh my, the Louvre and the White House just slipped past—was something I could work with. An airplane bathroom became the deck of a masted sailing ship. A sultry flight attendant was suddenly a pirate ready to buckle her swash with a willing, captive wench.

I realized I'd been watching for several minutes. Time for a little action of my own. I plugged my ears to the sound of the wench's joyful moans—they were quite lovely to hear and seemed so real—and a soft white rope appeared to hold the panting woman more firmly in place.

The pirate almost laughed, she liked the idea that much. Well, this human could hear me just fine. Now to show her who was boss.

The pirate was whispering, "That's right, my love, we're not going to stop until you can't move."

The wench, between gasps, answered, "I know you'll take care of me, please don't stop."

I bent the setting to my intent, drawing again on that Irish dungeon. My little writer had liked the ropes, so how about some shackles and chains?

For just a moment, the small captain's cabin shimmered to the walls of my fantasy dungeon. Then the cabin solidified again. The pirate was still a pirate, the wench still a wench.

Frustrated, I was about to try something else when the pirate raised her head and looked at me.

She said, "Enough of that for now. Maybe sometime soon." And then she went back to her panting, moaning wench, and took care of her, I might add, until neither of them seemed able to move.

If I had a body, I suppose my jaw would have hit the proverbial floor. This fantasy was so strong in her mind, even while she was preoccupied with speaking to a crowd, that I couldn't sway it.

I tried several times, let me tell you. I informed little-miss-love-those-ropes that I was a succubus, damn it, and nobody tells a succubus what to do. I told her my whole long, sad tale. Every thought, every discovery. My witch's plans and the irony of her failure. I emphasized that I was, to use the language of the sex play session being held in one of the nearby booths, the ultimate Top. I knew precisely where consent ended, and fulfilled fantasies to perfection. No trumped-up excuse for a sexual being was going to change that.

The battle was on, because, well, she had to sleep sometime.

The march ended, the booths all closed. She talked to friends and non-friends and all the while her rich background fantasies were playing for me to examine. Every once in a while, as with the ropes, I succeeded in slipping something into the mix. She was hot and wet and heavy with desire when she got home.

She lived alone—what a surprise. Someone so bossy was sure to piss everyone off. She opened the trunk at the foot of the bed and to my delight showed me she was no stranger to wonderful accessories. She selected a few.

And we went to bed.


Her fantasies had been rich and real while she was distracted with other things. Free to focus now completely on her wants, she unfurled a depth of sexual desire and abandon that took my breath away. Was it the most outlandish range I'd ever seen? No. The most varied or perverse? No.

But it was easily the most real. She described everything in her mind with detail that left me ever more aware of how long it had been since I'd felt my witch's moaning body under me. She pictured every whorl and ripple on a woman's hand, kissed the fingers, the palm, the knuckles. She imagined the faint taste of salt on her tongue as she flicked it over a lover's soft earlobe. From the depths of her love of women rose twining lights of need and fulfillment, around and around, swirling like lovers in a soul dance.

She gave me the shock of hot, wet, clasping flesh around a cool fingertip.

My lips felt coated with the proof of a woman's passion and I had forgotten how sweet, how primal, how luscious and delicious it tasted.

I gave my infiltration of her fantasies one last try. I wanted to stay in them for a very long time. I was as close to real as I could be.

She rubbed her lips on her fantasy lover's hand, a vibrant yes swelling her body. She drew it to her pulsing cunt and closed her eyes, willing the fingers to go inside her. Sliding in . . . slow . . . stopping to savor the feel of flesh, soft and taut and so slippery.

"Please," she whispered. "Please."

*Please what, honey? Please this?* I nudged the fingers with my mind and her fantasy body gasped as she was taken, filled. "Is that better?"

"Yes."

"Are you ready for me? Ready to do this?"

"Yes."

She was all yes. Wonderfully yes. I had control of the fantasy hand in her vision and I could feel her heat against me. It was my hand pleasuring her and I dipped my mouth to where my fingers were sinking further and further into her swollen depths. I tasted, I drank, and she was all yes.


"Is that what you wanted?"

It was her question to me, when she at last was sated. Her mind was still in a fantasy place where I was real. I didn't want her to stir, to wake up. I wanted to stay like this forever.

Softly, I murmured, "Yes."

"Good, because it was what I wanted, too."

She turned over in bed to face me. "Poor thing, you've traveled so far. Been so alone."

I could only nod. Some part of her saw far more than the fantasies I shared. Her eyes were open and the blue-green heat in them was warming parts of me I could not deny had been cold and empty.

"I have to admit, I'd not thought of the pirate tying the wench to the bunk. That was inspired. I think we'll work well together."

She kissed me.

I felt her mouth on mine. Smelled her on my face as she kissed me.

A little laugh escaped her and she whispered in my ear, "I wonder what a succubus tastes like."

My body trembled in her arms. She was no witch, but this was magic. She was imagining me into reality.

I wanted to be real for her. I wanted to be real and forever with her. "I can't linger," I said, desperately trying to find some kind of truth.

"Don't worry about that," she murmured. Her teeth nipped at my shoulder. "Your witch might not have known where to find her off switch, but I do."

"I'm the one who needs an off switch, or I'll drain you completely."

Her blue-green gaze fixed me in place then. "The flaw in the programming isn't that you can't help being what you are. The flaw is assuming that I am not in control of who I am. You're a being of intent, not power, right?"

She showed me a fantasy book in her head, where she'd written down everything I'd told her in my long, sad tale. "Right there— you said you were a being of intent."

"What's your point?"

"You have no power over me. You intend to give me pleasure, but I control me. You will overwhelm me only if I forget that. Your witch forgot. Your, uh, test subjects, didn't have a chance to prepare. But you told me all your secrets." She closed the book in her mind. "You didn't know you had your own passwords all the time, did you? You gave them to me."

She was not a witch, but she was all magic.

"And when I sleep you will be real, here, in my head where it really matters. People will wonder where I get the inspiration. But we'll know, won't we?"

She took my hand and I could feel the reality of her warm skin on mine. I could not tell if she was asleep or awake and it did not matter to me. I had someone to whom I could tell my tales and who would tell my stories, all of them. Someone who knew I was there. Someone who saw me, wanted me for exactly what I was.

Demons do not cry, yet my cheeks were wet. She said something and I didn't catch it. So she said it again.

"Lilith, come to me."

# By the Light of the Moon
## Radclyffe

"Come on, J.," my best friend Trudy said. "We need a fourth."

I set a glass of wine by her elbow and glanced at the object in the center of the card table, then at the three women eagerly studying me. "I never heard there was a quota."

"Come on," she whined, half cajoling, half hurt. "You said you'd play."

"No," I said with exaggerated politeness. "I did *not* say that. I said you were all welcome to hang out here and watch the eclipse."

That particular night was one of those rare confluences of science and superstition, when even ordinarily rational people surrendered to mysticism. It was All Hallows' Eve, the moon was full and bright in an otherwise inky-dark sky, and there was about to be a total lunar eclipse. Everywhere around the world, I was certain, Wiccans danced naked in tree-bordered glades and pagans prayed to the goddesses of yore. That was fine with me, and I sincerely hoped that they had a magical experience. My problem was that three of my good friends sat with a Ouija board poised between them, waiting for me to join them and summon a spirit from across the great divide. Presumably, the Ouija board was the vehicle to open the gate between our world and the other dimensions that some believed coexisted side by side with our own. Trudy insisted that everything was conspiring to ensure our success. Success at what, I wasn't entirely certain.

"You three go ahead. I'll light the candles."

I turned off the room lights and opened the drapes, exposing the floor-to-ceiling windows in the French doors, beyond which lay the gently rolling slope of lawn behind my house. The moon was a huge, shimmering globe above the treetops, and silver light immediately suffused the room with a warmth that was tangible. Even as I watched, a tiny sliver of midnight inched its way over the edge of the moon, marring its perfect beauty. I struck a match to the candles in several ornate silver candleholders that had been my grandmother's, knowing that in just a few moments, the room would be cast into total darkness. When I finished, I turned to find three sets of eyes still regarding me hopefully. With a sigh, I took the fourth seat at the table. I wasn't entirely certain of the source of my reluctance, and it seemed churlish to ruin their fun.

"Well," Trudy began with an eager note infusing her soft Southern accent, "y'all put your fingertips lightly on the planchette. Now remember, don't press too hard."

The instant my fingertips touched the smooth, varnished wood, I felt it. Some shift in the air. A faint tingle in the back of my throat. The barest stirring of blood deep, deep inside me. The sound of my own heart beating magnified inside my head. Of course I knew that it was only the involuntary rush of epinephrine prompted by my surprise as a faint breeze flickered the flames in the candles on the far side of the room. *Breeze?* It was early fall in New England. I didn't leave the windows open at night. I would have searched for the source of the cool breath against my face if all of my attention had not been riveted to the Ouija board. As I watched the planchette rock gently back and forth in a small semi-circle, I heard Trudy's voice, muffled and soft, as if she were speaking from a great distance. For some reason, I could only catch every few words through the low hum in my ears.

" . . . friends . . . welcome . . . visit . . . lonely . . . "

One after the other, the candles guttered and went out. The moonlight, which moments before had illuminated the room nearly as brightly as sunshine, was quickly fading. I knew without looking that the shadow of the night now nearly covered the face of the moon. The planchette vibrated, sliding in an ever-widening circle on the board, jumping from letter to letter too quickly for my eyes to decipher. Was it spelling something in its frantic race from place to place, or merely reflecting the chaos of our own hidden secrets and desires?

" . . . waiting . . ."

My arms shook with the effort to keep the small pointer from flying into the air. Energy poured through my fingertips, along the avenues of my muscles and nerves, stirring anticipation in my depths. Anticipation that was surprisingly sensual, as if some memory of a touch long past had been awakened. The darkness was so complete I could see nothing, the silence so dense I could hear nothing, not even the shuddering breaths of the women beside me. And then, with crystal clarity, I heard her voice.

"Can you help me?"

The planchette stopped moving. Someone gasped. In the same instant, a dull thud registered in my overstimulated yet strangely sluggish brain. I froze, my heart seizing. Then the sound came again.

Knocking.

"There's someone at the door," I said in a surprisingly steady voice, lifting my fingers from the pointer.

"Don't answer it," Trudy said sharply.

One of the candles burst into flame, and I could see my friends' eyes open wide with apprehension.

"Spirits don't use the door," I murmured as I rose.

For some reason, I felt no need to turn on the lights, making my way through the home of my childhood with the certainty born of having traveled the same path countless times before. Without hesitation, I pulled open the heavy wooden door and looked out.

"I'm so sorry," she said. "Can you help me?"

*Can you help me?* I recognized her voice, but I was certain I had never seen her before.

"My car . . . I'm afraid I've run it into a ditch. It was so dark . . ."

Her voice trailed off, and I realized that I was staring. There was almost no light reaching the tree-shrouded porch through a sky so black that even starlight did not penetrate. For some reason that I failed to comprehend and did not bother to question, I could see her face clearly. It was an ordinary face, if you could call simple beauty ordinary. Smooth, high forehead, wide, faintly almond-shaped eyes that even in the dark I knew with certainty were a pale shade of blue, prominent cheekbones tapering to her soft but well defined chin. She was slightly shorter than I and somewhere close to my age. She regarded me with a quizzical expression tinged with doubt.

"I'm sorry," she repeated. "If I could use your phone?"

"Where is your car?"

"Just up the road there." She pointed over her shoulder, although there was nothing to be seen in the dark.

"I didn't realize it was raining."

For a moment, she said nothing, then glanced at the damp blouse that clung to her slender shoulders and full breasts. With a self-conscious laugh, she plucked the material away from her body.

"It started just before I went off the road. The sky just opened and the entire storm struck at once. I couldn't see a thing."

I nodded. My porch was dry. From behind me, I heard the faint hum of conversation from the living room. My unexpected visitor shivered.

"Why don't you come in and get warm. I'll take a look at your car."

"Oh, no," she said immediately. "I'll just call a garage."

"Even if you can find someone to come out here this late, it will take several hours. And you look like you're freezing." I held the door open. "There's a guest room at the top of the stairs on your left. If you want to get out of your wet clothes, there's a robe behind the door in the adjoining bathroom. You can get a hot shower, too, if you'd like."

"That would be wonderful."

As she stepped inside, she ran her fingertips lightly down my forearm and whispered, "Thank you." It was the kind of innocent touch that people exchange every day. Innocent and casual. The swift surge of desire that seared through me nearly dropped me to my knees. I caught my breath in surprise, but she didn't seem to notice. I watched until she had climbed the stairs and disappeared into the dark hallway above. Then I returned to my friends.

"Who was it?" Trudy asked curiously.

"Just someone who needed directions."

In my absence they had begun to gather their things, and I made no effort to convince them to stay. I didn't question why I didn't tell them about my visitor. I only knew that I didn't want one of them to offer her a ride into town. I walked with them to the front door, gave all the appropriate responses about getting together again soon, and watched until their cars disappeared from sight. Then I removed the large battery-operated flashlight from just inside the foyer closet and walked rapidly down my driveway to the road. Less than two minutes later, guided by the wavering yellow beam of light, I saw where the bushes lining the road had been destroyed by a careening vehicle. Nearly the entire car was in the ditch, and nothing short of a tow truck was going to get it out. The driver's door stood open and, when I shined my light inside, I saw that the windshield was cracked.

In less than five minutes I had returned to my house. I hurried upstairs, and then was strangely reluctant to enter the guest bedroom. Tentatively, I knocked on the partially open door and heard a soft voice call for me to enter. Once again, I had no trouble seeing although the night outside was still pitch black and the room lights were off. She stood by the window, her back to me, in a thigh-length white robe that appeared far sheerer than I remembered. The outline of her breasts and hips was unmistakable. She did not turn as I approached or move at all as I rested my hands gently on her shoulders.

"Are you hurt?"

She leaned infinitesimally back against my body, her head resting lightly against my shoulder. "No."

"From the looks of your windshield, you must have hit your head pretty hard in the crash."

She reached up for my hands and drew my arms down and around her waist, relaxing fully into my embrace. Her hair smelled of shampoo and autumn. She fit perfectly into the contours of my form, as if we were reciprocal sides of the same mold.

"If I did, I don't remember."

"What do you remember?"

"Knowing that you would answer the door, that you would invite me in."

She turned in my arms and slid hers around my neck. The robe fell open as her mouth found my neck. Her lips were soft, warm, as they traveled along the underside of my jaw, her tongue a teasing ribbon of heat. I arched my throat, offering her more. Her teeth grazed my earlobe, and she laughed quietly.

"I can feel how fast the blood is racing through your veins. I'm not a vampire, but I almost wish I were."

"What are you?" I whispered, smoothing my palms over her collarbones and underneath the now nearly translucent material of her robe. Even as I watched, the last tendrils of material drifted into the darkness and left her pale skin glowing in the light of the moon.

"Does it matter?"

Her words were a wash of heat against my ear that stirred my blood even more. With a groan, I closed my hands over her breasts. They were full and firm and hot to my touch. She was no spectre, no illusion. She was flesh, and I wanted her.

I had thought myself a sensitive lover, but I barely recognized myself as I drove her back toward the bed with the force of my hands on her body and my tongue in her mouth. When she struck the edge of the mattress and fell, I was close upon her. I had a fleeting thought that it was I who had become the vampire. I hungered for her, thirsted for her, ached for the taste and scent and wild glory of her. Vaguely aware of her hands fisted in my hair, I pressed my fingers high between her legs and found her wet and open, waiting for me. Her passion inflamed me, and with my teeth against the tender skin of her breasts, I entered her—not slowly, not with the gentle care of a new lover, but with the raging need of the long starved at the first glimpse of nourishment.

She uttered a victorious cry and arched beneath me, tilting her hips to take me deeper. Fully clothed still, I scissored my legs around her thigh, squeezing to ease the pressure building dangerously deep inside me. I claimed her, hard and fast, but I knew even as she closed around me in the first shock of orgasm that it was I who was owned. Her pleasure tore through me like a sweet drug, curling beneath my defenses to burn its mark forever upon my soul. As she came, over and over, pulling me with her into sweet oblivion, I knew with absolute certainty that I would never again ache for the touch of any other woman.

When I awoke, the first hint of dawn limned the room. The bed beside me was empty, and only the ache in my body and the persistent beat of desire in my depths assured me it had not been a dream. The robe hung on the back of the bathroom door, just as I had left it weeks before. There were no stray hairs on the pillow, no scent of love or lust lingering on the sheets. Weak limbed and faintly disoriented, I retrieved my flashlight and stumbled out into the early morning in search of her. I found the spot where her car had left the road, but the bushes were intact and there was no evidence of an accident. I scoured both sides of the highway for a mile in either direction and found no sign of her. Exhausted, I returned and fell into a troubled sleep plagued by the sound of her passion and the memory of her desire.

When I finally emerged from the torpor that had suffused me for most of the day, I showered and dressed with the efficiency of an automaton. As I started downstairs, my eyes were drawn to a small white card on the table just inside the door. With a rush of wild anticipation, I clambered down the remaining stairs and snatched it up. My heart leapt into my throat. The words were scripted in a clear, delicate hand.

*Call me.*

Eagerly, I turned the card in my fingers and stared in astonishment. There was nothing else—no number, no address. Nothing. Slowly, I sat on the bottom step, turning the card over and over in nerveless fingers. The house grew still and dark around me, and still I sat. At last, I stood and opened the front door, half expecting her to be there. The night was nearly as deep as the previous one, although this time the moon was bright and gave no sign of ever having been overpowered by shadow. I waited, calling to her in my mind, but she did not come.

Finally, I closed the door and made my way through the silent house, more aware of being alone than I had ever been before. When I reached the living room, I stopped and stared, remembering that I had taken time the previous night for nothing but her. Slowly, I sat down at the card table and rested my fingers on the planchette in the center of the Ouija board. Closing my eyes, I let her memory take me. I saw her face shimmer with passion, felt the softness of her lips on my neck and the smooth silken heat of her skin beneath my fingers. The planchette moved, but still I kept my eyes closed. I listened to her cries of ecstasy, felt my own body stir and surge toward orgasm, only to falter before the peak. Without her, I would perish from longing. I trembled, breathless, so hungry for her presence I feared I would bleed.

"Please," I whispered. "Please."

"I'm here."

Her words were a wash of heat against my ear. I opened my eyes and found myself in the bedroom again, my arms around her supple form, nothing between us now but desire.

"What are you?" I asked, knowing that the answer did not matter.

"Not what others have named me," she whispered with her mouth against my breast. She moved beneath me, stirring the hunger. This time, I took her inside me as I lost myself in her.

Reality was the dream; she was past and future. I emptied my mind of all that had been as the first surge of orgasm captured us both and I followed her by the light of the moon into the dark side of the night.

# The Feast of
# St. Lucy
## Victoria A. Brownworth

That night had been deeper and darker than it ever seemed to get in New Orleans, a night devoid of moon and seemingly of stars, fog a thickened skin between what was and what had been. Out on the river, foghorns blew their melancholy glissandi, in funereal complement.

On that December night, the thirteenth, the feast of St. Lucy, Sandrine Mørdsen, an exchange student on a long-expired visa, had left home and never returned.

No one looked for her. No one found her.

When Sandrine awoke just before dawn on St. Lucy's day, sadness slammed her with wave upon heartbreaking wave. So many losses. Today meant yet another.

It wasn't that Sandrine would have donned the flowing white embroidered nightgown of her childhood and prepared the tray of tea and little sugared cakes. Nor lit the candles after she had ringed her long blonde hair with sprigs of holly and walked, tray in hand, lit in the endless dark of Arctic winter only by the candle, singing in her reedy alto of St. Lucy as she climbed the narrow stairs to her now-dead parents' bedroom. She was, after all, no longer a child—or that child. At twenty-five, she was now a good decade older than any Swedish girl who would be the Lucy of the house on that most important feast day so central to the melding of religious and pagan rituals. A feast all about light and forgiveness in a country in which light came for only brief glints throughout darkly tumultuous and harshly unforgiving winters.

This St. Lucy's day dawned dark, like home, and, like Sandrine's heart, unforgiving.

Sandrine had grown up in Sundsvall, a small seaside town on the east coast of Sweden, a town of biting winds, kippered *fisk* and the briny taste of the sea everywhere. When she had left for Uppsala and the university, she had not planned to go home again. Rather she had hoped to leave Sweden for good—go west to Europe—first the Netherlands, then Berlin, then perhaps the States.

It had all happened much more quickly, though. Uppsala had led to her affair with Hanne, and Berlin—Hanne's Berlin—had come within her first year away from home. Together they had gone to New York, exchange students in a pre-9/11 time when visas went untracked and blonde girls with European good looks could stay in the States on expired papers and rarely worry, their flawless if accented English granting them entrée and decent jobs in shops, restaurants and bars. Later, Sandrine had come to New Orleans. New Orleans, where on this morning she was reminded of Sundsvall, of home, in ways she could articulate to no one. Even if there had been someone to whom she could have explained it.

Sandrine got out of bed, pulled her robe from the chair and shrugged it onto her naked body. It was dark here, too, this St. Lucy's day, but barely chill. Nothing like the bone-snapping cold of Sundsvall. It was always damp, here, though, like at home. But where Swedish dampness crystallized to snow and winters were spent crossing the tundra-ed landscape on skis and snowshoes, here the damp became an animal of fog—a low beast that slunk about the streets and curled around you, knocking your breath away, grabbing you in its wet, briny grasp.

Sandrine walked to the bathroom, brushed her teeth in the near-dark. She could just discern the outline of her face in the mirror—her hair still as blonde as any Lucy girl and her creamy skin accented with the deep pink blush near her cheeks that was the hallmark of a Swede.

Last year she had played the Lucy part for Hanne—they were still together then, still together in the minuscule flat in New York above Columbus Circle where girls that looked like them stood out against the Pakistanis and Colombians and Jamaicans that lent the neighborhood the sounds and smells of a foreign land—but not *their* foreign lands. Sandrine had worn a diaphanous version of the Lucy gown, had brought her lover cakes and tea and more love than she could ever remember feeling. The candle had flickered as she sang low Swedish hymns, and then Hanne had pulled her back to bed, splattering her with candle wax, and licked the crystalline sugar from her fingers, her lips, her cunt, had pushed deep inside her, thrust into her again and again until it was light and the feast was well under way.

Sandrine splashed water on her face. Hanne was gone, back to Berlin, and she was still here—unsure of why, for without Hanne, big-city bred, worldly wise Hanne, she felt lost. Abandoned. By the love of her life. She slid to the floor of her little bathroom and wept. This St. Lucy's day would be longer and harsher than any winter day in Sundsvall.

Morning always comes hard in New Orleans. Dolores Gutierrez had never liked mornings. Had not liked them in the cruel sun of La Pesca, the small Mexican town on the Gulf two hundred miles south of the grim Texas border at Brownsville. La Pesca, the gritty, smouldering town where she had lived for years with her *familia* before she ended up on a string of *tourista* jaunts— to Cancun, Cozumel, Belize and then her downfall, Port-au-Prince. The too-extended foray to Haiti had inevitably led her here, to New Orleans, where the mornings were just as unkind, although differently so than in La Pesca. There was none of the predawn flattening of the corn, no pounding and rolling it out, yellow and brown paste splattered with flour. None of that early morning frying up of the tortillas here, no husks littering a dirt floor in a three-room adobe box made from straw and mud and tiles, chickens prancing about her bed, spiders and millipedes skittering through what served as cupboards. Here morning was a recovery mission—recovery from the night, which inevitably ended just before dawn, and from all that must, of necessity, recede back into the shadows until it was sunset once more.

Dolores stood naked and barefoot, her legs slightly splayed apart, the dark hair between them lush and full, and washed her face with eucalyptus soap. The shower had been quick and hot, but the water with which she washed her face was icy and crisp. She loosed the damp braid that had held her black hair in the hour or two she had slept and the cascade of silken black fell over her bare shoulders and across the left side of her face. She looked hard into the mirror, a solitary red candle wavering, nearly done, behind her on the shelf. *Where did that rumor about the mirrors get started?* she wondered. Was it just the Eastern European vampires who couldn't see themselves? *No.* She remembered Nadja standing with her at Antoine's one evening, their images had both shimmered in the long mirror in the entryway, watery and vague, but wholly *there* as they had glided into the room for dinner. No, the mirror thing had clearly been devised to give hope to anyone who thought they had ways to catch out those who walked the other side of life.

Dolores brushed her hair hard, twisted it up with a gold and magenta scarf, outlined her eyes with black and then began to dress. The shop opened at 8 a.m.—an ungodly hour, to be sure, and yet Dolores knew from all the years she had been doing it, that there would be *touristas* and even *locales* waiting outside the cypress shutters when she opened them, some still awake from the night before, alcohol infusing their breath. Others had risen early, to get there first thing as if it were a charm in and of itself, arriving on her doorstep so near to dawn. But each would be waiting for the same thing—waiting for a potion, a powder, a *milagro*—anything slightly tainted by the clash of this side and the other that might thunder their wishes and dreams into the crescendo they so desperately desired. And today was a saint's day—a big one. The feast of that young virgin Lucy who had given her life at the end of her would-be lover's sword. He had thrust it deep, like a stake, into her believer's heart and her eyes had glowed, incandescent, glowed at him like lasers until he had fallen, blinded by the light of her. The glow of her faith in herself, in her belief, had felled him.

Dolores looked once more in the mirror, her face a subtle oval, the features even, the lips full, the eyes luminous. By any standard, in this world or the other, she was beautiful. The candle sputtered softly, then went out, a thin line of smoke traveling upward as Dolores left the room.


The last night Sandrine had spent with Hanne they had smoked weed and cigarettes, drunk a delectable red wine and woven into each other's bodies deftly, as Hanne wove the fabric art she made on the criss-cross of looms at the back of their small flat. Sandrine had known Hanne was returning to Berlin; Hanne had asked her to come too, because it was for good. She wanted to be back in Berlin, needed the city that throbbed in her veins stronger than Sandrine could make herself do. But Sandrine did not want to go back to Europe, wanted to find a way to stay here, permanently, in America, in the anonymous bustle of New York where music and scents and food and bodies all pulsed together to form a heartbeat she had never been able to feel in Sweden, or even in Berlin. This was where she belonged now, Sandrine believed. But she had hoped it would be with Hanne. She had hoped everything in her life would always be with Hanne.

Sandrine had made a meal—a German meal, a Swedish meal— a *smorgasbord* of European-style meats and fish, chopped eggs and dill and little hard breads coupled with pickled this and that to signal the bond with America was breaking between them. Hanne had taken her to bed, her short, spiky hair had stabbed at Sandrine again and again, punctuating her sense of loss. Hanne bit lightly along her thighs and nipples, sucked her clit hard and slipped her deft fingers, the fingers that Sandrine had so often watched flitting with lightning speed between the warp and weft of the looms, deep between her hot, wet lips, making her pant and cry out, the sound muffled in Hanne's creamy shoulder.

Sandrine had not gone to the airport. Had stayed in their bed as Hanne rose, showered, dressed and left, her bags already packed, her things already gone from their place before they shared their last meal, their last sex together. It was a dark night then, too, as Hanne left for that even darker city she would always call home, no matter how alone she might be there without Sandrine. There had been a flood of e-mails after, and a few calls. Letters, postcards, weeks and even months of pleading by each in her turn to come back home, but for Sandrine home was in the States now, and for Hanne it would never be anywhere but the dark throb of Berlin.

Light had begun to creep along the edge of the windowsill in Sandrine's bathroom. She stood, slowly, a little stiff from the cold floor, and turned on the shower. She would go to that little shop today—what was the name, she couldn't remember. Could remember only the white python on the sign, its one eye wide and glowing and the commingling of bergamot, sweet olive and eucalyptus that had emanated from inside the shop when she had passed by yesterday on her way to work. Hanne was coming to visit at Christmas. Sandrine would find something to make her stay.


Dolores was hungry. Last night she had found no time to feed—or rather, nothing upon which to feast before she returned to her bed for the rest that had to come—that myth remained truth. After she had left—fled—Haiti, conscience had descended upon her. Her subsequent choices had been limited by this decision: Kill only the deserving, cross over only those worthy and truly desirous of the pain and pleasures of immortality. She'd gone home briefly—a fortnight, the longest she could go without feeding—and then left La Pesca forever. She'd landed in Brownsville for a time—there was so much misery there on that border between worlds, that barren hole without electricity or water or breath of *espira* that she had grown fat as a tick from gorging herself on those who preyed upon the hapless and had turned boys and girls with an almost reckless abandon to give them the strength to find a life, even if it was the death-in-life that she had found in Haiti.

Loudon had crossed her over. The devil himself, Pierre Loudon—dancing in front of the fire, his white python draped over his near-naked body agleam with bergamot oil. Later she discovered the oil relaxes the snakes, makes them drowsy and less likely to remember their keeper is also prey. He had danced to her, had pushed a young woman toward her and the girl—Elise—had shimmered and slithered around her like any snake, her hair woven with feathers and tiny conch shells. The girl had mesmerized her—her body shiny and blue-black, her hair a snarl of tiny snake-like curls and her eyes an eerie greenish amber. Elise had been almost intolerably beautiful and Dolores had given in to her desire, allowing herself to be led back to one of the scroungy tin and plaster huts that doubled for housing along the back streets of Port-au-Prince.

They had been entwined on Elise's ratty cot, their bodies limned with sweat, when Loudon had arrived. Loudon, her mentor from Cancun and Cozumel, Loudon who had found her at the harbor one day in La Pesca and told her all about the choices he could offer her. That had been nearly three years ago—three years of her catering to *touristas* and pimping herself, but never turning over the goods, throughout Mexico and Belize. Loudon never tired of telling her how good she was at sharking the *anglos*, with her smouldering good looks and her inherent wit. Dolores had been a small treasure for Loudon and he in turn had been her ticket out of grinding corn and even more grinding poverty. She had sent wads of pesos home to her *Mami* wound in scarves, imbedded in tins of spices. She and Loudon had been a good match. Then the Day of the Dead had come and she had made the little marzipan skulls for him and he had danced with the python and sent her home with Elise and now he was there, his white linen pants an evanescent pool at his feet, standing naked in front of them both, ready to collect on a long-owed debt—one Elise had apparently already fulfilled by bedding Dolores, but one which Dolores had yet to pay.

Dolores had known the day would come. Had awaited it, dreaded it, feared it and shrugged it off. Loudon had heated himself up with the dancing and the potions and the slithery animal sensuality of the snake. His eyes glowed black and dreamy in the hot, candle-lit room. Dolores felt faint looking at him, felt herself press into Elise's curvaceous flesh, involuntarily seeking a hiding space.

It had not been what she'd expected. He had not opened her legs, had not thrust into her, had not taken himself in his hand and pushed open her lips. Rather he had covered her and Elise with his body as if he were a cloak—his skin was slick with the bergamot oil and Dolores felt herself grow dizzy with the heat of the room and the candles and the heady scent. He had whispered into her ear— something, a mix of Spanish and French that was almost a chant— and then she had felt a sharp pain, quick and thin—there was no corresponding throb, no long pulse. Just the quickness, something hot, and Elise's hand fluttering between her legs and an irrepressibly strong orgasm as she involuntarily pushed back against Elise, her clit explosive and then . . .

Had she passed out? It was a thin, pink dawn when she awoke, sweaty and flushed, on Elise's tattered cot. She felt bruised and slightly sick, something thick in the back of her throat made it difficult for her to breathe and she tried to sit up, but the room spun and she lay back.

The room had an aqua glow to it, like the bottom of the pools in Cancun. From the doorway Dolores could hear a low chanting and smell something sweet cooking, like her *Mami's tamales*. She closed her eyes and seemed to sleep.

Elise had come to her later, after it was dark and the hunger was so intense, Dolores was sick with it. Elise gave Dolores a bowl filled with something red and steaming and Dolores ate it, ravenous in a way she hadn't been since childhood. Elise laid Dolores back down. She stood, pulling the sweater and skirt from her body. Dolores could sense rather than smell the tang of her flesh as she lowered herself onto Dolores, spreading Dolores's legs with her knee, pressing her thigh hard up against Dolores's lips and then putting her whole hand against Dolores, her fingers slipping slowly inside as her teeth bared sharp against the faint pulse in Dolores's neck.

It had gone like that well into winter—Elise and Loudon feeding off her until she was nearly dead, then rebuilding her strength with their well-cooked pieces of liver and beef, blood puddings and steaming stews mixed with god-knows-what. She had lived in a languorous dream state broken only by rabid sex with Elise and pyrotechnics in the square with Loudon, his pythons and his retinue of minions much like Elise.

The day Dolores had fled them both, she had feared the stake through her heart would materialize, hot and deadly, like St. Lucy's lover's sword. She had cajoled a *tourista* who seemed enchanted by her now wraith-like beauty. He was headed to Kingston, Grand Cayman, then Juarez on a form of business Dolores knew simply from the places involved was at least as dangerous as what she was fleeing. And he was eager for a companion—for her. Her choices had winnowed down to nothing. She had to leave.

Dolores opened the register, took a last look in the mirror behind her that reflected everything in the shop into another mirror angled across from it, and went to open the door. Too late to regret what was unchangeable. Too late to regret not knowing that she had already been turned, that she was in her novitiate state as vampire when she fled Haiti and nearly died from not knowing how and when and how much to feed. After Kingston, once they found the drug-runner's body, she had made the pact with herself. She had not regretted that kill; still didn't. She had never given in to the *touristas* before; he would not be the lucky first. Even Loudon had not taken her—at least not like that.

The shop stayed dark during the day, lit only by a scattering of amber lamps here and there—Dolores liked it that way. She never fully opened the floor-to-ceiling cypress shutters that lined the French Quarter, the *Vieux Carre*, and made the city look like Old Havana or Juarez. The harsh light of New Orleans day coupled with the heat could sicken her. She had long ago learned to keep the shop as dark as dusk. The customers liked it that way, too. It lent the atmosphere that made them believe everything they had come for would be realized.

It was nearly closing time when Dolores saw the blonde girl come into the shop. She had seen her earlier—she'd been there first thing, milling about with the others lined up out front when she'd opened, but she hadn't come in. She'd stood like a revenant, unable to cross the threshold without permission. Dolores had considered actually inviting her in, but had become distracted by other customers. And then the girl was gone. Now she had returned. Obviously her desires had gotten the better of her. A little smile played at the corners of Dolores's mouth. It was time to close the shop, but Dolores would not close until this girl got what she was looking for.

Sandrine had stood outside the shop with the python sign for what seemed a long time that morning before she continued on to work. *Voodun Loudon* the sign read. She wasn't sure what that meant, exactly, or if it meant anything at all. She had paced back and forth between it and the coffee bean shop two doors down for more than fifteen minutes when she decided she needed to think about this more. Somehow even entering the shop meant crossing a line.

All day Sandrine had thought about Hanne. She had gotten three e-mails from her—all written as she had slept and Hanne had been going about her morning. Hanne was eager for the visit—she had never seen New Orleans, but couldn't wait to share the music and food and atmosphere with Sandrine. Couldn't wait to bed Sandrine again. Had made her a beautiful fabric piece with thickly interwoven threads, a hanging that she knew Sandrine would love. Hanne always wrote as if they had never truly parted, as if they were still lovers, as if she knew it was only a matter of time before one convinced the other to go home—whichever home that turned out to be.

*Voodun Loudon* was a dark little shop, filled with small tables arrayed with bottles and boxes and vials of every size and shape, their labels foreign or obscure or mostly blank. This was no shop for the uninitiated, like herself, Sandrine had thought immediately and had hovered near the door, thinking perhaps she should just leave. But something about the woman inside drew her in.

The woman was dark—her hair was truly black, as were her eyes, and her skin looked polished. It was whiter than Sandrine would have expected, given her hair and eyes, but it had a burnished look to it, like something that had once been in the light for a long time and now was hidden away. She wore a long teal skirt with a long, white, man's-style shirt over it. In her hair was wound a scarf that was gold and a purplish-red and around her neck was a heavy necklace of turquoise and silver. Long silver earrings hung from her ears and one very long tendril of black hair played along her neck onto her breast. She was lean, but her breasts were full and the shirt accented her cleavage.

She was very, very beautiful and of no discernable age.

Dolores watched the girl as she wove her way between the little tables and picked up this and that, obviously clueless as to what she was looking for. She was tall and large boned with pale blonde hair that was twisted up in the back and then fluffed over, like a waterfall. She wore black trousers and a dark red shirt. The leather jacket looked very old and was worn through at the cuffs. A line of piercings ran along her left ear and she had a small red and black tattoo Dolores couldn't quite discern on her left hand. The girl didn't look American, but then she might have been from one of those Midwestern places to which Dolores had never gone. It was past six and Dolores was hungry and this girl was looking more lost and also more desirable as the little clock ticked away behind her on the mantel.

Dolores walked toward Sandrine.

"Do you know what you are looking for?"

The question—and the Latin accent in which it was framed—startled Sandrine. This was not the way American shopkeepers spoke. Each always posed the same query: "May I help you?" Sandrine really was out of her depth here. Perhaps she should just go. Or should she say exactly what it was she wanted?

The girl took a step back and Dolores moved closer. "Perhaps something for work or money or"—Dolores picked up a small blood-red vial with a green stopper, took Sandrine's hand (it was *so* warm) and laid it within the hollow—"love?" The smile came and went again on Dolores's beautiful mouth.

"Love, I think." Sandrine both blurted and stammered her embarrassed answer, unable to look away from the too-black eyes and Mona Lisa-smile of the Latin woman. She had come because of Hanne, but desire had begun to pulse and she knew it was not for Hanne—at least not right at this moment.

When the girl spoke—was her accent German? Scandinavian?—Dolores felt a frisson of pleasure. It had been a while since she had taken a risk outside the realm of the always risky business of her daily life and tonight seemed like as good a night as any to take a risk. Feast of St. Lucy and all that. She suddenly felt a risk might be in order. She stepped a little closer to the girl. There was another tattoo along the crest of her right shoulder. Just below the pulse of her neck, which was rapid, Dolores could smell the scent of the blood, she was that close.

"A man? Young or old?" Dolores asked, already knowing as she watched the girl's discomfiture that it was no man she wanted to trick into submission with potions and *milagra*. Men required little when it came to trickery, after all. But women—

It was fully night now, and from the short distance of Jackson Square the cathedral carillon had begun the six o'clock chime, long and beautiful—the Angelus, a call to vespers. A call to the succulence of the night, as Dolores always heard it. Beyond that was the river. Would this girl like to take a walk, have a drink, a meal, a cozy evening in a room filled with candles scented with bergamot followed by a languorous bath and then the slow descent into the other realm?

Images of other girls and other places, different accents and longer, shorter hair, curvier, straighter bodies, younger, older faces ran in a quick montage before her as she watched the girl watch her.

"Not a man." Sandrine had not stood this close to anyone since Hanne had left. *Hanne.* She really should leave this shop. It was too hot and she felt a little faint from not eating lunch and—

Dolores put the back of her cool hand to Sandrine's cheek. "You seem a little flushed, *amiga*. Come, sit for a moment. I'll get you some water." Dolores led Sandrine to a small upholstered chair off the counter and disappeared behind a curtain for a few seconds. She handed Sandrine a small blue bottle. *Volvic.* Sandrine felt a sudden, peculiar and unfamiliar pang of homesickness. She broke the seal and drank.


Sandrine lay on the stark white sheets, the maroon duvet pulled across her legs and wondered what had led her to Dolores's bed. They had closed the shop and left, walking along the river for a good half hour before going into a small, dark restaurant Sandrine had never seen. It was redolent of spices and no one—neither customers nor staff—seemed to speak English except when ordering. The food had been intense—tangy and hot and unlike anything Sandrine had eaten before. She hadn't really asked and Dolores hadn't offered information on the food. Mostly they had eaten and touched each other under the table and Sandrine had felt the heat of the food and the heat of her own body propelling her closer and closer to Dolores.

They had talked, had learned they both came from fishing villages, hers cold at one end of the world, Dolores's hot, at the other end. Sandrine had asked how old Dolores was and the other woman had laughed and put a finger to Sandrine's lips and whispered, "Older than you, *amiga*."

Dolores had talked about her shop, about the customers, and Sandrine had blushed. Dolores had leaned over and kissed her, then, her lips soft and cool, spicy from the food. Sandrine had asked Dolores why she had gone into such a business and that mysterious smile had crossed her face and she had said only, "I had some debts to pay."

They had walked slowly back to Dolores's shop and when she had locked the door behind them, Dolores had grabbed Sandrine's shoulders and pushed her against the wall and kissed her hard, so hard that Sandrine's breath seemed to stop and she felt weak. They climbed the stairs together, Dolores's arm slung around Sandrine's waist, Sandrine's head against Dolores's shoulder, her lips moist and hot against Dolores's cool neck.

Dolores had undressed Sandrine slowly and laid her on the bed. The room was redolent of bergamot. Red and white candles lined the walls in sconces, along shelves and on torchieres. The bed, too, was red and white and the heavy drapes over the windows that looked out onto the Mississippi were a deep arterial color. Vials and bottles much like the ones in the shop were scattered throughout the room and in one corner stood a black statue that looked like a Madonna.

Sandrine lay, naked, on the cool, smooth sheets, the downy duvet over her legs, her thighs slightly apart. She resisted the pull of desire that urged her to touch herself—she ached for Dolores on top of her, inside her, her beautiful mouth all over her. She felt such intensity for this strange woman she had only just met—it was like when she had met Hanne at Uppsala, but this heat was explosive, she had felt it the moment Dolores had first spoken to her in the shop.

When Dolores finally stood next to the bed, dressed in a long white Mexican nightgown, her dark nipples outlined under the sheer muslin, Dolores looked like a dark, sensual Lucy girl, a halo of candles behind her. Sandrine felt a deep pang of loss, tears edging out from her eyes just before Dolores lay down beside her and covered Sandrine's mouth with hers.

It had been passionate, lusty lovemaking. They had taken each other quickly at first—hands and mouths everywhere, touching, kissing, licking, sucking. Dolores was an accomplished and seductive lover and her body was lush and full and open in a way Sandrine had never experienced. Sandrine couldn't get enough of her, couldn't get enough of Dolores touching her, fucking her, taking her over and over, whispering to her in Spanish, running her tongue along the pulse in Sandrine's neck again and again, teasing her, slipping her fingers into Sandrine's mouth, the tang of their spicy dinner still sharply apparent.

In the blood-red and amber glow of the heated room, Sandrine cannot believe how much she aches for Dolores over and over. She gives herself over to Dolores, opens her legs wider than she ever has, touches herself when Dolores tells her to, wraps herself around Dolores, slips in and out of her and kisses her deeply, hard. They are ravenous for each other.

Midnight comes, the carillon chimes through the foggy distance. Sandrine is half-asleep as Dolores begins to bite lightly along her clavicle, runs her tongue up toward her earlobe in a way that nearly makes her come from the intensity. Dolores stops, looks into Sandrine's Delft-blue eyes with the deep, impenetrable black of her own and asks Sandrine what she really wants, why she came to *Voodun Loudon*.

Sandrine tells Dolores the story, tells her of Hanne, of how much she loves her, of how Hanne left her for Berlin, that she loves the place she calls home more than her, who should be her only home. There are tears running back toward the pillows. Sandrine tells Dolores how she came upon the shop, how she was overwhelmed by her desire to keep Hanne in New Orleans, in the city she herself found by accident on a weekend trip with acquaintances from New York soon after Hanne left for Berlin. New Orleans, the city she now knows she could never leave because it is everything she wants—the darkness and the light, the heat and the fog, the river and the sea, the smells and sounds of a foreign land but the comfort of home, somehow. New Orleans ran in her blood immediately. Like Hanne, like Dolores. Sandrine takes Dolores's hand, kisses it, recounts how she came here that weekend and within two weeks had moved everything from her small studio to an equally small flat at the edge of the Faugburg-Marigny. She knew no one, still barely knows anyone. It didn't matter. She was home.

"I live near Elysian Fields now," Sandrine tells Dolores. "I want Hanne in that place with me. In Elysian Fields." The reference is not lost on Dolores.

"I can give her to you," Dolores whispers, her voice thick with desire, her accent more apparent. "But you must choose, you must want it. It must be like it was for your St. Lucy—faith must lead you to death so that you can have the life you desire."

Dolores sits up on the bed, her body softly exquisite in the glowing amber of the flickering candles. Sandrine can just see a hint of black hair between her legs. Finds the cascade of silken black down her back, the tendrils mussed and wound into each other like so many small snakes intoxicatingly sensual. She wants Dolores again, pulls her back onto her, puts her hand, with the silver snake ring and the long tapered fingers so like Hanne's first on her breast, then hard against her cunt.

"Do it," she tells Dolores, the heat of the other woman and her own heat overwhelming her. She aches to be taken again, can feel how wet she is, her nipples hard in the coolness of the room. She takes Dolores's arm, turns the wrist toward her lips, sucks hard at where the vein should be pulsing furiously, looks up at Dolores in time to see the teeth, white and sharp and glinting in the light. She feels a light frisson, spreads her legs wide, the widest she can ever remember spreading them, and waits to feel Dolores plunge inside her.

Dolores has only slept a few hours, but she is sated. She stands in the bathroom, the daily ritual of eucalyptus soap and bracing cold water on her face bringing life to her body. She can still taste Sandrine on her lips, a faint scent of her remains on her fingertips. Her cunt, her blood. *Her.*

This is how it was for Elise and Loudon, she thinks, still intoxicated by the fullness of the night before. She has turned many in the last forty years, but she hasn't turned anyone like Sandrine.

Sandrine is *her* Dolores, Dolores thinks. Sandrine will always be here, just like Dolores. They will be *compañeras*—with or without Hanne—in this city so full of transience, this city that lives for body, for night, for all the things on Dolores's side of the divide.

Sandrine still lies in the bed. She appears to sleep, but she has been dead for several hours. At dusk she will awaken, ravenous, when Dolores brings her a rich, spicy blood stew. Dolores will feed it to her slowly and then they will feed on each other. Dolores will cover them in szechuan oil to make them both warm again. They will make love, they will walk out into the night, they will be together. Dolores will feel complete again, as she did with Elise, before Loudon—

They had talked first. Sandrine had been too eager—Dolores needed to be sure she was turning a friend and not a potential enemy. She didn't want to be threatened by the thought of someone stalking her, cross in one hand, stake in the other, looking for revenge. Dolores had told her everything—about Loudon and Elise and her time in Brownsville. How she had come to New Orleans with a girl named Marisol, one of Loudon's minions who had left him, too. She and Marisol had opened the shop and worked together for more than a decade. Then one night—the Day of the Dead, for he had a keen sense of irony—Loudon had come and taken Marisol away with him. She had gone willingly, Dolores had seen that, and it had crushed her. Loudon had taken so much from her. Neither he nor Marisol had ever returned. It had been more than twenty years.

There had been others, Dolores told Sandrine—two girls, Odette and Miranda, and a gay boy, Jack. But they had not stayed, had wanted to serve their own desires, not share in hers. A writer had come to her and they talked a great deal. They liked each other immensely. Like Dolores, the writer had lost much—a daughter to a blood disease. They had shared their losses and Dolores had told her all she knew about her side of the world. They had come close, but Dolores had never turned the woman, who had written down everything she had told her. Now her books were everywhere and the two do not see each other much. Distance and embarrassment has built between them, Dolores thinks and it makes her a little more lonely.

Dolores needs a friend, she tells Sandrine, one hand resting lightly on the pale blonde hair between Sandrine's legs, the other stroking Sandrine's flushed cheek. "I need someone close, *amiga*. This life is not meant to be lived alone." Dolores stands, walking to the draped and shuttered windows, opening them just enough to let in the briny scent of the heavy fog outside. The feast of St. Lucy is over. But the night is still incandescent.

Dolores turns back toward Sandrine. The young blonde woman holds out her arms. "I want it," Sandrine tells Dolores, desire heavy in her lightly accented voice. "I want *you*. If I don't have Hanne, I *will* always have you. We will be something for each other against the darkness, won't we? We won't be alone."

Dolores had covered Sandrine with her body then, had lowered herself down, trailing her lips along Sandrine's lush, silken skin. *She was so warm.*

The bite was so quick, so clean, Sandrine barely felt it. She was close to coming, Dolores tonguing her fast and hard, nipping lightly at her lips and clit before she bit into her femoral artery and began to drain the life from her. The intensity of the pleasure as Dolores sucked on her and fingered her clit, was almost unbearable. The orgasm rocketed Sandrine into unconsciousness and Dolores bled her out. The blush in Sandrine's cheeks began to fade and soon she was as starkly white as the sheets. Dolores licked lightly at the tiny wound near Sandrine's groin, curled around the girl's still-warm body and slept.


Dolores hates these mornings, but they are the penance for the tantalizing night. It is nearly Christmas and business at the shop is brisk—from near dawn to after dark they come, each needing that special something for the holiday, the charm that will make them feel blessed and sated by the New Year.

Sandrine opens the shop early for Dolores now. It is, she says, the only job she wants. They have been working together for only a week, but Dolores knows it will last, that she has found the right partner, that there will be trips through Mexico and Guatemala and even to Haiti. They will find new elixirs and potions and there will be ever more *touristas* at their cypress shutters every morning. Hanne comes tomorrow, Christmas Eve, and the three of them will have dinner together, walk past the cathedral—the crowds, Dolores and Sandrine will say, will keep them outside—and listen to the Mass and the music, cover their ears when the burst of the carillon rings loud and long at midnight.

Dolores imagines that they will come back with her. Sandrine still has her little flat, but she has not been back to it, except yesterday, to get more clothes. She stays with Dolores, upstairs, in the little garret space that would be too hot for mortals in the summer, too chill in winter. Dolores has sent for a small quantity of earth from Sundsvall and sewn it into a pillow for Sandrine to sleep upon. She has another, from Berlin, just in case.

Sandrine will close the shop early tonight. Hanne's flight comes in at five and she wants to meet her. Dolores has a dinner planned, and Sandrine has ringed the garret with candles, she has bergamot oil for the bath. The sheets are scented with eucalyptus. Everything is ready. A little stack of gifts stands in one corner. Dolores says there is a gift for Hanne from her as well, but Sandrine does not know what it is.

Sandrine is happy, happier than she ever could have imagined. Her desire for Hanne has lessened—it is no longer an unbearable catch in the back of her throat threatening to choke her—but it has also deepened. She has learned so much from Dolores about love and life. Dolores is her world now, more than Hanne, but there is space for them both and Sandrine is ready—ready to take Hanne to her or let her go. For without Hanne now, there is still life: there is Dolores. But with them both—

Hanne waits at the airport for Sandrine and her friend Dolores. She paces, running her hand through her short hair again and again. She has smoked a half dozen cigarettes, is surprised by her own nervousness. She made her decision on the flight over. She wants to stay with Sandrine. The time without her has been harsh and bitter and the beat of Sandrine has vied day and night with the beat of Berlin in her blood. They are warp and weft of the fabric of her and she will have to find a way to have them both. That is her Christmas present to Sandrine—that she will stay.

She has re-read all of Sandrine's letters. The pull of this place, New Orleans, is awesome, palpable in them. But when she spoke to Sandrine on the phone last week, Sandrine sounded dreamy, far-off. She talked about Dolores too much, Hanne thought, and yet had not felt jealous. What was between them was not what was between Hanne and Sandrine, of that she was certain.

Sandrine sees Hanne through the airport window, standing near the baggage check, already deplaned and gone through customs and waiting for her, only for her. Sandrine sees Hanne turned in profile, so striking, so lean and strong and handsome and Sandrine remembers what it was to have her heart race. Dolores touches her shoulder lightly and Sandrine turns toward her and smiles, a smile not unlike Dolores's own. "Mi compañera," she whispers to Dolores, putting a finger to the other woman's lips, a finger that smells vaguely of blood. Then Sandrine opens the door, pushing past airport personnel, jostling against visitors and passengers and runs—full lips parted, teeth sharp against her tongue, the taste of blood lingering in her mouth. She runs, toward Hanne.

# The Tomb of Neru-Ra

**Alison Laleche**

"Come, come," the tour guide kept insisting as he walked several hundred feet ahead of the last stragglers. The bouncing beam from his torch grew fainter and fainter on the walls of the narrow, low-vaulted corridor. "Follow the light. Very dangerous here. Don't fall behind."

Wanda crouched down once more, hurriedly scouring the dusty ground. Where had that damn bracelet gone? She should never have put it on this morning; it was always falling off. But she had been thinking of Darryl when she woke up, unable to forget his parting words back in New York: "There's no passion in you, Wanda. It's like making love to a refrigerator. Don't expect to find me here when you get back from Egypt." The silver bracelet with its tiny engraved *W* for *Wanda* had been a gift from him last Christmas. She could not bear to lose that too.

They must be deep within the tomb here, she thought, finding the echo of so many feet disorienting. It was surprisingly cold at this depth and getting darker by the second.

The last man passed her, glancing down. "You okay?"

"I dropped something."

He hesitated. "You want me to wait?"

"No," she said quickly. She did not want to have to explain the significance of her bracelet to a stranger, however well-meaning. "I'll catch up in a minute."

It was only once the man had continued on that Wanda realized her mistake. Now she was alone in the dark and could no longer see the far end of the corridor as it sloped back toward the main entrance to the tomb. The last of the tour group and their tall Egyptian guide had vanished from sight. The only illumination came from a handful of lights set high into the walls at intervals, barely enough to see by, let alone search for a bracelet that might have rolled into any one of these shadowy corridors to her left and right.

Wanda stood for a moment, trying to remember exactly where she had been when she felt it slip from her wrist. Had they been passing this narrow passageway to the left? It was possible.

She took a couple of steps into the passageway, frowning. What was that she could see shining, a few hundreds yards away in the darkness? Groping her way toward it, she reached the glinting object and bent to investigate. But to her disgust, it was only a twisted piece of metal, thick with dust, probably discarded here years ago. Crouched there in the passageway, Wanda began to get confused, struggling to regain her bearings. Had she come from the left or the right when she bent to pick up the metal object? It seemed just as dark in either direction.

Panic rose in her like a black silent tide and she forced it back with an effort. It was important to stay in control. It was not as though she could be left behind, she told herself coolly. Heads were sure to be counted on the coach back to the hotel, names checked against the list. The man who had stopped might mention their conversation. Sooner or later, someone would be sent back down to find her.

She took a few steps forward, frowning. There was another faint gleam ahead, a suggestion of light in the distance. Picking her way toward it, she eventually came to a low-ceilinged chamber lit by a single bulb, the entrance hewn roughly from the rock as though no door had ever existed there. In the center of this chamber was a sarcophagus on a platform, its lid pushed to one side as though for display.

Unlike the other sarcophagi she had seen on her tour of the Valley of the Kings, this one was startlingly plain. There were no decorative hieroglyphics on the lid or sides, no gold or other ornamentation to indicate this coffin belonged to a person of status. It stood alone, plain and oddly humble beside a collection of sealed pots and wooden containers, presumably filled with provisions to accompany the occupant on his or her journey to the Afterlife.

Well, she thought, there's nothing to do but stay in this room and wait to be rescued.

Idly, she approached the platform on which the sarcophagus stood and ran a hand around its high sides. The wood felt smooth, well sanded, not rough and ready as she had expected from such a lowly coffin. She leant over the edge and peered inside, expecting to find it empty. But her eyes opened wide and her heart gave an odd little lurch as she realized the Egyptian mummy was still inside. Stiff and mute, the body was turned slightly toward her instead of lying flat on its back, its bandage-like burial wrappings brownish and discolored.

Wanda examined the mummy in a reverent and fascinated silence. She had never seen one at such close quarters before; they were usually kept under glass or roped off from the public. Her eyes moved down the close-bound body in its stained wrappings. Could those be breasts under the tight fabric? She thought so, eyeing the gentler curves of the lower body, slender yet unmistakably female. This mummy had been a woman, she realized, many thousands of years ago.

With a tentative hand, aware that she was not meant to touch any of the exhibits, she leant over the coffin and brushed her fingers across the small high breasts, stroking them in wonder. How could a human body preserve its shape so perfectly through so many millennia? It was a miracle of primitive science that the Egyptians had been able to embalm their loved ones with such precision.

She had not intended to touch the body so intimately, had never even touched a live woman like this, yet her fingers seemed to do so of their own accord. Her hand moved lower, investigating the prominent mound above the dead woman's sex. She imagined how the once vital flesh between this woman's legs must have withered and blackened to a dry husk of bone and skin fragments thin as parchment. Yet there was something disquietingly erotic about the mummy, as though—even long dead—she was still somehow a sexual creature.

Some of the burial wrappings across her face seemed to have come unravelled. Wanda leant over and tried to tuck them back into place, feeling a strange empathy with this woman in the unmarked coffin. But time and exposure to the air had weakened the fabric; it fell apart in her hands, loosening yet more of the wrappings. Her clumsy attempt to remedy the situation only resulted in more of the rotten material falling away to reveal something which looked—to her shocked disbelief—like smooth, dark skin beneath.

Living flesh! she thought with a start, and jerked her away.

No, she told herself firmly, that was impossible. Her racing heart began to settle again. It was just her imagination working overtime; she had become separated from the rest of the tour group and was on edge, that was all. This poor woman, whoever she was, had been dead for thousands of years.

Then a tiny movement, glimpsed out of the corner of her eye, left Wanda frozen, staring down in horror. Had the fingers of one stiff, bandage-bound hand twitched?

"Now you're just being ridiculous!" she said into the silence, half laughing at her own superstitious fear, half frightened.

But if she had hoped to dispel her fears by speaking them out loud, it had the opposite effect. Instead, her voice echoed around the chamber, sibilant whispers flying back at her from every unlit corner. A deeper fear struck her heart as the whispers died away. Had that really been her own echo, or was there someone else here? Her eyes searched the shadows, glancing over her shoulder toward the yawning darkness of the entrance passageway, that disorientating maze of corridors leading nowhere. But she could see no one. The chamber was empty and she was alone.

Hearing a creak from the sarcophagus, Wanda spun in horror to see the mummy's arm lift slowly from its side as though reaching out toward her.

Color drained from her face as the wrist turned slowly in the air and the slender hand seemed to flex, wrappings falling away to reveal long, tapering fingers that stretched and gradually uncurled from their claw-like posture.

Too frightened to move or even make a sound, Wanda watched in disbelief as the mummy's hand grasped at the loose edge of the burial wrappings around her face and pulled, beginning to unravel them with terrifying speed and efficiency. First the dusky forehead emerged, broad and noble, then both eyebrows, finely plucked into a pleasing arc. Then one eye was revealed, two eyes, staring back up at her from inside the sarcophagus, kohl dark and glittering strangely.

Finding a scream in her throat at last, Wanda turned on her heel to run but it was too late.

That dead hand shot up and seized her by the upper arm. She found herself held in a powerful grip, struggling to be free, while the mummy continued to unravel the burial wrappings off its face. The mouth had been uncovered now. Those sensuous lips parted and the mummy spoke, a single unintelligible phrase that hissed around the chamber like a thousand snakes. The words were in some language Wanda did not recognise and could not understand. When Wanda did not respond, the mummy tightened its grip on her arm and repeated the phrase in a tone of command.

"I don't know what you're saying," Wanda cried, her body shaking violently. "Let me go, please let me go!"

Abruptly, the hand released her and Wanda fell backward to the floor, winded and in shock. Before she could crawl away, the mummy swung itself determinedly out of the sarcophagus and down from the platform, most of her body still bound in the stiff discolored wrappings. Landing with astonishing agility on the rough stone, she tore at the remainder of her bindings. The ancient fabric seemed to disintegrate at her touch, dropping away to reveal a woman in her late twenties, completely naked, her skin dark and gleaming as though she had just been anointed with precious oils. She stepped out of the last tattered shreds with disdain, standing there proud and beautiful, her high breasts jutting out above a flat belly.

Staring at Wanda, the woman intoned "Neru-Ra," in a guttural voice, touching herself solemnly between her breasts.

Still shaking uncontrollably, her legs so weak they could barely support her, Wanda stared back at the woman in fear and incomprehension. Then she lifted a trembling hand to her own chest, copying the same gesture.

"Wanda," she managed, her mouth so dry she could hardly speak above a whisper. "My name . . . Wanda."

Neru-Ra smiled, apparently satisfied with that response. She came gliding toward her, hips rolling, moving with the supple grace of a dancer. Her hand reached out to stroke Wanda's pale cheek. To her surprise, the dead woman's hand was not cold, but warm and alive, disturbingly sensual as their skins touched for the first time.

"Wanda," she repeated slowly, her tongue stumbling over it as though the name was difficult to pronounce. "Wan-da."

Finding it hard to meet that penetrating gaze, Wanda lowered her eyes and found herself staring at the woman's bare breasts. The dusky nipples were larger than her own, the skin milky brown, puckering slightly in the chill air of the burial chamber. A strange desire began to come over her, the desire to reach out and stroke those beautiful breasts. It must have shown in her face for the woman uttered a soft laugh and took her hand, placing it directly on her left breast. The electric shock that burnt into the nerve fibers of her body at that contact was indescribable.

The woman was saying something again, her voice huskier now, almost pleading; though Wanda could not understand the words, she understood the tone.

Obediently, she increased the pressure of her fingers, squeezing the breast until it seemed to swell into her hand. Both nipples tautened to firm peaks and the woman sighed with pleasure, watching her with those strange magnetic eyes. Wanda stared down at the stiffening nipples, a flush on her cheeks. She could not believe what was happening. Had finding herself lost in the dark labyrinth of the tomb turned her mind?

It was the first time she had ever touched another woman's breast, and it felt good. That was undeniable. Yet this woman was dead, long dead. She was making love to a corpse.

Seeming very much alive for a corpse, Neru-Ra dragged up Wanda's T-shirt and frowned at the lacy white bra beneath. She muttered something and Wanda, moving as if in a dream, reached behind her back to unhook the bra. It took the woman another few seconds to push its restrictive underwire up, freeing Wanda's breasts. She began cupping them and stroking her nipples, massaging them this way and that, squeezing and examining them like fruit on a market stall.

Moaning with a sudden compulsive desire, Wanda found herself touching the woman's shoulders and slender neck, her fingers sliding up to the dark coarse hair. She seemed unable to stop herself, her body trembling with excitement and fear. Had the woman cast some sort of spell over her with that magnetic gaze? Then, with both arms linked about the woman's neck, her eyes fell on the empty wrist where Darryl's bracelet had been and she closed them in pain and confusion, shaking her head.

"I can't do this," she managed in a broken voice. "Darryl . . ."

But the woman merely laughed and laid a silencing finger against Wanda's lips.

Her other hand moved lower, slipping beneath the waistband of Wanda's white denim shorts to find a thong blocking her way. Before Wanda could protest, she had pushed the lacy thong aside and was stroking her pussy lips. Every nerve in Wanda's body jangled at such an intimate touch, her pussy responding with intolerable need as it moistened and grew hot under Neru-Ra's fingers.

Slowly, her eyes still closed, she felt herself being lowered to the dusty floor of the burial chamber. They lay together in a breathless silence, Neru-Ra's fingers still working inside her, so clever, so knowing. It was as though the other woman knew exactly where to touch her, how to manipulate her flesh for the maximum pleasure. Wanda groaned. She ran her hands down the naked back, stroking the smooth firm buttocks and feeling the muscles contract as Neru-Ra suddenly pulled away and knelt up.

The woman reached into a basket below the sarcophagus and withdrew a bracelet. Fashioned from some tarnished metal in the shape of a serpent, it was quickly fastened about Wanda's wrist. Wanda stared at it, uncomprehending. Was this a love gift?

Neru-Ra smiled down at her, murmured something in that thick guttural tongue, then leant forward and kissed her on the mouth. Their tongues met—the woman's probing fiercely, Wanda's shy and uncertain. Those clever fingers slipped back between her legs, burning into her flesh, turning her insides to a quivering mass of desire. She could feel the Egyptian's breasts brushing against her, taut nipples hard and insistent. Unable to resist, she lifted her head to catch one between her lips, sucking it into her mouth and exploring the dusky puckered skin with her tongue. The woman above her moaned, her own arousal evident from the perspiration breaking out on her body, the way her hips had begun to move in a languid rhythm. Their kiss deepened as Wanda cried out against her mouth, the sound muffled. She could not bear this intimacy a moment longer; it was too exciting, too intense.

Wanda climaxed, head falling back and her eyes closing as a sharp bittersweet pleasure possessed her body. "Oh my god," she breathed, realizing she had never experienced anything like this with Darryl, that her adult life so far had been wasted on sterile kisses and cold, stilted lovemaking. "I never knew . . ."

A noise behind them made her stiffen, coming back to reality with a shock. She heard loud footsteps in the passageway, saw the glare of a torch beam bouncing off the walls as someone approached. Then a voice called her name, a familiar mispronunciation.

The guide had found her at last!

Neru-Ra backed into a crouching position and stared at her, the dark eyes wide with some unfathomable emotion as she shook her head. Then the smooth dark skin began to wrinkle—first her face, withering fast around the eyes and mouth, then her breasts, shrinking to grey skin hanging on paper-thin ribs. Within a matter of seconds, the rest of her body had begun to disintegrate as well. Her mouth opened in an anguished cry, then those lips that had kissed her so passionately shrivelled to curling ashen wisps of skin.

As Wanda shrank back, one arm lifted to shield her from the horror, the tattered remains of Neru-Ra made one last desperate lurch toward her and crumbled into a heap of fine white dust on the floor.

The guide came rushing into the burial chamber at her terrified cries. He helped her to her feet, his face concerned. "You are unwell, Miss Wanda? You should not have left the group. This is a dangerous place. Some chambers not safe yet."

"Did you . . . see her?"

He was frowning. "Her?"

"The woman."

Clearly confused, the Egyptian guide glanced round the empty burial chamber and shook his head. "You are the only one here, Miss Wanda. I check the list, you were not on the coach. So I come back to find you. Now, if you please . . . the others are waiting."

Feeling more than a little foolish, Wanda brushed herself down. Her clothes were covered in white dust from the floor and she could not help noticing that her shorts were still fastened and her bra very firmly in place beneath her T-shirt. It was as though Neru-Ra had never existed, as though Wanda had fallen asleep here and dreamt the whole thing.

"Of course," she stammered, her face red with embarrassment. "I'm sorry if I've held everyone up. But I dropped my bracelet and I had to find it."

He nodded. "It's very beautiful, your bracelet. But now we must hurry back to the coach, yes?"

"No, I couldn't find it in the dark. I meant to . . ."

Stopping dead as she realized what he had said, Wanda gazed down on the bracelet on her wrist. It was not the one Darryl had given her, a plain silver bracelet with its neat W for Wanda. This bracelet was quite different—dark and ancient-looking, it curled around her wrist in the shape of a serpent. Her skin crept as she looked back over her shoulder at the sarcophagus, sealed now as though it had never been opened, the heavy lid concealing its secrets. The pots and baskets that had stood below it had vanished, the floor swept clean.

"What . . . is . . ." She cleared her throat with an effort. "Who was buried in there?"

The guide shot a dark glance at the sarcophagus, a frown on his face as he escorted her toward the narrow entrance. "That was a queen called Neru-Ra. An unfortunate lady. She deceived her husband with many women lovers. He had her buried alive down here, about five years before he died himself."

"Buried alive?"

"A terrible punishment." The guide nodded grimly. "According to the texts we found with the body, Neru-Ra was drugged and wrapped tightly in the burial cloths, then the sarcophagus was sealed. The burial chamber itself was walled up. We only discovered it by chance last year, during new excavations."

Wanda could barely speak. "And is she still . . . ?"

"No, no. Her remains were moved to the museum as soon as they were found. The sarcophagus is there for show. We open the exhibit to the public next summer."

They began to walk back toward the surface, the passageway lit up by the brilliant beam of his torch. Wanda stared down at the bracelet and remembered those firm hands on her body, the mouth that had met hers so compulsively as they made love. It was not possible. And yet, how else could she account for the bracelet?

"You say this Neru-Ra took women lovers? That must have

made her husband very angry. But to bury her alive like that." She shuddered. "Such an appalling fate."

The Egyptian guide smiled. "Some of the people who work here, they are very superstitious. They believe she is still angry, that her ghost walks the tomb. Ridiculous!" He laughed dismissively, pointing her toward the bright reassuring glow of sunlight ahead as they neared the tomb's main entrance. "Did you see the ghost of Neru-Ra, Miss Wanda?"

"No," she said slowly, tracing the serpent round her wrist with a wondering finger. "I certainly didn't see a ghost."

# Visitation
### Julia Watts

"I have come here against my husband's wishes." Mrs. Selby twisted her lace handkerchief in her small, white hands.

"I see." Sylvia Forrest poured an amber stream of tea into a china cup and offered it to her guest. "Mr. Selby does not believe in spiritualism, then?"

"Heavens, no." Mrs. Selby accepted the cup, moving her lips in the shape of the words *thank you*. "Charles says it's all stuff and nonsense—the sort of foolishness only women believe."

"Oh, but your husband is mistaken," Sylvia said, pouring her own cup now. She recalled an especially successful séance she once attended at which a gentleman had acted as medium. She had watched with amazement as the gentleman wrote down a letter dictated to him by the spirit of a dead woman. He had written the entire perfectly legible page with his eyes closed! "There are quite a few very fine spiritualists who are gentlemen."

"Really?" Mrs. Selby's blue eyes were wide. "I can't imagine talking with a man about such things."

"Well, I hope you feel comfortable talking with me." Sylvia felt she should nudge Mrs. Selby toward explaining the reason for her visit, as she seemed like the type of client who could take up a great deal of one's time without actually saying anything.

"Oh, I do, Miss Forrest. And I'm so relieved just to have someone who will listen and offer some guidance. I am at my wit's end."

"The note you left me alluded to some sort of problem in your house—a problem that might be caused by spirits?"

"Yes." Mrs. Selby set down her teacup and took up twisting her handkerchief again. "The problem is in one room in our house—the bedroom that serves as the quarters for the children's nurse. But you see, Miss Forrest, the children don't have a nurse now. I have hired three different girls over the course of a month-and-a-half, and with each one, it's been the same." Mrs. Selby's eyes welled up, and she dabbed at them with her handkerchief. "The first night each girl stayed in her quarters, and shortly after midnight, my husband and I were awakened by screams. Each time we ran to see what was the matter, and each time the new nurse was trembling and crying and already on her way out the door."

This was certainly more interesting than the usual "I want to talk to my dead husband" case that was Sylvia's most common type of business. "Did you ask any of the girls what had happened?"

"All but the first one. She left so quickly I didn't have time to ask her anything. The other two girls, though, both kept saying 'the room, the room,' and neither of them would go back into the room, not even to retrieve their belongings. The third girl . . . she kept saying something about cold hands, but I couldn't make much sense of it."

Sylvia looked closely at Mrs. Selby. She was a well-dressed, prosperous-looking young woman who seemed sane despite her obvious distress. Sylvia decided that there must be something to her claims. "Well, this is all very strange," she said, jotting down some notes. "And how long have you and your husband lived in this house?"

"Only two months. We bought the house from its original owner, who took a job in another city."

"And have you yourself noticed anything unusual about the nurse's quarters, Mrs. Selby?"

Mrs. Selby smiled shyly. "To be honest, Miss Forrest, ever since these strange happenings began, I've been afraid to set foot in that room. After the second nurse ran away, though, my husband said he was going to get to the bottom of all this nonsense, so he spent the night in the room. Nothing at all happened. He said he had a fine night's sleep—that all this screaming and fussing was just women's hysteria, nothing more. I wanted to believe him, Miss Forrest, and so I hired another nurse. And her first night in the house, it was exactly the same—the screams, the terror, the running away."

"Well, Mrs. Selby," Sylvia said, snapping her notebook shut. "I'm not a great believer in hysteria in the first place, but even if I were, it would seem to me that when three unrelated women have the exact same terrified reaction to the exact same place at the exact same hour of the night, something besides hysteria is involved."

"Oh, Miss Forrest, I am so glad you believe me!" Tears spilled from Mrs. Selby's eyes. "Charles thinks I have grown so nervous, I need to take a rest cure! And I've been too frightened to tell anyone else about this. I've been in so much distress, Miss Forrest, and then, too, not having a nurse for my two little ones is very difficult."

"I would imagine it is, for you," Sylvia said, thinking these spoiled upper-class women didn't know what difficult was! Sylvia's own mother had raised her and her five siblings besides, without even knowing what a nurse was. The whole family had lived in two cramped rooms and slept on pallets on the floor. It was only because of Sylvia's considerable talents as a medium that she was now able to afford such comfortable lodgings and to send money home to her family as well.

"Oh, Miss Forrest, you can't imagine the difficulty!" Mrs. Selby was nearly sobbing. "And so I am prepared to pay you handsomely if you can help me. I have some money saved that Charles doesn't know about."

"Clever girl," Sylvia said, trying to imagine what it must be like to depend on a husband for every penny and nickel. It was much better for a girl to earn her own money to do with as she pleased. "Well," Sylvia said, "the only way I can possibly help you is to examine the room that has been causing you trouble. If I could be there at the time of night when the trouble tends to occur, it would be even better. But I'm not sure how I can be in your house without your husband knowing about it."

"On Friday evenings he goes out with business associates," Mrs. Selby offered. "He stays out until the wee hours and sleeps late on Saturday morning."

No wonder, Sylvia thought. A Friday night at the brothel must be exhausting for the poor man. But she held her tongue. "Well, then, Mrs. Selby, if you will write down directions to your home, I'll be there on Friday night around eleven o'clock and will leave early Saturday morning after having solved your problem."


The Selby house was exactly as Sylvia imagined it—large and white, with a turret and heavy with gingerbread trim, like an elaborately decorated wedding cake.

Mrs. Selby answered the door before Sylvia so much as raised her fist to knock. "I heard your steps on the porch," Mrs. Selby half-whispered. "I was afraid if you knocked, it might wake the children."

Sylvia could tell that Mrs. Selby was quite nervous; apparently, she was not accustomed to deceiving her husband. "Of course."

"Do come in." Mrs. Selby stepped aside so Sylvia could enter the lavishly decorated foyer, with its green-flocked wallpaper and gilt-trimmed mirrors. "The nurse's room is on the third floor. May I offer you a cup of tea before you . . . begin?"

"No, thank you, Mrs. Selby. I am very anxious to see the room, if you would show me the way."

Sylvia followed Mrs. Selby up two winding flights of stairs into a hallway that was painted plain white, a far cry from the fancy flocked wallpaper of the first floor. Clearly this was where the servants were housed. "Is anyone else staying on this floor tonight, Mrs. Selby?"

"No. The cook and the maid both go home at the end of the

day. Ever since the troubles started in the nurse's room, everyone is too frightened to stay the night."

"I see," Sylvia said. "This is the room, is it?"

Mrs. Selby nodded.

"Well, then, good night, Mrs. Selby. I will give you a full report in the morning."

In the dull glow of the gaslight, Sylvia saw this was the kind of uncomfortable room in which the financially comfortable boarded their help—windowless, with an iron bed, an unwelcoming straight-backed chair, a cast-off bureau, and a cracked washstand. Sylvia sat on the edge of the bed, closed her eyes, and tried to sense the presence of a spirit—a spirit that, given the reactions it had provoked, was quite possibly malevolent.

But Sylvia sensed nothing—no variations in the temperature of the room, no feelings of an unseen presence, none of the uneasiness that usually overtook her when she was in the presence of a restless spirit.

Could Mr. Selby be right? Could it be that the only presence in this room was a figment of the imagination of three hysterical females? She certainly hoped not. Mr. Selby sounded thoroughly unpleasant, and she would love to have the opportunity to prove him wrong. She lay back on the lumpy mattress and waited.

She had begun to doze when a whoosh of cold air hit her in the face. She opened her eyes and sat up to see a hazy figure floating near the foot of the bed.

It was a woman, or rather, it was the spirit of a woman. Sylvia had talked with spirits who had answered her by rapping on tables, had heard noises made by spirits, had seen candle flames blown out by spirits, but she had never seen a fully formed apparition standing before her—what those less conversant in the spirit realm would have called a ghost. Looking at the apparition, Sylvia felt no fear, only amazement, like a scientist gazing at a new discovery.

Perhaps she would have felt differently if the apparition had not been so lovely—if it had been a black-robed spectre rattling chains and moaning, but instead it was a beautiful woman with long, heavy hair loose around her shoulders, wearing a dressing gown as if she were coming to bed. The dressing gown was filmy, but so was the apparition, which was not transparent but translucent, with the soft glow of moonstone. Its face was as daintily formed as a profile in a cameo brooch, and the features were those of a young woman. Sylvia would have been surprised if, in life, this lovely woman had been much older than twenty. The spirit's face broke out in a smile—not a cruel smile, but one of pure joy. "Darling," it said, and its voice was like the wind in the trees, "you've come. I am so glad! And everyone else is asleep—no need to be afraid."

Since no one else was in the room, Sylvia assumed the apparition was speaking to her, though why it would call her "darling" and seem so happy to see her was a mystery. Before Sylvia could think of a reply to the apparition's strange words, it had floated across the room and lain down beside her and was stroking her face with its cool fingers. The touch felt like a human touch, but lighter, softer, like being stroked very gently by a feather. "My love," the apparition whispered in Sylvia's ear, "how I've longed for you!"

The breeze of the apparition's breath blew in Sylvia's ear, and the feathery touch of its hand on her throat made her break out in goose bumps. But these weren't the goose bumps of fear, but rather the anticipation she felt when she watched the curtain rise at the theatre. Only now, Sylvia wasn't certain what it was she was anticipating.

The apparition waved her hands over the buttons of Sylvia's long dress, and they unfastened themselves one by one—pop, pop, pop, pop, pop. Sylvia was trembling now, perhaps even a little afraid, but something—was it curiosity or something baser than curiosity?—kept her from screaming or moving from the bed.

Her dress slipped off and discarded, Sylvia felt the laces of her corset pop loose. She felt the freedom she always felt at the end of the day when her corset came off—the liberation of her soft flesh, the sudden ease of breath and movement. But of course, this was not the same as undressing alone in her own quarters; it was the apparition which was undressing Sylvia and which floated above her, sighing, "So beautiful."

The apparition lowered herself onto Sylvia's body. It weighed nothing more than a light blanket, yet Sylvia could feel the swell of its bosom, the softness of its flesh, the tickle of its hair against her shoulders. Its lips pressed to hers felt like chilled velvet.

Sylvia was no stranger to kisses. She had been out with gentlemen before, gentlemen who probably would have married her had she not always found fault with them. These gentlemen had given her rough-lipped goodnight kisses scratchy with stubble and stinking of tobacco, but this kiss—the kiss of the apparition—was as light and sweet and delicious as cool meringue on a hot day. She was lost inside this kiss, and no matter how long it lasted, it was not long enough.

The apparition's mouth moved from Sylvia's lips to her throat to her collarbone to the swell of her bosom where no one had ever kissed her before. The touch was so light, so gentle, so ethereal, and yet so intense at the same time. The apparition's cool hands moved over Sylvia's bosom, belly, and legs, and she shivered and sighed at the sweet strangeness of the touch, her head leaned back and her eyes closed.

Soon the apparition found a part of Sylvia's body with which Sylvia herself had only the most passing of acquaintances. Sylvia did not know what the apparition was doing, but the sensation . . . It was as if she had lived her whole life thinking she couldn't carry a tune and then suddenly discovered she could sing with an unearthly beauty, like the Sirens of the sea on a heavenly choir of angels. Her whole body was singing, releasing music more perfect than she ever dreamed possible.

When Sylvia opened her eyes, the apparition was lying beside her, a beatific smile on its lovely face. "You," it said, stroking Sylvia's cheek, "have set me free."

Sylvia could only find one word. "How?"

The apparition placed its hand on Sylvia's. "Now that I am free, I am also free to tell you my story. This room was my room when

I was alive. I was the housemaid here. This room was mine alone, but I often shared it with Maggie, the kitchen maid. You see, with me and Maggie, it was like it was with you and me just now. I loved her, body and soul."

"And did she love you?"

The apparition smiled, but the smile quickly faded. "For a time she did, yes. And when she did, it was all the happiness I could have asked for. But then there was another . . ." The apparition gazed off into the distance.

"Another girl?" Sylvia asked.

"No." The apparition let out a bitter laugh. "A boy. The new gardener. He was sweet on Maggie from the moment he got here. It took her some time to come around to him, but she did . . . once she saw he could give her a wedding ring and a place of her own she could clean instead of somebody else's."

"So, she broke your heart?" Sylvia asked, feeling sorry for this sad spirit.

"She did more than that. She was terrified, you see, that I'd tell her little gardener about her and me . . . terrified I'd ruin her reputation and her chance at being a respectable wife. So she didn't tell me about her friend, not at first . . . she kept right on with me like she always had, sneaking into my room, bringing me sweets from the kitchen. 'Here, have a bit of cake, Tess,' she'd say, and fool that I was, I always took it."

The truth of the spirit's fate hit Sylvia like a fist in the stomach. "She poisoned you, didn't she?"

"That she did. Arsenic, it was. I never suspected her of anything because I loved her so dearly, but I kept getting sicker and sicker until I wasn't able to get out of bed. The mistress of the house called the doctor, but he couldn't find anything wrong with me. And all the time, Maggie was pretending to take such good care of me, bringing me tea and broth to sip, all of it laced with poison."

Sylvia took the weightless apparition in her arms. "You poor, poor girl."

"Oh, but the poison wasn't the worst part," the apparition sighed. "The worst part was the curse."

"The curse?"

"When I was very near death, so ill I couldn't move or speak, Maggie came to my room. She told me she had been poisoning me, had been doing it because she wanted to marry Toby and didn't want me to destroy her chance of happiness. 'You thought you could ruin me with your unnatural love,' she said. 'But I have powers which you cannot know.' She tossed a handful of foul-smelling herbs in my face and said, 'Death is only the beginning of your suffering. This room will be your spirit's prison, and the only way you will ever be free is if a living woman submits to your desires. Until then, you will never see the world past these walls.'"

In her studies of the occult, Sylvia had heard of spells and curses, but this was her first proof that such things actually held power. It was turning out to be an extraordinary night. "And so you've been trapped here."

"Yes, until tonight. I have approached each woman who has slept in this room the same way I approached you, but each one has run away screaming." The apparition stroked Sylvia's hair. "Why were you different?"

"I don't know," Sylvia said. "Perhaps because I am not frightened by the spirit world. Perhaps because I wanted you to . . . to touch me."

"Thank you," the apparition whispered. It brushed its lips against Sylvia's, and when Sylvia opened her eyes, it was gone.


A knock on the door jolted Sylvia awake. "Miss Forrest?" A voice that, after a moment of disorientation, Sylvia identified as Mrs. Selby's, called, "Are you all right?"

"Yes." Sylvia sat up, noticing that her underclothes were still in disarray from the night before. "I'll be with you in a moment, Mrs. Selby." It took longer than a moment to right her underclothes, button her dress, and pin up her hair, but when she stepped outside of the room, Mrs. Selby was still waiting in the hallway.

"I am sorry if I woke you, Miss Forrest, but it is almost nine o' clock, and my husband will be up soon."

"Almost nine?" Sylvia was shocked. "I never sleep so late. I must have been exhausted from last night's . . . exertions."

Mrs. Selby's eyes grew wide. "Last night, was there—"

"A visitation?" Sylvia interrupted. "Yes, there was. But you won't be troubled any more, Mrs. Selby. Her spirit has been released." A pleasurable shiver ran through Sylvia, and she felt that somehow last night's visitation had released her spirit, too.

# Loving Ophelia

## Barbara Johnson

She came to me in the deep hours of the night, skirting along the edges of my nightmares. There, but not there. I remember the first time, a whisper of a memory, like her, along with a faint whiff of lilacs. I felt a slight indentation, as if a cat or a small dog sat on my bed; just the barest dip of the mattress. My consciousness toyed with me, making me aware but not letting me fully wake up. But I know no one was with me.

In the morning, I thought I'd simply had a bad dream, but I checked my doors and windows just in case. All were locked tight, as I'd left them the night before. I dismissed the dream, getting ready for work as usual and having an uneventful day in my capacity as a fashion buyer for a department store. It was my dream to someday work for an upscale establishment like Barney's or Saks, where I would buy from only the best—Versace, Gucci, Gautier, Badgley Mischka. Instead, I concentrated on buying clothes with "Made in the USA" labels for wannabe Britneys and Christinas. It wasn't very exciting, but it paid the bills, barely.

My friends Kim and Therese insisted that night that I go to dinner with them. I said no at first. The rent was due and I was down to my last $20 until next Tuesday. Kim can be very persuasive, however; plus, she promised it would be their treat, and I never turn down a free meal. There have been plenty of nights when all I had was just enough for a grilled cheese sandwich.

We went to a mediocre Italian place and somehow the talk turned to dreams. It didn't even occur to me to mention mine from the night before, that's how insignificant it had become. But as Kim talked about a nightmare where she was devoured by a monstrous snake, I felt an unease creep along my spine. My breath felt tight in my lungs.

Therese's hand shot out. "Are you okay, Ophelia?"

Startled by her touch, I pulled away. She looked surprised. "Yes. Why?" My voice sounded fine to my ears, though there was a trembling inside me.

"You're pale as a ghost."

Ghost. It was funny she should use that term. And yet, I knew my dream was not of a ghost. I laughed nervously. "It's nothing. Really."

I couldn't tell them about my dream. What was to tell? A fleeting sensation of someone in my room? A common phenomenon of someone who lived alone they would tell me, dismissing my anxieties as couples are wont to do. And as I sat there in the bright light, playing with a glass of cheap Merlot, I too dismissed the dream and heard my laughter quietly, as if I stood in another room.

The next few nights I didn't remember my dreams, good or bad. I awakened in the mornings, seemingly refreshed, yet with a feeling of heaviness. If I'd had a cat, I would have suspected her of sleeping on my face, making me feel suffocated, yet not. And then, the dream came back. When I felt the indentation on my bed and smelled the lilacs, I tried hard to waken to full consciousness but could not. Through half-lidded eyes, I tried to see if someone was there. I saw only darkness, no shadows of someone's presence.

The dream returned night after night. I was powerless to do anything. And each time it happened, my fear grew. I managed to stay awake one night, watching TV while I sat on the couch with all the lights blazing. I got up and walked around when I felt myself falling asleep. I must have drunk at least two pots of double-strength coffee. The next day, my work colleagues told me I looked like hell. Little did they know, I felt like it too. I barely made it through the day before going home and collapsing. Mercifully, the dream did not come to me that night, but then it soon returned in the nights that followed.

At first, the dream came sporadically. I never knew from one night to the next if I would have it. The dread almost became worse than the dream itself. My work suffered. My social life, what little there was of it, suffered.

But then the dream came nightly. In fact, it soon became routine and almost a comfort. I no longer dreaded falling asleep. And in the middle of the night, she would sit next to me. I don't remember when I decided "it" was a she. How to discern a female presence from a male one? I couldn't say, but perhaps it was what I wished, so I could justify no longer being afraid. It was a grave mistake, but one that I would not identify until it was too late.

I don't know how many weeks had gone by when the dream changed. Her presence accompanied by the smell of lilacs woke me as usual, but this time I felt something on my body—the barest sensation of a touch. Light and feathery. I heard my own intake of breath, felt the goose bumps rise on my flesh. My fear returned, sharp as the sting of my mother's hand against my cheek. I stared into the darkness, willing myself to see whoever or whatever was there, but there was nothing. I wanted to turn on the light, but I was immobile. She left as quickly as she'd come, and all I could do was weep.

She came to me again the next night, her touch gentle yet insistent, possessive. And as the nights blended into days and back into nights again, the tenderness left her. There were no more whispering caresses, only what felt like cat claws raking across my skin. But in the mornings, my body was smooth and unmarked. I don't know how I managed to wake up, follow my normal routine, and make it through the workday. One day melded into another. I did my job by rote, responding to people when they talked to me, yet not even knowing what I was saying.

"Is everything okay with you, Ophelia?" my supervisor, Mrs. Carlson, asked one day. "You're looking haggard."

Haggard. What a strange word. I associate it with ancient crones or women who have six children clinging to their skirts.

"I'm fine," I replied, "just busy getting ready for the spring line."

"How long's it been since you took a vacation?"

I shrugged. I didn't remember and I didn't really care. "Don't know."

"I want you to take a week off."

Startled, I looked up from my purchase order. Mrs. Carlson stood exactly like my mother had when she was irritated with me— one leg in front of the other, weight on the back leg, and arms crossed. She had the look too—tight lips, one eyebrow cocked. I fully expected one foot to start tapping.

"I feel fine. Really."

"I insist. You've got the vacation. I want you to come back refreshed. I've not said anything because you're one of my best employees, but your work has really taken a turn for the worse. You're distracted, tired, snippy . . ."

Hmmm, snippy? No one had called me "snippy" since my little brother. I heard Mrs. Carlson's voice in the background, but I had already tuned her out the way I used to tune my mother out.

"Okay," I said. I pushed the purchase order toward her. "You just have to tally up the totals."

This time it was her turn to be startled. "You're not going to finish it before you leave?"

"Nope."

And with that, I left, not even knowing or caring if I'd ever come back. Dinner that night was a hard-boiled egg and a package of Oodles of Noodles. I tried to watch some TV, but I was restless. Nothing held my interest. Reading didn't work either. I threw the book down and got up from the couch. I was more than restless. I was nervous and afraid. I didn't want to admit it, but I knew she'd come tonight, and it would be different. I was scared and eager at the same time. I looked at my watch. Two hours until dark. She'd come then, like a vampire of folklore slinking in as soon as the sun set. I felt a shiver along my spine and the hair on my neck prickle.

And then a sudden calm descended upon me, and I knew I had to get ready for her. Perhaps tonight she'd reveal herself to me. She had no corporeal body, of that I was certain. She would be ethereal, a mystical being come to life for me alone. And she would be beautiful.

I put on some soothing music, something with chirping birds and running water in the background. It was probably one of Therese's meditation tapes. She'd loaned me one or two a few weeks ago, thinking they would help me sleep. I couldn't remember the last time I'd seen her and Kim. I made a mental note to call them in the morning.

I never had been much of a girly-girl. Not that I was a tomboy either. I'd always considered myself kind of neutral. But tonight was special. I wanted to look pretty for her. When I ran the bath, I added essence of lilac to remind me of her. I soaked in the tub for a long time, taking the extra effort to scrub my skin until it tingled and turned bright pink, like the blush of a new bride. A bride. That's almost how I felt. And what I looked like after I finished. I gazed at myself in the mirror.

The room was lit only by candles. I didn't know I owned so many of them, but I'd found candles hidden away everywhere, and now they covered every available surface in my bedroom. They flickered in some unfelt breeze, casting dancing shadows along the walls. In the mirror I looked pale, the bridal flush long gone. My reddish-brown hair, still wavy from dampness, fell softly to my shoulders. My ordinary brown eyes tonight seemed luminous and beautiful. My lips looked full and berry stained. The finishing touch was a long nightgown of black silk, not bridal white. The lace bodice was such that it revealed just the right amount of flesh, hinting at rounded womanliness. I wanted to touch myself, but I needed to wait. She would touch me tonight, as she had other nights.

I glanced out the window. Darkness had come. Not even the moon dared show its face tonight. I carefully closed the curtains before I lay down on the bed like some sacrificial virgin. I smiled at the absurdity of the thought. Although I'd never been with a man, I doubted I qualified as a virgin. There was more than one way to lose a hymen.

I don't know how long I'd slept, but I woke when I sensed her. The aroma of lilacs was almost overwhelming this time. Most of the candles had burnt out. I had no idea how late it was. I felt the first familiar rush of dread. It didn't matter how many times she came to me; in the first few seconds I was always afraid. I stared hard, looking for her. In all these months, she'd never revealed herself to me in a form I could see.

"I want to see you," I whispered.

In answer, her soft caress on my arm turned harsh. I winced at the slice of pain. I took a deep breath, willing the fear and the pain away. As if sensing my acquiescence, her caress became gentle again. I closed my eyes, feeling the touch of her fingers along my body—face, neck, shoulders, breasts, stomach, hips, thighs, legs. Somewhere along the way, I lost my nightgown. Naked and vulnerable, I let her have her way with me. Desire and revulsion warred within me as she took me.

Her mouth alternately kissed and bit me. I would cry out at each bite and moan at each kiss. My skin felt worshipped and then as if I was being flayed alive. Pleasure and pain, pain and pleasure. Who knew where one ended and the other started? The minutes and hours melded into one, as she both tortured me and revered me. And then, something new. She spread my legs, and I screamed as she thrust into me, pounding deep again and again until I was certain the wetness flowing between my legs must be blood. Then, her mouth and tongue warm and soothing against me, taking the place of her hand. Licking me and sucking me until this time I cried out with joy as wave after wave of orgasm sent me spiraling into sheer bliss. A moment's rest as I struggled to catch my breath. My throat felt parched. I wanted water desperately. Her fingers fluttered against me, then entered me, gently this time. I could feel them inside me as she drank from me. I cried out as I came again, my body seeming to dissolve into crystals of light. I knew then that no mortal woman would ever satisfy me. I would be condemned forever to wanting only this unearthly presence who tormented me in more ways than one.

Then, the barest whisper. "Do you want me?"

The sound sent chills of fear through me. I clutched the covers to me. Wasn't this what I'd been wanting? Some physical manifestation of this phantom, this female being who'd come to me in a dream all those months ago?

I felt the faintest hint of a kiss against my neck. Nails light along my arm, then across my breasts. My body responded on its own, forgetting the pain, wanting only the pleasure. Her fingers traveled down, across my belly to the inside of my thighs. I couldn't help but raise my hips, urging her fingers to once again plunge into me.

Her fingers stopped their caress. "No," she said, laughing softly. "You have to tell me you want me."

Again, that crushing fear. Of course I wanted her. I'd wanted her for days, for weeks, for months. But I was terrified to say yes. And what would I say yes to? I saw nothing, and until tonight, I heard nothing.

"I want—" I couldn't say it.

The silence was more frightening than ever. I could feel her anger, her hostility. I wanted to feel her love, her desire. "Let me see you."

Her fingers pressing into me were like hot coals. I screamed. Or at least, I thought I did. Surely the neighbors would hear? Would they come bursting in and save me? I could feel the tears on my cheeks. I didn't want her rage. Then, the pain faded away as her touch once again turned soft. Why did she torment me so? I gave her everything she wished. I took a deep breath. I would tell her what she wanted to hear.

"Tell me you want me, and I will let you see me."

"Will you stay with me? I don't want you to leave me."

Laughter again. I fought against the panic. Why should I fear her still? An animal's instinct is strong, but we humans have learned to suppress our instinct. We let our reason or our desires control us. Right now, my sexual desire, however distorted, controlled me. I wanted to feel her mouth on me, her hand inside me, her body on mine. I wanted her to love me. Ophelia.

"I want you."

The last candle sputtered out, and the smell of lilacs disappeared as if sucked out by some powerful fan. I felt a brief sense of unease. What had I done? A small, glowing light appeared beside my bed, calming me. It grew in brilliance. I reached out my arms to it. At last, we would be together in every way. The light began to take shape. I smiled as I saw the unmistakable form of a woman, but then wrinkled my nose at the sudden smell of decay. With a bright flare, she materialized. I opened my mouth to scream as I beheld the apparition before me.

Pale, rotting flesh hung from a naked body seemingly long dead. Hollow black eyes in a white face framed with matted, crawling hair. Bloodless lips and razor sharp teeth. Long, bony fingers tipped with pointed nails. The stench of her breath brought tears to my eyes. She was my own worst nightmare come to life. I could smell my own terror. Paralyzed, I could only press into the mattress as she floated over me, more mist than substance, and lowered her ice-cold body onto mine.

"You're mine now," she said, "forever." Then, all faded to black.


"Funny how Ophelia just disappeared like that last year," Kim said to Therese as they looked through an old photo album. She pointed to a picture of all three of them in happier times.

"Something was really bothering her," Therese replied. "I just wish she'd been able to talk to us about it. Do you think she killed herself?"

"I wish I knew." Kim flipped through to another page of photos. "Hey, I never noticed that before."

Therese leaned over. "What?" She followed Kim's pointing finger. Photographed one night after a dinner at her place, Ophelia sat on her couch and smiled at the camera. "Who is that behind her?" Therese peered more closely at the photo and shuddered. "That's gotta be some kind of flaw in the film or the developing."

"I've never seen anything so creepy. Look at that face. Looks like something Stephen King would conjure up in one of his novels."

"I'll bet they had some punk working at the film place who decided to have some fun with Photoshop."

"Yeah," Kim said as she took the photo from the album and ripped it in half. "How annoying. I'll just have to find the negative and have it remade." She turned and kissed her lover. "Thanks for the lilacs, by the way. They smell terrific."

# Dream Lover
### Therese Szymanski

"Oh no you don't," Nikki said to me when we entered the bar. "No moping about the past. Cori is evil and deserves to die. And with any luck, she'll be here tonight when some gorgeous butch sweeps you off your feet."

I gave the doorman my cover charge. "I've never met a woman worth dating in a bar, and I really don't expect that to change suddenly tonight. As for Cori, if she's here, then I'm leaving—no matter who I have to pull you off of."

Just then a woman jostled into me. "Excuse me," she said in a deep, rich voice. Her eyes were dark and hypnotic. "Have we met before?"

"I . . . I . . ." I tried to remember who and where I was.

"ID please?" the doorman asked.

"What? Oh, yeah, okay . . ." I pulled out my driver's license and handed it to him, then turned back toward the woman. She was gone.

"Who was that?" Nikki asked after the doorman gave us back our IDs and stamped our hands.

"I don't know." I gazed around the bar, searching for the woman and not finding her.

"Well c'mon then, let's find her." Nikki grabbed my arm and led me through the crowd. "Just remember not to *look* for her. You can't try too hard or it'll be obvious."

Nikki led me on a circuit of the bar, smiling and saying hey to friends we hadn't seen in a while. I didn't see the woman anywhere. She had disappeared like magic. But I kept looking over my shoulder anyway because I felt as if someone was watching me.

"I just don't know what you ever saw in that androgynous vanilla wafer anyway," Tracy was saying to me, "C'mon, girlfriend, somebody like you can easily find a nice butch who'll take care of you."

"Oooo, speak of the devil," Brenda said, nodding toward the railing near the dance floor. I turned to see Cori watching me. She looked away as soon as she realized she was busted.

"Hey c'mon, no getting all down now," Nikki said, grabbing me by the arm and leading me right to the dance floor.

"I told you I'd leave if she was here."

"Not when such a great song is playing. Besides, she's gained weight and you look fabulous! So it's time to rub her nose in it!"

I would've just left, but I kept hoping I'd see that butch again. So I danced. Nikki was a good dancer, and we'd danced together ever since high school, so I soon lost myself in the beat . . . and one song drove into the next and the next . . . I felt as if I could dance all night, but Nikki stopped moving mid-song.

"I'm parched," she said, "I'll be back in a minute."

I wondered why Nikki had suddenly fled, then became aware of a presence behind me. It was the mystery woman. I just knew it. I slowly rotated my hips as I pulled my hands up through my long red hair, shaking it out. I ran my hands down over my halter top and denim-clad hips. Her hands slid under mine as she pressed up behind me. She ran her hands up to my just-exposed middle, then down to briefly hook her thumbs into my low-riders. She grasped my hips and yanked me back against her.

We moved as one, with her guiding my every move. I wanted to see her, to look into those amazing eyes again, but she was the one in control, and she was making me know it. Her lips were on my exposed shoulders, teasing me. Her teeth gently nibbled my neck.

She could've taken me right there on the dance floor if she wanted to. I would have let her.

Hell, she could've shown Cori how it was done.

Finally, she let me turn around. She pulled me up close, her well-muscled thigh lodged between my legs on my already aching wetness. My hands found her hips, enjoying the feel of her well-oiled leather pants.

She moved quickly and surely, leading me into a stream of sophisticated dance moves, including lifting me up off the ground and spinning me around her as easily as if I was only a bottle of beer. Her arms were reassuringly thick with a bit of definition, but not so large as to destroy the feeling of a sleek and sinewy black panther. She wasn't much taller than I, but her strength and sureness made her feel much larger.

I was almost afraid to look into her eyes again, afraid they'd freeze me again, especially since I now wanted so much to appear smooth and sophisticated. It felt almost as if the entire world had disappeared and it was only the two of us, the beat of the music guiding our hearts, making them beat in time together.

The music went into house-mix, transitioning to a new tune. She pulled me in close and whispered into my ear, "How about a breather, gorgeous?"

I nodded and allowed her to guide me to the table a Cheshire-cat grinning Nikki had commandeered. I glanced down and saw the woman wore heavy biker's boots and could only wonder how she could move so gracefully in such shoes.

She pulled out a chair for me, then leaned down to ask what I'd like to drink. She leaned across the table, picked up Nikki's drink, sniffed it, and headed to the bar.

"You go girl!" Nikki said to me.

I could only stare after her until she faded into the crowd. Above her tight, black leather pants she wore a slightly loose, black V-neck T-shirt that complemented her short, mussed-up black hair.

"So what's her name?" Nikki asked, bringing my attention back to her as my mystery butch disappeared into the crowd by the bar.

"I don't know. We were dancing."

"Yeah, I noticed, and so did almost everybody in the bar. I'm surprised no one told you to get a room."

"I wouldn't have noticed if they did."

"So you don't know anything about her?"

"She's a great dancer, hot as hell, and a damned good dresser. That ain't some Fruit-of-the-Loom T she's wearing."

"Nobody knows anything about her," Nikki said. I turned to look at her. She shrugged. "I checked around while you two were out there tripping the light fantastic. I wonder what she does for a living?"

Nikki was very big into money. She realized her dreams of a sugar butch to take care of her were only dreams, but she hated that the ones she really fell for usually slept on a smelly mattress in the middle of the floor of some roach-infested room. She also hated getting ripped off when she asked them to spend the night with her. "I don't know. She's gotta have a decent job to dress like that."

"You'd be surprised. Some spend all their money on clothes, jewelry, their wheels, and drugs. But I think you're right about her. I bet she's into computers. Maybe a hacker of some sort."

"Hackers don't have arms, and style, like that."

"But look at how pale she is, she must be inside all the time."

I had noticed. All the black made it that much more noticeable. "You were the one telling me to flaunt it in front of Cori. I think I'm doing that admirably. So don't piss on my goddamned parade!"

Suddenly a heavy leather jacket landed on the seat next to me. "Here you go," butch said, placing a drink next to me. She put a drink next to Nikki, "Slow Comfortable Screw, I believe?"

"The bartender remembered, huh?" Nikki replied. "Thank you." Nikki changed drinks every night. The bartender hadn't remembered; somehow butch had known from a single sniff just what she was drinking.

The butch sat down with her jacket and hefted her Miller-Lite-in-a-bottle to her lips. She placed a pack of Marlboro Lights on the table, along with a gold Zippo engraved with a devil with a horn, halo and fangs.

I picked up the lighter, flicked it open and inhaled. I don't know what it is, but I really enjoy the smell of lighter fluid. I flicked it shut and studied the engraving. "Interesting design."

"Some folks have an angel on one shoulder, a devil on the other. They're combined in me." She had a truly devilish grin.

"And the fangs?" Nikki asked, leaning forward. She loved getting the scoop on anyone new to the scene.

Butch turned and looked her right in the eye. "I don't get out much during the day." She shrugged. "It's made some of my friends refer to me as a 'vampire.'" She raised an eyebrow as a dare. And then a teasing grin wound its way across her lips.

Nikki was my best friend. I trusted her with all my innermost thoughts and feelings. But I didn't trust her with a woman I was interested in. I could trust her with my girlfriend, my butch, but until that "my" was attached, I couldn't trust her. We had the same taste, after all.

I put my hand on butch's, bringing her attention back to me. But then I had to come up with something to say. "I'm sorry, I didn't catch your name."

"That's because I didn't throw it." She took my hand in hers, which was strangely cool and dry, stood, and bowed slightly. "Allow me to introduce myself." She looked into my eyes, and I was lost. "My name is Daron Silvers." She kissed the back of my hand. "And you are?"

I was mesmerized by those eyes. I had to force myself to reply. "Victoria. Victoria Hayes."

She took my hand in both of hers, and then ran her fingers up my naked forearm. "The pleasure is all mine." Her hand found my exposed shoulder, sending chills coursing through my body. She touched my cheek, and lifted my face so my lips met hers.

I met her lips with mine open. Hers were soft and gentle, but her tongue was forceful in my mouth. I lifted my arms around her neck, trying to draw her in, wanting to share our heartbeat again, wanting to share the air I breathed with her . . .

She pulled away far too soon, leaving me breathless in my chair.

She took a long draw on her beer, and a short one on her smoke, which she held like a joint. She picked up her jacket and put it on. She put her smokes in her pocket, then took another long draw from her beer, draining it. She knelt beside me, ran her thumb over the side of my face, down my neck, and across my breast.

Then she yanked my head to the side and put her mouth next to my ear. "Next time, wear a dress," she whispered into my ear.

She picked up her cigarette and left.

I still couldn't move when Nikki picked up the lighter. "She left this."

"She meant to." I took it from Nikki and ran my fingers over the engraving, not looking at it.

"Cori's staring right at you."

"I don't care," I said, standing. "It's time for me to leave." I kept the lighter clasped in my hand the entire way home.

"Are you okay girl?" Nikki asked when we pulled up in front of my building. I nodded. "She really got you, didn't she?"

I turned to her and smiled, still holding onto that lighter. "Yeah, she did." Then I turned and walked into the two-bedroom apartment I shared with my sister. I knew Nikki watched me until I went through the front door. I locked it behind me, and flicked the light twice, knowing that was the sign people always gave when they were home safely. And I was home safely.

But I didn't want to be.


I fell asleep immediately. I can't remember what I did before falling into my bed, but . . .

I remember the dreams.

I walked into the bathroom at the bar. Daron walked up beside me, watching me while I washed my hands. She stood just to my side as I checked my makeup, wanting to make sure I looked my best for the handsome butch with whom I was flirting.

I turned to look at her, and she took my hands in hers, then pulled me up close. I looked in the mirror, and saw only me.

I looked at her, but I was in my bed, realizing it was all a dream. I sat up and realized I wasn't alone.

I looked up to my right and gasped, pulling my covers up around me and starting to scream.

She laid a finger against my lips. "Shhhhh . . ." she said, sitting next to me. She caressed my cheek. "Are you her?"

I wanted to lose myself in her warmth, but she wasn't really warm. I pulled away to ask her about it, but when I did so, I became lost in her eyes. Her eyes stopped me.

They made me lose all thought, all intention, all ability to speak.

And she looked deep into my eyes, seeing everything about me. I felt more exposed than I ever did when I was naked.

"Who have you been?" she asked. "Are you the one?"

"I . . . I don't know. Am I?" I wanted to be, with everything I was, I wanted to be.

She leaned forward and brushed her lips against mine. Her hands were on my waist underneath my T-shirt, on my skin. I parted my lips, practically begging her to enter me. She did. Her tongue was possessive, taking me over and letting me know who was in charge.

"Who are you?" I finally asked, having to break away to breathe. She didn't seem to need to breathe. She hadn't been sweating at the bar, in fact, she never even seemed really warm at all.

She didn't respond. Instead, she pulled off my shirt in one swift movement. She kissed my neck while she felt me up with her hands, caressing my breasts and lightly pinching my nipples.

She sucked on my neck before biting. Hard. I cried out.

She muffled my cries with her mouth. She pushed me down on the bed, her hands guiding my hips. She was neither gentle nor hurtful; she was aggressive as only a woman who really knows what she wants can be.

She ripped off the boxers I slept in, leaving me naked. She ran her hands over my body, as if learning the territory. "Rebecca," she said, tracing small circles on my skin.

I didn't care what name she called me. It was a dream after all.

She lay half on top of me, her powerful thigh between my legs, opening me and pressing against me. I whimpered and arched against her, pressing against her with all I was.

I moaned out loud and she moved down my body, sucking my neck, biting my nipples, her hand going down between my legs and touching me. I was so wet even she gasped.

"Please, I need . . . now . . ."

Her fingers slid up and down me. She entered me with two fingers while her thumb played with my clit, causing me to writhe under her.

She went down between my legs, tasting me even as she spread my legs wider with her powerful shoulders. Her hands explored my breasts, squeezing my hardened nipples while her tongue gingerly explored me.

She was exquisite. It was like she knew exactly how I wanted it.

"Rebecca," she moaned as her fingers slid up into me.


The next morning I curled around her body, and found only a pillow as my mind came to consciousness. It was chilly. I got up and pushed the window closed the rest of the way. I sometimes left it slightly open because I liked the coolness when I slept.

I went about taking my shower and getting into my nylons, heels, skirt and blouse for work.

I was an automaton, still wrapped up in what had happened the night before—both at the bar, and in my dreams.

"So what happened last night?" Veronica, my sister, asked.

"Nikki pulled me out, wanted to have some fun, no big." I grabbed my jacket and pulled it on.

"Then what was all that moaning about?"

I put my hands into my pockets. My fingers automatically locked around the lighter. "What moaning?"

"That I heard in the middle of the night. Sounded like somebody was having an awfully good time. So who'd you meet?"

"No one." And I closed the door behind me.

Veronica pulled the door open, calling down the stairs, "Today's Sunday. You don't have to go to work."

I stopped in my tracks. "I'm meeting Nikki for coffee," I said, finally.

"Not dressed like that you're not."

I wondered what I might do at this hour on a Sunday morning and came up blank. I sighed and trudged back up the stairs to face the inquisition. "I came home alone last night. I met a woman but she didn't come home with me."

"Huh, must've been some woman to have you moaning like that . . . all night."

Finally I grinned. I couldn't hide anything from Veronica. We had always been close and she knew me far too well. I shook my head. "I was alone last night. But I dreamt about her."

"Oh really, all that from just a dream? I almost had to turn on the radio to cover the sounds and get some sleep."

"Why didn't you?"

"Are you kidding? I haven't seen any action of my own for far too long. I made the most of it."

"You are so nasty!"

"You bet I am. So wanna share?"


I met her on Saturday night. I dreamt of her the first time on Saturday night. And I kept on dreaming of her. Almost all night, every night.

By Tuesday night, I was sleeping in the nude, expecting the nightly dream, anticipating it.

I wanted to feel her cold hands on me, bringing warmth to my body, bringing me fully to life. All my exes combined never brought me to such heights, never gave me such ecstasy.

"I know you're going through a hard time," my boss said to me on Tuesday. "Just let me know if you need someone to talk to."

"I'm fine," I insisted for like the umpteenth time. I felt alive again.

She indicated the dark circles under my eyes. "Looks like you need to sleep a bit more."

And every night I studied her lighter before I went to bed, wondering what it really meant, and what it might all lead to.

No one knew Daron Silvers. And I asked around. Every evening, after work, I went home, changed and ate, and then did the rounds. I was obsessed.

Finally on Thursday night, I found her.

I felt her at Maxxie's before I saw her. And I knew from the moment I walked in that she knew I was there.

I gave the doorman my cover and showed him my ID, getting the obligatory stamp on my hand in return, and then I slowly slipped my ID and cash into my handbag. Then I looked up and directly into her eyes.

I advanced on her, panther meeting panther. I was dressed to kill, stiletto heels and all. I met her, eye to eye.

"Who are you?" I asked.

"I already told you, Daron Silvers."

"Nobody's ever heard of you."

"Not my fault." She reached into my purse and drew out her lighter. "I believe this is mine."

"I've been carrying it to return it to you."

"It's mine again now," she said, tucking it into the pocket of her leather pants. This time she wore a collarless black silk shirt above them.

She took me to the dance floor. I felt like I was under her power, like she controlled my every movement.

I was hers.

We danced till I started sweating, then I took her hand and led her from the dance floor. I led her out the back door and into the alley.

She threw me against the wall. The brick was cold against my exposed shoulders, and I realized my dreams were accurate: her hands were not warm. But she was as good as I had dreamt. In fact, I was not sure all this was not a dream. That this moment was real.

"Daron, Daron please, now!" She took me, wholly and completely. She possessed me. She owned me.

She left me panting in the alley by myself. She left me fulfilled, but still wanting.

It didn't matter. I pulled on my clothes and went to my car, with the feeling of her fist inside me, keeping me warm. I knew she wouldn't have gone back to the bar, so there was no reason for me to return.

But it didn't matter. I knew she'd still come to me tonight.

After all, she had yet to release me.


That night, I dreamt she came as usual through my closed bedroom window and loved me yet again. I didn't want that to happen so quickly, so easily. I wanted to speak to her, at least in my dreams, but that wasn't to be.

But in my dream, I stayed awake afterward long enough to ask her, "Stay the night."

"I can't."

"I love you."

"You shouldn't." She touched my face, pushing a loose lock of hair behind my ear.

"I do." Then, when she didn't reply, "Stay. Hold me."

"You're not her."

"I know." There was a lot I didn't know, but I did know I wasn't the Rebecca she longed for. "I don't care. Use me, pretend I'm her, I want you so badly I don't care."

"But you should."

I realized she wasn't coming back. She came tonight only to say goodbye, and although she hadn't said it, it was what she meant. "I don't." I sat up. I wasn't going to let her go so easily. I reached forward and ran my hands over her muscular shoulders, and down her arms. "Why don't you get more comfortable?" I started unbuttoning her shirt. She stopped me.

"No." She pulled me into her arms and lay down with me. "Go to sleep."

She wasn't a dream, she was real. She came to visit me every night. And now, she was here. She had no body temperature, no reflection, and didn't need to breathe. "Bite me."

"What?" she asked, pulling away.

I drew her back down, leading her mouth to my neck. "Bite me. Drink from me."

She touched my body and it was electric. I responded immediately, leading her hand down between my legs. I didn't want to let her go.

She slowly caressed me, working me back up into a frenzy until she slid her fingers up inside of me.

I couldn't see the end of this, but I knew this was it. I knew I'd never see her again. I hated Rebecca, whoever she was, and still desperately wanted to be her, whoever she was.

This time Daron looked into my eyes as her hands worked their magic.

I wanted to wake up with her, wanted to live with her, wanted her to look into my eyes when I came, wanted to see her body, naked. I wanted her to taste me as I came.

She gazed into my eyes as I neared my climax, moaning under her touch . . . I could see the raw desire, want and need in her eyes. I wanted to make her feel like she made me feel, but I couldn't. I could never, and she wouldn't let me even try . . .

I reached up, grabbed her by the back of her head, tangling my fingers in her short hair, and brought her mouth down to my neck.

"Please . . ."

I felt her lips on my neck, then I felt a moment of pain as her teeth pierced the tender flesh.

The pain only added to my excitement, and then it grew. As she drank my blood, it grew . . .

Her hand between my legs, her fingers inside of me, her mouth pressed to my neck drinking from me . . .

I exploded, screaming.

It took her a moment to pull away from my neck. I felt faint, either from the orgasm or from the blood loss. I wasn't sure which.

"Vicki! Are you all right?" I heard Veronica at my door.

"I'm fine," I yelled immediately, not wanting her to enter.

"Are you sure?" She worked the door, which I had locked.

"Yes. I'm fine." I looked at Daron. "Will I see you again?"

"No."

"Why can't you just pretend, imagine that I'm her?"

She smiled sadly. "I met her centuries before you were born. And someday, I will find her again."

She caressed my cheek, lightly kissed me, and stood.

I was desperate. "Please . . . this can't all have been a dream."

She touched my slightly bleeding neck. "You'll know it wasn't tomorrow." Then she reached into her pocket, pulled out her lighter and put it on my bedside table.

She leaned down, brushed my hair aside, and kissed my forehead. "I wish you were her." She went to my window, pushed it open, and jumped.

I lived on the sixth floor.


The next morning the alarm went off and I threw it across the room. I wanted to be left in my delicious dreams of the butch I was going to hook up with.

I stared at the ceiling, trying to relive my dreams, and finally got up and went to the bathroom. I started the shower and, while it was heating up, looked at myself in the mirror.

The left side of my neck was bloody. I grabbed a washcloth and cleaned the wound. There were two clear puncture marks. I went to my bedroom and looked at my bedside table.

A lighter was there. A very distinctive lighter.

"Yo, Vicki," Veronica said. "You going to work today, or can I hit the shower?"

"Why wouldn't I go to work?"

She stopped and looked at me. "Those nightmares are getting really bad. Maybe you should . . . I dunno, see a doctor or something."

I stared at her. I guess she saw something in my eyes because she waited for me to say something. So I did. "I did scream last night, huh?"

"Oh, hell, I thought somebody was killing you or something. So . . . what the hell happened to your neck?"

I turned from her and picked up the lighter. "Nothing."

# The Dream
## Amie M. Evans

I have a reccurring dream. I am on a street made of large purple stones cut into rectangles and held in place with white cement, long since gone gray. The stones, like hopscotch blocks drawn over and over, are framed by long purple curbstones. The street-lights glow warmly with textured light that only real fire can produce. The houses are closed up with wooden shutters and it is sometime in the early 1800s. I have on a black silk evening gown, a brooch with a diamond cross is pinned in the center of my breasts where the neckline plunges exposing my cleavage, the bodice is sheer black lace covering my exposed neck and shoulders. I have on long black gloves and black hook-and-eye boots. I am not wearing any panties or petticoat. I am lying on my back, my head crammed against the curb, looking up into the sky. The air is heavy with the smell of the sea, moist and salty. The sky is cloudy but the stars and a full moon break through between them.

Water pours over me, covering my body, my face—it is as cold as ice.

It pours into my mouth, entering my lungs. I breathe in deeply, trying to fill my lungs with air—only water enters. I strain to sit up, to raise my head above the curb, out of the water's flow. The air is only a few inches above me. All I need to do is raise my head a few inches. I cannot. I am drowning. The beats of my heart pounding are mutated through the water—reverberating in my ears, sounding as if they belong to someone else. From somewhere outside and above my body I see myself—head extended back, neck exposed, chest arched forward, pelvis thrust backward, mouth open in a silent gasp for breath, but I am taking in only water. I am drowning. I am unable to lift my head and save myself. I know I am dreaming that I am drowning. I know I cannot sit up, I know I will not die. I know also that I cannot breathe, that only water is entering my lungs. I know it is a dream I dream. I am drowning still the same.

The water begins to recede slowly, exposing my face, allowing air to enter my lungs. I inhale deeply, greedy for the air to fill me. I am wet and out of breath. My heart is pounding. My breath turns to mist as I exhale into the cold air. I am lying on my back in the darkness of the street; there is no one around. Silence except for the stream of water still running over the cobblestones, the low scratch of rodents, and the heaving of my own breathing. A thick fog rolls in quickly off the bay enveloping everything—distorting the light from the streetlamps causing halos to encircle them; making houses appear like unfamiliar objects; obscuring my vision; and transforming the familiar sounds of the urban night into eerie, unidentifiable noises. There is a dog baying in the distance. My skin is numb from the cold water. It stings as the night air hits it. My wet silk gown clings to my breasts, thighs, and stomach. I am disoriented. My chest heaves as I strain to catch my breath. My nipples form small points in the wet silk. Someone is watching me. I feel their eyes fixed on me.

I get up from the street and start to walk down it. My legs are heavy, my step is unsure; I wobble on the pointed heels of my boots. I don't know where I am going. I walk in the center of the street away from the direction of the dog's howling. Water splashes up my legs. A few rats scurry across the street, stopping once they reach the curb stone, rising on their hind legs, sniffing the air, looking up the road from where I had come, from where the sound of the dog whimpering comes. I am not alone—I sense someone is on the street with me. I look around, see no one, nothing. Dark houses, small walkways, stillness. My heart pounds in my chest, my breath comes in quick, short, uncontrollable gasps. The dog is suddenly quiet; the rats have retreated out of sight. I wrap my arms tightly around my chest, clutching the wet lace that covers my shoulder with my silk-gloved hands.

I feel someone moving in the fog toward me. I go to one of the houses, pound frantically on the door with both my fists. No one moves inside, no one answers, no candle is lit, no door opens. Tears well up in my eyes and fall sliding down my cheeks despite my efforts to control them. Something is out here. Something is stalking me. I feel it moving, watching. I continue down the street, walking faster. The heels of my boots catch between the stones of the street, slowing my progress, causing me to stumble. I hear a noise, a soft, full throaty *grr*. I stop. My skin tingles with terror, my heart beats harder, the sound of blood pumping fills my ears, making it hard to identify the noise or the direction it comes from. I look around, straining to see someone—something—in the fog. Clearer, the throaty *grr* followed by the sound of breath being forced out in a huff. I walk faster, clutching my arms around my waist. I hear it again closer, stronger—*grr*, no huff, more of a curling sound at the end. *Grrrrr*, more intense, dragged out, louder. My heart thumping, the blood pounding in my head, I run. I can hear the throaty noise and the sound of steps behind me quickening to match my pace—then stopping, waiting, as if it could easily overcome me and wanted to prolong the excitement and satisfaction of the hunt. And again hard-soled boots against the stone pavement suddenly replaced by padded, scratching paw steps.

My head throbs, my hands are numb, my nipples erect, my heart pounds, my clit tingles, my mouth is dry. I can smell it now. It smells like dog—no, not dog, but something *like* dog only much more dangerous. The smell of menstrual blood, but not as metallic—more like women's sex. I can feel it moving closer, pursuing me, hunting me, playing with me. I run. I can hear it behind me: its four paws hitting the pavement; its warm, moist breath turning to steam vapor as it hits the cold night air; its tongue, hanging out of its mouth; saliva dripping from its fangs; its heart beating in excitement; its eyes glowing; the low raspy curling in its throat,

*GRRR*, and a small whine—of satisfaction and anticipation. The hairs on the back of my neck stand up. I turn into a side alley—stumble and fall facedown. Looking up, I realize it is a dead end—a brick wall blocks my way. I roll onto my back, my knees bent, legs apart, I lift my trembling wet body up on my elbows and—I see it.

I see it for the first time—a silhouette in the fog at the end of the alley lit only from behind by the glow of a single streetlamp. I see it for only a second. It is massive and low to the ground: hunching, the fur standing straight up on its back, it creeps toward me, slow, precise, barely controlling its excitement, its powerful hind leg muscles quivering with restraint, its lips curling up exposing its teeth. A low growl escapes from deep in its throat.

She is slender and tall, walking toward me erect on two legs, her firm breasts exposed, her hands clenched. She is slow, precise, barely controlling her excitement with her lips pressed together and her eyes intent on me.

She lunges toward me. I am overcome and unable to do anything about it. I am on my back and the beast is on top of me. I can feel her breath against my neck, warm, moist. The beast's weight pins me down. My breath comes in fast, shallow gasps. My chest strains against the beast as I struggle to pull air into my lungs under its weight. Its fur brushes against my face. Fear seizes me, sending an electric tingle through my body, making my clit throb, making the wetness in my cunt spill out. Its mouth is inches from my face; I can feel its breath. It curls its lip as it growls—a low, strong, slow growl from deep in its throat—a string of saliva drips slowly from its exposed front canine, landing on my cheek. I close my eyes, turning my face away from its open mouth.

The scent of wild animal and women's sex rushes into my nostrils. I struggle, squirming under its weight, pushing against it with my thighs, pelvis, and shoulders in a frantic but vain attempt to free myself. My erect nipples rub against its chest. For a moment, I do not know if a woman or a wolf is holding my arms down. I feel the unmistakable force of fingers against my wrist, the pressure of a thigh pressing hard against my pelvic bone and clit. She releases one of my wrists. I struggle, pushing against her upper body with my free hand, desperately pushing my whole body against her trying to dislodge her. Urgently she rips open the lace top of my dress, exposing my neck, shoulders and breasts. She presses her body hard against mine, immobilizing me. As her leg grinds against my clit, a moan escapes me and is forced into a gasp as her hand clamps tightly around my neck, momentarily blocking the flow of air. I struggle under her, gasping for air. She controls my entire body. She releases my neck, seizing my wrist again, pinning it against the hard, cold road. I feel her teeth biting at my exposed nipples, her moist, warm breath first on my breast then moving up. Pausing at my neck she exhales deeply, her hips grinding against me, her open mouth pressing the soft flesh of my neck in a hard kiss. I feel the wetness of her tongue, the wetness of my cunt. My body throbs with fear, excitement, desire. My hips move against my will, meeting hers in a rhythmic grind. Her tongue licks my neck, sharp canine teeth pierce my flesh, ripping away the skin of my neck; paws pin my wrist; the muscle of a powerful hind leg presses against my crotch.

I feel the tearing of my skin and muscle, the veins and arteries in my neck exploding as the teeth rip them apart; the warmth of my blood as it spills from the open wound, pouring down the back of my neck and running across my exposed breasts, staining my flesh and hers; my head extended back as I struggle against the teeth; my chest arches forward as the pain blends with the pleasure; my hips thrust against her thigh searching for friction; my mouth is open in a scream of passion as I come. I submit as the rush of fear turns into waves of ecstasy. Light tongue work laps at the stream of blood. Her tongue pushes harder in her greed to ensure none of the blood is lost. Human teeth bite at my nipples and a bloody hand caresses my face, soothing me. I smell the scent of her skin, feel her flesh against mine. My blood and her power have purified both of our souls. My body and blood have sustained her and she has finally transformed me into something divinely spiritual.

# In the Blood
### Patty G. Henderson

Eleanor needed just one more touch of her lover's tongue in the right place for total orgasm. She screamed in ecstasy as she dug sharp nails into her lover's sweat-soaked back, letting her wetness come freely. The lovemaking had been slow, sexy and totally satisfying.

Both of them relaxed, dropping exhausted in a tangle of limbs. Eleanor looked at the strawberry-blonde woman beside her. It wasn't Lola. It hadn't been Lola in a long time. Lola was dying. Lola, her beloved partner of five years, was diagnosed with stomach cancer last spring. The doctors were generous when they gave Lola one year.

Seven months later, the cancer had fully ravaged Lola's body. She was bed bound, barely able to walk for more than ten minutes before becoming so exhausted she crumpled back into bed like a broken rag doll. Eleanor had stuck by her partner, caring for all her needs. Thank God for hospice. They at least offered some relief for Eleanor, watching Lola while Eleanor was at work.

It was November, and there was a cold chill in the air, scattering multi-colored leaves of red, gold, brown and green on the ground like a thick carpet. It was Eleanor's worst nightmare for Lola to die during the Christmas season. Losing a loved one during the holidays was traumatic. You would forever associate the scent of Christmas trees, twinkling lights and cheap Santas with pain and loss. Forever torn between happiness and a deep blue.

Lola was dying and Eleanor was having steamy sex with a complete stranger. Eleanor's and Lola's relationship had been good—in every way—but they hadn't had sex since Lola became too ill. Three months was too long for Eleanor to be celibate. For her, sex was an absolute necessity. A powerful and healing experience. She rationalized away her affairs and guilt by convincing herself that it really wasn't cheating. Not at all. It was her only release from the pain gutting her insides. Her Prozac. She cared deeply for Lola and still loved her fiercely, but Lola didn't expect her to live a virgin lifestyle, did she? She couldn't.

Eleanor left her one-night stand with barely a good-bye and walked home. After Lola got sick, the bills started piling up. They'd had to move into a cramped efficiency in a low-rent brownstone building.

The apartment was dark when Eleanor got home, with only the flickering candles creating jagged, dancing shadows on the walls and even deeper darkness in the corners. Lola had gone to sleep without blowing out the candles again. Eleanor had warned Lola about the candles. Lola had become obsessed with gothic culture and literature. Things like vampires, the occult and dark and morbid oddities. Eleanor brought Lola books home from the thrift stores and Lola consumed them with an insatiable appetite. It wasn't something Eleanor approved of, but it seemed to be making Lola more alert, happier even, if that was possible. And so Lola wanted to burn candles. Eleanor didn't want to hide them from her, but if Lola wasn't going to be responsible when using them, Eleanor would have no choice.

They'd had to get twin beds because most of the time, Lola was in so much pain, she couldn't handle even the slightest touch of Eleanor beside her. So Eleanor put the beds right next to each other.

Eleanor tiptoed to Lola's bedside, not wanting to wake her. Lola had lost most of her hair, so she wore colorful bandannas.

Eleanor ran her fingers across her partner's sallow, sunken cheek and fought back the tears that came every night. Lola opened her eyes at Eleanor's touch.

"I love it when you touch me." Lola's voice was a whisper, her blue eyes pale. She turned in bed and reached for Eleanor's hand. "Did you just get in?"

"Yes, and I'm really mad at you." Eleanor pointed to the candles burning in the room. "I can't leave you and worry all night about you catching yourself and the apartment on fire."

Eleanor walked away and began undressing. Lola watched her intently. "Did you have a good time with your work friends?"

This was the tough part. There had to be an explanation for Eleanor staying out so late. The easiest was the old-and-tired friends-from-work routine. Eleanor liked to think of herself as a good and honest partner and lover to Lola. So Eleanor made it a point to invite co-workers for happy hour. She suffered many a happy hour drink with co-workers she detested just so that she wouldn't be lying to Lola. Of course, after that one happy hour drink, Eleanor would hit the lesbian bars. What Lola didn't know wasn't a lie.

"Yeah, I had a nice time. Sometimes though, they can get so chatty." Eleanor pulled up her pajama bottoms and caught a scent of something alien to her nose. Was it perfume? She didn't want to sniff herself, besides, that dyke she'd slept with tonight wasn't into perfumes.

"Lola, did we get a scented candle recently? It smells a bit like patchouli or something like that in here." All of their candles were of the cheap variety. Eleanor had never bought scented candles. Too expensive.

Eleanor let it slip from her thoughts and started to blow out the candles before getting into bed. A shadow near the window opposite from Lola's bed distracted her. Did the inky blackness move?

"No, Elli, don't blow them all out yet. I want to look at you a bit longer. Please?" Lola asked.

"Sure, baby." Eleanor walked over to kiss Lola goodnight as she always did. She noticed that Lola looked weak, the dark circles under her eyes more pronounced. Lola had bundled herself up to her neck in clothes. "Lola, honey, are you cold? We can turn the space heater on if you want."

"No." Lola wrapped her arms around herself. "I'm fine, really." Lola's gaze didn't leave Eleanor's face. Something that might have been a smile tried to tug at Lola's lips. "Elli, are you sleeping around?"

The question landed like a killing punch in Eleanor's stomach. Her heart was thumping so loud she could hear its beats in her ears. This was the moment she'd hoped would never come.

"Why do you ask that question, Lola? Do you think I am?"

Again, Lola tried to smile, but was too weak to manage it. "Yes, I do. I have one question, though, that I want you to answer me honestly."

"Baby, I've been honest with you." Eleanor fumbled her words.

"I know, Elli. Please, it's okay." Lola motioned for Eleanor to sit on the bed beside her. "I understand you can't live your life like a nun just because I'm dying."

"Lola, I don't want to have this conversation now. It's late—"

"We need to have this conversation now," Lola cut her off. "I won't be here much longer."

Eleanor shook her head hard, wanting to shut her ears. "Stop talking like that, I won't listen." Eleanor cast a quick glance at that darkened corner. The smell of patchouli was stronger.

"You will listen because I need you to answer this question for me. Please, pay attention to me." Lola's eyes blazed with an intensity Eleanor hadn't seen in a long time.

"Eleanor, do you love me?"

"I can't believe you need me to answer that." Didn't Lola understand that if Eleanor didn't love her, she wouldn't be here?

"Answer me, please."

"I love you, okay?"

"Would you love me in death as in life?"

Eleanor looked at Lola, confused. "What kind of question is that? Lola, honey, you've been reading too many of those books."

"Elli, if I died today, would you still want to love me?"

"This is crazy, Lola. I'm getting rid of those books. I thought they were good for you, but now I'm not so sure." Eleanor started to get up, but Lola grabbed her arm and held on. Eleanor was surprised at the strength in Lola's grasp.

Lola pulled her face up to Eleanor's. "I can be with you forever, Eleanor, if you just say the word."

Did something move in the corner? "Lola, you're starting to scare me. Please, let me go. What's gotten into you?"

Without warning, one of the candles blew out, casting the room into the hands of growing shadows.

"I can be with you forever, Eleanor. Tell me you want that."

"Of course I would stay with you, Lola." Had the pain of the cancer started to eat away at Lola's mind? Eleanor started to strip away some of Lola's layers of clothes. "C'mon, let me take some of this off you and make you more comfortable."

As she snatched the throw blankets away, she noticed glaring, red blotches on Lola's neck and arms. Lola grabbed the extra blankets from Eleanor's hands and pulled them up to her neck.

"What are those marks?" Eleanor asked, fearful that Lola had begun to hurt herself.

"My salvation." Lola turned away from Eleanor.

"I think now it's your turn to be honest with me. I can't help you if you won't let me."

"You no longer need to help me. She will be all I need." Was that a smile?

Maybe Eleanor needed to speak with someone about Lola. She wasn't making any sense. Maybe if they both went to sleep, tomorrow would make tonight disappear. Eleanor began blowing out the candles.

"Elli, when you blow out the last candle, the darkness will come and she will come to take me away. But I'll be back. To be with you forever."

Eleanor had had enough. She didn't blow out the last candle. The room, almost in total darkness, was deep, black, and waiting. "This is enough, Lola. You're not going to die tonight."

"I want to die tonight. I have to die in order to come back to you. She promised me that I will live forever after dying in this life."

"Who is this 'she' you keep talking about? Are you seeing someone?" The words sounded so stupid after they tumbled out of Eleanor's mouth. Of course Lola wasn't seeing anyone, except maybe in her fevered mind.

"Her name is Melora. She's a vampire. I found her in one of the books you bought me. I wrote to her."

"A vampire?" Eleanor shook her head. She wanted to scream. "A vampire has been coming to see you and promised you that you would live forever after you die? Vampires don't freaking exist!" Eleanor did scream.

Lola flung off the blankets, exposing the raw marks on her body. She pointed at them. "She comes and takes my blood. I help her survive and she helps me die. But I won't die, so don't cry for me, baby. I'll be with you forever. I promise I will never leave you."

Lola coughed hard, her wasting frame shaking in pain. She looked at Eleanor with defiant eyes. "Now blow out that candle, Elli, because Melora is waiting in the shadows."

Eleanor looked around the room, for the first time, frightened. She couldn't believe she was letting Lola get to her.

"I'm calling the doctor tomorrow and asking him about those marks you've got. I don't want to hear any more of your crazy talk." Eleanor blew out the last candle, sending the room into total darkness. The moon was only a sliver in the night sky, so very little light seeped into the apartment.

Eleanor crawled into bed and pulled up the covers. She turned on her side, punched her lumpy pillow into shape, and got comfortable. She was exhausted and drifted into sleep immediately. Lola was there, making love to her like the countless times they had in reality.

"You're my little nymphomaniac," Lola teased, as her wet, hot tongue traveled down Eleanor's naked stomach, while her hands moved slowly up to Eleanor's erect and waiting nipples. Eleanor released a soft moan, as Lola's mouth tasted fully of Eleanor's breasts. Lola cupped both of them then and opened her mouth, sliding her tongue smoothly between them.

Eleanor's breathing came in quick gasps. Lola worked herself down in between Eleanor's open legs, pried her fingers into Eleanor and found a flow of wetness. Eleanor arched her body into Lola. The aching and swelling was almost painful. When Eleanor felt her lover's tongue pushing inside her while her fingers moved faster and faster against her enlarged clit, Eleanor couldn't hold her screams back any longer. She held on to Lola's back and released her orgasm. "Lola. Lola," she repeated, flushed with satisfaction.

And then she heard the loud slurping sounds that woke her from that erotic dream. Her heart was still beating hard when the strong smell of patchouli stung her nose again.

She looked at Lola's bed and although her eyes were groggy from sleep, she could see a dark form lying on top of Lola. It was moving.

"Holy shit." Eleanor jumped out of bed and ran for the light switch near the door. The room was bathed in 60-watt light. Eleanor screamed and couldn't stop screaming.

Lola was completely smothered by a pulsing mass of blood, but God in heaven, the blood had the shape of a woman with long, matted hair that wrapped itself around her totally naked body. And Lola was drenched in blood. She had rips along her skin as if sharp nails had slit her flesh.

But it's what they were doing that made Eleanor throw up all over herself. The bloody woman's tongue was like a snake, buried deep into Lola's crotch, plunging it deeper and deeper into Lola, tearing and drawing blood and sucking it up with loud slurping sounds. And each time she did, Lola arched up in total ecstasy, moaning loudly.

Eleanor stood frozen, sickened by the obscene sexual act before her. All she could do was scream. Again. The woman turned toward Eleanor and Eleanor's scream choked in her throat. Blood dripped from the woman's mouth and obsidian eyes locked on Eleanor.

Lola's neck was ripped open, her final orgasm nothing but a gurgle. Blood spurted out in red streams. The smell of death was overpowering in the tiny room. The woman with the flowing, blood-soaked black hair was slowly moving toward Eleanor.

The room began to swirl and Eleanor could no longer focus. She couldn't hear her heart beat.

"She is yours forever. Feed her well." The voice was thick with blood.

Then everything went black.


Two months of intense therapy had done nothing for Eleanor. Lola had died and been buried. Lola's good-for-nothing mother had taken care of everything. She'd never been there for Lola in life but guilt was a pretty strong power. At least she took care of her daughter in death.

Eleanor had woken up in a hospital. They said she suffered from severe shock. She was admitted into a mental hospital for two months of extreme therapy. But they couldn't help her forget what she saw that night. And what she sees each and every waking night of her life.

Eleanor continued to make the rounds of the bars. She took every pass that came her way from every good-looking dyke who wanted a good time. That's what Eleanor wanted too. A good time. That's what Lola needed.

In the shadows of every bar, Lola waited. Sometimes Eleanor would catch glimpses of her. Watching. And each and every lover that Eleanor went to bed with, Lola was there. In the shadows. Waiting. To feast on Eleanor's sex and the flesh of the aftermath.

And in the darkest hours of the night, when Eleanor laid her head to rest, Lola was there. In the shadows. In the blood.

# The Haunted Haunted House

## Rachel Kramer Bussel

As the visitors poured in, I scoured the incoming line of guests, looking for the one girl who would be my main course for the night, who would go home with more than just scary memories for the night. Or perhaps, scary memories that she treasured. Ever since I arrived here at New Orleans's most famous haunted house, the day after I died, I've found it the perfect milieu to find girls who are secretly seeking that edge, that push from being scared to being chillingly thrilled, pulled into a sexual underworld they can only dream about from the comfort of their soft beds. And that's when my gaze landed on her—she looked young, probably a college girl, her hair dark, her face pale, typical Goth attire, sleek black pants and a skintight black top, the darkness somehow suiting her perfectly. She entered with her classmates but had a superior air, like she was just humoring them by going through the motions. I could already tell—for her, Halloween was for babies with no imagination. But I could also see beyond the mask she wore, carefully protected by all that pancake makeup, but visible nonetheless. Because of my supernatural powers, I could sense that underneath her tough-girl exterior, she was ripe and ready, looking for a real woman who could show her exactly what being afraid could make her body do. And thankfully, I was just the woman, or at least, ghost, for the job.

While the customers walked through the scariest part of the mansion, where everything was absolutely pitch black and decidedly creepy, even for me at times, I made my way through the crowd, picking her out. I heard her friend call her Beth, and as I sneaked by, I whispered the single soft syllable lightly in her ear. She looked around, startled, and reached out to grab the hand of whoever stood next to her, trying to get her bearings in the dark. I beckoned to her, running my fingers through the air around her, gently leading her away from her peers and into a corridor. "Hello?" she whispered, and the word echoed through the still air. She could tell that she had lost her group, but not surprisingly for her, she didn't seem scared like most other people would have been. People come here to be scared, but not really; they want to rest on the side of fear that's safe, just edgy enough to give them a momentary jolt, but nothing that would actually shake up their existence. But within every crowd, there's one who is seeking something more, and for them, I'm here to give them what they're looking for.

"It's okay, you're safe," I crooned, letting my voice get a little bit louder.

"But who are you? Where am I?"

She didn't seem eager to get back to her friends, simply curious. I took a bold step and brought my hand in between her legs, knowing exactly how wet I'd find her. I may be dead but I can still tell when a girl is turned on, and this one certainly was. Even through her tight pants, I felt the current of heat pulsing from her pussy, the warmth and movement that were oh-so-close.

Once she had calmed down, and I knew her shivers weren't from fear but trembles of excitement, I teased her, stroking my nails all up and down her legs and the back of her neck, sucking her ears into my mouth and blowing on her tender skin. She wasn't fragile, but she wasn't entirely sturdy either, and holding her in my arms after so long felt wonderful. Not being able to have that daily contact with another person, having to sleep alone instead of curled alongside a woman's warm, breathing body, has been one of the worst parts about this afterlife, though don't get me wrong, it's far better than what most get.

"I've lived in this mansion for a very long time, but only show myself to those who I know will appreciate my presence, and you, Beth, seem like a girl who could use some guidance from beyond the grave. Believe you me, in my day, I was quite the stud, and all the girls wanted me. They still would, if they could see me. But they can certainly feel me," I said in my most seductively throaty voice as I continued to massage her pussy. She let out a moan and before she could speak again, I slid my hand sideways into her mouth, and felt her bite down on my fingers. "I'm going to make you feel like nobody else ever has, and not just because I'm a ghost. I bet you don't even know you're a dyke yet, you just think you're 'different.' I bet no one's ever showed you what your pussy's really for, just hinted at its potential. I bet late at night, in your dreams, you let women take you, let them shove their greedy fingers so far inside you, you think you'll die. Don't worry, baby, I'm going to make you feel things you'll never feel again."

With that, I tilted her head back, her lips still wrapped around my fingers, and drew a long, pointy nail across her neck, lightly raking the delicate skin, intimating more. I felt her shiver beneath me, and nudged her legs apart with my foot. I leaned forward and suckled her earlobe, ravishing it with my mouth, so grateful for the human contact that I practically devoured it. It's not every tempting morsel I can approach safely, without having her run screaming, potentially shutting us down. The bulk of our business is optical illusions, tricks that nobody would ever be able to guess but that really don't take much time to construct, and once you know they're there, they're beyond easy to spot. A ghost can get really bored trying to drum up her own tricks, so I've had to find ways to amuse myself, and playing with cute girls looking for their very own thrill ride has been just the diversion I need.

I took a deep breath, relishing the way she felt, the way her skin radiated that special warmth, a combination of fear and arousal that was particularly intoxicating. I pinched one nipple and then the other, my other hand going to lightly stroke her neck. She whimpered against me, all thoughts gone from her head as she succumbed to the sensations I was tempting her with, relaxed into my arms and let me have my way with her. Her skin was radiating heat, the warmth that comes only from the most potent form of arousal, and I pinched her nipples harder, drawing them away from her skin and slipping a finger into her mouth for her to suckle, to keep her quiet. I delicately peeled off her clothes, placed them in the corner, stroked her nakedness all over until her whole body was squirming with need; she'd have let an alien fuck her by then, she was so horny. I kicked her legs apart with my own, my feet tucked inside hers, her pussy now bare and open to the wind, with nothing at all to protect her. Then I brought my hand down and simply held it as close as I could to her pussy without touching it. She could certainly feel my presence, and when she didn't escape, I pressed my hand closer. I knew that it would take her a while to truly process what was happening, it might not even be until later that she realized who I was or what I stood for, but for the moment, I wanted her to simply need me so desperately she'd be willing to die for me, to run naked through the house, to suffer any humiliation as long as I would fuck her deep and hard.

When I finally did start to stroke her, she practically came right then, and I felt that same righteous glow of pride I did every time I made a girl come, but this time even more so. That she had overcome her fear and let her mind and body go in such a way, showed that I had what it took for the long haul. I didn't have to rely on what I had used in the past—a sort of girly macho swagger, a bit of intimidation perhaps—no, this was pure, raw lust, and it spoke to something that went much deeper than her pussy. But back to that pussy, which I continued to work even after she'd squeezed my fingers so tight I thought I might have permanent damage. It was almost as if I knew her from the past, but that was impossible, she was much too young, yet somehow, every touch made her more and more familiar to me. The way her cunt wrapped around my fingers, gripping them, then letting go, sent shivers of arousal throughout my body, made me long to escape this place I now called home. I almost wanted to cry as I shoved my way into her deepest reaches, twisting and turning to find the one spot, the one stroke, that would make her go absolutely wild. When I found it, I stayed there, stilling my hand and simply holding her, feeling every minuscule movement she made as she tried to get me to go deeper, to force my hand, as it were, but I simply kept her there, waiting and needing, dying a little bit until I took pity on her and plunged my fingers back inside. I shoved into her, fast and hard, wishing we were in a more comfortable spot, with a bed and light and pillows, but as I fucked her deeper and deeper, I realized we didn't need any of those creature comforts. Her pussy was the only blanket I needed, and I pulled her close to me, inhaling the scent of her perfume, her sweetness, her girlness as she pressed her ass against me while my fingers continued to plunder her. I could feel her getting restless with desire, but I didn't care.

I kept going, massaging her clit, giving it slow, sensual strokes, then pinching it roughly, making the blood rush in and out, torturing her poor nub in a way I knew was making her whole body throb right at that pressure point, making her lightheaded with desire. I tapped my fingers against her clit, feeling her whole body tense with the need to come as I toyed with her, shoving my fingers into her dripping-wet pussy, only to pull them out moments later and messily smear her juices along her leg. I kept right on, ignoring her breaths of air and huffs of frantic indignation, pushing her body past its level of comfort, past anything she'd known before, determined to wring out every final drop of pleasure, to leave her sagging and wilted and utterly unable to forget what had happened here today, no matter what logic would later tell her. I wanted her to wake up in the middle of the night and feel my fingers on her, to know that somewhere out there in the world was a woman, all right, a ghost, something, someone, who could do this to her, who could give her back to herself.

I hadn't spoken to her since the fucking started, so when I spoke directly into her ear, she jumped against me, sending my fingers even deeper inside her. "Are you ready? Of course you are, you little slut. How badly do you need to come?" I asked her, a rhetorical question at best, since her pussy was practically fucking me with its fierce spasms. I felt a few lone tears fall from her eyes onto my arm, and those drops made me slow down. She didn't need a roller coaster of an orgasm, but a wave she could ride long into the night. I knelt down in front of her, sucking her hot, hard clit into my mouth, tending to it with warm, slow strokes of my tongue. I slid my fingers back inside her, gently this time, savoring every wet fold, memorizing the feel of her cunt to save for later. I held both hands below her, sliding one in, then out to make room for the other, crisscrossing until she had no idea where one started and one ended, while my tongue continued its oral assault. Then I pulled her clit between my teeth, nipping gently, just enough to make her truly tremble. As she did, I moved my tongue away and slid eight fingers inside her, my thumbs kneading her clit as my fingers made her open as far as she could go.

I could hear her hissing, "Yes, yes," and moments later, felt the entire room shake and sob along with her. Maybe I imagined that, but somehow I don't think so. She shook and shook and I held her like that, my hands inside her, my face pressed lightly against her leg. When she finally stopped, I wrapped her in my arms, then helped her get dressed. I didn't say goodbye, just sent her off to her friends. I didn't look at her, couldn't stand to see if she looked elated or heartbroken or a little bit of each. I sank to the ground, too flustered to try to scare any more visitors that night. They'd have to find a way to scare themselves for the night; I'd already done my part.

# The Call
## Vicky "Dylan" Wagstaff

Nicole dropped her bags the moment she crossed the threshold of her room. She was exhausted but relieved she'd finally made it, out of her parents' home and their control. Well, at least to some extent.

She was still living by their standards in regards to a lot of things, but this was something they had absolutely hated the idea of: Nicole getting her own place and attempting to stand on her own two feet.

Her parents were thoroughly disapproving the move, and the location. They had wanted to help her out, with the offer of a nice apartment overlooking the river Thames, but Nicole hadn't wanted that. She wanted to strike out on her own. She was nineteen and really didn't want to be tied to her parents' apron strings any longer.

The room she was now renting wasn't great. It had no views, barely any furniture, and was in a less than desirable area of London, but it was all hers. Well, the small room she was renting was hers; the rest of the old Victorian town house was rented out to four others, that she knew of.

She looked around her, recalling the first time she had been shown the room. Nothing much had changed. The room was still dingy, dark, and dusty and in need of a good clean. Sorry looking, and highly impractical, blinds hung limply at the lone window, almost looking like they didn't belong there at all.

Nicole walked over to the blinds that were shutting out any hope of light from outside. She pulled the cord to the right, instantly sending dust particles flying around her, making her sneeze. Every corner of the room remained shrouded in shadow, with peeling wallpaper and long-forgotten cobwebs that even the spiders avoided.

She sighed, running her fingers through her long dark hair, attempting to straighten the kinks that insisted on appearing, no matter how much she did her best to keep it straight. She walked slowly over to the bed in the middle of the room, sliding past the small couch squeezed into a space that was protesting its appearance long ago.

The mattress perched on top of the stiff springs of the bed looked far from appealing, in fact, it looked on the brink of suicide. Like it had spent the entire morning struggling to free itself from the murk of the room, toward the window, in order to hurl itself out to the dark and dirty yard below.

Nicole shrugged her slender shoulders and convinced herself that she had made the right decision, despite the dire surroundings she currently stood in the center of. She knew she would get used to it, and it wouldn't be hard to clean.

She took a deep breath, coughing as dust filled her lungs, and retrieved her notebook from her small backpack. She grabbed a pen and set about noting down everything she would need to do in the small room to make it habitable.

A week passed by quickly, and Nicole could safely say that she had managed to create herself a nice little living space. She had bought a new mattress, taking pity on the old one and leaving it out for the bin men to take it to the mattress heaven it deserved to be in. It had obviously had a hard life, well used, and now thankfully gone.

The shadowy gloom of her surroundings had mostly gone too, with a few well-placed lamps and some blinds that had more spaces in them than dirt, so the light could actually make its way through. The place was almost worthy of being called her home, for now at least, until she finished her photography degree and started making some money.

Getting somewhere bigger and grander wasn't a high priority though. Enjoying actually being in the world was. And the world was looking a lot less daunting than her parents had made out it would be.

Nicole smiled at all the improvements she'd made to the place, then turned her attention to herself, glancing at her reflection in the mirror to ensure she looked okay for her night out. Her long hair fell in soft waves about her face, framing its natural beauty, and accentuating her dark eyes and lightly tanned skin, a gift from her father's side of the family. The Mediterranean look ensured that even the cute dimples when she smiled didn't detract from her sexyness.

She checked over her full red lips for imperfections in her lip-gloss application, running her tongue over her teeth, and her hands down her slender frame to ensure no wrinkles marred her clothing. She took a second just to gaze at herself, realizing that she was looking happier than she had ever done before. Her eyes practically twinkled in the gentle light of the room, and she felt good. Arching a perfectly sculpted eyebrow, feeling satisfied that she also looked good, she grabbed her denim jacket from the bed, and combed her fingers through her lush dark hair one last time.

As she placed her key in the lock of her door to secure it behind her, Nicole heard a telephone ringing. At first it made her jump, as it was loud, unlike any telephone she had ever heard. A deep tone of a ring that was insistent, and coming from her room. She didn't have a phone though, and even if she did, nobody would have her number.

Turning the key back in the old lock, Nicole slowly opened her door. The trilling telephone was definitely coming from inside, so she stepped in, looking around, shaking her head because she was sure there wasn't a phone in there.

Searching with her ears as much as her eyes, the confused student ended up near her bed. Getting annoyed now at the constant ringing, she blew out an exasperated sigh, and got down on her hands and knees. And there it was, an old black telephone that looked like it had been there since sometime back in the 1920s, chirping away at her to pick it up.

Nicole pulled it out from under her bed, her nose protesting at the amount of dust that came with it. She realized she had neglected to clean under there, and tut-tutted at her own carelessness, placing the ringing phone on her knee as she sat on the edge of the bed.

She had an unusual urge to pull the short cable it was attached to out of the wall. She didn't know why, but felt a foreboding sensation sweep through her. Chuckling to herself, she realized there was no reason to feel anything other than annoyance at being halted in her plan to leave the house.

Tucking her hair behind her ear, she lifted the heavy receiver and answered before she had any silly thoughts of phantom phones. "Hello?" She spoke more softly than she had meant to.

There was a moment of silence, and Nicole thought maybe whoever it was had realized they'd dialed the wrong number, or that she wasn't who they were seeking. But then she heard a gentle, steady sigh, escaping almost wistfully, regretfully. It intrigued Nicole rather than had her jumping to conclusions that the as yet mystery caller was a heavy breather type.

She repeated her hello, and waited again—wanting to know now who the caller was, feeling her curiosity take over.

"I'm not sure if I have the right number." The voice was quiet, feminine and sweet. It seemed devoid of accent, but was similar to Nicole's own, apart from the fact that Nicole had a much huskier tone to her voice.

"Who were you calling?" she asked, setting the base of the phone down onto her bedside table, being less abrupt than she normally would have been to a stranger.

"I'm not too sure. What's your name?" The unknown caller

questioned tentatively, the softness of her voice practically whispering, like a caress, into Nicole's ear.

She felt a shiver run down her spine, catching her off guard. She looked over her shoulder to check if she had left her window open, but it was shut firmly. She could feel a chill, however, sweeping through her like an internal breeze. Like a touch to her skin. It instantly put her on edge, but she kept hold of the receiver.

"Um, my name? It's . . ." Nicole felt unusually light. Unusually lost for words. "Nicole." She had no idea why she had given the girl her name, and she had no idea why she was still talking to her and not making her way out to meet her friends.

The girl spoke again, and Nicole gripped the receiver tight in her hand. "Nicole." Her name rolled off the other girl's tongue like she was tasting it, wrapping her lips around it and testing its flavour and texture.

Nicole had never heard her name spoken so seductively.

She ran her fingers through her hair, doing her best to keep her hand from shaking, and not having a clue as to why she wasn't putting the phone down on the girl. She was aware that giving a complete stranger her name, and having a voice affect her in a way she didn't quite understand, was not something that normally happened in her day-to-day life.

She had certainly never felt herself become completely intrigued and captivated by so few words before. In fact, she had never felt that at all, ever.

The thought frightened her, like the feeling of foreboding she'd had before answering the phone. It made her stop and think, and Nicole instantly felt uncomfortable as she listened to the gentle breathing of the girl on the other end of the slightly crackly line.

"Look, I think you've probably got the wrong number, or the person you're looking for doesn't live here anymore. I'm kind of in a rush so I—"

"That's a shame. You have a nice voice. It would have been nice talking to you, and listening to it," the caller said, pausing for a reaction maybe.

Nicole didn't know quite how to react. She had no clue whether to hang up abruptly, or feel flattered that the girl liked the sound of her voice. She rubbed her fingers across her brow, telling herself to put down the phone and go.

"I'm sorry, I really have to go," Nicole apologized, standing in the gloomy light of her room.

"Can I call you again? I'd really like that," the girl said, the same soft caress of her words being far more enticing than Nicole cared to think too much about.

"Yes, I guess." Nicole winced at her own words, completely unsure of why she had said what she had.

She didn't want strangers phoning her, but she didn't take back the offer.

"I'll talk to you soon then, Nicole. Take care." The sweet lilt of the girl's voice washed over Nicole as she listened to the other end of the line go dead.

Replacing the receiver back on its cradle, the student gazed at the telephone for a minute or two. She then turned to go, but quickly spun back, lifting the receiver to her ear, just in case. Putting it back down as soon as she assured herself no one was there, Nicole breathed out a small laugh.

She shook her head, attempting to regain her usual composure as she picked up her keys, trying to understand why she hadn't just reacted in the way she normally would have with a wrong number: by being curt and to the point, and slamming the phone down. Not giving the person her name, and agreeing to having them call back.

Again Nicole laughed, but it was a nervous laugh, as she closed the door to her room, keeping one eye on the old telephone as she did so. She wondered if she should tell her friends about the call, but decided against it as she didn't want to explain how the girl's voice had sent chills down her spine. The good kind of chills that pointed to one thing—arousal.

She had never felt so captivated by another girl before, and it was a little embarrassing. But strangely, it didn't feel wrong. It just felt . . . different.

Nicole left the warmth of the old house, and strutted out into the chill of the street with her usual assured gait. She couldn't allow her worries, and the fact that she'd just had a very strange encounter on a phone she hadn't even known was in the room, to upset her. It was pointless.

Slumping down into the silky sheets of her bed, allowing them to cool her skin and envelop her in their velvet caress, Nicole sighed. She was tired from her late night out, and she had drunk a little too much, feeling the need to forget about the strange but appealing voice of the girl who had called.

She was still thinking about it, and about her, however. Wondering if she really would ring back, and wondering just as much, if she wanted her to. It was all too confusing and tiring, so slipping an arm under the soft pillow against her face, Nicole allowed the tug of sleep to pull her into its warmth

Just as she was about to fall into the dreams she longed for, Nicole was disturbed by the ringing of a telephone. The telephone next to her bed. It seemed to be ringing less loudly than it had before, less urgently, but still trilled enough to yank her back to reality.

Nicole propped herself up on her elbows, looking over at the vexing black phone on her small table. She stretched over and placed her hand on the receiver, her tight grey T-shirt slipping up and exposing her slim waist to the cool air. She stopped then, wondering just why she was about to answer the ringing.

It was midnight and nobody knew she had a phone, so it had to be the stranger who had rung earlier. She was calling because Nicole had told her she could.

Letting out a deep breath she hadn't been aware she had been holding, Nicole lifted the handset and brought it to her ear. "Hello," she said, her voice even huskier than normal with the burr of sleep.

"I'm glad you answered, Nicole. I knew you would though." The lilting singsong charm of the girl's voice rolled over Nicole.

She felt herself shiver, but put it down to the fact she was no longer fully under the sheets, because she didn't want to acknowledge again that the voice of somebody she didn't even know had an effect on her that ran deeper than just confusion.

"How did you know I would answer?" Nicole asked, her tipsy and sleepy state causing her to enter into conversation, when she really didn't think she should.

"I just had a feeling. You're probably thinking you should hang up though, right? Possibly thinking I'm a little crazy for calling you back."

Nicole relaxed back onto the headboard, resting against it as she pulled the covers up around her a little more. "Maybe. I mean, I don't normally get phone calls from people I don't know. I don't usually *talk* to people I don't know."

"Yet you're talking to me." The caller sounded a tad smug, like she was well aware of how her voice drifted down the line in a tender and intriguing tone, only to flush over the person on the other end, immersing her in its warmth.

Nicole tried to fight the fact that whoever it was on the other end sounded sexy as hell, but she couldn't. She could feel her body reacting in ways her mind was telling her not to, but her hormones were driving without her permission.

"So, what is it that you want? To talk about?" Nicole asked, hearing a slight chuckle on the other end. A chuckle that gave her goose bumps for more reasons than one. It sounded not only incredibly alluring, but also a bit unnerving. She frowned, shifting in readiness to put the phone down, coming to her senses a little.

"You're not thinking of putting the phone down are you? I thought you were keen to hear what I wanted . . . to talk about." The girl's voice grew ever more seductive with each word, and Nicole became ever more uneasy.

"Well, you've rung for a reason, obviously. I'm intrigued to know what that reason is," Nicole said, squinting at the shadows in the dull light creeping in through her blinds.

"Do you really believe there would be any other reason than you? I wanted to hear your voice again. Didn't I say that I liked it, and that I'd like to listen to it a little more? That's why I'm calling, Nicole. To hear you." The girl's voice became more breathy, and certainly more intriguing, with every syllable.

Nicole found herself slipping lower under her covers, holding the phone close to her ear, feeling the darkness of the room wrap around her just as much as the soft sounds of breathing on the other end of the line.

"Who are you?" Nicole asked, finding herself not wanting to end the call quite as quickly as she imagined she should. "If you want to talk, it would be nice to know your name."

"My name isn't important. The way you're making me feel is." There was a pause as the caller sounded like she was moving around, a rustling of cotton, or something similar, travelling down the wire with a crisp crackle.

"The way I'm making you feel? What exactly do you mean?" Nicole asked, her sensible side telling her in no uncertain terms to put the phone down.

Of course, her sensible side was going largely unheard, as she was too busy wondering what the caller was now doing, shuffling around, wherever she was.

Once again Nicole felt her body reacting in a way she hadn't consciously given it permission to. The tingles running down her spine with the gentle but insistent breathing of the mysterious caller, shooting through her, aiming for one destination. She shifted on the bed, not wanting to allow herself the perplexing pleasure of being turned on by a stranger.

"If I tell you, do you promise not to go?" the caller asked, so softly that Nicole barely heard the whispered plea.

"I'm not sure. Just tell me." Nicole's curiosity was far out-weighing the weirdness of the situation now. She waited in the quiet, hearing only the faint murmuring of the wind blowing against her window, the odd creak and groan of the old building around her, and the enchanting tones of the other girl as she began to speak again.

"You, your voice, makes me feel tingly in all the places it feels good," the girl said with a slight sigh. "It makes me . . . want to touch myself for you."

Nicole nearly dropped the phone. She hadn't quite expected to hear that. Fair enough, her inner voice was squealing "I told you so," but her common sense was busy trying to explain why a random girl on a phone she herself didn't even know the number of, was telling her she wanted to touch herself because of her voice.

"Nicole, are you still there? I hope I didn't offend you." The girl spoke a little louder, trying to catch Nicole's attention.

"No. I mean, you didn't offend me." Nicole wasn't actually sure if she had been offended or not. She was certainly feeling rather amorous, but was still holding off on believing it was because of the sweet seductive sound of a mysterious girl on the other end of the phone.

"You don't sound too sure, Nicole. Maybe I should go," the girl suggested rather dejectedly.

"No, don't go," Nicole replied a little too quickly, wondering when she had gone from thinking it was a good idea to slam the phone down, to keeping the caller talking to her. She was sobering up slightly, her mind becoming clearer, beginning to realize the implications of wanting to continue talking to the other girl. She wasn't completely sure where the conversation was headed, but certainly the way the caller was practically whispering down the phone to her, and what she had said, had loud alarm bells ringing.

"I won't go, but I'd like you to tell me something," the girl said sensually. "Tell me what you look like, and what you're wearing right now."

Okay, there were lots of alarm bells going off inside Nicole's head now. What was she wearing? It sounded so cheesy, yet she found herself becoming a little overheated with the prospect of the conversation heading into areas she'd never been to before.

"Um, I . . . this is odd." Nicole ran a nervous hand through her hair. "Okay, I'm not tall. I'm slim. I have long dark hair and brown eyes. And I have no idea why I'm telling you this, but I have on a small grey T-shirt and a pair of matching shorts." Nicole let out a slow and slightly shaky breath, knowing she was far into unknown territory. For not only was she entertaining the thought of talking fairly intimately with somebody she didn't know, but that person also happened to be female.

"You sound nice. I bet you're very attractive, going by your voice. I bet your T-shirt is straining to keep your breasts within it." The girl sighed, almost sounding like she would have moaned had Nicole not let out a little gasp of shock.

"Pardon? I . . . I don't know what you mean." Nicole looked down at her chest, only really just noticing that her breasts *did* seem a little packed within the confines of her clothing.

She knew she wasn't a particularly large girl in the chest area, but Nicole was aware that her breasts were nice and full. Firm in appearance, yet delicately soft to the touch. She blushed at the realization that her nipples were swollen and hard to little pin-points in affirmation of her arousal.

"I think you should squeeze one of your hard little nipples for me, Nicole." The girl breathed out.

"How did you know they—never mind. I really don't think we should carry on this conversation," Nicole stated, doing her best not to notice that her breasts were now aching to be touched.

"Why? Because you're getting wet for me?" she asked. "I'm getting wet for *you*, Nicole. Your voice is slipping over me like warm silk, and caressing me in places I'd rather your hands were." A small moan filtered down the line, instantly proving to Nicole that the caller was indeed arousing her, as she felt herself become wet between her legs.

She couldn't believe she was reacting to the other girl in such an overt way. She had never been so easily turned on, but there was just something about the caller's voice, her soft reassurance that maybe it was okay to allow whatever was happening to happen.

Nicole still felt compelled to resist as much as she could, but it really wasn't working.

"I can't . . . I can't do this," Nicole told the girl rather shakily, whilst lifting a hand to her chest. It seemed to be moving without her consent, placing itself on her left breast and gently stroking.

She licked her full lips and brushed her fingertips over a painfully erect nipple, feeling tiny bolts of pleasure shoot through her as she rubbed a little harder. Her legs parted under the warm covering of her blanket, hopeful of something to ease the ache there. But Nicole didn't want to slip her hand into her shorts and start relieving some of the tension that had built up without her knowledge or permission, whilst she was on the phone with someone whose name she didn't even know. It didn't matter that it was because of the girl that she was feeling the need to pleasure herself.

"I can hear you touching yourself, Nicole. Stroking your fingers over your tender nipple. I'd love to be there to kiss it, to suck it into my warm mouth." The girl moaned with barely restrained desire, and it washed over Nicole, heating her to her very core.

"Stop, you're—"

The caller interrupted. "Am I arousing you, Nicole?"

Before Nicole could answer in the negative, she heard footsteps outside her door. The soft shuffling sounded like somebody approaching her room from down the corridor.

She sat up, still clutching the phone. "Hold on," she said, pulling the receiver away from her ear and watching the dim play of light from under the door.

The footsteps were creeping nearer, whispering closer to her door. Then they stopped, but Nicole couldn't see a shadow in the light. Couldn't detect any other noise giving away that whoever it was now stood outside her room.

"Nicole?" The caller's voice drifted from the receiver.

Ignoring the caller for a second, Nicole put the phone down and got out of bed, padding slowly to the door as her sheets dropped loosely over the phone. She reached out for the door handle, holding her breath, unsure why she was feeling so nervous.

Nicole strained her ears to detect any sound, and she knew she could now hear the soft breaths of somebody close by.

Taking a slow and steady breath herself, Nicole pulled her door open in a rush, staring out into the inky blackness of the corridor. No one was there. Nobody stood on the other side like she had expected. Nobody breathing heavily, shuffling nearby.

She looked up and down the dark corridor, listening, squinting into the shadows and finding nothing to confirm the fact that she was sure she had heard somebody there, waiting outside.

Frowning deeply, she closed the door, locking and bolting it and double-checking the integrity of her security. She almost wanted to laugh. It had probably just been the creaking of the old house. The floorboards groaning, or the windows rattling. Whatever it was, it had stopped now anyway, so she made her way back to the comfort of her bed.

Lifting the sheet to slide back under, Nicole picked up the large black receiver of the telephone. Settling herself back down into the patch of warmth she had left behind, she placed the phone back to her ear, unsure whether her mystery caller would still be there.

She didn't speak, but listened, and detected the soft breathing of the girl on the other end of the line. She sounded like she was waiting patiently. Maybe lying in her own bed somewhere, her own body now aching to be touched just the way Nicole's was.

She couldn't deny it. She was aroused and it was all because of a caller whose name she didn't even know. She could picture her; it was as if she knew what she looked like. Knew that her hair was soft as silk and shimmering blonde. Her body slender and naked under a delicate fabric that draped around her feminine beauty.

Nicole didn't know where the image was coming from, but it felt right, and it felt good. It made *her* feel good. She took a deep breath, cursing herself for even daring to continue the conversation, but doing so anyway.

"Are you still there?" she asked, hoping she didn't sound like she was shaking quite as much as she felt she was.

"I'm still here, Nicole. Waiting for you. Are you okay?" the caller questioned, her concern pulling Nicole even further under her spell.

"Yes, I'm okay." She paused, before deciding to plunge right ahead into something she had no experience with. "You are, by the way. Arousing me I mean." She bit her lower lip, not knowing quite why she felt compelled to confirm the fact that she was aroused, but she just couldn't seem to help herself.

Maybe it was the slight adrenaline rush of thinking somebody was creeping around outside her door. Maybe it was just the fact that she wanted to feel the touch of the girl so much she just couldn't hold back any longer. Whatever it was, her resolve had gone, and she could practically feel the smile of the caller down the crackly line.

"I'm glad, because I'm aching to touch you. To kiss you. I can almost feel you against me." The mysterious girl sighed gently, her voice once again caressing Nicole, firing her body up as if she really were being touched.

As if the caller was there, beside her. Her hands hot and tender, whispering over her body as Nicole craved the sensations she could bring her. She wanted the sensations. Felt herself needing them as she lay back with the phone in her grasp.

"Touch yourself, Nicole. Touch yourself for me," the girl practically demanded, and Nicole obeyed.

Placing the phone down momentarily, she struggled out of the restriction of her tight T-shirt, throwing it to the side as she felt the cool air harden her nipples even more. Holding the phone with her left hand, she slid the fingers of her free hand across her stomach, enjoying the tickling sensation from her nails as she moved them closer to her breasts.

"I'm touching myself. Caressing my breasts." Nicole hadn't a clue what was possessing her to act the way she was, but she was lost to it.

Lost to the now heavy breathing of the caller, and her own eager body, as she swirled a finger around the stiff and dusky skin of her nipple. Teasing it. Stiffening the little nub so that it was begging for the soft wet feel of lips. Of a mouth possessing it.

"Does it feel good, Nicole? I want you to feel good. I want you to slide your hand down. Down toward your shorts." The girl melted Nicole with her tone, dissolving her reality into a heady mist of arousal and need.

She did as she was told, gliding her fingertips slowly down toward her heat. Down to the barrier of her shorts. Lifting up her hips, Nicole slipped off the shorts, wiggling her small backside to free herself from their confining restriction. They went the way of her T-shirt, and she was left naked under her light sheets.

"Tell me what you want me to do. I need to . . ." Nicole groaned as her hand descended to the small strip of pubic hair covering her already soaked sex. "I need to . . ."

"Touch your pussy, Nicole. Slide your fingers over yourself. Let me hear you enjoying your touch."

"Shit, that feels good," Nicole hissed, as she slipped her fingers into her wet folds, spreading herself open as she abandoned any hope of stopping what was happening.

"How does it feel? Tell me how your pussy feels," the girl requested, her voice raspy with obvious arousal.

Nicole shifted slightly, opening her legs wider so she could slick her fingers over herself freely, feeling her clit jump to attention as it throbbed for her to swirl the tips of her fingers over it. To have her give it the pressure it demanded.

"It feels hot, and wet. God, you've got me so wet," she moaned quietly as she dipped into the flow of arousal seeping from her slippery pussy hole.

She wanted to thrust her fingers inside. She wanted to feel her pussy open for her as she fingered herself, listening to the alluring voice of the mesmerising girl. But she didn't because for some reason, she wanted to wait. Wanted to wait to be told to do it, so it felt more real. Felt like it was the other girl gliding her fingers into her, fucking her.

"Nicole, I can almost hear how wet you are. I wish I was there to feel it. Would you like that? If I was there, with my fingers on your pussy. Sucking on your delicious breasts. Touching you. Fucking you. My fingers buried inside you." The caller moaned as Nicole whimpered in her desperate need.

"Yes . . ."

"Yes what, Nicole? I need to hear it from you." The girl's voice became more demanding as Nicole began circling a finger over her hard clit, her hips reacting to the touch as she searched for relief.

"I want you touching me. I want you here." The phone slipped a little from her grasp as she arched her back, needing more than what she could offer herself.

She was vaguely aware of a misty draft as she bit her lip to keep from moaning too loud, then fingers not her own began touching her, replacing hers in the silky stickiness of her hot pussy. She felt a warmth envelop her as the bed seemed to shift with more weight, and her skin felt the brush of someone else against it.

Nicole opened her eyes to the dim light, fearful of what she would see, but needing to witness what was happening as she groaned out loud with the fingers deftly rubbing her drenched slit. She took in the sight before her, unable to pull away as a warm, wet mouth descended on her nipple.

She was in the arms of a beautiful blonde girl. Her hair as soft as silk as it swept over her. Her hands attentive and skilled as she carried Nicole toward the release she craved.

Nicole knew she should be afraid. Knew she should be questioning. But with hot skin against her own, and the delicious intoxicating scent of the girl above her wrapping around her senses, she was unable to feel anything but desire.

"Oh, God," she called out, as the small blonde trailed her fingers lower, teasing around her opening as Nicole bucked up to the touch.

Lifting her hand to the girl's head, losing track of the phone completely, Nicole tangled her fingers in flowing blonde hair and gave herself up to the sensations of hands and lips teasing her, caressing her, making her crazy with desire. She couldn't think beyond that. Didn't want to think beyond it.

Using her other hand to grasp at the girl's back, Nicole pulled her closer, craving her skin. Seeking out hungry lips in the dark with her own. They kissed. Hot tongues dancing in a frantic kiss that seemed to arouse both girls equally as they moaned for one another.

The fair girl pulled away slightly, her eyes a piercing green that mesmerised Nicole as she felt fingers enter her slowly, spreading her drenched pussy open as they slid inside her. She sighed loudly to the quiet of the room and opened her legs further, giving herself to her mystery lover.

The girl began slowly sliding her fingers in and out, the wet sound of Nicole's pussy mingling with the scent of her need. Nicole gripped the girl, keeping their eyes locked as she arched her hips to meet the deepening thrusts of the fingers within her.

"Oh, fuck . . . you, you're her," Nicole breathed as the blonde girl quickened her pace, her fingers penetrating harder, filling Nicole's tight pussy as she rubbed up against the soft spot deep inside.

"Yes. You asked me to come to you." She swirled her thumb up over Nicole's erect clit, causing her to quiver with her oncoming orgasm. "I'm sorry, but you invited me." As she spoke in her soft tone, her eyes grew dark, and before Nicole knew what was happening she felt a rush of come gush from her pussy over the girl's fingers as she became swept up in overwhelming sensations her whole body was experiencing.

She trembled as the girl fucked her, thrusting her fingers deeper and harder as Nicole moaned out into the night. Then, as she attempted to clear her mind, to pull the girl's hand from inside her, she realized something else was happening. Something else was keeping her trembling, and as the night seemed to fade to an even darker shade of black, Nicole knew what it was.

The blonde had her gripped by the throat, her teeth feeling like impossibly sharp needles digging into the vulnerable flesh. Her hot mouth sucking and body quivering with its own rush of sensation.

Nicole couldn't break free. She couldn't scream. And as her surroundings dissolved around her, she felt the fingers leave her cold as they withdrew and gently caressed her cheek, soft whisperings of apologies and sorrow cradling her gently as she fell into the enveloping darkness.

A final shiver. A final tear splashing on pale skin, and Nicole became lost within the suffocating, lifeless air of her passion-filled demise.

The victim of a lustful legacy.

# All Hallows' Eve
## A Chain Gang Chronicle
### Peggy J. Herring, Laura DeHart Young and Therese Szymanski

Roth looked out the window, enjoying how the night held the world in its tendrils of darkness, hiding all of its secrets. Even without the bright full moon she'd have been able to look over the surrounding countryside without problem.

The conjunction of a full moon with this most auspicious of holidays was certain to be a potent mix and it was something she hadn't been able to savor in thirty years. The swollen belly of a full moon always brought something special out of so many different people.

A wolf howled in the distance. She wondered if it was anyone she knew, but then realized that was a pretty ridiculous thought. She wasn't still in Romania; this was supposedly a much more civilized area of the world with a far less prevalent nightlife.

She slicked her recently dyed jet-black hair back with the butchest gel she could find, donned her white tuxedo shirt and black tuxedo pants, and turned to the mirror to tie her bow tie. All of these newfangled clip-on theses and clip-on thoses mostly just annoyed her. If you were going to do something, you might as well take time to do it right. She'd always tied all her own ties, and she'd go to her dustpan doing just that, goshdarnit. (There was one exception to her anti-clip-on rule, but of course, it just wasn't the same. It was strap-on, not clip-on!)

She loved dressing as a vampire for All Hallows'. It was her all-time/always costume, and she did it well, down to her long black velvet cape and the cheapest fake teeth she could find.

She loved this holiday. Some thought it was way overdone, but she thought of it more as an . . . all-you-can-eat buffet. Granted, people were always running around rather like a 24/7 smorgasbord, but on All Hallows', they *expected* people to have elongated canines. They *expected* folks to do the unexpected. They wanted to be scared out of their pants. Wits. Whatever. (Although, truth be told, Roth kinda liked it when cute girls got scared out of their pants. She just simply could not find the bad in that. Unless it was her. Being the Big Bad in a cute girl's pants. She grinned at her own funny.)

Yuppers, Roth was all with the "Yay, Halloween." Others might stick around inside by the Telly because they found it tawdry and Hallmarkey, but she tried to make the most of every minute—after all, people just assumed any dead bodies they might run across were mannequins, and no one would ever believe them if they mentioned a vampire bit them in a haunted house.

Hell, they wouldn't even believe it themselves.

She took one last look at her clothing in the mirror, ensuring all her little shirt studs were in place, and that she appeared perfectly appointed. She scoffed at those who imagined that both she *and* her clothes should not appear in a mirror. Just because she put on clothing didn't make it invisible, after all. What sort of sense would that make? (Entirely too little for her taste.)

She smiled to herself as she left her house. She so enjoyed Daylight Saving Time, since it meant leaving her abode early on All Hallows' was not necessarily fatal.

After all, she didn't just play a vampire on Hallowe'en.


It still didn't look right, even with the spell she had cast upon the old, black dress with its lace bodice and cascading satin. Veronica Annabelle Lee, witch of Old Salem, stood before the mirror studying the blue eyes that stared back from a young face, a beautiful face. Another spell had taken the deep wrinkles and gray hair away into ages past. It was All Hallows' Eve—a night when anything could happen, when spells and dreams meant gathering with old friends and bewitching the living.

The lace and satin of the dress flowed with the body of a young woman. There were no scars from the stake's flames and embers. They, too, had vanished for All Hallows' Eve. Her powers were still strong, her spells still potent. For one brief moment, the terror of the stake and licking flames flashed through her ancient memory. She felt the fire, blazing hot, creeping up her body—the flames that had taken her mortal life more than three centuries ago. The eyes in the mirror blinked, willing away those terrifying last moments. No time to think of the past now—at least not until she arrived at the party. Then the past would present itself in a far more beautiful form. Yes, it was All Hallows' Eve and her friends were waiting.

To the mortal eye, Veronica walked the two-mile gravel road that wound toward the old Stanford mansion. Actually, she was floating just above the ground—gliding on the night breezes that also blew her long, red hair away from her face. The lights in the old Stanford mansion were already on and she could picture its endless corridors, creaking floors and luscious decay of years ago. But all had changed now.

The once-abandoned mansion on the Massachusetts hillside had been renovated in a single summer season. Trucks carrying workers up the winding dirt road came daily to complete the old mansion's transformation into a dwelling habitable to the human form. For several years now, mortals walked the halls, cooking mortal food and speaking in the mortal tongue Veronica had long forgotten. Oh, she could still manage the cumbersome syllables of the human language—but human voices sounded like fingernails moving slowly down a chalkboard. Except on this day (All Hallows' Eve) when the human and inhuman were invited to descend upon the mansion to dwell on the pleasures of the flesh in whatever fashion pleased them. Wasn't it a party after all? And all of the neighbors had been invited. Excitement coursed through her witch's blood. This year, the human flesh she sought was here in the old house and well within the power of her spells, as it always was. If only she didn't have to share this pleasure with her ghostly and other nonliving friends who inhabited the hills and valleys nearby. Veronica licked her lips. Yes, being alone with her lady-in-waiting was what she really wanted. But spells, spirits and the powers of life and death could not be kept completely separate. There were always trade-offs when mixing the mortal with the immortal, who were now gathered in the old drawing room, busily decorating for the party that was about to begin.

As a youngster Kit loved Halloween for the candy . . . the *good* kind of candy. Not that peanut-butter-wrapped-in-orange-or-black-wax-paper crappola some of the houses liked to pass out. Or popcorn balls! Yuck! The popcorn was usually stale before they even got any of the "ball" part of it done. If it wasn't a Snickers or a Milky Way—at least something close to being sort of expensive—then that house could expect a *real* trick.

One year old man Patterson gave the neighborhood kids each an ice cube. They couldn't really see very well with those scary masks on, and it was great hearing the sound of how heavy his candy was when he dropped it into the bag. Usually, as a general candy rule, the heavier the "clunk" it made in the bag, the more expensive the candy was. A group of kids behind them caught him doing the ice-cube thing. Then the rest of the kids checked their candy bags and they *allll* had a fresh ice cube in there! As a matter of fact, old man Patterson still had toilet paper in his trees because of being so cheap. The next year they all got 3 Musketeers bars!

Even now in Kit's ghostly form, she liked to see what old man Patterson handed out for Halloween. If it wasn't good and at least a little expensive, she set off his fire alarms every two minutes or so just to irritate him.

Her friends said she was too restless—that she should settle down. They said she needed to get over life's disappointments. Her friends said a lot of things and it was always fun meeting up with them. They might think Kit was immature and nothing but a prankster, but they all *loved* hearing about some of the things she'd done to her old lover when she was going at it hot and heavy with her new girlfriend. Yes, indeed. They couldn't wait to hear some of *those* stories!

Roth strolled down the street, whistling a merry version of a nice little head-smashing number she'd learned in Transylvania in the late nineteenth century. She wanted to hum the throat slashing/decapitating tune she'd liked so well in the 1400s, but couldn't remember the words or tune. Yet another thing to Google during those long daylight hours when she was unable to sleep. Insomnia was truly an evil thing for one such as her. Even insomniacs in the inner city could go for walks if they had a big enough gun. (Of course, the very idea that some people thought vampires had to sleep in a coffin during the day was humorous to Roth. She for one was most thankful it wasn't so, since she was extremely claustrophobic.)

Decades ago (or was it centuries?) no one owned this old manse. Now, for years, the same lesbians had owned it and held a Halloween party every year.

But now, she got to town a week ago, and discovered the mansion'd been sold, which was a somewhat worrisome development, but then she discovered it'd been again bought by lesbians and, as luck would have it, they were also having a party tonight—this most sacred of all nights.

She was a lesbian, she was in costume—getting in was *so* not going to be an issue. C'mon, she was all debonair and shit with the tux and really over-the-top fangs.

She loitered by the bushes, smoking, until a couple came up that she could follow to the house, as if she was with them.

"Cori, Ann!" the woman who answered the door said, "about time you got here!"

The two women went in, but Roth hadn't been invited. Yet. She paused at the threshold and looked expectantly at the host.

"Do I know you?" the woman asked.

"No. Not at all. I'm an evil vampire who needs an invite to enter your abode." Roth held her arms out, trying to look innocent. She bowed her head for extra effect.

"Oh. Well. Now don't you need an invitation from someone who actually lives here?"

Roth looked up. "Oh, well. Yeah. Could you possibly find someone who lives here to invite me in?" She pulled her cape up in front of her face and grinned. "I've come to drink your blood!" She dropped her arm and looked beseechingly at the woman. "C'mon, I'm *hungry* already."

"Get in here, you goof," the woman said, waving Roth in.

Roth knew folks would get freaked if she couldn't actually enter—or if sparks went off when she tried. So she said, "Do you live here? Cause, y'know, an actual resident has to invite me in and all."

"Okay, fine. I lied before. I'm Christie and I live here, so I can invite you in. So come in. I invite you to enter," Christie said, looking Roth over from head to toe (and apparently liking what she saw).

Roth pushed a foot over the threshold, keeping eye contact with Christie so she wouldn't notice if Roth couldn't enter. "I'm Roth."

"Roth? What an interesting name."

"It was my father's," Roth said, sidling into the elegant home. She was immediately aware that she was not alone—meaning, yeah, there were mere mortals here, but there were others who were more than that as well.


"Do you have some plumbing problems with this old house?" the woman dressed as Little Red Riding Hood asked Christie as they both made selections from a relish tray on the buffet table.

"No. Why?" Christie asked. "I've spent a fortune getting this place rewired and the plumbing updated."

"I was in the downstairs bathroom adjusting my hood in the mirror when the toilet flushed all on its own. It sort of freaked me out."

Kit was standing by the punch bowl refreshing the contents of her cup when she overheard the comment and nearly blew punch out her nose. She loved doing things like that! Old man Patterson had three different plumbers out to his house over the last month trying to find the cause of all that unneeded and extra toilet flushing.

"It just flushed by itself?" Christie asked with a touch of skepticism in her voice.

"All by itself," Little Red Riding Hood confirmed. "I thought perhaps you had some sort of remote-flushing-apparatus thing you liked to use to give us a bit of a scare."

"I'm not much of a prankster. Besides, that's a little over the edge. This is a costume party where mingling and exchanging phone numbers or e-mail addresses is highly encouraged. It's not meant to be scary."

"Well, you might want to have that toilet checked out then. It shouldn't be doing that on its own."

Kit finished playing with the ladle in the punch bowl and gave Little Red Riding Hood a nice, slow once-over. She wondered when her vampire friend Skeeter would get there. It had been a year to the day since they had seen each other.

Kit was toying with the idea of going into another room and changing out of her Casper the Ghost outfit and into a werewolf's costume. *Little Red Riding Hood might like that*, she thought. *It would almost make us look like a couple!* Kit glanced around and noticed that there was no one in the library. It would only take her a few seconds to change her form into something more wolf-like.

When she came back into the huge great room, Kit felt taller and more buff. *No more Casper for me on All Hallows' Eve*, she thought. *It's too wussy.*

"So Christie," someone in the group said. "How much did this place set you back?"

Kit stepped up and joined them, managing to nudge her way beside Little Red Riding Hood.

"So far, just fifty thousand," Christie said. "There's still a few more things I want done yet."

"Fifty grand," someone dressed as a witch said. Kit recognized the voice of her old friend. Veronica smiled and winked at Kit.

"Twenty thousand of that went to rewire this place," Christie said.

Kit looked up at the chandelier high above their heads and blinked. Every light in the house flickered, causing a few guests to giggle and another one to yell. However, it made Christie's eyes widen in surprise. She never seemed to notice how truly extraordinary her Halloween celebrations were.

"Excuse me," Kit said to Little Red Riding Hood, "but may I ask what you have in that basket you're holding?"

Red turned to Kit and broke into a smile. "My, what big eyes you have."

"All the better to see you with, my dear," Kit-the-wolf replied.

Each woman in the group threw her head back in a hearty laugh. *Oh, this is going to be fun*, Kit thought. *I can hardly wait until Skeeter gets here.*


Veronica sidled up to the big bad wolf and whispered, "How many different people do you plan to morph into this fine evening? Personally, I thought Casper was deliciously cute."

Kit laughed, placing one hairy paw on Veronica's shoulder. "So sorry to disappoint you, dearest Veronica. But I was trying to make an impression on Little Red Riding Hood."

"I think you did. I noticed her goody basket quivering."

"Ha! I'd like to get into her goody basket!"

"Patience, my carnivorous friend. All in good time. The party's just getting started. Have you seen Skeeter yet?"

Kit scanned the dining room. "No, I haven't. But I feel her presence. Know what I mean? My fur is standing on end."

"Yes, you're absolutely right. She's definitely here . . . somewhere. And that means the party's headed in the right direction." Veronica rearranged the flow of her dress, allowing the dark shawl to fall from her shoulders to reveal her ample cleavage. She caught Kit staring. "Now listen. You need to behave, darling. Your job is to ensnare your own unsuspecting mortal while I draw mine to me."

"Yeah, but I have to look at all the goods, ya know. Mortal, immortal. Flesh is flesh."

"Mine is a bit aged, but still tender."

"Better not talk that way around Skeeter. You'll set her tuxedo pants on fire."

"Her pants are always on fire," Veronica said with a snicker. "That's what makes her so irresistible, don't you think?" Veronica felt a sudden chill, then a faint breath along her neck—cool and light like a breeze running up from the ocean. "Skeeter? Is that you?"

"Who else, babe? You look good enough to eat tonight," Skeeter hissed through the fake plastic teeth, her fingertips sliding across Veronica's shoulder.

"Haven't you eaten enough women already?" Kit interrupted.

Skeeter ran her hands through her slick hair. "Never, my ghostly friend." Eyeing Kit more closely, Skeeter said, "This is a new apparition I haven't seen before, Kit. A sheet in wolf's clothing? HA! I like it. Proves what I've always said. There's a little butch in everyone. Even Veronica, don't you think?"

"Only when I have my broom close at hand," Veronica interjected before Kit could reply. "Now, what do you say? Shall we mingle? Select the chosen few and make sure they're the last ones here when the night is over. Well, when the night is over for everyone but them—and us of course!" Veronica whispered, her eyes glowing red. Many a spell passed through her brain as she scanned the old house now crammed with chattering women. "Once you've selected your prey . . . uh, I mean, dates for later this evening, give me the usual sign and I'll spike the punch, if you know what I mean! Now, get to work!"

Skeeter rolled her dark eyes and muttered, "Damn, the bitch is getting bossy in her old age."

Kit flicked a moth out of her fur. "No shit."


Roth had finally given up correcting the nut-case ghost about her name. Several years ago when she had first come to this party, Kit had run up to Roth, wrapping her arms around Roth and calling her *Skeeter*, saying how concerned she was that *Skeeter* was so late—she'd been sure *Skeeter*'d gone and gotten a stake through the heart, making her something far more Pledgeable than Kit wanted for her dear friend.

It was only when Veronica burst into laughter that Roth realized she'd been had. Apparently Veronica'd told Kit she might as well dress as a chicken next year since that was what she was, and one thing led to another and so Kit had to hug the next vamp that came to the party and call her *Skeeter*.

"You two are really rather . . . different," Roth had said that year. They really were, but there was something enchanting and playful about them nonetheless. "However, the name is Roth, not *Skeeter*. I've never met or known a *Skeeter* in my life or since."

"Roth, what sorta name is Roth?" Kit said. Veronica simply stood back, watching with an amused look. It was almost like she knew exactly what Roth was in for.

"It's short for Hrothgar."

"That's even worse!" Kit said, her ghostly form shimmering brighter beneath her sheet.

Roth was annoyed. "It was my father's name!"

"You took your father's name? No, wait, your father's name was Hrothgar and still you took it?"

"You would've taken it too, if your name was Æðelœryð."

Kit looked at Veronica. "I can't spell that. Can you spell that?"

"Listen, *I* can't even spell it," Roth said. "We were a mostly illiterate society. Thus, the needing to take my father's name."

"Hrothgar indeed. You look like a Skeeter—don't she look like a Skeeter?" Kit said.

"Skeeter it is," Veronica decided.

The worst of it was that occasionally Skeeter . . . Roth . . . would be in a different part of the world and somehow someone there would know her as *Skeeter*. Damned ghost and witch got around far too much.

Ah, well, perhaps a new identity for a new millennium wasn't so bad . . . and *Skeeter* seemed a bit more playful than Roth had ever been. So now, tonight, Roth went buh-bye and Skeeter came out to *play*.

She scanned the room, quickly appraising the wide buffet of delights set out for her appreciation—tall, short, light, dark, full-figured, slender, and all the ranges between. She briefly thought about making like a Chinese restaurateur and sampling all the dishes, but decided some might frown upon such.

But hey . . . she was *Skeeter*! She grinned evilly and dove into the melee, running her hand lightly over Wonder Woman's firm rear, and waggling an eyebrow at the brunette when she looked up. Having just come from Romania, she was in the mood for something a bit . . . lighter . . . though, so she glanced around the room and pointed to Ariel, bringing the redhead to her without any magick at all. They finished the current disco song, but as soon as Monster Mash came on, Skeeter slipped away. Ariel wasn't quite right. Not quite what she fancied tonight.

Tonight was a night for something special . . . Not Barbie . . . no Glenda . . . not in the mood for Little Red (not this time, not tonight—plus it looked like Kit was having an ectoplasmic episode for the little innocent) . . . and no matter what, Skeeter'd never be in the mood for Paris Hilton! Sheesh . . .

She did a quick turn around the dance floor with Rapunzel, running her tongue lightly up the woman's tasty neck and taking just a spot of blood from her earlobe ("So you do bite," Rapunzel had said with a wicked grin,) before walking up to the bar for a glass of wine (red, of course).

Skeeter continued looking, knowing she'd recognize the girl when she saw her. The girl for her special night.

"Hi! I think you're looking for me!" a voice from behind her said. Skeeter whipped around to face the petite blonde. "I'm Buffy!"

Skeeter set her wine down quickly before she dropped it. Moving her head ever so slightly to the right, she was able to see around the young woman to squint menacingly in Kit and Veronica's direction.

Kit leaned closer to Veronica and whispered, "Wow. Did you see that?"

"You mean Skeeter's eyes rolling back in her head?"

"Sometimes she doesn't have much of a sense of humor."

Veronica smiled and took a sip of punch. "She knows who sent that young blonde thing over there."

"Maybe if we pretend we didn't see anything—"

"Too late," Veronica said. "Here she comes and she knows we've been watching."

Kit looked up and blinked slowly, making the lights go out again. She could hear Veronica's low chuckle just before allowing the lights to come back on again.

"Bad wolf," Veronica said.

Kit nonchalantly strolled over to the buffet table and carefully selected an assortment of hors d'oeuvres with her paws. Within seconds, Skeeter and Veronica were there beside her.

"That was good, Kit," Skeeter said. "My upper lip still has an annoying twitch to it thanks to you."

"It's all part of the festivities, my friend," Kit said. "When your cape came up to hide those adorable fangs, I thought I was going to howl!"

Kit heard Veronica snicker again as the three of them stood there randomly selecting a varied assortment of stuffed celery, miniature quiches and pickles.

"Well," Skeeter said with a sigh, "it's obvious you're still not over that Ghostbuster incident that took place a few years ago."

"Unlike what just happened with young Buffy over there," Kit said, motioning toward Buffy the Vampire Slayer with a carrot stick in her paw, "the Ghostbuster incident was *not* funny."

Veronica's delightful laughter made the other two eventually laugh as well.

"I *so* look forward to seeing both of you each year," Veronica said. "I would suggest that you two just call it even and forget about this little good-natured rivalry that's developed between you, but I enjoy it too much to ever want it to stop."

"At least one of us was amused this evening," Skeeter said with a touch of boredom in her voice.

"Not quite true," Kit said. "It was quite amusing wondering just how far those Transylvanian boxers of yours would ride up when that cute little vampire slayer showed you some attention."

"I hate being predictable," Skeeter said as all three of them laughed. They stood there pretending to snack on finger food, each carefully surveying the guests in costume.

"What strikes your fancy, Veronica?" Kit asked after a moment. "June Cleaver with the tray of cookies, or Lizzie Borden over there wielding the axe?"

"Come now. You know I have a very particular taste. She'll be here soon," Veronica said.

"What about you, Skeeter?" Kit asked. "One of each?"

"Not tonight. I want something special."

"What could be more special for a vampire than Buffy?" Kit asked in mock innocence.

Skeeter hissed, which made the wolf fur stand up on the back of Kit's neck.

"Okay, okay," Kit said. "I was trying to do you a little favor. I overheard her say she worked at the local blood bank."

Skeeter hissed even louder this time, but it was drowned out by Veronica's laughter.

"I thought we were supposed to be mingling," Kit reminded them, changing the subject. "I'm sticking with Little Red Riding Hood. We're kind of cute together."

"That you are," Veronica agreed. "I guess it's time for me to get to work as well. But that won't take long."

"Excellent!" Kit said. "Let's get going then. You'll be okay without us, right, Skeeter?"

Veronica and Skeeter both looked at the Big Bad Wolf and couldn't help but shake their heads and chuckle.

"I'll manage," Skeeter said dryly.


Veronica shot a glance at the art deco clock on the living room wall. It was 11:30. Only thirty minutes until the bewitching hour! With an imperceptible nod, she cast some quick spells that rippled like waves through the adjoining rooms, as well as the punch bowl. Kit had wasted no time and was already baring her canines at Little Red Riding Hood again, and Skeeter had disappeared, pouring herself like an intoxicating liquor into the crowd. It took but a few seconds for the spells to weave their magic and then *she* walked into the room—already looking for Veronica, *compelled* to look for Veronica. *She* was medium height with dark hair and smoky, gray eyes—and a smile that was bewitching even to Veronica. Dressed as G.I. Jane in tight camouflage pants that accented her enticing hips, she coyly flipped her curly hair away from her forehead, leaning one hand on the mahogany buffet. The dog tags hanging from her neck swung hypnotically. Veronica knew her name even before the woman said, "Hi, I'm Liz. Have we met before? It's so odd, but I feel like I know you."

Veronica smiled and shook the woman's hand. It was warm and slightly damp. From nervousness? "Is that the best you can do for a pickup line?"

"I'm sorry," Liz replied sheepishly. "That was completely lame.

But the feeling I'm having is so odd . . ." She shrugged, as if trying to play it off. "No more rum cake for me."

"Well, I don't think we've met, but it is a pleasure," Veronica said, knowing in her own heart that they had met a thousand times before—the same two spirits adrift in the fog of ages past, destined to meet again and again. Through the sheer will of Veronica's spells and longing for the touch of Liz (Elizabeth, Bette, Eliza, Beth as the generations passed), they stood and searched each other's eyes to reconnect once again. It was in Old Salem that Liz and Veronica had first been lovers. Liz had not been cast to the fire like Veronica because she was not a witch but an earthly creature— a beautiful and delicate lesbian trapped, as they both had been, in a Puritan society. Veronica took Liz's hand. Flashing her most charming smile, she asked, "Care for some punch? I hear it's delish."

"Thank you. I'd love some."

While Liz was sipping punch in her Marine muscle shirt and chatting about her job at the local chamber of commerce, Veronica was scanning the crowd for her friends. It was now midnight and many of the women were slowly filing out. The few remaining diehards were out back on the heated porch, trading renovation stories.

"Have you seen the upstairs?" Liz asked Veronica, staring suspiciously into her punch glass. "Either the rum cake is taking effect, or this punch has a powerful kick." Liz shook her head as if to clear the cobwebs. "At any rate, I overheard some conversation earlier that they completely transformed the upstairs rooms."

"Do take me on a tour," Veronica said in a sultry tone, gesturing toward the old wooden staircase. With Liz in tow, she nudged Kit on her way by and whispered, "Get a message to Skeeter. I'm headed upstairs. Plus, I think it's time for you to get your paws on Little Red Riding Hood's basket."

Kit winked and nodded. "I see you've found an old friend. Ever get tired of the same woman year after year?"

"Never," Veronica replied, her face flushed with excitement.

"I'd never pass up a chance to be with Liz, even if it meant facing the stake again!"


"Okay, so Christie says you said your name was Roth, but your friends keep calling you Skeeter. What's up with that?"

Roth suffered a sudden identity crisis as she turned to face the voice. "Well"—she started, but then hissed and raised her cape up in front of her as a barrier when she saw who it was. She slowly started backing up.

Buffy laughed. "God, serious about your costume much?"

Roth lowered her cape and stopped in her tracks. "So you're not carrying any pointy wooden objects?"

"Just this one," Buffy said, pulling a really sharp stake out of her sleeve.

Roth hissed and leapt back, right into the punch table.

"Smooth move there, Fang," a sultry voice said, coming up beside Roth and steadying the table just before it tipped. "Ya gotta problem here, B?" she said, using the nickname that Faith, the *other* vampire slayer from the TV show *Buffy the Vampire Slayer*, had for Buffy. This girl was a luscious brunette dressed in black leather pants and one of those rather small and tight white tank tops known as a *wife beater*, which was exactly the sort of outfit the TV Faith would have chosen.

"Dear God, is this place lousy with slayers or what?" Roth said, looking at the two girls.

"Didn't you get the memo?" Faith asked. "B here keeps mackin' on the vamps." Her gaze slowly moved over the other girl's body, obviously undressing it.

"Sssh, *F*, don't go telling all my secrets," the Buffy-wannabe said, making fun of the nicknames and absolutely oblivious to the look *F* had given her. Roth thrilled to the subtext and what it could all mean. Especially tonight.

"She said we had to come as the"—the Faith-wannabe made quote marks in the air with her fingers—" *'chosen two'* just so she could get the attention of tall, dark and butch, whom she's been drooling over for the past two Halloweens."

"Okay, so I'll just put the stake down over here," Buffy said, laying said sharp pointy object a few feet away on the punch table. Her cheeks were slightly red. "Now, can a girl get a dance?" She looked at Roth and raised an eyebrow. "After all, you just heard my . . . eviler half . . . tell how I'm quite the undead groupie."

Roth wondered just how lucky Veronica's spell would help her get. She went to the punch bowl, poured two glasses, handed one to Faith and one to Buffy, and then circled Buffy, running her hand along the slender waist. When she wrapped her arms around the girl from behind, she felt her shiver just slightly and lean back into the embrace. Roth pulled a hank of blonde hair back over Buffy's shoulder so she could whisper right into the lovely girl's lovely ear. "I hear the upstairs is quite the tour these days. Would you like to go exploring with me? Or perhaps we can make it a . . . *chosen*-two-for-one?"

Faith and Buffy silently met each other's gaze and sipped their punch. Their heart rates had sped up noticeably, however.

Roth wrapped an arm around each of them and said, "Okay, so no more sharp wooden objects then?"

"Just this one," Faith said, pulling one out of her waistband.

"Let's just leave this down here, shall we?" Roth said, grabbing it gingerly between two fingers and dropping it on the table before refilling their punch cups and leading them upstairs.

Buffy giggled. "This punch is making me all loopy."

"Ah, you're just a lightweight, Allie," Faith said, apparently using the other girl's real name.

Allie giggled again. "Look who's talking, *Lisa*."

This all made Roth feel immeasurably better. She *knew* there were no such things as vampire slayers, just like so many *knew* there weren't any actual real vampires. So she was glad to know their real names. To know they were just girls.

Really hot, cute, femme girls. Girls she was leading directly to her favorite room at the far end of the third floor.

"That's wicked," Lisa said as they walked by a mirror. "Roth, dude, I can only see your clothes in the mirror. Where are you?"

Kit looked up when she heard the door open. She smiled, seeing Veronica and Liz coming in holding hands.

"I was beginning to wonder where you were," Kit said.

"Did you start without us?" Veronica asked with a wink.

"You were right about my girl-in-the-hood over there. Her basket has definitely been quivering."

Veronica stood in the middle of the huge, brightly lit room and slowly took it all in. Kit watched her friend's gaze settle on the far right corner near a heavily draped window.

"You waited for me?" Veronica asked Kit.

The Big Bad Wolf's eyes softened; she nodded.

"You pick where you'd like to be," Kit said. "It doesn't matter to me where Little Red and I are when the fun begins."

Veronica put her arm around Liz and led her to the section of the room where the rows and rows of blue velvet pillows were scattered about on the huge Persian rug. Kit blinked, instantly causing the bayberry-scented candles to flicker to life. The lights in the corner dimmed just as Veronica slowly pulled Liz down to her among the pillows.

Kit turned to find her companion for the evening standing there without her basket and looking delicious in nothing but her red cape with the hood.

"Wolfie, I might need some more of that punch I had earlier," Little Red said.

Kit smiled. "I'm sure you've had plenty."

There was giggling in the hallway just before Kit saw Skeeter and the two vampire slayer impersonators enter the room. The giggling stopped as the three of them came in and glanced around at the orgy-inspired décor—the pillows of every size and rugs so soft and inviting that there was no denying what they were to be used for.

"You waited for me?" Skeeter asked. She had a beautiful woman on each arm. The blonde toyed with the hair on the nape of Skeeter's neck, while the other ran her tongue along Skeeter's earlobe.

"I did," Kit said. "Veronica chose blue. You and your entourage can have your pick of the other three areas."

Skeeter smiled her pleasure at Kit's thoughtfulness and generosity. In the past, the first one to the room got to pick where they wanted to entertain for the evening.

"We'll take the white," Skeeter said. "My lovelies will show up ever so nicely on it."

Kit blinked and lit the white candles in the white corner of the room. The regular lights in the area dimmed and set the mood for a most enjoyable time for her blood-sucking friend.

"Wolfie," Little Red called. She had an adorable pout on her full, glossy lips. "I want more punch."

"I have something even better than punch," Kit said. As she made her way toward the girl-in-the-hood, Kit took her time and let her wolf persona revert to a form composed of less fur and more flesh. *More like a five o'clock shadow,* she thought as she inspected her arms.

"What big ears you have, my Wolfie," Little Red murmured.

"All the better to hear you with, my dear," Kit said. She took the woman in her arms just as soft music began to play. *Thank you, Veronica,* Kit thought. She slowly danced Little Red Riding Hood over to the corner of the room where a row of pillows the color of gold were lined up waiting for them. Kit pushed the hooded cape from Little Red's shoulders and let it fall on the golden rug beneath their feet. Kit pulled her closer and nuzzled her neck and was promptly rewarded with a deep sigh.

"You know there's a rule, don't you?" Kit whispered as she moved her lips along Little Red's bare throat.

"What rule?" Little Red asked with a weak, husky sigh.

"Never moon a werewolf, my love."

Little Red's lips found Kit's and she pulled her down and wrapped her bare legs around her.

"My silly, silly, Wolfie," Little Red cooed as she continued to kiss Kit's face and mouth. "You're not a werewolf."

"Yeah, you're right," Kit whispered before flicking her tongue over one of Little Red's hard nipples, "but you just never know who's gonna show up in here."

Holding Liz once again on All Hallows' Eve was like a dream, the kind Veronica wanted to escape into forever. As she held Liz close, she cast another spell that sent a warm breeze cascading through the room (and a bit of fog, too), leaving her and Liz alone. Oh, the others were there—but she and Liz had been transported into another dimension where the sounds, touches and pleasures belonged only to them. Being a witch was sometimes damned convenient.

Liz ran her fingers through Veronica's hair and Veronica couldn't help but smile. No spells were needed now. "I don't do this on first meetings. I've never done anything like this before. But I can't help myself," Liz stammered, trying to compose herself. "I want to say that I love you. But that's impossible, isn't it?"

"Nothing is impossible, my darling," Veronica replied, turning Liz over on her back. "Perhaps we've met in a previous life." She slid her hands across the fabric of Liz's khaki shirt, imagining the warmth of her skin beneath. The same soft skin she remembered from those long-ago days in Salem when they held hands while walking the wooded trail outside of town, and rolled like school-children across grass warmed by the sun. Liz's nipples grew hard as Veronica pressed her lips against them, teasing them through the fabric of her shirt. She wore no bra. "I love you, Liz. And I've waited so long to say it."

"Then I'll say it, too. I love you . . . my God! I don't even know your name!"

"Veronica."

"Of course. I did know that. Didn't I?"

"Yes, darling. You did." Veronica kissed Liz deeply, her hands sliding underneath the shirt, fingers running across Liz's firm breasts. Liz sighed and quickly pulled off the shirt, tossing it over her head onto one of the many blue pillows. They held on to each other tightly, and sank into that boundless ocean of blue velvet far away from anyone or anything. Their kisses were tender but insistent—as though the kisses they shared were the first and last they would ever know of each other. Suddenly, they locked eyes and for that brief instant they understood that time had been defeated. Staring deeply into the blue eyes of Veronica, the barrier of time was swept away and Liz awakened. Yes, Liz's soul was there in that room and Veronica gasped with joy.

"Veronica, how I've missed you. It's All Hallows' Eve at last."

"I've missed you, too, Liz. Yes, at last."

Veronica kissed the creamy white skin along Liz's thighs and felt Liz's arms encircle her. They were melting together, two lost souls of centuries past—complete once again. Liz's fingers raked over her back, as Veronica's tongue moved in loving unison with Liz's hips. The taste of her woman after so long made Veronica woozy. She closed her eyes and listened to the long-awaited sound of Liz's moans and ran her hands up and down the smooth creaminess of Liz's breasts. Then Liz cried out and sighed again in dreamy satisfaction, sinking back into the pillows, her arms wrapped tightly around Veronica's neck.

"Oh, what you do to me, my darling. Remember Old Salem—how we used to make love in that cornfield beyond the woods and the old town road?"

"I'll never forget," Veronica said, kissing the lovely curve between Liz's neck and shoulder. "We used to run all the way there just so we could be together."

"And by that time I was so wet, I'd beg you to fuck me. Didn't even care that I had corn husks digging into my back. I always ached for you, just like I do now."

"Then I won't disappoint you."

Liz unzipped Veronica's dress, pulling it down over her shoulders while Veronica twirled her tongue in and out of Liz's belly-button. Liz laughed, spying the dog tags that hung to the left of her neck. "How will you like fucking a Marine?"

Veronica stared into Liz's gray eyes and replied, "I'll like it just fine."

Liz ran her lips across Veronica's nipples and then bit them softly, sucking them until they were hard between her teeth. Veronica closed her eyes for a brief second. Then she heard the low, familiar whisper. The same whisper she often heard in her dreams. Liz's voice pleading softly, "Fuck me, Veronica. Fuck me hard like you did in that cornfield when I could scream as loud as I wanted and no one could hear me." Veronica slid one arm around Liz's waist, and the other between Liz's legs, her fingers slipping easily inside her lover, moving slowly at first—then rapidly as Liz began to respond. Veronica felt her own orgasm rising, knowing that she was fucking Liz, hearing her lover's moans, feeling Liz pushing Veronica's clenched fist deeper into her burning thighs.

"Harder! I can take all of you. You know I always could," Liz moaned.

They came together as Liz emitted a low growl that morphed into a scream, her body shuddering in Veronica's arms.


"Your friends are gonna be in the room with us?" Allie said, glancing around.

Roth had an arm around each of her girls as she led them to their area. "I hope you don't have a problem with that. I'm pretty sure you'll forget they're even here." Without releasing either girl, Roth leaned down and ran her tongue lightly down Allie's neck, stopping briefly to place a kiss on her pulse point, which beat deliciously against her lips. Allie shivered slightly.

Meanwhile, Lisa pressed up against Roth's other side, practically riding Roth's thigh. "Hey, is that a bottle of wine in your pocket, or are ya just glad to see me?" she asked, feeling said bottle in Roth's tux pocket. She pulled it out, took a swig, and handed it to Allie.

Allie took it, and took a more ladylike swig. "Mmm, punchy goodness!" She giggled.

Roth gently nudged them toward the pillows, so they lay next to each other. "You know what I'd like to see?" She knelt by their feet, putting her hands on their ankles, and slowly feeling up their beautiful curves. She squeezed gently just below their knees, making circles with her thumbs. Lisa was in leather, but with Allie, in her pastels and short skirt, she got to luxuriate in the feel of warm flesh beneath her fingers.

Allie closed her eyes and took Roth's hand in her own, to guide it upward over her body.

Lisa, on the other hand, was staring directly at Allie. "Tell me," she said, flipping her long dark hair over her shoulder, "whatcha wanna see."

Roth inched forward, moving her hands to their luxurious tresses. Allie was oblivious, but Lisa, even though she was apparently enjoying Roth's attention, kept her eyes on Allie.

Keeping her eyes closed, Allie put Roth's hand on her breast.

Roth was never one to say nay to a woman, girl, female . . . so she acquiesced.

Lisa's eyes were glued to Roth's hand, which was gently caressing Allie's breast, her thumb flicking over Allie's rapidly hardening nipple.

"I want to see you two kiss," Roth said. Allie's eyes shot open and she stared at Roth, panicked. Lisa's jaw dropped open and she looked panicked as she stared at Roth.

Roth leaned down and lightly kissed Lisa, letting herself briefly taste the fullness of Lisa's lips, then she leaned up to quickly nip at her ear, and ran her tongue down her neck. She caressed her ass, rested her hand on Lisa's hip, and pressed her thumb into Lisa, just inside her hip bone, and finally slipped under the wife beater to run up the naked flesh of her ribs briefly.

"I just want tonight," Roth whispered into Lisa's ear. "Give me that, and I'll get you what you've always wanted. Plus, well, you'll also get a helluva ride." She nipped Lisa's ear enough just to taste a drop of thick, rich blood.

"Ow . . ." Lisa moaned, not pushing her away.

Roth turned to Allie. She started by just exploring Allie's lips with her own, then bit her lower lip and slid her tongue inside the other woman. Allie moaned and put an arm around Roth's neck. Their tongues were warm and slick against each others. Roth reached around Allie to unzip her dress. Unsnap her bra. She felt Allie gasp, and she pushed her onto her back.

Roth began nibbling on Allie's ear even as she pulled her dress down to her waist and removed her bra. Lisa pushed into Roth's back, as she began licking and biting Roth's ears and neck.

Roth shoved herself up, taking Lisa with her. Roth looked down at Allie, letting her gaze wander over the smooth, soft flesh. "You are so beautiful." She turned to look at Lisa, who was propped on her elbows staring at Allie. "Isn't she?"

Allie suddenly became aware of her best friend's gaze on her naked form and she grasped at her clothing.

"No," Roth said. "Relax." She kept her gaze locked with Allie's and used her hands to keep Allie's in place—away from her clothing, leaving her exposed. She leaned up enough to take one of Lisa's hands in her own and run it over Allie's body, from the slender column of her neck, down to the plush fullness of her breast.

Lisa started moving her hand herself to run her thumb over Allie's hardened nipple.

Allie stared up at the two women and . . . looked afraid. Scared. But then both women were touching her intimately at the same time, and she moaned and closed her eyes.

Roth slid over her body so both she and Lisa could enjoy Allie at once. Lisa seemed to catch her cue, and she bent down to run her lips lightly over Allie's, even as her hand continued to play with Allie's nipple.

Roth bent to tongue Allie's other nipple, swirling her tongue around the hardening bud until she pulled it into her mouth and sucked it . . . then bit it. Her hand moved down Allie's body—

caressing her stomach, cupping each hip in turn, then sliding beneath the thong to trace circles along the tender flesh in ever-closer proximity to the heat Roth could already smell.

As if reading Roth's mind, Lisa finally pulled her lips from Allie's and moved down her body, sucking on her neck, nibbling her ear, licking down to her nipple, which she ended up biting.

Allie moaned, groaned, wriggled and squiggled.

Roth sat up on her haunches to pull Allie's dress, thong, and fashionable, stiletto-heeled boots from her, leaving her naked except for her earrings and . . .

. . . oh God . . .

. . . bulky silver cross necklace, which lay between her breasts. How had Roth managed to miss seeing that . . . and touching it?

What the fuck. She was the butch here.

"Cross. Get rid of it, blondie," she said, growling slightly.

Allie's eyes shot open. Her cheeks turned bright red as she realized it was Lisa sucking on her nipple.

"Take it off," Roth said, running her fingers lightly up Allie's inner thigh. Lisa had seen Allie's reaction and was now pulling away, so Roth grabbed her hand, entwined their fingers, and laid their clasped hands on Allie's naked belly. "You do want both of us inside you at once, right?" She inched their hands down.

Allie twitched and squirmed slightly. Her eyes were wide, staring at the hands moving down her body. She reached up hesitantly to remove the cross from her neck.

Roth ran her and Lisa's fingers through Allie's wet, feeling not only with her own hand, but also with Lisa's. And slowly she guided her and Lisa's fingers into Allie.

"Oh *God!*" Allie said, arching, watching what was being done to her and experiencing the first of her orgasms.

Roth leaned forward to kiss Lisa briefly, then Allie, before she started licking, biting and nibbling down Allie's beautifully firm body. She knew she was going to have to have Lisa, too. That girl'd be a wild ride.

Roth and Lisa were acting almost as one as they sucked Allie's nipples, took turns fingering her and eating her out, licking her thighs and tummy, nibbling her neck, and having her as she came again and again.

Lisa leaned over Allie and kissed her deeply. Roth knelt between her legs, pushing them further open.

"I . . . can't . . . any . . . more . . ." Allie gasped while Lisa caressed her breasts.

Roth used her hands to open Allie up to the cool night air. She ran her thumbs up and down Allie's tender flesh, enjoying her wetness and her heat. She rubbed her entire hand in Allie's wet and then entered her, one finger at a time . . . one . . . two . . . three. Then she laid her head on Allie's stomach and breathed deeply of the intoxicating smell of her arousal. Roth ran her tongue slowly, very slowly, up and down Allie's clit.

And then she put her entire mouth on her, shoving a fourth finger in. Then her entire fist. She sucked her, using her shoulders to push Allie's legs ever wider.

Allie bucked against her, wrapping her legs around Roth's shoulders.

Lisa was still kissing Allie. Roth grabbed one of Lisa's hands and put it on Allie's spread pussy, while keeping her fist inside Allie, and shoving a finger into Allie's ass.

"Fuck!" Allie screamed, coming.

Roth allowed her teeth to turn into fangs and she leaned forward and bit into Allie's neck, puncturing the flesh and sucking on the wonderful nectar from her neck. Roth felt the blood flow through her, into her.

Allie arched up into her. "Oh . . . Oh . . . God . . . Fuck!" she screamed, coming again. Hard.

It was . . . it was blood. She had to . . . pull herself from Allie. She licked the wound to help close it, licked her lips clean of blood, and looked up to Lisa's fascinated gaze.

"Oh, God, no more," Allie moaned, when Roth and Lisa lay down against her, each stealing a kiss before nuzzling into her shoulder.

Roth lay there for a moment, then took Lisa's hand in hers, so they could both again caress Allie. Then she sat up and said, "I loved watching you touch her," to Lisa. "But you know you're next."

Lisa looked right at her. "What're you gonna do to me?" There was nothing shy about this girl. She actually made that statement sound more like a challenge than anything else.

"I'm gonna make you come. Then I'll bite you. So take off that cross and get naked," Roth instructed.

Lisa stared at her for a moment, then stood. She pulled her top off. She didn't have a bra on. She took off one boot, then the other, tossing each to opposing sides. Then she peeled off her leather pants. She wore no underwear.

"Really got into the part, huh?" Roth asked. The girl was gorgeous. Nice big breasts with sweet, dusky nipples. She was totally shaved, leaving herself bare and exposed (Allie'd had just a thin sliver of hair left down there). Even now she stood, naked and proud, with her legs slightly apart.

"You got that right," Lisa said, taking off her necklace and wrapping it around her hand. "Just in case, yunno?"

Roth stood and stepped over Allie, who was momentarily passed out, to pull Lisa up onto her. Lisa immediately wrapped her legs around Roth, even as an intoxicating fog began to swirl around them.

"You're butch," Lisa said, feeling Roth's thick biceps.

"Yeah, I am," Roth said, reaching between their bodies to pull down her zipper and pull her toy out.

Lisa looked down at it and her eyes widened in amazement. "Oh fuck."

Roth slid her fingers along Lisa's clit and then rubbed them against her toy, lubricating it. She lifted Lisa and impaled her on her dick. She shoved Lisa against a wall, where she could fuck her good and proper.

"Oh God, oh God . . . I . . . I didn't . . ." Lisa mumbled as the fog swelled around them.

Roth held her hands above her head against the wall as she slammed into her, fucking her with her dildo. Then she held the two hands with only one of her own so she could explore Lisa's beautiful body with her other hand—from her firm, plush breasts, down her trim stomach, over her sweet ass . . . She wrapped Lisa's legs around her even tighter. Then she leaned forward to devour Lisa's mouth with her own, fucking her with her tongue as well.

And just as Lisa hit climax, just as she began screaming her release, Roth let go and bit deep into her neck.

"Oh, *FUCK ME!*" Lisa screamed, coming even harder.


Kit felt as though she were floating. With Little Red Riding Hood snug in her arms and her blond head resting easily on Kit's shoulder, there was a wonderful sense of peacefulness and tranquillity spreading through Kit's body. Veronica had done her magic earlier by sending an intoxicating fog through the room. Kit opened her eyes to find gold veils moving over them, flowing easily in the breeze that circulated near the ceiling. Kit reached over and groped for the cape her lover had worn earlier. She covered them both with it and pulled Little Red deeper into her arms.

"Your lips are so warm," Red murmured into the crook of Kit's neck as she nestled closer to her.

"Use your Little Red Riding Hood voice," Kit requested.

Red ran her hand slowly across Kit's chest. "Oh, Wolfie. What warm lips you have."

"All the better to kiss you with, my dear." Kit moved her head a little and kissed her lover on the forehead.

"I feel so . . . so . . ." Little Red Riding Hood seemed to be struggling for just the right word.

"So heavy?" Kit finished for her. She imagined they were both probably feeling the same way. It was all Kit could do just to open her eyes and focus on the swirling fog and lazy flowing veils. It was one of the spells Veronica enjoyed casting the most . . . that sleepy-fog spell that took away all inhibitions and left them woozy with pleasure. Skeeter always referred to the fog as the Love Cloud, but Kit liked thinking of it as Veronica's very special gift to her friends.

Kit could tell that Little Red was getting aroused because she kept pressing her ample breasts against Kit's body. Then it seemed as though Red breathed in a nice, healthy dose of the fog, which woke up her senses and injected a bit of playfulness, since she slid her bare foot up and down Kit's leg.

"You know what I'd like, Wolfie?" Red whispered.

Kit smiled and opened her eyes. "Another wolf ride, perhaps?"

Little Red's laughter was contagious. Kit propped herself up on an elbow and leaned over to kiss her again. Red's laughter slowly turned into shy giggles as they rolled around on the pillows.

"Wolf-sex, wolf-sex, wolf-sex, wolf-sex," Little Red began to chant.

"You want a ride, little girl?" Kit asked in her best wolf voice.

"I do! I do!"

Kit sat up and moved several of the gold velvet pillows out of the way. She got down on all fours and slowly rocked back and forth.

"Get on!" Kit said gleefully.

Little Red scrambled up and was ready to mount her wolf's back.

"Throw that cape on me like a saddle," Kit suggested.

Little Red giggled again, but before she knew it, Kit felt the cape being put on her back. Red rearranged it several times before she decided to mount up! Once she was on Kit's back, Little Red tried to get more comfortable.

"Oh my," Little Red commented.

"Are you ready?"

"The hood on this cape is in a very nice place right now."

Kit could feel her lover squirming around and slowly rubbing herself into the hood portion of the cape on Kit's back. Turning her head in an attempt to see Little Red's expression, Kit said, "Don't get too tired back there."

"Tired?" Little Red whispered. Biting her lip as she squirmed against the cape, she muttered, "We're just getting started, Wolfie Baby."

Kit encouraged her lover by continuing the rocking motion like a hobby horse in a wolf suit.

"Bad wolf," Little Red whispered in a low, throaty voice. "Baaaad wolf," she said again as the grinding and rocking increased the intensity. Then as if Little Red had no control of herself any longer, she smacked Kit on the arse with her bare hand in order to make her go faster. "Bad wolf! Bad wolf!" she yelled while continuing to slap Kit's butt. " BAD WOLF!!"

Kit threw her head back and let loose with a howl that seemed to shake the entire house's foundation. Little Red squeezed her legs together and rubbed herself into the cape as if her very life depended on it. At last she slumped forward and pressed her breasts against the cape and Kit's back.

"Bad wolf," Little Red whispered in exhaustion.

Kit slowly crawled over to the pile of gold pillows with a limp Little Red still slumped on her back. Kit leaned to the right and deposited the spent Little Red Hoodless Rider on the pillows. With an effort, Little Red extended her arms and pulled Kit down to her again. The fog was back now, creeping slowly all around them. Little Red gently kissed Kit on her wolf lips.

"You're a bad, bad wolf," Little Red whispered with a sleepy smile.

It was all Kit could do to keep her eyes open. "I bet you say that to all your wolves."


For a long time, Veronica and Liz held each other—floating in that other dimension, never wanting to let go of the precious moments that remained. During those moments, Veronica thought about how they had first met in Salem Village. Liz was a schoolteacher and Veronica a midwife. They met along Essex Street in the middle of a cool autumn day with maples ablaze in red and orange. They were walking toward each other when Liz dropped her basket of vegetables (or perhaps was *compelled* to drop her basket of vegetables) and a potato rolled and stopped at the toe of Veronica's black-laced boot. They spoke for only a few moments, exchanging the expected greetings and pleasantries typical of that time period. It was 1659 when they fell in love and began their secret rendezvous—three years before the witch trials began and Salem was written into history forever.

And now, as in all the many years past, the evening was fading into morning and Veronica understood how little time remained, even as her heart screamed, "No! I can't let go of my Liz!" Veronica glanced down at Liz. Liz's head was resting on Veronica's shoulder and her eyes were closed, but she wasn't sleeping. "What are you thinking, darling?"

"That we're lucky. We somehow keep finding each other. I wonder if others have been so lucky." Liz's eyes opened and she smiled, those adorable gray orbs melting into tears. "But I guess others don't have the powers you have."

Veronica kissed Liz lightly on the forehead. "Oh, you'd be surprised at the powers others have. Sometimes I find it difficult to keep up with the antics of my friends. But the one thing that I have—and they don't—is you. And remember, darling, my spells would be meaningless if you didn't want to be with me as much as I want to be with you."

"Then we'll be together again."

"Always."

Veronica took Liz by the hands and lifted her from the pillows. "One last kiss to get me through until next year." Closing her eyes, Veronica used all of her will to hang on to that last moment—to remember Liz's warm body against hers and the beautiful kiss that made her heart race.

"I love you, Veronica."

"Thank you, darling Liz. I love you, too. Shall we go?"

"Until next year."

"Next year."

"You'll find me?"

"I'll find you."

With a nod of her head, Veronica escorted Liz back into that earthly dimension they had left behind earlier that evening. The fog in the room slowly dissipated. And then Veronica cast the final spell that sent the soul of Liz back into the ages until next All Hallows' Eve. "Good-bye, my love," she whispered softly. The woman to her right looked dazed.

"Hey, did I fall asleep or something?" Liz asked.

"Must have been the punch," Veronica said, forcing a smile to her face. "They make a wicked punch here in the old mansion."

"Gosh, I can usually hold my liquor pretty well," Liz mused. "But I don't remember a damned thing about the party. Did we have fun?"

"Depends on your point of view, I guess."

"Say, wait a minute," Liz said indignantly. "Nothing *happened*, did it?"

"Happened?" Veronica replied, opening the door to the upstairs hallway. "All Hallows' Eve happened! I'm already looking forward to next year."

*In 1999, Peggy J. Herring, Laura DeHart Young and Therese Szymanski began writing* **The Chain Gang Chronicles** *for WomanSpace, a San Antonio, Texas, lesbian publication.*

*For the shorter pieces, one author begins a story, passes it along to the next, who does her part, then hands it off to the last to finish. For this one, they kept passing it around . . .*

# A Ghost of a Chance
## Lynn Ames

Sweat, warm and sweet, trickled between her breasts. Elizabeth blew out a breath, unconsciously brushing the thick auburn hair from her face. With a sigh, she ripped open the next moving box. She sifted through the contents, organizing the clothes according to type and style before settling upon a home for them. It was hard to believe she was really here. She'd been beyond flabbergasted when she'd received the call from the lawyer telling her that a childhood friend had died, leaving a huge estate in historic Savannah, Georgia, to her. She had questioned the man twice, just to be certain she'd heard him correctly.

Elizabeth hadn't seen Lynda for nearly ten years—hadn't received so much as an e-mail or a letter in at least eight—why would the woman bequeath such a generous gift to her? Try as she might, Elizabeth couldn't think of a reason. Yet here she was, sitting in the middle of what had been Lynda's bedroom, putting her belongings away.

She sat back on her heels, wishing for even the slightest hint of a breeze from the open windows. She chuckled mirthlessly. It wasn't as if she hadn't been warned.

*"Elizabeth, do you have any idea how hot Savannah can be in the summer?"*

"*Stop, Vance. Stop right there. I'm going, and nothing you can say—*"

"*Not just hot, but sticky. Take one step outside and you'll feel like you put your clothes on straight out of the washing machine . . .*"

"*Vance—*" *As usual, he plowed right over her words, as if nothing she said was of sufficient consequence to merit consideration.*

"*. . . Before the spin cycle has even finished. No, Elizabeth, this is all wrong for you.*"

"*Goddamn it, Vance. I didn't ask for your opinion, nor do I care what you think.*" *Anger suffused her, catching both of them off guard. It was not in her nature to let loose her temper. She made a conscious effort to rein in her emotions.*

"*You still don't get it, do you? This is my life, Vance, and I will live it the way I see fit.*"

*She was almost to the door, almost free of his oppressive meddling and the arrogant presumption that he knew what was best for her—or that he knew her at all, for that matter.*

"*This is a big mistake, Lizzie.*"

*She hated when he bastardized her name. She rounded on him, unwilling, perhaps even unable, to ignore the wave of fury any longer. "The mistake, Vance, was ever believing that you and I had enough in common to make a life together. The mistake was allowing you to control me for too many years of my life. The mistake was thinking you could honor and respect me. That, Vance, was the mistake. What I'm doing now is something I should have done years ago. You never wanted someone to love, you wanted someone to control. Find some other willing victim, Vance, because that someone isn't me.*"

*She slammed the door with a resounding thud.*

She was so deeply lost in thought that the shrill sound of the telephone ringing made her jump.

"Hello?"

"Hey, cutie. How's the new place? Is it a palace, or what? Anything go bump in the night yet?"

Elizabeth laughed in spite of herself. "Let's see . . . the place is lovely, it's not a palace, which would denote that royalty lived here, but it is a mansion. Tonight is the first night I will sleep in the house, so I can't answer the spooky question, and I wish you'd get off that."

"Can't help myself, honey. Elizabeth, doesn't it bother you at all that a woman *died* in that house?"

"Jess, we've been through this at least a dozen times already. Mom died in our house and we continued to live there. Nothing weird happened to us. Death is a part of life."

"True, but we didn't live in Savannah, where there are more haunted houses per capita than anyplace else in the country."

"Why Jessica Marie, I'm surprised at you."

"Um, groan, sis. Your southern accent needs more work than my love life."

"You're a scientist. You're supposed to know better than to believe in ghosts."

"There is plenty of scientific evidence to support the existence of specters. Do you want me to send a team out with a Room Guardian?"

"No, Jessica, I don't need any security; I feel perfectly safe here."

"What? No, you idiot. I'm not offering you protection. I'm talking about a Room Guardian—it's a passive infrared motion detector that senses temperature changes, shock waves and physical movement. It's used to detect paranormal activity."

"Oh. I don't need that, either, thanks. In truth, I'd prefer that you just change the subject."

"Okay, but you might change your mind after tonight."

Elizabeth rolled her eyes. "If I do, you'll be the first to know. 'Bye, Jess."

"I miss you already, Flash. Don't be a stranger."

The use of her childhood nickname made Elizabeth homesick for her sister's company. "You, either. You can always come visit, you know."

"What, and stay in that haunted mansion? No way."

" 'Bye, Jess."

Elizabeth shook her head as she hung up the phone. She didn't want to think about the fact that Lynda had died less than ten feet from where she now sat on the floor. The lawyer had said that Lynda's instructions were very clear: she wanted to finish out her last pain-wracked days in a place that she loved above all else. The cancer had robbed her of so much, so soon; at least this she could have control over.

Elizabeth tried to conjure an image of her childhood friend. When they were eight, they'd built a tree fort with the help of their fathers. Lynda was small for her age, and wiry. Elizabeth was long and lean. Their fathers dubbed them Mutt and Jeff, after the cartoon characters. This irked the girls, since they already had nicknames they had picked out for themselves. Elizabeth was The Flash. Lynda called her that because she was such a fast runner, and because of the redness of her hair. Elizabeth called Lynda Wonder Woman, after Lynda Carter, who had played the part in the old TV series.

They spent most afternoons in those early years in their hideaway, talking, laughing, pretending, and reading old comic books they had pilfered from their parents. As they grew older, they continued to seek refuge in the fort, reading Nancy Drew mysteries, doing their homework together, and struggling through those awkward pre- and mid-teen years.

They were going into their junior year in high school, and Elizabeth thought they would be best friends forever. She told Lynda so one lazy Sunday afternoon as they reclined on the bean bags they had added to the fort some years before.

*"Wonder Woman, I don't know what I'd do without you. No matter what else is going on in my life, I always know I can count on you."*

*"Always."*

*Elizabeth, who had been looking at the book she was reading, turned her head to regard her friend. There was something different in her voice, something compelling. Their faces were just inches apart. Elizabeth swallowed hard. Her pulse was pounding and an unfamiliar warmth spread through her abdomen.*

*"I—I want us to be friends forever, to grow old together, sharing everything."*

*"Me, too," Lynda said. As she had done on many occasions, Lynda reached over and tucked an errant strand of hair behind Elizabeth's ear.*

*Elizabeth, confused by the response of her body to Lynda's simple touch and the undisguised look of hunger in her eyes, recoiled as if she'd been burned.*

*Lynda, stung by her best friend's reaction, rose.*

*"I have to go. I promised my mother I'd help her with dinner." She was gone before Elizabeth had time to speak.*

From that moment on, Lynda began spending less and less time in the fort. Elizabeth often asked her friend to do things, but she always seemed to have a ready excuse. Hurt, Elizabeth finally gave up, turning her attention to the many boys who asked her out on a regular basis. She compared every boy she spent time with to Lynda, and they all came up lacking. None of them were as good friends, or as interesting, or as much fun. They only wanted one thing from her, Elizabeth discovered, and she wasn't willing to go there yet.

She missed Lynda terribly, but nothing she said or did seemed to bridge the ever-widening gulf between them.

*"Hey Lynda. I'm having some trouble with the advanced calc. Can you help me later? We could go to the fort and hang out."*

*"Sorry, I've got to get right home."*

*"Lynda. Hey, Wonder Woman, wait up."*

*"Can't, I'll be late for class."*

*"Have lunch with me third period?"*

*"Sorry, I'm tutoring then."*

And so it went. The last time she saw Lynda was on the night they graduated high school. Elizabeth found her old friend standing off by herself, apart from the crowd. Lynda always seemed to be apart from the crowd, she thought.

*"Hey, Wonder Woman."*

*"Oh, um, hey yourself."*

*"That was a really great speech you gave. Usually the valedictory address is dry and boring. You even managed to make old Mrs. Banks laugh."*

*"Thanks."*

*Elizabeth, by then well familiar with the signs, knew that Lynda was about to bolt. She put a hand on her friend's arm, surprised to discover that she was trembling.*

*"Lynda . . ."*

*"Um, I've got to go."*

*"Wait," Elizabeth pleaded. "Please."*

*Lynda looked at her anxiously.*

*"I . . . I just wanted you to know . . . I really, really miss you. Now you're going off to Harvard to be the genius I always knew you would be, and I'm afraid I'll never see you or hear from you again. Whatever happened to our friendship?"*

*"Nothing. I've really got to go."*

*"Wait. You can't just walk away like that. Lynda, please. I wish to God I'd never said whatever it was I said that hurt you, or scared you away. It's the biggest regret of my life. I'm sorry, Lynda."*

*"There's nothing to be sorry for. It's fine. You didn't do, or say, anything wrong."*

*"Will I ever hear from you again?"*

*"Of course."*

*"I love you, Lynda."*

Even ten years later, the shocked and wistful expression on her friend's face was the thing that stuck with Elizabeth. Following that visceral reaction, Lynda had simply shrugged, mumbled an apology, and literally run away. Apart from a few very general e-mails their freshman and sophomore years at college, Elizabeth never heard from Lynda again. Until she reached out to her in death.

Sitting in the middle of the hardwood floor, Elizabeth shook her head sadly. "I'm so, so sorry, my friend. I wish I had understood you, and myself, then. I miss you still, Lynda." She wiped a tear from her eye. "There was never anyone who understood me the way you did—never anyone who brought me such joy or taught me so much. I don't know why you left me this place that was so very important to you, but I'm honored and touched. I promise you I'll do everything in my power to keep it and love it as you did."

Elizabeth got up and walked over to the large antique dresser on the other side of the room. It was made of a deep cherry wood, the kind of fine, heavy piece of furniture that belonged in a place like this. She ran her hand over the smooth surface, her fingers caressing the grain. She opened the top drawer and placed her underwear inside, repeating the process with shirts, shorts and sweatshirts until all the drawers were full.

When Elizabeth had finished, she wiped the sweat from her forehead with a hand towel liberated from the bottom of one of the boxes. For a moment, she stood under the ceiling fan that spun slowly some eight feet above her five-foot ten-inch frame. The relief it provided was minimal, but it was better than nothing. Checking her watch, she was surprised to find that the day was nearly done.

She made her way down the wide, sweeping staircase into the main foyer, turned left, passed the formal dining room and entered the large, surprisingly modernly equipped kitchen. She intended to make herself some dinner, return to the bedroom to finish unpacking her personal items, and fall into bed. But her gaze fell upon the leather-bound journal the lawyer had given her that morning, when he had turned over the keys to the house. When Elizabeth had questioned him about it, he had shrugged, remarking that it was Lynda's instruction that the journal was for her eyes only.

Intrigued, Elizabeth had hefted the journal, turning it this way and that in the sun's hazy light. It was gilt-edged and ornate—just the sort of journal Elizabeth had always wanted as a young girl. The lock was opened by an old-fashioned key. She had set the book on the kitchen table, intent as she was on supervising the movers unloading her possessions. Spying it again now, her curiosity was piqued.

She reached into the stainless-steel refrigerator, grabbed the leftover pizza from lunch, and placed it in the microwave to heat. Fumbling around in her shorts pockets, she found the key for the diary, sat down at the table, and, with a mixture of eager anticipation and dread, fit the key in the lock.

There was a snick as the clasp popped open, and Elizabeth absently placed the key back in her pocket. She rubbed her hands on her shorts to remove the perspiration before gently opening the heavy cover.

Elizabeth easily identified the writing on the front page as that of her friend. Lynda had always had distinct handwriting—elegant, yet simple, economical yet stylish. She spared a moment to remember the hours they had spent practicing their signatures just in case they ever got famous. Elizabeth laughed to herself. In the end, their practice sessions had come in handy.

Before the cancer had robbed her of her life, Lynda had been the equivalent of a rock icon in the combined fields of Web technology and advanced medical science. Her Web-programming innovations paved the way for doctors to save thousands of lives. Elizabeth proudly followed Lynda's career as a young phenom, celebrating with her from afar when she won a Nobel Prize for Science and international acclaim, reveling in her friend's successes, happy for the riches and accolades her talents brought her.

Elizabeth focused her eyes on the page.

*"Dear Elizabeth,*

*"When you read this, I will be gone. It's freeing to finally be able to share with you so much that I couldn't in life."*

"Oh, Lynda." Elizabeth sighed.

*"As you no doubt remember, there are very few things I ever do without a reason, and so I'm sure you've figured out that I chose this journal very carefully. I know you have more than enough money to buy thousands of these, but, knowing you, I doubt that you ever did. You always were a procrastinator. I've left the pages at the back then, for you to fill, Flash, much as we used to finish each other's sentences in the good old days.*

*"I want you to know that I've followed your career assiduously, and that no one could be prouder of your Hollywood success than I am. I knew right from the very first time I met you that your star would burn brightly—such imagination, such passion, so many dreams. You were meant for the silver screen in every way.*

*"As you leaf through this book, you will find many articles about you that I clipped and saved over the past six years. I promise you I wasn't an obsessed fan, just a proud friend and your most ardent supporter."*

Elizabeth's head snapped up. The last movie she did had run so far over budget that the studio had threatened to stop production. It was a blockbuster and a breakout role for her that many other actresses had coveted. Elizabeth was heartsick over the possibility of the set closing down. At the eleventh hour, just as the producers were about to pull the plug, a mysterious benefactor provided the monies needed to finish the project. Although there was much speculation in Hollywood about where the financing came from, no one was ever able to follow the money trail successfully.

"Oh, Wonder Woman, you didn't . . ." Tears clouded Elizabeth's vision. For a split second, she could have sworn she felt a hand squeeze her shoulder.

"It was worth every penny and more. You were magnificent, as I knew you would be. Watching you on the screen made my heart stop."

"Wha?" Elizabeth whipped her head from side to side, looking for the source of the voice she thought she'd heard, or was it in her head? "Great, Flash," she mocked herself, "now you're imagining things."

She shook her head to clear her vision and returned her attention to the words in front of her.

*"Congratulations on your Oscar—it was well deserved. I was thrilled to get to see that while I was still able to concentrate. I can't tell you how moved I was that you remembered me in your speech. It meant the world to me."*

Elizabeth replayed the moment in her mind when she had accepted the sparkling statuette, in front of thousands of her peers, and millions of TV viewers. *"I want to thank someone very special in my life for this,"* she said as she waved the trophy aloft in her fist. *"Wonder Woman, wherever you are tonight, I want to share this with you. You encouraged me, fired my dreams and indulged my imagination, always telling me that I could be anything I wanted to be. Thank you, I love you. I haven't forgotten."*

"I haven't forgotten, Lynda. I never will. If only I could tell you everything you meant to me, everything you are to me still. I'd give anything to have you back for just one night, so that I could tell you everything I've learned, and how much I've missed you in my life, and that I wish with all my heart that things could have gone differently between us. I made so many mistakes. I was young, and scared, and stupid. You were the best thing that ever happened to me. After you, nobody measured up. I married Vance because he was strong, self-assured and powerful. Just as you were. I thought he could be the male version of you. What a fool I was. He was nothing like you. Nobody was."

Elizabeth got up and paced around the kitchen.

"I kept trying to replace you, and never could. The answer was so obvious; it was staring me in the face the whole time. You were the only one for me, Lynda. The one I really wanted. I was too afraid and too immature to deal with it back then. And I've been ashamed ever since. I always thought—hoped, really—there would be an opportunity to tell you that in person. I figured you could never forgive me, but still, I wanted you to know."

"I'm here now. And I know. There's nothing to forgive."

Again Elizabeth looked around, certain she had heard the words, but unable to fathom where they came from. "Lynda?" She waited a beat, but heard nothing more. "Wishful thinking, Flash," she muttered.

She carried the journal up the stairs to the bedroom, the pizza in the microwave long forgotten.

*"I wish I'd been able to give a similar style speech upon winning the Nobel. Trust me when I tell you that you were the first person I wanted to share it with. Pride—that insufferable beast—and fear, stood in my way. Just as I was afraid you would see what was in my heart when we were sixteen, so too, was I sure that you would see the truth if I gave in to my impulse to celebrate with you, my dear Elizabeth, upon receipt of the Nobel."*

"Oh, Lynda."

*"I suppose it is safe now to come clean—to spill the secrets I guarded for a lifetime.*

*"You know that I never married—was never, in fact, involved in any sort of serious relationship. There were rumors, of course, that I was a lesbian, but no one could ever find proof. I never said, one way or the other.*

*"Silly, I know, that I never took a serious lover, but I could never move on when my heart and soul were already taken.*

*"From the time we were ten and you cradled my head in your lap after I fell out of the tree house and broke my arm, stroking my hair and telling me stories until help came, I was in love with you. I never stopped loving you. But I knew that you didn't love me in the same way. That much was clear when we were juniors. I couldn't bear to be so close to you, knowing that you would never be truly mine, and that I would always want you to be. It wouldn't have been fair to either one of us.*

*"So, darling Elizabeth, please understand, at this late date, that it wasn't that I didn't want to be close to you—quite the opposite. I wanted to be too close to you, and I couldn't bear the rejection that would surely have been the result if I had told you how I really felt. Or worse yet, if I had leaned over those few inches that day and kissed your mouth as I wanted to so very badly.*

*"I spent almost my whole life loving you, and, even in death, I don't think I could stop. I hope this doesn't scare you too much. I would never do anything to hurt you, or frighten you.*

*"Which brings me to the gift of this house, my beloved throwback to a bygone era. I bought this house with my very first royalties from the development of the Web-based programming that allowed doctors to assist with an operation remotely, while stationed physically thousands of miles away from the operating theatre.*

*"I remember so vividly all of the evenings we spent planning the 'Tara' we would own, just like in* Gone with the Wind, *when we were old enough and rich, too. How many hours did we spend imagining every single detail of the house, inside and out?*

*"I hope, my darling Elizabeth, that I got the flavor of the place right. I worked night and day with the architects to make it as close to our*

*dream as possible. I wonder if I have succeeded, or if my memory was
accurate on the fine touches.*

*"Perhaps it was the whim of a dying woman, or perhaps your tastes
and dreams have changed. If so, the disposition of the house is completely
in your hands, of course. You are under no obligation to keep it. It is yours
to do with as you wish. Take it out for a test spin as we used to do with the
go-carts we built, and see how you like it. I will understand if it weirds
you out and you'd rather be rid of it."*

"Never." Tears flowed freely down Elizabeth's cheeks. "This
place is a part of you, Lynda. I could never sell it. It's as close as I'll
ever be able to get to you now." She pounded her fist on her thigh.
"Damn it all. Why did I have to be so weak? Why didn't I know
what I wanted back then? My God, what a fool I was."

"No, you were just a sixteen-year-old girl, confused and unsure
of your feelings."

Elizabeth sniffled. "That's no excuse."

"You always were too stubborn for your own good."

This time when she heard the words, Elizabeth registered them
as thoughts. They appeared internally, were not spoken aloud, but
were also clearly not her own. Although she imagined she should
be afraid, she was not.

She answered silently, "And you weren't stubborn Miss-Do-
This-My-Way-I-Know-It-Will-Work?"

"Was I ever wrong?"

"No."

"I rest my case."

"I see you haven't gotten any less smug."

A chill, like a slight breeze, passed through Elizabeth's hair.

"And you haven't gotten any less beautiful."

"Lynda? Can it really be you? Is that possible?"

"Yes, my love. It's me."

Elizabeth sobbed. "I miss you so much. I wasted so many
years."

"Don't, sweetheart. Don't beat yourself up so. You came to your
own truth, in your own time."

"But it's too late."

"Only if you believe that it is."

"What do you mean?"

"Close your eyes and clear your mind."

"But . . ."

"I swear to God. Just do it, stubborn girl."

Elizabeth closed her eyes, and rotated her shoulders. "Okay."

For a moment, she felt nothing. Then gradually, she became aware of a warmth encircling her cheek, running along her jaw-bone, outlining her lips.

"Can you feel that?"

"Yes," she answered, surprised. "Was that you?"

"Oh, yes. Is it okay?"

"Mm. More than okay."

"Shh."

Elizabeth felt the warmth return, and this time, when it reached her lips, she envisioned sucking Lynda's fingers into her mouth. In her head, she heard a gasp that was not her own.

"You felt that?"

"Yes."

"Wow. Is there a picture of you in the house?"

"There's one on the mantel in the living room, from my brief vacation in Stockholm following the Nobel ceremony."

Elizabeth was up off the bed and moving in an instant.

"Where are you going?"

"First of all, can I just tell you how strange it is to be talking to you in my head? How many times did I tell you growing up to 'get out of my head'?"

Elizabeth heard the unmistakable sound of laughter. "Too many."

"And here I am welcoming it. I must be nuts."

"You haven't answered the question. Where are you going?"

"I need to see you. I want to touch you."

"You don't need a picture for that."

"Apparently not, but you know I always was one for visual aids."

"I see some things never change."

Elizabeth arrived in the living room, went directly to the fireplace, stood on the hearth, and removed the pewter-framed picture from its perch. It showed a laughing, smiling Lynda, looking rakish and for all the world like a Peace Corps volunteer.

"You were beautiful." Unconsciously, Elizabeth caressed Lynda's features. "I was always captivated by your eyes. They were so honest and intense. They were the windows to your soul."

"That's what got me in trouble in the first place."

"No. I always felt like I'd come home when I looked into your eyes."

"Except for that day . . ."

"No." In her mind, Elizabeth pictured putting her fingers to Lynda's lips. "Especially that one day. That's why I got so scared. If I had only had your courage, Wonder Woman."

"My courage? If I'd been truly courageous, I would have done what I'd been dying to do, to hell with the consequences."

"I guess we both missed opportunities, huh?"

"I suppose we did."

"And now it's too late."

"Is it?"

"Isn't it?" Elizabeth's eyes closed involuntarily as she felt the sensuous touch on her lips. It began as a light pressure, expanded into her mouth, where her tongue felt as if it were being enveloped in a heat-searing battle with another, and built until the flames were stoked into a bonfire. She gasped when the sensation went away.

"Shall I ask you again?"

"Only if you're going to show me proof again."

"I want you so much, Elizabeth."

"I want you too, Lynda. Can we?"

"Do you trust me?"

"Of course."

"Clear your mind again and follow the thoughts that suggest themselves to you."

"Are you sure . . ."

"Hey, I've never done this quite this way before, but if we both believe, and trust, I'm confident we can breach any barrier—even death."

"Okay." Elizabeth closed her eyes and tried to still her mind. Her pulse raced, the blood pumping wildly through her veins. Concentrating with all her might, she followed the prompts as they appeared in her mind.

Slowly, teasingly, she unbuttoned her blouse, freeing one button at a time, lingering over the swell of her breasts, running her fingers along the rigid muscles of her abdomen and under the waistband of her shorts. Carefully she freed the shirt from its cloth prison, pausing to caress the soft, sensitive skin beneath.

Languidly, she reached behind her and unfastened the clasp on her black lace bra. She lingered over one breast, then the other, stroking, fondling, teasing, until her nipples were rock hard and painfully erect. She gasped. As if in a trance, eyes closed, head thrown back, lips parted, she continued to make love with her hands. She liberated first one arm, then the other. Soundlessly the bra and shirt fell to the floor.

Her fingers found the snap on her shorts, and the pads of her fingertips caressed the fine hairs below her navel. She grasped her zipper, and in slow, measured movements, teased it open to reveal matching black lace panties. The shorts joined the shirt and bra on the floor, leaving only the one barrier.

Her palm played over the silk fabric, pausing ever so briefly over her distended clitoris. She moaned and gasped as her fingers played through the wetness of her folds. With exaggerated care she removed the panties, both hands returning to her center, one thumb and forefinger squeezing her clit lightly, the other entering her, stroking rhythmically in time with the thrust of her hips.

"Argh. Oh my God. I don't think I can stay upright."

"Yes, you can. I've got you. Let yourself go."

As if by magic, Elizabeth felt herself enveloped in a warm, strong embrace, breasts pressed against her back, lips tasting her neck, hands briefly caressing her nipples. She felt herself transported, and as she began to come, she felt the second set of hands cover her own, sliding in and out of her slick center, stroking her clit, urging her to an ecstasy she had only ever dreamed about.

She screamed out her pleasure, waves of bliss overtaking her, tilting her world on its axis. Even as she peaked, she was dimly aware of a shuddering sensation coming from behind her—a feeling of deep satisfaction and release above and beyond her own registered somewhere in the recesses of her mind.

Somehow, she did not know how, she found herself in Lynda's bed—their bed—wrapped in a blanket of love and tenderness.

"Are you all right?"

"Mm. Never better."

"I'm glad."

She felt fingers feather lightly through her hair as it splayed on the pillow. "Did I do that, or did you?"

"We did that, darling. Together."

"I like the sound of that."

"Me, too."

As she drifted off to the sleep of the sated, Elizabeth mumbled, "Lynda?"

"Yes?"

"Are you bound by the walls of this house?"

"No, my love. You are my home."

"That's good. Because, while this will always be the place I return to, I'm still a working girl, and I always, always want you with me."

"I like the sound of that."

"Mm, me, too."

"Good night, my love. Welcome home."

"Good night, sweetheart. Sorry it took me so long to get here."

# From the Sea
### Crystal Bareia

I am not afraid of death. Death is more welcome than an existence where she is not. If I cannot touch her body, there is no place for me. If I cannot breathe in the sweet scent of the sunshine from her skin, there is no point of living. If I cannot hear the sound of her laughter drifting through our house, there is no home. Parisa has returned to the sea.

As is my wont, I love to wander at night. I would not recommend this to those who are strangers to these parts, but I know every crag and hill by heart. The Orkney Islands are alight with stars, so bright that if I stretched a little more, I could bring one home with me. On this night, the moon was full, lighting my path as I started down the rocky incline toward the beach. As I approached the shore, I heard voices and slowed my steps. There, dancing in the surf, were eight of the most beautiful women I had ever seen. They were tall and lithe, with skin the color of alabaster. They laughed amongst each other, splashing and teasing in the cold waters. I knelt down on the sand and my eyes took in their graceful play.

One of these gorgeous creatures stood and stretched her arms toward the heavens. Her hair was a dark sheet that sparked with brilliance under the moonlight. Her lips turned up in a generous smile as she brought her hand in front of her. A moonbeam fluttered in her palm, sparkling with light. She turned her back to me, and I felt my pulse race at the sight of her full hips and dimples just above the curve of her posterior. She made herself comfortable on a crop of boulders that jutted from the sea, lengthening her body under the night sky, and the light of the captured moonbeam accentuated her every curve.

One of the other women swam out to the rocks and climbed up to lie beside her, draping her arms and legs over her body, nuzzling her neck. Then another came and curled around the other. One after another they joined the object of my interest. All lay in a comforting pile, gently touching and breathing together. I was drawn to them.

I stood and removed my sandals and skirt, wanting to be as they were. As I walked toward the shore, I took off my shirt and tossed it to the sand; I froze. My shirt lay amongst the skins of seals. I knelt, picking up one of the pelts; it was the softest fur I had ever touched. I rubbed my cheek against it, my eyes not leaving the mass of beauty upon the rocks. They were Selkie. My grandfather had lulled me to sleep with their stories. My heart jumped, and I clutched the skin to my chest.

"Release the skin!" Her voice carried across the water to my ears, yet it sounded like a whisper spoken in my head. I clutched the skin tighter to my breasts and backed away. They dove from the rocks into the water as one, their heads bobbing to the surface as they reached the beach and rose out of the water in a graceful wave. They quickly gathered their skins from the sand and pulled them over their heads. They slithered into them, twisting their bodies back and fourth, breasts bouncing and hips swaying. The skins molded around their torsos, covering their backs first, and enveloping their limbs and chests until you could see nothing of their former humanness. They leaped into the sea and swam out to where I could barely see them. All accept the Selkie I had admired earlier.

She stood, her eyes fierce and lips drawn. I swallowed hard as I watched the beads of water traverse her body. My eyes greedily took in her full breasts, the gentle curve of her belly, and the down at her center. I wanted her.

"Look your fill, mortal," she ordered, "then give back what is mine."

"No." I knew the curse that plagued all Selkie. If I did not give back her skin, she would have to come with me. She would live docile and do my will. She would please me for as long as I kept her skin from her. So strong was my desire that I didn't care if it was wrong. All I could think of was her long limbs wrapped around me. Her beautiful face staring at me from across the dinner table. Her laughter would be a song as I worked in my garden.

"*Please*, return my skin," she demanded again. I picked up my shirt and tossed it to her. I turned from her and went to where my skirt and sandals were. I knew she would follow. Her hand found my shoulder and she squeezed hard . . . not in a friendly way. I looked over my shoulder and our eyes held. "Remember this. If you bring me to your home and make me your lover, you will die on our parting. That is the cost."

I knew what she said was true, but her hand on my shoulder sent electricity through my body. The warmth of her skin so close called to my own. A Selkie could not leave unless she had her skin. I would be sure that she could never find it.


"Is this what you seek?" she growled, pushing me against the kitchen table as we entered the house. A vase fell to the floor with a crash. Her lips were hot and insistent on mine. She swallowed my voice as our tongues tangled and my hands sought the curves of her body. She was warm and soft like the sun; all heat and energy beneath my palms.

"Or this?!" she insisted, her hand pushing up my skirt and squeezing my thighs. She nailed me to the wood of the table with her hand. It swam in my juices, diving in and out like a dolphin. I couldn't move, couldn't breathe . . . the air was thick with the scent of my need. She laughed against my thighs, her lips joining her hand. Her tongue swept my cleft then latched onto my clit . . . sucking and pulling until my ceiling opened and the sky exploded above me. Then darkness.

I awoke to the sound of crying. I had passed out on the table. The house was torn to pieces. Everything was pulled from cupboards and tossed to the floor. Furniture was overturned. "I cannot find my skin!" she wailed, her breasts heaving with her angry sobbing. I arose groggily as she collapsed on the bed of feathers from the shredded pillows. They hung in the air, drifting about the room in an unnatural snow, and covering her fetal form upon the mattress. I crawled through the bedsheets and curved my body around hers as I had seen the Selkie do on the rocks. I weaved my arms and legs with hers until you could not tell where I began and she ended.

That was the last time she cried in front of me. True to what legend had told me, she remained in my home, seemingly content. She did all that she thought would please me. She woke before me and put the coffee on to brew. She crawled back into bed and snuggled with me while it percolated. She laughed at my jokes and held my hand when we went on walks. She talked of all my interests and pleased my body in every imaginable way. But I could not please Parisa.

Having a love slave, constant companionship, and everything I ever wanted in a woman is not as satisfying as it might seem. It became my heart's foolish desire to grant her every wish.

That spring, I caught her staring wistfully out the window toward the sea, as she often did. She was sure to hide it as soon as I noticed.

"Let's take a walk," I said, putting down my sketchbook. She grabbed my hand and pulled me out the door. She took me on a familiar path; one we had worn into the ground over the past two years. Where there was once grass, there was now dirt and sand. Rocks and shrubbery had been ruthlessly thrown to the sides of the path, leaving a beeline to Parisa's favorite haven.

"Come on!" she called, tugging my hand like an eager child. She broke free to rejoice amongst the waves. I watched her dance as she did that first night. Arms stretched toward the sky and hips swaying. The white linen of her dress was plastered to her body from the spray. The rouge of her nipples, the shadow of her belly button, and the hair of her sex winked at me through the sheer fabric. She took my hands and drew me into the circle of her arms. We twirled and laughed until we were dizzy and falling against each other.

Our mouths met. We drank the salt of the sea from each other's lips and our tangled hair caught on our fingers. The rough grains of the sand became our bed as we fell to the earth and gloried in being alive. I rolled her onto her back and pushed my way under her dress. The blanket of linen embraced me, leaving me to shower her flesh with my attentions. I licked and nibbled my way around her body. I suckled her toes and breasts. I lavished her pussy with my respect, letting my tongue become a tool for her pleasure. I relearned every fold, every hair. My nose nudged her clit while my tongue dove into her depths. Her noises were aquatic, like the songs of mermaids. Granules of sand mixed with her juices, lending a welcome grittiness to our lovemaking. She writhed beneath me, tugging at my hair and calling my name. Joy washed over me at her coming. Her body was an altar for my happiness.


I was in the garden, trying to get my stubborn vegetables to grow in the rocky soil, when I found a pile of sea shells. Parisa had been gathering them on our many visits to the beach but was afraid that I would disapprove. I began collecting them myself and leaving them around the house in places where I thought she might find them. She had thousands of them. She strung the shells together and hung them from the ceiling; row after row hung over our heads so we lived under a tinkling canopy of pearly white. When the windows were open, they rang together like wind chimes.

When we slept at night, I listened to her breathing as it mingled with the sound of the shells and I was comforted. She had made this her home.

"Tilt your head down a bit," I suggested. Parisa did so, and she was forced to look up through her lashes. "You are divine," I murmured, pushing a strand of hair behind her ear. She smiled and pursed her lips at me. She was the perfect subject. She could lie for hours without moving. Bright-colored silks framed her, teasing us with the promise of revelation. She loved my worshipful brush. I stood back and loaded my palette.

"Do you not tire of this?" she asked as I mixed my paints.

"What?"

"Capturing me." My eyes darted to hers and she held them.

"No. And I never will." I turned from her and stroked the canvas with my brush.

"I am beautiful, am I not? More beautiful than any woman you could find in your world?" I met her eyes again and she continued. "Am I not more intuitive?" I concentrated on shape and form, letting her ramble. "Do I not anticipate your every wish? Your every need?" She shifted so her hip lifted slightly. She winked at me and I gritted my teeth. I hated it when she could read my thoughts. "You only hate it when you want to keep something from me." Her voice was cold, and I pretended I didn't know what she referred to.

Ψ

She laughed as she tightened the belt around her waist. She stood, the dildo waving at me as she walked. "I could learn to like this," she said, grabbing a fistful of my hair. "Lick it!" she commanded, pushing my face against the rubber. I dutifully ran my tongue along its length, lapping at the tip like a kitten. "More!" she ordered, and forced it between my lips. I gagged as it hit the back of my throat and she laughed again, pumping her hips against my face. I swallowed as much as I could and reached my hands around to cup her ass. I kneaded it, loving the firm roundness. Sometimes I would ask her to bend over with her back to me and play with her pussy. She was so sexy; her breasts framing her pussy as she brought herself pleasure.

Now she wanted me to bend over. "Be still," she whispered near my ear and I trembled at her voice. She let her fingers trail along my spine, then tease the crack of my ass. She tickled my thighs and laughed as I squirmed under her electrifying touch. "You will do as I say!" she demanded. I jumped as she slapped my ass, and moaned as she soothed away the redness with her lips.

Parisa brought herself flush against me and leaned over my back. "You will give me all that I desire," she murmured, adjusting her prick so it teased my needy cunt. I could hear slight sucking sounds as she nuzzled the entrance. I moaned, wanting her to ram me. I wanted her to fuck my brains out.

"As you wish," she cooed. She drove the 10 inches into my welcoming cunt over and over, punishing my needy hole. I pushed back against her as she pressed her hands into my back. Because I was draped over the couch, I could not reach my clit. The force of her thrusting kept me from moving. "Tell me what you want!" she ordered.

"Please touch my clit!" I pleaded. She kept fucking me, not satisfying me or allowing me to do so myself. I begged over and over, and she would not stop slamming into my pussy. I gasped her name and bit my lip, drawing blood. She stopped. The length of the prick filled me, and my muscles clenched around it ravenously. This was more torturous than when she was screwing me. At least then I had the friction of the couch. She leaned over my back, letting me feel the hardness of her nipples and the sweat of her exertion. She took a firm grip of my hair.

"What do you want, darling?" she cajoled, kissing my neck. I moaned and tried to move my ass. She slapped it and asked me again, yanking my hair.

"Touch my clit," I groaned. She laughed softly, nibbling her way to my other ear.

"What will you give me?" she asked. She rotated her hips, causing my clit to rub against the sofa. I moaned, feeling tears in my eyes.

"Anything!" I croaked, and she eased up.

"Is that a promise?" she asked softly.

"Yes! Anything . . . anything!" She lifted her weight from me and slipped her arm around my waist. She pumped the dildo into me slowly as her hand found my clit. In a couple of deft movements I came, my juices running in rivulets down our legs. Every part of me felt expanded, hairs on end, skin sensitive to the air. "My heart stopped," I whispered. I was crying uncontrollably. It was too much.

"No. That was my heart," she corrected, licking the tears from my cheeks.


In the bedroom we snuggled close and I told her all that I loved about her. Her generosity of spirit, her passion, her extravagant thought, her perfect body. And as sleep claimed me, I heard her say that she loved me too.


I awoke to find her watching me. She was wringing her hands and smiling tremulously.

"Please give me my skin," she said excitedly.

"What?" I asked, wiping the sleep from my eyes.

"You said that I could have my skin."

"I said no such thing!"

"Last night, you said that I could have anything." Panic cata-pulted my heart as I got up from the bed and went to the bath-room, closing the door. "You said I could have anything!" she insisted, banging on the door. I splashed water on my face and stared at my haunted features. My eyes latched onto the overly quick flaring of my nostrils as I tried to breathe. It will be okay.

I opened the door, nearly tripping over her. "No," I said firmly. "But . . ."

"NO, Parisa!" She shrank back and seemed to wilt before me. She collapsed on the floor like a rag doll. No tears, just great dry sobs that shook her body. I gathered her up. She shook her head in protest and lay in my arms like a lifeless doll.

"Please understand, Parisa," I whispered, rubbing circles into her back. "I can't live without you."

"I warned you," she hissed, meeting my eyes with her listless ones.


After that day, she never spoke to me again. She was a shadow of the woman I had grown to love over the past four years. The shells I collected grew into an uncontrollable heap. When I brought her to the beach, she sat with her chin resting on her knees, staring out over the water and watching the seals frolic amongst the waves. When we made love, she lay there and thought of the sea. My broken promise had stolen her will.

There was nothing I could do but give the skin back to her. Her happiness had become my own, and the woman who lived with me was no longer the woman I had grown to love.

I went to the garden, where all of my plants refused to flourish. I dug with my hands, not wanting to harm her fur. That's how she found me, covered in earth, sodden with the damp air, tears falling down my face. The skin was clutched to my chest, much like the first day I saw her.

Parisa took my hand and helped me rise. She led me into the

house and through the living room, a trail of dirt and mud in our wake. She turned on the bathwater and filled the tub. I stood there like a helpless child as she undressed me. She helped me into the bath and climbed in behind me, enveloping me in her body. Our smooth wet skins caressed each other. I lay my head on her shoulder while she soothed me with her touch. Her hands caressed my small breasts. Her palms journeyed in long sweet strokes, bringing my nipples to hard points. She massaged my stomach in great sweeping lines. She rubbed my thighs and cunt lips, bringing a gentle hum to my body. Nonsense words filled my ears, calming me, until our hearts were a steady thump. The porcelain tub became a cocoon filled with our love as we gently rocked against each other. Water splashed on the floor with our soft movements. Her fingers were an extension of her heart, moving to the time of its rhythm, bringing me home in her arms.

She put me to bed. She sat beside me like a mother would a sick child and stroked my head until I fell asleep.

How could someone who apparently loved me so, leave? And leave knowing that her departure would bring me death? But that's what she did. While I slept with the hope she would be there when I woke, she walked out the door. I awoke to silence. Emptiness. Naked, I ran from our home, to the beach where I had first seen her, and I screamed her name. I called out over and over and saw nothing but the turbulent waters. In desperation, I swam out to the rocks where she had lain all those years ago.

It's where I lie now. My heart pains me so that I can hardly move. The sun has burnt my skin to a crisp redness. I will be food for the birds soon; and what they don't eat, I am sure the fish will as I am washed away into the sea. Every time I lick my cracked and bleeding lips, I taste the salt of the sea and think of Parisa.

# Samhain
## (The End of Summer)
### Jane Vollbrecht

"Thank you for being so understanding about this, Anna. I know it's a lot to ask." Rosalie stood next to her lover in the kitchen of their Cape-Cod style house. She wrapped an arm around Anna's shoulder and kissed her lightly on the cheek. Anna dropped the overnight bag she was holding and pushed it out of the way with her foot.

"No big deal," Anna lied in reply. "You told me right from the start that there would be things about your relationship with Louise that might seem out of the ordinary. I just wish, though—"

Rosalie held up her hand.

"Don't, Anna. You know I won't discuss it. This is a promise I made to her the night she"—Rosalie drew in a breath—"the night she left. I've kept that promise for four years. I'm not about to break it now."

Anna sighed. She and Rosalie had been together just over five years—all in all, a good, happy, harmonious union, if she discounted the immediate issue. In those five years, she had gained insights into any number of Rosalie's idiosyncrasies, but this Halloween ritual of Rosalie's was still beyond her comprehension. Rosalie wouldn't even refer to October thirty-first as Halloween; it was All Hallows' Eve.

Anna studied Rosalie's face. Rosalie would be sixty-one on her next birthday. They didn't blunt the truth to themselves or each other about what the decades had done to their looks. The wrinkles, the puffy eyes, the sagging chins—all just part of the glory of growing old. Still, Rosalie looked somehow younger and more vital today. Anna found that odd, given what the ultimate agenda of the day would be, but she had sense enough to keep the thought to herself.

"Well, I suppose I should get going," Anna glanced at the clock above the sink. "Heaven forbid I'm not at the reference desk of the North Salem Middle School library the moment the little darlings pound the door down." She retrieved the overnight bag from its resting place by the table and gathered up her shoulder bag that was hanging on the back of a kitchen chair. "I'll see you in the morning."

"Right." Rosalie pulled Anna back so she could kiss Anna's neck. "You're an angel."

Anna gave Rosalie a half smile. "Have a good day at work." She moved to the carport door. "And a good evening." She hoped the words didn't sound as bitter to Rosalie as they tasted in her mouth.

Anna tossed everything into the backseat of her road-weary sedan and walked around to the driver's door. She looked up toward the kitchen window. As she did every day, Rosalie had pulled the curtain back just enough that Anna could see her face, backlit by the overhead fluorescent light. As always, Rosalie blew her a kiss and Anna made the usual pantomime of catching it and tucking it next to her heart.

She cranked the engine and backed out into the street. She knew she should feel worse about the subterfuge she was about to engage in, but she soothed herself with clichés and platitudes. "God helps those who help themselves," she muttered. "Pray for wind, but row toward shore."

Anna drove a half-dozen blocks up Lombard Street, turned onto Exeter Road and parked facing Lombard. A fog hung low over the naked trees, distorting the thin sunlight. She watched and trembled. It was cool, but warmer than it often was in New England on the last day of October. Anna knew the shaking in her body had nothing to do with the temperature. The reaction would have been just as pronounced on the Fourth of July.

She scrutinized each vehicle that passed the intersection of Lombard Street and Exeter Road. In ten or fifteen minutes, Rosalie would go by on her way to her job at the Home Improvement Warehouse. Anna willed herself to slow her heart rate and to take a few breaths that filled more than the top third of her lungs. While she waited, she reflected.

She and Rosalie had met at services at the Unitarian Universalist church. One of Anna's friends had suggested that Anna might benefit from the open, embracing worship services there. Lord knows she had let her soul shrivel down to a lump of skepticism. Like opposite poles of those old U-shaped magnets she played with as a child, she and Rosalie had been pulled to one another that first Sunday morning in September five years earlier. After the service, they went out for lunch. By dinner the next night, Anna knew she had found the miracle worker who would heal the gaping hole left in her heart when she and Sarah (her partner of twenty-three years) had broken up three years before.

Displaying the wisdom of their advancing years, she and Rosalie dated for almost six months before moving in together. When the time came, Anna surrendered her apartment and took up residence in Rosalie's house on Lombard Street. Of course they had told one another appropriate details regarding previous lovers and all the relevant life events that brought them to their present states. Rosalie's only lover, Louise, her partner of some thirty-four years, had died of a rare kidney disease four years before. Rosalie spoke of Louise with such abiding affection and reverence that Anna felt compelled to temper the rancor she usually spewed about Sarah's departure from her life. In her heart of hearts, Anna knew it was wrong to be jealous of a dead woman, but she couldn't always help it. To hear Rosalie tell it, whatever the afterlife might hold, Louise surely occupied an exalted place in it.

Anna recalled how taken aback she had been the first Halloween—All Hallows' Eve—she corrected, and then chided herself for doing so—when she had asked Rosalie to spend the night at her apartment so they could greet the trick-or-treaters together.

"Oh, no. I couldn't possibly," Rosalie said. "I've promised that night to Louise."

Anna tried to be patient and non-judgmental, but how in the name of anything holy can someone promise a night—or anything else, for that matter—to a dead person? After much prompting, Rosalie finally told Anna that Louise had died on the thirty-first of October and her dying request of Rosalie had been that, for as long as she lived, Rosalie would devote that night to Louise's memory.

And so, each year when Halloween came, Anna packed a bag and stayed overnight with a friend. The next morning, she'd return home in time to have breakfast with Rosalie and head off to work at the school's library. Anna had tried every angle she could think of to learn more about what Rosalie did in honor of Louise's memory every Halloween, but Rosalie steadfastly refused to talk about what she did, how she felt, or why Anna couldn't be part of whatever form the remembering took.

This year was going to be different.

For at least the hundredth time that morning, Anna traced the outline of the key tucked in the pocket of her slacks. Her plan for the day went against everything she had ever believed about herself, but it was as though she was powerless to stop the chain of events she had set in motion.

"I have a right to know," Anna stated out loud. "It's not like I'm a casual girlfriend. We've been together five years and I pay half the expenses of that house, I never pry, and I vanish like some unwelcome visitor every Halloween, and . . ." Anna struggled to find plausible rationales, but there were none to be had. She wanted to respect Rosalie's request—the only one she had ever made, truth be told—but tonight Anna would break that trust and satisfy the curiosity that gnawed at her insides.

"There she goes." Anna saw Rosalie's blue Toyota with its mismatched tan back passenger door (a repair from a minor accident two years back) pass by on Lombard Street. Anna felt her adrenaline surge as she engaged the key in the ignition.

She drove home and left the car running while she scooped the overnight case and shoulder bag from the backseat and hastily shoved them into the house through the kitchen door. She got back into the car and drove to a house two streets up and three blocks over. The owners were out of town and Anna was watching their house while they were away. She parked in the garage, closed the door, turned her collar up against the increasing drizzle, and hurried back on foot.

At home, she hung her jacket in the hall closet. Just as she was shutting the door, she caught her mistake. "Idiot! If you're spending the night at Lisa and Janet's, what's your coat doing in the closet?" Anna grabbed her damp jacket and returned to the kitchen. "Pay attention to what you're doing," she admonished herself. "This is your one chance to find out what's so damn special about Halloween. Don't mess it up."

She took the overnight bag into the smaller of the two bedrooms on the main floor. Like most Cape Cod–style houses, this one was woefully inadequate in closet space. There was no hope of Rosalie and Anna keeping all of their clothing in the same room, so Anna used the little room for her things while Rosalie used the bigger room for hers. Anna stashed the contents from the decoy bag, knowing that even if Rosalie looked in drawers and the hanging closet, she'd never detect things being back in their accustomed places. She crammed her jacket as far back in the closet as it would go. She hid her shoulder bag under the heavy comforter that was still lodged on the shelf above the hanging bar in the closet. She closed the top of the overnight bag and slipped it under the guest bed, way up in the corner, out of reach and out of sight.

Anna slipped out of the slacks, blouse, and vest she had ostensibly been wearing for work. Her supervisor at the library thought Anna was taking care of her annual physical check-ups that day, so her absence from work was excused. Rosalie almost never called Anna at the library, and today of all days, there was no likelihood that she would. Anna pulled on a sweatsuit and opted for soft-soled house shoes. She extracted the key from the pocket of her slacks and gazed at it in the palm of her hand. She wrapped her fingers tightly around it as though the gesture could steel her for the hours ahead.

When she uncurled her fingers, she saw that her hands were sweating. Then she realized her ears were ringing, her heart was racing, her knees felt like Jell-O, and her muscles ached from the anticipation pumping through her. She tried to calm herself. She breathed in through her nose and exhaled through her mouth. "You've come this far; don't lose your nerve now."

The key Anna was holding was a copy of one that Rosalie kept in a small, hinged box in the top drawer of the night stand on her side of the bed. It fit the lock on the garret room under the peak of the roof on the second floor. Anna had found the key when she was tending Rosalie, who had been laid low with a bad bout of the flu. When Rosalie was knocked out from fever and medications, Anna lifted the key from its box and had a copy cut at the hardware store, returning it before Rosalie even stirred.

Anna had been in the room only a handful of times—once was shortly after she moved in and on one or two other occasions since. As Anna stood in the bedroom on the main floor, she pictured the room above.

One wall was lined with three four-shelf bookcases, all with drop-down doors to conceal the books within. Next to the book-cases, was a small door that led to a sloped storage space tucked tight under the eaves. Against the opposite wall, there was a tall file cabinet with a lock bar on the front of it. A multi-drawer cabinet like Anna remembered seeing in her dentist's office when she was a little girl stood in one corner. On the far side of the room, there was a double bed with a lace coverlet looking like a throwback to the previous century. A three-legged table draped with a floral cloth sat beside the bed. Two objects sat on the table. One was an empty bottle of Guerlain Shalimar perfume. The other was a framed photograph of a somewhat younger yet undeniably beautiful Rosalie in profile with her arms around the waist of a woman Anna could only describe as intriguing. She looked to be Rosalie's age, and yet somehow seemed ancient. Probably it was the salt-and-pepper hair clasped into a grandmotherly bun at the back of her neck.

"That was taken on our twenty-fifth anniversary," Rosalie explained on Anna's first visit to the room. "Louise never was one much for pictures, but she humored me for this one. I hope you don't mind that I've kept it."

What could Anna say? "No, of course not," she managed to utter. Anna picked up the empty perfume bottle in an attempt to deflect any further comments from Rosalie.

"She loved Shalimar," Rosalie said. "In the first weeks and months after she was gone, I'd take the cap off and inhale the fragrance. I could sometimes still almost—" Rosalie cut the thought short. "The bottle has been empty for so long now there's not even a hint of the fragrance left." Rosalie took the container from Anna and pulled the stopper out. "See?" She offered the vial to Anna. She was right. For all that was left of the scent, it could have been Evening in Paris toilet water or Blue Waltz cologne.

"What's in the file cabinet?" Anna asked.

"Just Louise's old research," Rosalie replied.

"Research on what?"

"Lots of stuff. She was fascinated by unusual happenings and strange coincidences."

"Why do you keep it?"

"Oh, I don't know. I keep thinking I'll pass it along to someone with similar interests, or maybe it's a way of hanging on to her memory." Rosalie gave a half laugh and then added, "Or more likely just because I've been too lazy to get up here and clean this room out. I'll do it one day."

"What about the books?" Anna asked.

"More of the same," Rosalie said with a shrug. "Louise had a passing interest in the occult, and she just never could bear to part with a book she thought might be useful to her or someone else."

"And this storage cabinet?"

"Louise did some work with natural healing. She studied to be an herbalist back in the early nineties."

But Rosalie wouldn't let Anna open the bookcases or look in the files or see what was in the drawers. Yes, Rosalie answered her questions—sort of—but Anna knew there had to be something more to it. Not only was this shrine to Louise still in the house, but Anna surmised this was where Rosalie went every Halloween to keep her promise to Louise.

One day not long after Rosalie had given Anna that first brief tour of the room, Anna noticed a new deadbolt lock had been installed on the door. Anna never let on that she had seen it and never—almost never—even mentioned the room at all.

Now, at long last, even before the sun came up tomorrow, Anna would know for sure what Rosalie kept locked away in that room and unravel the mysteries of Louise's memory.

Anna circled through the kitchen, living room, and bedrooms of the main floor to ensure she had left no telltale traces that she was there. Satisfied that her tracks were covered, she made her way up the stairs. Two rooms—one on either side of the hall at the top of the stairs—served as offices and hideaway space for each of them. She looked to the far end of the hall.

Anna had to will her feet to propel her to the door that stood between her and the answers she was determined to unearth. She pulled the key from the pocket of her sweatpants and watched her hand shake as she put the key into the lock. She took in a deep breath and turned the key. The deadbolt barely whispered as it slid free of the jamb. She turned the knob and pushed the door open. She fumbled for the light switch on the wall.

The room looked exactly as she remembered. Since it was directly under the peak of the house, there were no windows to provide natural light. The switch was for a floor lamp that stood between the bed and the multi-drawer cabinet. Anna waited while her eyes adjusted to the dim light.

Her heart pounded in her ears. She forced herself to cross the room and examine the bed. The lace coverlet lay as if it had just been tatted. There wasn't a crease to be seen. She expected it to be yellowed with age, but it was as white as an angel's robe. The photograph of Rosalie and Louise and the Shalimar bottle sat in the exact same spots on the bedside table.

From the bed, she went to the cabinet and opened several of the many drawers. As Rosalie had told her, the cabinet was filled with vessels of herbs and dried plants, each labeled and dated. Many also bore cryptic notes like "good for headache," or "boosts fertility." Satisfied there would be no insights gained there, Anna went over to the bookcases.

She was surprised to find the cover over the top shelf slid back readily when she lifted it. She could barely make out the titles on the books' spines in the diffused light. At random, she pulled a book from its place. A *Complete History of Witchcraft in Colonial America*. She replaced it and pulled out another one. *The Role of Witchcraft in Midwifery*. And then the next: *Europe's Purge of Witches—Three Hundred Years of Persecution*. Each book Anna drew from the shelf proclaimed the same subject matter. The other shelves revealed more books on related topics. What was it Rosalie had said—"Louise had a passing interest in the occult"? If this was a passing interest, the Pope had a passing interest in Catholicism.

Anna pulled yet another book from the bottom shelf. It slipped from her hands as she shifted for more light. When the book hit the floor, it opened and a folded page dropped free from the back cover. Anna could see it was a lineage chart, much like the one she had seen in her grandmother's Bible. Oddly though, this one only contained women's names, and the last one was Louise Coombs. Stranger still was that there were no dates of death listed, only dates of birth. By quick calculation, Anna discerned that the woman listed at the top of the chart was born more than two hundred and forty years earlier. Why would anyone keep a lineage chart that showed only the date of birth and not the date of death? When the obvious answer presented itself to her, Anna jammed the book back on the shelf and felt the blood freeze in her veins.

She wanted to bolt from the room, but stanched the urge. "Don't be a fool, Anna. You'll hate yourself tomorrow if you don't go through with this." Her legs felt as though they were dead weight as she left the bookcase and went to the file cabinet. The lock bar down the front of it was in place, but there was no padlock on the bar.

Anna folded the bar out of the way and pulled the first drawer out. She was greeted with an array of file folders, seemingly in no particular order. She extracted one labeled "Yule." Inside were articles clipped from books and magazines. "Yule is from the Gallic 'gule' which means wheel . . ." began one clipping. Others went on to explain the concept of Winter Solstice, God's rebirth from the Goddess, signified by lengthening days. She dropped the file back in the drawer and yanked another out.

This one was labeled "Imbolc—February Second." The materials there told about how that date marked the first stirrings of spring and the growing of light as the Goddess recovers from giving birth to the God. It is a time of spiritual cleansing, or the Second Cross Quarter Day, when the sun reaches fifteen degrees of Aquarius, symbolized by Spirit. Before the calendar was changed by Pope Gregory, it was Valentine's Day, the arrow in the heart not a sign of love piercing a soul, but of a phallic symbol entering female genitalia.

Next, she took a file marked "Ostara, the start of spring." Fertility symbols of eggs and rabbits abound; Pan dances with Esther. Anna skimmed through the contents and found some interesting details, but nothing that knocked the earth off its axis.

And on it went. Anna lifted file after file from the drawer and scanned the contents. Okay, so Louise had information—lots of information—that described the Pagan origins of every major religious holiday. Big deal. And she had other files full of data about how modern medicine conspired to marginalize midwives. And there were files about covens and warlocks and aliens and topics generally regarded as paranormal, but it wasn't shocking news that had to be kept hidden away in a locked room.

Then another file caught her eye. The tab said "Samhain—October 31." Now maybe she was getting somewhere. Anna began to read: "the summer's end; the beginning of winter; New Year's Day for Pagans. The death of the Sun God to await rebirth. Bid farewell, reflect over what has transpired; meditate over what is yet to come." The next words flung themselves off the page and seared themselves into her brain. "The gates between Life and Death open to each other. A time to reunite with those who have passed over and to remember and rejoice."

The door to the garret room slammed shut and Anna all but shucked her skin on the spot. She checked her watch. "Oh my god. It's after one." She hadn't realized how mesmerized she had been by the herbs and books and files. Rosalie was only working a half day. That was why the door had suddenly swung shut. Rosalie had gotten home, opened the door from the carport into the kitchen, and the draft had pulled the door shut because it was at the end of that long upstairs hallway. Just the vacuum pressure of the down-stairs door opening, or so Anna assured herself as she gulped for air.

And now she had another problem—or maybe two. If Rosalie had heard the upstairs door slam, she'd know Anna was home. Anna's plan had been to scout out the room before Rosalie got home and then to relock it and hide in her office on the second floor until Rosalie let herself into the room for her memory cere-mony with Louise—assuming the locked room was the site of the ceremony. Now Anna doubted she could get out of the room at all. Every board on the second floor creaked at the slightest pressure. She was trapped.

She crammed her hands into her pockets and felt a fear unlike any she had ever known begin to rise from deep in her core. Part of the fear was that Rosalie would find her in Louise's shrine and that would be the end of things between her and Rosalie. But there was a bigger horror, something unfamiliar and unnameable. Anna fought to regain her composure. Her fingers wrapped around the key in her pocket.

"Damn. She'll wonder why the room is unlocked." Anna felt her heart fall to her feet. Then she remembered how easily the lock had turned. Maybe, just maybe Rosalie wouldn't notice the deadbolt had no resistance. Anna could only hope that would be the case. What choice now?

With catlike caution, Anna slid the file drawer closed and pushed the lock bar back into place. Willing herself to be lighter than air, she padded across the room to the light switch on the wall. She looked hard at the room trying to memorize the exact location of each piece of furniture and gauging the distance from the place she stood to the tiny cubbyhole closet next to the bookcases.

Anna turned off the light and eased down onto the floor. Like a woman who knows the lake she's ventured out onto hasn't a thick enough layer of ice to hold her, she flattened herself to spread her body weight to its thinnest, hoping the floorboards would keep silent, and began creeping toward the cubbyhole closet in the dark. What felt like an hour later, she felt her fingertips touch the edge of the door.

"Please, let this door open easily," she prayed to an unspecified goddess. The hinges heeded the goddess's command and the door swung open silently. Anna edged into the cubbyhole and pulled the door closed. She worked herself into a sitting position, her back against the boxes that were stacked under the shortest part of the eave.

"I'll probably die from oxygen deprivation," she thought derisively. "Serve me right, too."

Anna had no idea when Rosalie would come upstairs or when she would begin whatever it was that she would do to honor Louise's memory, if, indeed, that room was the site for whatever she might do. She tried to read her watch, but it was impossible in the tiny, sealed enclosure.

"Don't think about being claustrophobic," she warned herself, too late to do much good. "Don't think about how you've ruined things forever with Rosalie." Another caution that came too late.

And so, Anna waited. And waited.

The next thing she was aware of was the sound of voices in the garret room. One of them was Rosalie; the other, a total stranger. Incredibly, Anna realized, she had dozed off. Had she slept for a minute or a lifetime? What difference? This was what she had come for and all her senses were electro charged.

She could hear Rosalie's voice clearly. And she detected the shift in her tone—the one that always caused her labia to swell and moisten.

"I've missed you so much, darling," Rosalie moaned. "I need to feel your whole body against me."

"I've been with you every minute, dearest. That's the promise I made you. We're never really apart from one another." The stranger's voice was husky and evocative. Anna could almost feel the heat from her breath as she pictured her murmuring the words against Rosalie's throat.

"But not like this, my love. It's the touch of your hands and the feel of your lips against me that I ache for."

"I know, Rosie. I know."

Anna bristled. How dare this woman call Rosalie "Rosie?" That was Anna's name for her when they made love.

"But it's not like you don't have a lover, Rosie. I've seen and heard you with Anna. She's good for you. She loves you very much."

"Yes, Anna is wonderful. She's been a godsend to help me past my sorrow."

"Like you haven't found other ways of getting past your sorrow, bitch," Anna cursed silently from her lair. "All this crap about honoring Louise's memory. This is the last time I fall for any of that bullshit."

"I need to feel you inside me," Rosalie urged. "It's been forever since I've known your magic. Please, baby, do me now. I can't wait any longer."

"I never could say 'no' to a woman in need." The stranger's voice was like velvet. Anna was sure she could hear the other woman shift on the bed. Anna knew she was poised over Rosalie. She sensed what would happen next. Rosalie would start to breathe faster and faster. She'd start to rock in rhythm with the other woman as the woman slipped her fingers in and out of Rosie's deep, wet vagina.

"Take my breast in your mouth. You know how I like it." The urgency in Rosalie's voice stirred Anna in spite of herself. She didn't feel like a fifty-seven-year-old woman lodged in a closet spying on her lover. She felt like a teenager caught in a rush of passion that had to be satisfied. The contractions of her own vulva made her even more acutely aware of the burning desire consuming her beloved Rosalie. Anna anticipated what was happening in the room.

Soon Rosie would make low, guttural sounds that came from a place of total abandon and then, in a sudden arching motion, she would climax and whimper, "Yes, oh thank you, yes. Yes."

"Yes!"

The shout startled Anna because it was her own voice she heard as an orgasm unlike anything she had ever known swept across her and left her gasping. Then she heard Rosalie's voice echo her own. "Yes, yes, my eternal love. Yes. It was perfect."

Without thought to consequence or explanation, Anna sprang out of the closet, ready to confront Rosalie for the liar and cheat she was and learn the identity of Rosalie's clandestine lover.

She was rendered dumbfounded to the point of near hysteria when she found herself greeted by a totally empty room. A lighted candle stood on the bedside table and the door was open, but there was no one in sight.

"They can't have gotten out of here that fast," Anna reasoned, but reason seemed a feeble tool. She detected a sound coming from the main floor. She primed her ears and listened intently. It was the music Rosalie listened to when she meditated—she was sure of it.

Anna avoided the worst of the creaking floorboards and edged to the top of the stairs. She crouched down and looked toward the living room through the balusters of the handrail. There, crossed-legged, fully clothed, and obviously in a deep meditative state, sat Rosalie. Scattered around her on the floor were old photo albums and other memorabilia from her three-plus decades with Louise. The placid, vacant expression on Rosalie's face told Anna she was mentally, emotionally, and spiritually—and for that matter, meta-physically—light years away. No way in hell had she been upstairs fornicating with a stranger not two minutes before.

Anna stole back to the room. She had to have imagined the whole thing. What the deuce was wrong with her? She must be losing her mind.

And then it hit her. Shalimar. The fragrance was unmistakable. It was Arabian nights and jasmine and ginger and myrrh. Potent and heady and intoxicating. The room was infused with the bouquet. Anna hurried to the bedside table and snatched up the bottle. Empty. She pulled the stopper and inhaled. Nothing.

Then she set the bottle back down and her gaze fell on the framed photograph, poorly lit by the flickering candle. How could it be? The two women were in the same pose, but Rosalie looked like a college girl. There were no streaks of gray at her temples and no laugh lines around her mouth. Louise looked different too. What was it? Of course, the hair. It was hanging free, not pinched in a bun at the nape of her neck. It was dark brown, flowing down her back like a horse's silken mane. And in this picture, Louise was smiling, not standing stone-faced like in the other one. The picture Anna had seen there that morning was the one Rosalie had told her was taken on their twenty-fifth anniversary.

This just didn't make any sense.

Anna paced. "Think, Anna. There's got to be an explanation." She pictured Rosalie downstairs in her trance, reminders of her life with Louise gathered around her. "She must have swapped the picture for one that was taken when they were younger," Anna decided in relief. She turned back to the bedside stand. Her heart stopped cold when she saw the picture she had remembered, the one that had been there that morning when she let herself into the room.

She sat on the bed, not sure what was real and what was illusion, not sure if she were alive or dead. Nervously, she swept her hands back and forth across the top of the lace coverlet, the immaculate coverlet that she had carefully inspected hours—or maybe a century—ago.

She felt her spine dissolve into mush. She didn't want to look at what was caught around her fingers, but couldn't help herself. She lifted her hands so the light from the candle fell across tangled strands of long salt-and-pepper hair woven into a gossamer net. It felt as though she was bound on the brink between two worlds.

Anna lifted her eyes to the photograph. The last of the smile faded from Louise Coombs's lips just as her hair lost its luster and curled into a bun pinned to the base of her head.

# Van Helsing 2005
### Lynne Jamneck

Stakes, three all in all. Two feet long with a smooth flat top and tapered down to a razor-sharp point. Two of them were hawthorns, the other an ash for good measure.

I sat on the polished wood kitchen floor, marking down my supplies with a chewed pencil on the ragged notepad I carried with me everywhere. I stopped my ritual to light a cigarette and turn up the radio. There was something decidedly spooky about Creedence Clearwater Revival. I liked it.

Mirror, check. Cross, check. A Bulgarian priest had given it to me after I'd helped him stake a particularly wicked vampire roaming the craggy foothills of his village. It was silver and plain looking. It evoked the fear of God in everything undead. I smiled to myself. Sometimes I loved my job.

Holy water, two silver daggers and my Beretta for good measure. The pistol wasn't for killing vampires. The circles I moved in, there was more to look out for than the undead. I holstered it and strapped it snugly beneath my arm.

I tossed the notepad aside and zipped up the sleek leather carrying case I used to conceal the paraphernalia of my trade. Then I picked up the crossbow at my feet. It was solid and heavy and felt comforting in my hands. I'd bought it from a Russian merchant when I was twenty; that seemed like a lifetime ago. It was beautiful; dark oak with decorative gothic silver inlay.

A sharp knock on the door made me look up, scowling. Now who in the name of fuck could that be at two o' clock in the morning? I had told no one that I was coming to New York. Then again, cities had ears and eyes and sometimes they had mouths, too. Lonely statues atop skyscrapers gave away secrets to one another, and the word spread.

I freed the pistol from its holster and stepped through the darkened hallway to the front door, trying not to curse the creaking wood floor beneath my boots. I leaned closer to the door to cast a look through the peephole, hand on the doorknob, ready.

Who I saw on the other side was the last person I'd expected.

*Was it? Really?*

A disorienting rush blitzed through my body and I felt my grip relax on the butt of the pistol. Leaning back against the wall as my heart beat faster, fluttering dangerously, my thoughts rushed. *What the fuck? Like I need this now?*

Of course I wasn't going to open the door. Not at two in the morning, with my body warm from too much whiskey, and most definitely not to the woman standing on the other side of the door. Not with what just a mere fucking glimpse of her through a peephole had provoked in my body.

She knocked again and my heart leaped at the sound. *Please, for the love of fuck just leave. I can't open the door to you. Please don't make me. And how did you know where I was anyway? GO AWAY.*

I didn't dare look out into the hallway again for fear that she'd see the shadow of movement. I wanted to. I was haunted to see her again—her blonde hair kinking on her shoulders, setting off the dark of her blue eyes. She must have just finished her rounds at the hospital.

I kept quiet, back rigid against the wall and my eyes closed, willing her to leave. There was no more knocking. Just the sound of muted footfalls taking her away from my door and steadily dying down the hallway. I slid to the floor, my body hot all over and the gun falling from my hands to the floor. The need and craving that throbbed in my veins was like the sudden onset of a fever.

My legs were weak and my palms sweaty, while other more primal needs blared jarringly for attention. Blood. Blood and sex.

I got up shakily and stumbled to the bathroom where I opened the cold-water tap full burst. A momentary hesitation held me back but only for a second. Instinct. I have learned to control it.

I plunged both shaking hands beneath the shockingly cold water as the ancient pipes creaked and groaned, then splashed water on my face, a second time followed by a third. The tap squeaked a feeble protest when I closed it. I allowed myself only a quick flash of a look in the mirror above the sink. It's not comforting. Even I'm shocked by the ghostly look behind the smoky-brown of my mother's eyes. I stood with both hands on the rim of the washbasin, steadying myself, waiting for the rush of lust to dwindle until finally I'm left with only the memory of anticipation on her face as she waited for me to open the door. Even that is bad enough, still.

She should have known better. She should *never* have come to my door. What was she thinking? All it added up to was the lingering of memories and a feeling akin to gut-rot in my stomach at what I'd never get from her.

Laura O'Connor.

I could hardly ignore the rush of excitement that refused to leave me in peace. The thought of her echoed in the stillness.

I picked up my gun and returned to the kitchen to gather the tools of my trade. I swept the keys of the beat-up Volkswagen mini-bus off the counter and, crossbow slung across my shoulder, made my way downstairs. No one looked at me. I could have been invisible.

After all—this was New York.


There was dried, caked blood on the dangerous-looking heels of my leather boots, splattered carelessly on the buckles running up the insides. It came with the job and there was piss-poor precious little I could do about it. Sure enough—*that* people would notice. The blood. Humans are enthralled by it, the letting of it. It conjures a certain ambivalence in them that I have rarely seen elicited by anything else. It attracts and repulses them at the same time.

I stood against the wall beneath the sign that read EMER-GENCY in warning red letters. There is an ambulance parked in front of the swinging doors. They are branded with the same word in stark green capitals. A paramedic walks out and briefly but long-ingly looks at the cigarette between my fingers. I implore him silently to look the other way. I'm in no mood to talk to anyone. Except *her*. I desperately want to talk to her, and that's why I'm standing here in the cold at just before five in the morning, waiting until I notice her come through the swinging doors. Shrouded in moving shadows, away from the emergency parking lot street-lights, I can watch in peace. No one approaches me. No one looks at my face. They know not to.

And then one of the swing doors open and she steps out into the predawn light, lighting a cigarette. I had no idea she smoked, and smile into the counterfeit warmth of my gloved hands as I blow into them, cupped round my mouth. She's contradictory. I liked that. I bet she hides her habit from her colleagues. She seemed the type to keep her vices private. I could relate to that.

*Maybe we could be good, Doctor O'Connor.*

"Alex? Alex, is that you?"

I heard her voice clearly. As if it was a sign from someone above it began to rain again. I retreated, quickly, the shadows of the city swallowing me, spiriting me away from her. I noticed blood on the concrete where I'd been standing. I heard her telling me to wait. I watched her as she looked about uncertainly.

*Alex, wait—*

I read her mind.

*Alex, I—*

*No.* No more. Nothing more. I dare not listen anymore.

Ψ

"Forgive me, Father, for I have sinned." I pondered the sentence, then asked, "Can I call you Father? Since, you know, you're a woman. Jesus—no wonder people don't come to church anymore. These benches are hell on your arse."

Robyn turned her head sideways to look at me. The massive, vivid stained-glass window in the wall behind her cast an ethereal glow on her face. Behind the sternness of her spiritual pose hid the innuendo of a smile, teasing the corners of her lips. There was a counseling look in her eyes, though.

"Don't be facetious, Alex. You know Episcopalians don't go to confession. Why don't you just tell me what you're doing here."

I shrugged. "In New York, or in church?" I wasn't going to make it easy for her just because she happened to be an ordained minister. Screw her. Robyn has contributed her own brand of torture to my life. Maybe not on purpose, but that didn't detract from the severity of its impact.

She waved a hand dismissively, explaining for my benefit. "Alex, you're here with me—in church—because you're Episcopalian. We're like childlike moths drawn to its blessed flame. It's in your blood. It's what you're doing in New York that has me concerned."

I felt chided that she saw straight through me. "What? I can't endeavor to visit my favorite priest?"

Robyn shivered as a cold draft crept past our feet. "Sometimes you're so full of shit, Alex."

"Robyn!"

She gave me a satisfied look. "What? You're the only one allowed to swear because you're undead and couldn't give a damn?"

"No—you're a priest, an ordained servant of God. You're not allowed to. Besides, I'm not *undead*."

"Whatever. God has more important things to worry about, take my word for it."

"Like me?"

"Don't be pompous. More important than even you." Robyn was looking at the raised altar in front of us, seemingly contemplating some mysterious, godly thought by the looks of the severe frown forming on her brow.

Robyn Westenra has had her fair share of secrets and lies. She hasn't always been a priest. Her life too has been stained by blood. But unlike myself, she's been careful not to be psychically marked by it.

She looked back at me then, her face softening somewhat. "I don't mean to sound unhappy to see you." She smiled genuinely. "Quite the opposite."

"Then be happy I'm here."

"Of course I am."

There was a moment of silence before I asked, "What was she like? My sister?" Robyn seemed surprised by the question. I'd been persistent in the past about my determination not to speak much of my family history.

"Rachel? A scholar as much as she was anything else. Anthropologist, parapsychologist . . . vampire hunter. It's a pity the two of you never got to know one another."

"How could I have? I only found out I even had a sister after she was dead." I crossed my arms resolutely, petulant at the anger in my voice. "Ancient history, anyway. I don't really want to talk about it."

*Then why did you ask?*

Robyn said, "She would've liked you."

"I doubt that."

"She would have appreciated your ballsyness."

"Bollocks. She would have told me to get an education and do something proper with my life."

Robyn gave me a look that said *you clearly know nothing.*

I shrugged. "Whatever. I didn't know her, she didn't know me. My adoptive parents only told me my real surname at seventeen, and then only because I found out by mistake."

"You ran away from home. The best thing you could have done for yourself."

"That's a nice sentiment, coming from a priest. Aren't we supposed to obey and honor our parents?"

"Not if they lie to you or keep you from the truth."

*Even if withholding the truth might have been better?*

I felt uncomfortable suddenly. Thinking of my life and my habits and trying to reconcile them with the stillness of where I found myself at that instant. And the woman next to me whom I'd first come to know at thirteen as a teacher of gifted children when I'd been sent away from home to live in a dormitory with twelve snotty brats who tortured me every fucking day because I had no interest in pretty clothes and seducing boys.

I could think of those years now and feel a fondness that I would only admit to myself. It had been character building in more ways than one. And there had been plenty of time to research my interests—the occult, archeology, medieval weaponry.

It was after a mild autumn day in September when Kelly Sowalski told me—with much glee and a good deal of derision—that I was descended from practitioners of witchcraft that everything changed. Not necessarily for better or worse, but for the first time, so many things suddenly made sense.

"You were brilliant, you know?"

I offered Robyn a smarmy cocked eyebrow. Compliments made me feel ill at ease. "Sod you. You told me I was a pain."

"And you were. But you were also exceptionally bright."

"Kelly Sowalski didn't think so."

"Kelly Sowalski was a stuck-up kid who cared more about her outfits than her natural talents."

I snorted amusedly. "I had such a crush on her."

"I know."

We watched as a young teenage girl approached the church altar, framed by the outstretched arms of the Virgin Mary. She placed her backpack on the floor next to her feet and lit a candle. She bowed her head and I watched. Her lips moved mutely. She seemed oblivious of Robyn and me. Her vigil reminded me of when last I held my own hands together in prayer. A long time. The inevitable guilt followed the thought hotly and I shut it out.

Then I said, "I miss her." I was sorry almost immediately after the words left my lips. A part of me felt as if I'd lost something by saying the words out loud. It made me feel weak and I hated it. "I'm not even sure that 'miss' is the right word."

Robyn said matter-of-factly, "Laura came to see me."

Robyn's voice had been low and even during the whole of our conversation, yet the words she had just spoken echoed loudly in my ears.

"She did?" My mouth was dry.

I saw a look in Robyn's eyes that I thought was tantamount to blame, but I couldn't be sure. I didn't know whether I wanted to be sure. She would have every right. But so had I in what I'd done to Laura O'Connor.

"When?"

"Must have been about three weeks ago. Alex, you have to talk to her."

"I don't know if I can do that."

"You saved her life. From a very unconventional threat, I might add. In a very unusual way too, I might add."

"Isn't that favor enough?"

"Alex—"

"No!" The word reverberated obstinately against the concrete walls of the how-many-hundred-year-old building. The young woman at the altar turned to look at us, her prayer either interrupted or finished. There was sorrow in the way she held herself. I looked away when her eyes sought mine.

*. . . some days I don't know if God . . .*

I stopped myself from accepting her thoughts, tuning out yet another person's misery. The girl picked up her backpack and left us alone again.

I was afraid to open my mouth and blurt out the wrong thing. Insubordination boiled dangerously in my blood, always has. Mostly, I didn't give a flying fuck about what anyone thought. But Robyn was one of less than a handful of people that I respected— sometimes to my own annoyance. I wasn't sure whether it was because she'd helped me realize my own potential all those years back, or whether we were both Episcopalians or because her intelligence and strength of character so powerfully attracted me.

Respect or not, I was still angry. And I had a truckload of shit to be angry with right then. I fucking didn't need anyone stepping on my toes as well.

"It's always the same," I said hotly. "I come here to ask for guidance and you tell me off."

Robyn laughed. "That's not true. You tell yourself off, Alex. And don't look at me like that. Please, keep your pithy anger to yourself."

My skin prickled and it wasn't from the light of dawn slowly creeping toward me across the hardwood bench.

"Can't you be on my side for a change?" I felt on the spot, venting my anger with a statue of the Mother Mary looking on. Saints and sinners alike turned their heads toward me from the colorful window displays. I was sure they didn't approve of my supernatural aura contaminating their holiest of holies. Well they could kiss my arse, twenty-four-seven. They got a rough deal? Well, they certainly weren't the only ones.

"I see you're critical of your faith again."

I jumped up, turned my back on Robyn and started walking out. It was unfair. Robyn didn't even need any supernatural powers to read *my* mind.

"You're being unreasonable, Alex. If you won't give it to yourself, at least consider it from Laura's perspective."

I kept walking, pretending not to hear, and she kept speaking. "Is it so difficult to allow yourself something for once? Stop being such a martyr—you're a Van Helsing, for the love of God!"

I breathed a sigh of relief as the heavy church doors slowly swung shut behind me. The sound disturbed pigeons nesting in a window. They took off into the sky with a flutter of wings, cursing me. Vermin. Bloody rats with wings.

At the bottom of the steps an old wino wiped at his bulbous nose with a grimy handkerchief.

Only then did I realize my breath was coming fast and low. I felt hot and unhinged. The awakening rays of daylight were unbearably bright. I reached inside my leathers and took out my sunglasses. The fresh air and sunlight made my skin tingle in a curious way. Evolution doesn't have to be a slow thing. I could now almost refer to sunlight as a pleasant experience. My resistance to it seemed to go with my mood. Like drugs. I found it ironic.

The wino looked up at me. I could smell the sickly vinegar of week-old wine as it wafted off him. He looked anemic. Without doubt I noticed the puncture wounds just below his collarbone. They looked sloppy, too. Probably a youngster; overeager and devoid of skill.

The old man's eyes were laced with yellow. "They come at night, you know." He spoke without the intention of someone trying to persuade. "The shelter won't believe me, the doctor won't believe me. Sometimes even I don't believe me." He went back to wiping his nose. Those puncture marks were fresh. Soon he would give up the curious struggle within himself and stalk his first victim. It was inevitable. I walked down the steps, pushing a tenner in his dry, cracked palm as I walked past. They could say what they wanted about London, these Yankees. Sure it was noisy. Hell yes it was dirty. In some places it was downright fucking filthy. But this place? It sucked. Big time.

I do so miss getting shitfaced.

Ever since I lost half of my humanness, the alcohol refuses to have the same effect. Drink after drink after drink—the closest I'll come is a mellow, blurred recall of what it used to feel like when I was too drunk to trust myself getting off a barstool at the end of an evening.

As if that wasn't tragic enough, I happened to be sitting next to one of those glamorous blood doll kids that kept coming on to me with bad vampire jokes. She couldn't have been more than eighteen.

*Why do vampires never get divorced? They prefer to bury their problems.*

*What's it like to be kissed by a vampire? It's a pain in the neck.* And she said that with a tease of course, like it was a good thing. Her jokes and transparent comments became more overtly sexual as the night progressed and her numerous gin and tonics were refilled.

*Maybe you like being sucked, too, Van Helsing.*

I've stopped trying to figure out how they ferret the places out. The bars. Vamps are always cocky about these things, so I guess it's only a matter of whom you end up talking to. There was a place I knew of on Lexington Avenue called *Plasma*—not too subtle. They had their hangers-on, and so did we. Sometimes they were a pain in the ass and sometimes they were a valuable source of information. Vampire hunters were not a sociable lot, and most of them hated any sort of taint on their reputation as champions of good. Even though most of the time, the lives they led were anything but. For me personally, I was careful whom I talked to.

I'd be lying if I said that bad-vampire-joke-girl didn't look . . . tasty. It was fun toying with her. I made comments about her being out her depth and fucking about with something she really had no idea about. Still, she wanted me to take her home because she'd get it twice for the price of one. She could see the desire in my eyes. We'd fuck. Afterward I'd drain blood from her neck. She'd get off on it, but not half as much as I would. The blood is the Life.

I don't need much. But I need it, nonetheless. The woman who bit me three years ago had been careless. She'd underestimated my strength, both mentally and physically. Lucky for me. Or unlucky, depending on how you'd like to look at it. Before I fought back, I gave in. She offered me her wrist and I took it because I couldn't help myself. I was weak. There is no other excuse.

It was after I had tasted her, when she wanted more of my blood for herself that I managed to fight her off. By then, the blood bond had formed. She'd infected me with the need.

Two weeks after, fever ridden and delirious, I tracked her down and killed her. Drove a stake right through her blackened heart. I vowed never to become what she'd been. And if not for Robyn Westenra, I might have failed in that objective a long time ago.

That of course, didn't stop my anger from being inflamed at the way she interfered in my life.

When I turned the moody-lit corridor of the apartment block and looked up from where I'd been fumbling to get the keys from my pocket, I stopped dead. A debilitating shiver coiled up my spine and rooted my feet to the ground.

She'd come again. Why had I not entertained the thought that she would?

Laura blinked slowly before she said, "Why did you come to New York? You hate it here."

My mouth was dry but I found words somehow. "I know. It's colossal, silent and grim." It sounded like a stupid reply at the time, but the more I think about it now, it aptly described my state of mind at the time.

Laura O'Connor.

Was she the only thing in my life I still deemed worthy to think about? I didn't weigh up my day-to-day trials anymore. I could stake a vampire in my sleep. And yes, that was because I had their blood in me. To that extent, I did not regret what I was. There were pros to having their blood in me.

Laura still hadn't moved from my door. "Why won't you see me, Alex?"

She was exceedingly attractive. And I was *inhuman*.

I couldn't help but think she had fallen in love not with me, but with the romantic notion that our love wasn't meant to be. Jesus, it hurt just to look at her. She didn't seem to be frightened. It only served to make me want her even worse.

I finally fished the keys out of my pocket. "You shouldn't be here," I said, hastily moving past her. Touching her would be thrilling. And detrimental to my defenses.

"Can I come in? Just for a minute?"

I couldn't help but smile. A resigned reaction, but it felt good nonetheless. The brass key slid inside the lock easily and I turned it. Did I really think that I had to *touch* her to feel it?

"Robyn told you I was here, didn't she?" I'm sure Laura knew I wasn't really expecting an answer.

Laura said, "I went to her before she told me that you were here. In New York."

I looked at her eyes and noticed again how ordinary they were. How human. Beautiful.

"Please don't do that."

"Do what?" I asked.

"Look at me like that."

"Does it frighten you?"

"No."

I wanted her.

I told her to go inside.

The night outside was black and blue. It illuminated the loft apartment in a hue devoid of softness but not atmosphere. It began to rain. I locked the door and patted my palms down on my jeans, then went to the big windows at the far end of the room and opened one. It had snowed lightly the day before. If the rain kept coming down the roads were going to be slippery as shit.

I turned around to ask Laura if she wanted something to drink. She was standing next to the kitchen table, running a cautious finger along the grip of my crossbow.

"Careful."

"It's a handsome weapon."

"Thank you. It's a few hundred years old."

"It suits you."

She wasn't even looking at me and my body reacted. "I really need some coffee. Want some?"

"God, yes." She smiled dismissively. "I just finished an ER shift."

I switched on the coffeemaker. My boots echoed loudly on the wood floor.

"I felt you. Here in New York, I mean." She said the words cautiously but with importance. She wanted me to understand. It was difficult for her, I could see. She didn't yet understand.

I spooned ground coffee out of a jar and soon the dark, aromatic smell punctured the cool, tight night air. Laura had come up close behind me. I could feel her. The energy linking us was intense.

"I wake up in the middle of the night and I feel as if I'm burning up with a strong fever."

I turned around to look at her.

*Is it so difficult to allow yourself something for once?*

"What does it feel like?" I willed myself to ask.

"Like I'm trapped. As if a vast heaviness is pushing down on me."

"Do you feel scared?"

"No." She seemed hesitant. "Rather the opposite." She moved her hand, as if to reach out and touch me, but didn't. "What did you do to me, Alex?"

Robyn was right, I knew it then. In that instant I realized that I could never have just left Laura to her own devices after tainting her the way I had. There would never have been peace for either of us. We would have gone through the rest of our lives like detached spirits.

I took her hand. It felt as if an electric current jumped from her into me and as I kept my eyes on hers I could see she was experiencing the same effect. Her skin was warm and smooth. I said: "The man who attacked you—that night when you left the hospital?"

"I remember. You staked him. I saw it, just before I passed out."

"Do you remember that he hit you?"

"Yes. I remember feeling the blow against my head. My ears rang and I fell down and I heard, I remember I heard him scramble, his shoes scattering gravel. And then I saw you . . . I couldn't figure where you'd come from, and you killed him, and then I lost consciousness."

"I should have just taken you to the hospital. I mean we were right there. I just . . ."

Laura took my hand and brought it up to her cheek. She smelled my palm. It was a refined, yet still somewhat animalistic motion.

"I didn't bite you," I blurted.

"Did you want to?"

"Yes."

"What did you do?"

The coffee machine was finally done when she took one of my fingers between her lips. The lust inside me rumbled madly and shook at its steel cage. I wanted to tell her to stop, to think, to take a step back, to return to her normal life and forget about me and my crossbow and that vampires existed and that I was—at least in a bastard sort of way—one of them.

"I—I bit myself, my wrist, and held it against your wound. It has coagulant properties. Our blood mixed."

I closed my eyes as she took two of my fingers inside her mouth. There was white noise inside my head, screaming and scratching reasons why I should get away while I still could—while Laura still could . . .

She released my hand and stood before me. *Exposed*, I thought.

"Alex, before that night I had nothing. My life was a series of day-to-day duties, things that had lost their meaning to me a long time ago. I know you were meant to find me. You've challenged everything I believed in. It's the goddamn strangest thing but, I feel like I've known you forever. Christ, that sounds clichéd, doesn't it?"

I took her wrists firmly in my hands and kissed her, holding her arms at bay, thinking that I could still control my actions as long as she didn't touch me.

My head swam as the atmosphere dipped in a slow, alluring charge of eroticism, making the kiss feel languid, smooth and drawn out. I felt too tight in my own skin. I felt her hands, pulling against the constraint of my grip, and let her go. I wondered what she would do with them. I wanted them on me. But I wouldn't ask. I didn't need to.

Her hands moved to my hips and she pulled me against her. I dared not close my eyes. There were images beating there I didn't wish to see, things that warned this was a transgression, that it was more than merely illicit—that it was against God. That *I* was against God.

And then Laura's mouth opened obediently beneath mine and her hands tugged at the pliable fabric of my shirt, unraveling my insipid protests. I brushed them away but they were there again, kneading the taut, tense muscles at the small of my back.

"You see so much death," she said into the space still separating us. There was something about the way she said it, something in her voice, which I hadn't expected.

What I was, what I did—it turned her on. Did that give me permission to give in to the craving inside me?

"We both do." I pushed my hands beneath Laura's shirt. "See death." She wore a tight tank top underneath. It accentuated her flat stomach hidden beneath the perfunctory cotton. "Difference between you and me is you try and restore life. I take it away." She shivered as my hands cupped her breasts, the nipples growing instantly hard.

Laura began unbuckling my broad leather belt, shaking her head. "I bullshit myself that I can do it. That I have any control over it. Some kind of nerve, right?"

My head was starting to get that funny feeling; as if something inside it was coiled too tight and in danger of snapping. All my senses were heightened. The air smelled of wet concrete, coffee and sex. And dear God, beneath all of that, I could smell her blood.

I pulled her against me and we kissed again, despite every part of me wanting to do something else. Not let go, no. That option was long gone by now. But to do something else *to her*. Part of me wanted to throw her down on the floor and fuck her. Another altogether different part sought to crawl my hand up her neck, cruelly tilt her head to one side and bite her.

Her warm hands moved up my back. I opened my mouth to let her tongue in and felt the first brief, sharp sting as my fangs protruded. I groaned—either pleasure or pain—or a combination of both. Laura expelled a tense breath of air into my mouth and I felt her hand unbuttoning my jeans, and then her hand slid down along the inside of my thigh.

She was breathing in my neck, hard. It sounded as if she was clenching her teeth. "I heard you calling me . . ." Her hand rubbing against my skin was like a charge. A bolt of energy that catapulted me from a state of wavering ambivalence to one of sheer determination. "Ever since that night, when you came, I've felt alive. Out of my skin." She eyed me intently with a strange, exhilarating curiosity. As if she was sure that I was hiding answers from her. An extraordinary riddle to be found somewhere behind the armor of my faded leather and the midnight of my eyes.

"My blood, Laura. It's contaminated. And now so are you."

"That's why I hear when you're not there. Why my body physically aches for you."

The last sentence she said as a statement, not a question. Laura was beginning to understand the events and sequences that had led her to my front door. Whilst she was certainly not a vampire—not in the fanciful storybook sense of it—we had merged with one another. We were bonded by blood.

I let her do what she wanted with her hands. They traced the jagged, healed scar on my stomach. It was unbearable. I wanted her hands everywhere on me, quick and at once. I didn't know how much longer I could keep myself from her. From her skin . . . Piercing it. The lust I felt for her was intolerable. I wanted to be inside her. I wanted to taste her blood.

I took Laura to the small bed on the other side of the renovated loft. She came readily and pulled me down on top of her with more force than I'd expected. Heat radiated from her as she moved against me. For an instant I recognized the unmistakable look of fear in her eyes, but the manner in which her hips moved up to meet mine told me it was acceptable. To be expected. Again, it made me want her even more.

I wasn't going to tell her not to be scared when I myself wasn't even sure of what I was doing. Or if it was the right thing to do. My hand tugged at the fly of her jeans, the other on her hip, holding her down against the unyielding mattress. The breath caught in her throat when I became impatient with the buttons and yanked the remaining three open. The sound sent a creeping shiver down my rigid spine. It trailed sinuously from the base of my neck to the dip in the small of my back. My nipples were hard, stiff even before she'd touched them. When Laura bent her head down and took one between her lips I thought I was going to come.

In my mind's eye I saw the wino on the church steps from earlier that morning. Saw myself sitting next to Robyn with the Virgin Mary looking down on us . . .

"No—" I didn't mean to say it out loud. Laura seemed to know that it didn't mean she should stop what she was doing. She took my swollen nipple between her teeth and grazed it, sucking the hurt sympathetically from it afterward.

Something in me coiled tightly, and when I opened my eyes I had my hand down across her throat, fingers splayed, feeling the pulse of her life force. Tantalizingly hypnotic.

"Do it," Laura said, her back arching and her eyes closed. The rain came down in a torrent and the wind was chiming in wolfishly. I wasn't sure what she'd meant by the comment. Fuck her—or bite her.

She had her hand on mine, guiding me down past the borders of her underwear. White cotton. I briefly wondered at the rousing innocence of it. Was she Catholic?

"Lutheran," she breathed to my unasked question. Her eyes flickered open, surprised at the confession. She didn't think about it long, but I knew. Our thoughts were merging. I was relieved she didn't pay it much attention. I didn't want her to have access at what I was thinking. Not now. The last thing I wanted to do was scare her off.

"Alex, please—fuck me, please . . ."

I felt as if I'd been slapped. The effect of those words coming from her mouth. My hand was working between her legs, and Laura was hard and wet and when she thrust her hips up I had no choice but to enter her deeply. She scratched at my back, her nails digging into my skin painfully. Combined with the agonizing last inch my canines protruded to their full length, the hurt was enough to make me cry out. Laura opened her eyes and I was thrilled to see that she didn't seem to be afraid of what she saw.

I remember my first time clearly. Seeing those sharp pointed teeth was nothing if not visceral. Nothing to make you feel like something's prey than getting its teeth sunk into you. Or to make you pray. I had prayed. It hadn't helped me at all.

Laura turned her head sideways, exposing the milky skin of her neck and throat to me. A tight ache ripped through my groin at the consent she gave. My hand settled into a deliberate, close rhythm. As I fucked her, I brought my mouth into the hollow of her neck. Coiled muscles moved tightly beneath her skin. Gooseflesh pearled on its surface from my breath. Noise thumped and rushed in my ears. I felt dizzy. I closed my out-of-focus eyes.

Laura's breath came in short, sharp bursts as I slowly sank my teeth into her neck, only halfway at first. The rhythm of my hand between her legs dissipated to long, slow, deep thrusts. I wasn't sure if she was reacting to that, or my mouth at her neck.

*Both. Yes. Don't stop. Do it.*

I let go then and sank my teeth all the way into her neck. She gasped, eliciting a sexual grunt from me. I had one hand on her shoulder, holding her down. I'd forgotten how strong feeding made me. The effects were instantaneous.

Laura's blood tasted coppery. There was a faint, musky undertone. Excitement. And the barely recognizable taste of citrus.

She went limp beneath me as a second spurt splashed against the roof of my mouth. My own need cooled to some extent as her blood came into me. I sucked at her neck unhurriedly, savoring the taste, the moment, the incident. Her cunt was starting to tighten around my fingers and low moans echoed from her mouth into the cold, crisp air. Her blood coated the inside of my lips, syrupy and dangerously fulfilling.

*Is this what you wanted me to do, Robyn? You who cling to the old ways even though you're no longer part of it? Is it fair for you to tell me what to do? Well fuck fair or not, because now I've gone and done it.*

Laura cried out, a guttural, secret confession to the pleasure she was experiencing, but quite possibly didn't understand. I licked across the two puncture marks, my lips still fastened to her skin, and took one last selfish taste before pulling away. I finally swallowed the last drop of blood and immediately felt loss.

To my surprise Laura grabbed me, her hand behind my neck, hot and clammy, pulling me back down to her. I wouldn't have thought she'd have that much strength. I pushed her back onto the bed, maybe a bit too rough but I practically couldn't help myself. She picked herself up again though and pulled me close, making me kiss her.

She must have tasted her own blood in my mouth. It started out cautious but quickly turned into a greedy fight for dominance, in the process of which, she bit my lip just as an orgasm ripped through her. She finally let go then, as did I. As I lay next to her panting, the wave began to wash over me.

It began at my feet and coursed slowly up my legs. Hot, bubbling like something with too much fizz, it rolled along up my thighs, through my pelvis, past my hips, knotting briefly—intensely—in my stomach before exploding pleasurably throughout my body. I jerked and twitched, grabbed at the nearest thing—Laura's leg. Then her hand was in mine and I clamped it, felt like I was crushing it, but she did not complain.

And I heard her.

*Now I feel free.*

I wanted to reply by saying,

*I'm sorry . . . I couldn't help myself . . .*

Instead I said—

*You're mine now . . . we belong. We are one.*

The last thing I saw was her smile. Delirious and deadly. There was blood on the bottom corner of her lip.


Three weeks later.

I tossed the binoculars on the van's dashboard.

Fucking Iowa. Of all places, they come here. Covens of them. Bloody typical. And they prance around without even trying to disguise themselves. Why do they have to be so goddamn cocky? Don't they know that vampire hunters love the Midwest?

As I put the cigarette between my lips, Laura reached out and lit it. She was giving me that look again. The one that made me want to sink my teeth into her.

*What the fuck have you done?*

That's what my conscience sometimes asked me since that night in New York. Then she'd do something—say something—in a certain way that gave me an answer. It would be enough, until the question rolled around once more.

Robyn tells me to stop questioning my own actions. It's easy for her to say. She has the assurance and consistency of the church on her side. She'll tell me I can have it too, of course. I may be Episcopalian, but that certainly isn't my fault.

It's nice to have someone with me again. I've killed almost twice as many vampires since Laura and I bonded that night. She finds it exciting. I think her family is of the assumption that she doesn't want to be found. They would be right.

All of it is still so new to her. She relishes her vampire traits. Unlike me she tends not to shy away from them. Maybe I let her drink too much. Why? I have no idea. There are things in my life I do not understand.

I think I'm in love with her. I think I was the first time I saw her. That's not a good thing, is it? Robyn would tell me to trust my instincts.

For now, Laura seems content to follow my lead. When she needs to have it, I give her some of my own blood. Some days it makes me weak, but on others it gets me off to see her depend on me like that. She likes it when I fuck her afterward. She can't let go of the physical pleasure yet. Eventually she will. In due course, she won't need it anymore. Some days I am afraid of what will happen when that day finally comes. Nevertheless, Robyn had been right about one thing. It would have been unfair of me to leave her like that for the rest of her life. Not knowing. Not understanding. I opened my heart for one moment. I wonder now if it was a fatal mistake.

# The Specter of Sin
## Kristina Wright

It was just a dusty little honky-tonk outside Amarillo. Nothing much to distinguish it from any other cantina, except maybe the broad strokes of red paint that had faded to the color of dried blood, splashing out the name *Diablo's* across the front of the dilapidated shack.

Allie swiped the heels of her hands across her jeans to dry the sweat. Texas heat was like nothing she'd ever experienced. "Hotter than hell" might have been a cliché, but she was willing to bet it wasn't far from the truth.

The place was quiet and still, as if death itself shrouded the property. The only thing missing was a few tumbleweeds blowing across the gravel parking lot. She shook herself. Stupid. It was three o'clock in the afternoon, the place was closed. Nothing more, nothing less.

She took the rickety steps two at a time, afraid the boards would give beneath her. Breaking a leg wasn't on her list of things to do. Hell, she wasn't sure what she was doing here in the first place. Diablo's had been a story from her youth, a legend told over late-night beers at more reputable establishments far from here. Truth was, she'd come to find out if the story was true.

"Place is closed," came a woman's drawl from the recesses of the bar as soon as she pushed open the surprisingly sturdy door.

It seemed as if the door was better constructed than the entire building. An image flashed through her mind—a tornado sweeping the place away and leaving behind only one thick door as a reminder.

"I figured," Allie said, not retreating. After scorching her corneas in the Texas sun, it was taking her awhile to adjust to the dimness. She didn't think she was missing much.

"Car break down?"

She was getting closer to the voice, which sounded vaguely familiar. "No. Actually, I wondered if I could talk to you."

A bark of a laugh. "Talkin's free, which is why this place barely breaks even. No one wants to drink, everyone wants to talk." She didn't sound especially perturbed about it.

"It breaks even?" Allie couldn't keep the sarcasm from her voice.

The woman stood behind the bar, nearly six feet tall if she was an inch. Her breast and hips were narrow, but her shoulders were broad and her arms were well-defined. Someone would have to be really drunk or really stupid to want to tangle with her. Allie thought of another cliché about things being bigger in Texas. Hell, maybe there was a reason they were clichés.

The woman had an easy grin, open; it hardly seemed to fit her otherwise intimidating appearance. It was impossible to place her age; her face was weathered from too many years in the Texas sun.

"Yeah, hard to believe, huh?"

"Tell you what, if you'll talk to me, I'll have a beer." Allie pushed back a stool and was thankful to see that it appeared to be as sturdy as the door. "Maybe two, if you talk slow."

"Honey, that's probably the best offer I'll get today." She was already pouring whatever was on tap. "What are you? Tourist or academic?"

"Pardon?" Allie took a long pull from the beer. Happily, it wasn't flat. This place just kept getting better and better.

"Well, see, tourists come in with their Nikons strapped around their necks, itching for a story to take back to Tacoma or Baltimore or wherever the hell they're from." She leaned forward against the counter, resting her long fingers beneath her chin. "Then there're the professor types. Studious geeks in their button-down shirts and loafers, asking the most asinine questions in the most serious voices. I don't know which is worse."

"And which am I?" Allie asked, feeling suddenly weary.

She folded her fingers inward, like the old "Here's the church, here's the steeple" rhyme Allie remembered from her childhood, and studied her for a long moment. "Neither. Both. You're hard to figure."

From her tone, Allie took it as a compliment. "I've heard the story about this place all my life. I was in the area, so I thought I'd check it out."

"Friend tell you? Or lover?"

"Does it matter?"

That easy grin slid away. "Only to you."

"Is it true?" she asked, voice barely above a whisper. She'd blame it on the dry Texas air if anyone would ask, but she knew better. "The story about the woman in black?"

The woman's fingers were steepled again as she looked at Allie. She didn't answer the question. "I'm Gina Mitchell, by the way. I own the place." She glanced at her watch. "For a full month as of today."

Allie blinked at her, realized she'd been holding her breath the entire time Gina watched her, and breathed. "Alison—Allie—Tyler."

"Pretty name."

She was getting impatient, weariness sinking into her bones like sickness. "Can you tell me if the story is true?"

"Why does it matter so much?"

Allie wished she knew. She wished she could explain to Gina, to herself, why it had mattered at all. Why did it matter when nothing else seemed to? Yet here she was, running away, running from her past, running from the pain.

She shrugged. "Curious, I guess."

"I was too. It's why I bought the place, probably." Gina walked to the end of the bar and gestured toward a table. "C'mon. Place doesn't open for an hour."

The table was battle-scarred from one too many bar fights. Gina kicked a chair out for Allie and she took it, feeling oddly irritated by her solicitousness. They sat there, sizing each other up, for a full minute. Gina finally took a swig of her beer and slouched in her chair, stretching her long legs out in front of her. Her jeans were faded in a way that had nothing to do with fashion, the fabric stretched taut across muscular thighs.

"So?" Allie prompted when it looked like she might be settling in for a siesta instead of a story.

"Is it true, you want to know." Another swig of beer, then a shrug. "Hell if I know. I've only been here a month and I ain't seen no ghosts. It's usually the truckers and welders from the plant, stinkin' up the place and pullin' a knife once a week just for shits and giggles."

Allie felt a keen sense of disappointment. She'd hoped to find something—what, she didn't know—by making this trip. Something to give her hope, or at least make her believe there could be hope.

She made to stand, to get the hell out of there before she started crying over something so stupid as a fairy tale ghost story, but Gina's gravelly voice kept her in her seat.

"I'll tell you something, though. Every night when I shut this place up tight, I feel like I'm being watched." The words were melodramatic, but her face was dead serious. "There's something here; I can feel it."

Allie waited for her to say more. When she didn't, she tried to prod her along. "She was supposed to be passing through, just here for a night or two." She searched back through her memory, piecing together the tidbits of the story she could remember. Strange how something so important to her now hadn't really stayed with her all the times she'd heard it.

"Passing through?" Gina shook her head. "Way I heard it, she was a whore. She was supposed to have fucked just about every guy in the place. And most of the girls, too."

It was Allie's turn to shake her head. That wasn't how she'd heard it, it didn't sound right. It wasn't right. "No, she was broken-hearted because her lover left her for a man. She came here to confront him and she was raped and murdered." Allie swallowed hard. "Now she comes back and dances for the men, hoping to escape the pain. Hoping her lover will return to her."

Gina laughed. "Seems you know this story better than I do."

Allie slid her hand wearily across the moisture her glass had left on the table, bone-tired and ready to go home. "I don't know anything."

Gina reached across and took her hand, bringing it to her lips in a gesture that was fiercely tender and somehow out of place here. "Spoken like a true wise woman."

"No one knew her name," Allie whispered. "She told the men to call her Sin, so it was probably something like Cynthia."

"You believe all this, don't you?"

Allie didn't know what she believed, she only knew how it felt to be loved and rejected and feel as if she would never survive the loss. She stood up, shaking off her melancholy. "It doesn't matter. It's the past. The past is as dead as Sin."

Crossing to the decrepit jukebox in the corner, she said over her shoulder, "Does this thing work?"

Gina nodded. "Barely. I can't afford to replace it with one of the new CD models."

Allie fished a quarter out of her jeans pocket and put it in the slot, hearing the soft "plink" as it hit the cash box. She punched a number she knew from memory, another little nugget of the story. In a moment, the old 45 record glided into place and the needle touched down, filling the air with the melancholy strains of some old country-western tune she didn't recognize at first. Then it was as if her soul remembered and she began to sway, dancing to a tune another woman had danced to, another woman had died to.

She held her hand out to Gina. "Dance with me," she murmured, her words not carrying above the music.

It didn't matter. Gina knew what she wanted and she stood, trance-like, and took her hand. Allie slid into her arms in one smooth, sensuous movement, liking the way Gina cradled her against her shoulder. They danced, slow and easy, pressed shoulder to hip, as the music surrounded them. Allie rubbed her breasts against Gina's chest, her nipples hardening.

"I can't do this," Gina said against her hair. "God, I want to, but I gotta open the bar soon."

She pressed her fingers to her lips. "Ssh. We're just dancing."

But it wasn't just dancing, and Allie knew it. The tempo of the song changed, becoming a driving beat of guitar and drums, and she swiveled her hips against Gina, wanting to make her ache the way she ached, wanting to fill her needs.

"Damn, baby, you're drivin' me crazy," Gina rasped, her Texas twang becoming more pronounced.

Allie didn't know what she was doing, or why. She was just so tired of running and looking for something that didn't exist. "I need you to fuck me. I need it."

This time, there was no argument, no mention of the bar that would be opening soon. Gina danced her back to the table, her strong hands gliding down Allie's back to stroke her ass. When the back of Allie's legs bumped the table, Gina steadied her, palming her crotch with her large hand.

Allie moaned and pressed against her, hooking one leg around Gina's hip. "God, I need you," she said again. How long had it been? How long had she been alone? It didn't matter now, Gina was what she needed.

Gina pushed her back across the table. Her fingers fumbled with the snap on Allie's jeans and she growled in frustration. Then, suddenly, the snap and zipper came undone, easily, readily. She yanked Allie's jeans and panties down while Allie braced herself on the table, raising her ass.

"My boots," Allie gasped, as Gina jerked her pants lower.

Gina stripped off her boots hurriedly, as if she'd done it a thousand times before. Then Allie's jeans and panties were on the floor, her bare ass on the rough-hewn table. Allie spread her legs and fingered herself, holding her lips open, showing Gina how wet and ready she was.

Gina stared at her, at her wide-open cunt, while she yanked the zipper down on her own jeans. "I'm going to fuck you so hard," she promised.

Allie believed her.

She reached out to Gina, wanting to feel her. Gina straddled Allie's thigh and Allie slid her hand down the front of her jeans. Gine was as wet and ready as Allie. She groaned at Allie's touch, and began to grind against her hand as if possessed.

They were both possessed, Allie thought. Driven by the same need, the same urge. Her skin prickled despite the heat, and she felt suddenly chilled.

"Did you feel that?" Gina asked, looking around. "Wind."

"She's watching," Allie whispered, guiding Gina's hand between her spread legs. "She wishes it were her."

Gina opened her mouth as if to argue, but Allie slid a finger into her cunt and stroked her G-spot hard, her finger curling up and forward. Panting, Gina leaned over her and palmed Allie's cunt, squeezing it hard before thrusting three—or was it four?— fingers inside.

Allie winced, but didn't tell her to stop. If it had been another lover she would have complained about her lack of subtlety. But now there was no need for gentle foreplay, no reason to take their time. She was hot and wet and aching, ready to be fucked.

Gina wasn't gentle or easy with her. Her fingers felt like they were bruising her insides, forcing their way into her body roughly even though she was slick and swollen and wet. She dug her nails into the table, leaving her own scars as she bit back a scream. The jukebox had long since gone silent and the only sounds in the bar were Gina's ragged breathing and the rhythmic squeak of the table legs as they fucked.

"So damn tight," Gina said through gritted teeth. "So wet."

Allie didn't need words or sounds; she needed only the fingers inside her, filling her, filling the ache with a solid hardness. "Shut up and fuck me," she said.

Allie slid her finger from Gina's drenched cunt and up to her swollen clit, stroking it steadily while Gina fucked her. She felt like her wrist was going to snap from the awkwardness of being pressed between Gina's crotch and her own thigh, but she kept stroking Gina, driven by her lust.

Allie felt her orgasm climbing up from her belly, spreading like fire through her veins. She bucked against Gina, taking her fingers a little deeper, forcing her to fuck her a little harder as splinters pricked her fingertips. The table groaned with the weight of them both as Gina's feet came off the ground, her body grinding against Allie's thigh.

Allie came before she did, but only by seconds. She opened her mouth and screamed, a banshee wail of pain and longing and desire so long unfulfilled. Gina was right behind her, quieter but coming just as hard if the fingers driving into Allie's cunt were any indication.

Gina propped herself up on her left arm and watched Allie as their breathing slowly returned to normal. Allie wanted Gina to move, but she didn't want to offend her, so she closed her eyes instead. Gina pulled away then, her fingers slipping from Allie's body so gently it made her gasp. Her cunt felt raw, abused. Empty. She drew her legs together, feeling the muscles protest, and sat up.

Gina kissed her softly and she stiffened in surprise. "Thanks, honey. You are incredible."

The words meant nothing, now that they were through. Allie bent to retrieve her jeans but Gina beat her to it, handing them and her panties to her. She mumbled a soft "thank you" and blinked back tears. She figured Gina thought she was embarrassed because she pulled her close and hugged her.

"You look exhausted. My office is in back. Why don't you curl up on the couch and take a nap." Gina stroked her hair gently, her hand curving around the back of her neck. "I'll wake you later."

Allie nodded, too tired to argue or be annoyed at Gina's unnecessary kindness. Scooping up her discarded boots, she padded toward the back of the bar. Exhaustion settled over her like a pall as she pulled her clothes on, not bothering to clean up. She fell asleep on the couch with the smell of leather and sex filling her senses.

She woke, not sure how long she'd been asleep. The bar was noisy, raucous, discordant. She shook off the remnants of sleep and pulled her boots on. She needed to leave. Now. Before Gina came back. Before she had to face what she'd done.

She peeked out the office door and saw Gina, her back to Allie as she talked to a washed-out blonde. Allie walked through the crowded bar, feeling conspicuous even though no one paid any mind. She slipped out the door, past two burly-looking bikers, and nearly lost her footing on the battered steps.

She felt cleansed, renewed. The tiredness of earlier had eased and she felt ready to run a marathon. The air was dry and still, missing the life and vitality of inside the bar. She walked past the cars and motorcycles, feeling suddenly disoriented. She had ventured beyond the gravel of the parking lot and now stood at the edge of the road. A car went by, lights bright and nearly blinding in such utter darkness.

"Oh my God." A woman's voice, high-pitched and frightened. "Oh my God, do you see her?"

Allie whirled, but there was nothing behind her. She was still seeing spots from the headlights, her night vision lost. "What?" she asked, voice sounding paper-thin. "See what?"

"Holy hell." It was Gina's voice, no trace of humor or intimacy now, only surprise and something like fear. "Allie? Alison?"

Allie. Alison. Sin. The names were a jumble in her head, she couldn't make out who was calling her anymore, couldn't hear Gina over the din of other voices, older voices. Frightening voices.

Something was wrong with her eyes, her night vision wasn't coming back the way it should. She stumbled forward, onto the gravel, going to her knees. Stones bit into her skin, even through the heavy denim of her jeans. She reached out, blindly.

"Please," she said. "Please." She fell forward, gravel beneath her cheek, hard and unyielding. Darkness engulfed her, pulling her down into a dizzying pit of pain and fear. "Please, no. Not again."

# Captus in Fuga
### Cynthia Glinick

From the time I was a child, I have always had a keen interest in birds and women. Year-round bird feeders in our suburban back-yard, and a comfy window seat, ensured hours of finches, robins, chickadees, cardinals, blue jays, and grackles. I had a babysitter, Annie, an ethereal young woman who also had a thing for birds. She wore feather earrings and flowing clothes and I liked to think that she flew to and from my house.

One day Annie and I were in the backyard. She was lying on a picnic blanket beneath my favorite shade tree and I was bored like a nine-year-old gets, pulling up grass with my toes and trying to get her attention.

Suddenly, all the birds flew off at once, as though someone had fired a starting gun. I knew, from my many observances, that it was more than our presence. A falcon was poised on a branch of the shade tree. Annie pulled me by the hand to sit quietly next to her. I wanted to please her and was as still as could be. A squirrel above us was motionless too. The falcon swooped down and back up within seconds, a mouse wriggling from its claws. I was thrilled at having my first out-of-the-ordinary birding experience with my bird-like babysitter.

I still love to watch and feed birds, but my long-awaited,

second, out-of-the-ordinary birding experience did not happen at a refuge or any of the migratory spots where hawks and falcons can be seen in this early autumn. It happened at the place where I was working.

I am a carpenter by trade and I was busily replacing some old, rotted boards on the wraparound porch of a summer home situated on Namquid Bay. Birds are easier to hear than to see and since I have a good ear I've been able to memorize the songs, chirps, and whistlings of my avian neighbors.

I heard a loud and plaintive bird call that day that was completely unfamiliar to me. I looked up toward the sound and there, clinging to the low roof, was a cockatiel. The gray body, white wing bars, yellow head and crest with the characteristic bright orange cheek spots betrayed his gender. Since cockatiels are not a native species, I had to assume it was an escaped pet. I was intrigued and watched as the bird flew down to the ground near me and waddled in my direction. I spoke softly and encouragingly as I held out my arm as a perch. He flew and landed on my hand, making his way expertly to my shoulder, anxious for familiar human contact. I sat on the edge of the porch, wondering what to do with this wonderful creature, who made his way from my shoulders to my head and up and down my arms, peeping incessantly. He was very composed as I called the Animal Rescue League and the Humane Society without any luck. I finally hit pay dirt when a veterinarian told me that she'd gotten a call about a week ago from a woman who'd reported her cockatiel missing. With her name and number in hand, I called immediately.

"Hi. I'm looking for Annie Covington?"

"This is Ani," the woman replied, pronouncing her name like Ah—nee.

"Hi, my name is Natalie Johns. Are you, by any chance, missing a cockatiel?"

"Yes, I am," she said in astonishment.

"Well, I think I may have found him." I described his plumage and asked his name.

"His name is Sammy."

"Sammy?" I called to him and he jumped around, animatedly. "Yep, it's Sammy all right."

"How did you find him?"

"He found me," I said.

"This is wonderful. I gave him up for dead. Where are you?"

I gave her the address of the house along with directions, and she said she would be here as soon as she could.

While I waited, Sammy continued to repeatedly walk up and down my arms and across my shoulders, nibbling at my earlobes and lips, which I took as affection until I realized he was probably very hungry. I found no birdseed in the house, but I did find some crackers and I gave him a dish of water. Who knew how long he'd been flying around hungry and disoriented? He ate avidly, all the while gripping my shirt and nibbling at the cracker. His repast done, I tried to put him down but he staunchly refused to leave his newfound perch. He sat on my outstretched arm, looking at me and "talking." I spoke some gentle words I thought a bird would appreciate and after an hour had passed, I thought we understood each other quite well. I'd grown fond of him.

I heard, before I saw, a vintage Volvo station wagon coming down the road. With the late afternoon sun in my eyes, I saw behind the wheel an older woman with shoulder-length dark hair. She pulled into the driveway and I walked over to meet her. As I stepped into the shadow of the garage I realized I was mistaken. The glare had played tricks with my vision because she was in her mid-thirties, with honey-blonde hair pulled back into a loose ponytail. She wore sandals and a floral print summer dress to mid thigh that flattered her slender figure. The features of her face were classic movie star; in other words, she was breathtakingly stunning.

"Hi," I said, "I'm Natalie." I reached out my hand, which she took warmly into her own, searching me with extraordinary green eyes. I was drawn into them and held her gaze. Then Sammy began peeping excitedly and jumped around wildly from my shoulders to my head and back again.

"Thank you so much," she said, looking at Sammy and then back at me with interest.

We spoke for a moment about Sammy's escape, his will to survive and good nature. She was relaxed and chatty.

"Where do you live?" I asked

"In Wilmont Cove."

I knew the area. It was a good forty miles across the bay "as the crow flies," even farther by car. I'd heard stories of birds getting blown out to sea and hitching rides on ships. Sammy's route was anyone's guess. As Ani reached out for him, he flew off a short distance to the roof, where he fluttered around nervously, still peeping animatedly. Ani reached up for him with her long slender arm. Her dress lifted and I could see more of her tanned thighs. A woman with leisure time, I thought. We waited for him to settle down.

"I hope he hasn't been too much trouble."

"He's been a little jumpy, I guess, and talked to me a lot."

"Talked to you?" she said with alarm in her voice and threw a cautionary look toward Sammy on the roof.

"Well, you know what I mean, that peeping."

"Oh, I see," she said, visibly relaxing. Sammy flew down to my shoulder again. "He seems to like you," and she added with a quick laugh, "he has good taste."

"Well, I've come to like him, too. He's been a wonderful companion," I said to her, and then to Sammy, "c'mon, it's time to go home." I tried to reach for him but he backed away.

"He does this sometimes," she said, looking at him sitting on my shoulder and pecking at my earlobe. She took a few careful steps forward and repeated his name slowly, even hypnotically. She stood very close to me, and I could smell her scent. It was lovely; a subtle mix of floral perfume and the sun on her skin. As she plucked him off my shoulder, she momentarily rested her hand on my forearm. I felt a thrill run through me.

Enveloped in her hands, Sammy was now completely docile. In fact, if I hadn't just seen his animation I'd have thought him fully asleep. It was a very curious thing. As we walked to her car, she said, "Thank you again. It was so kind of you to go to so much trouble."

"Oh no, it was no trouble, believe me. This was way more interesting than what I was supposed to be doing." I gestured toward the unfinished porch.

She placed Sammy in a cage in the back of her car. I opened her door for her but she didn't get in. Instead, she turned and perused the porch.

"You're a carpenter?"

"Yes."

"I thought so by your hands. They're rough, yet strong." She took my hands in hers and studied them a moment, then said, "I have some things that need work. Would you be willing to take a look at them?"

"Of course."

"Call me," she said.

"I will." I watched her slide into the driver's seat and glance at her perfect lips in the mirror. "I definitely will."

As I walked back toward the house I saw a white feather in the grass and smiled to myself that Sammy had left me a present. I picked it up and put it in my pocket.


I called Ani a few days later. In the background I heard the chattering of birds. She must have a house full of them, I thought.

"I was wondering when a good time would be to come see what you need done?"

"Can you come later this afternoon?" she asked. "Around five-thirty?"

"Um, yes. Yes, I can."

"Do you know Wilmont Cove?"

"Somewhat."

"If you follow the old road down toward the water, you'll see a lane on the left just before the road bends right. Take that. The house is set back."

Wilmont Cove was a small summer community on a crooked finger of land jutting out into the lower part of Namquid Bay. A couple of summers ago, a community of wild parrots took up residence there, disturbing the power and phone lines and generally becoming a nuisance. The authorities were eventually called in to "relocate" them, but when they arrived the parrots had mysteriously vacated.

It would be hard to get lost in such a small area, but her dirt lane was well hidden. I nearly missed it and as I was pulling in, a flock of crows blasted from a treetop with a terrible racket and settled on another tree across the road, all the while scolding me. My right tire went into a precipitous hole and out again with a thunk. I parked alongside her old Volvo.

The small house was nestled among hedges and bracken, and the tree cover was so dense I doubted the place got any sun in the spring and summer. It was damp and chilly, even on this warm autumn evening. As I walked up to the door, I heard a sound that made me look up. In the dimness, sitting about six feet above my right shoulder and silhouetted on a thin tree branch, was a beautiful white dove. It regarded me with curiosity, taking my measure, turning its head this way and that. I knocked on the door and waited. When there was no immediate answer, I knocked again. With a clapping of wings, the dove flew around the side of the house. I followed. All the windows were dark, and I saw the house was nothing more than a converted summer cottage with a series of rambling additions made to it. Around the back was a small ramshackle shed, which the dove entered through a small opening. I turned toward the back of the cottage, looking for another way in.

"Oh, I didn't hear you arrive." Ani emerged from the darkness of the shed. Her voice startled me. I stood for a moment, composing myself and taking her in, since I was always a person who noticed details. Her T-shirt outlined her small and supple breasts, and tight jeans emphasized her hips; her hair was up, with wisps of lovely strands caressing the back of her neck. She had a casual elegance about her. That was it; I couldn't place it when I first met her. An elegant ethereal quality, as if no one could really know her.

"Did I frighten you?" she asked. I smiled in reply. She went on, "I was just tending to my dove."

"Yes, I saw it as I came in. It's beautiful." I poked my head inside, and saw a cage, but it was empty. Standing this close to her sent a thrill through me.

She smiled and said, "This shed is what I need help with. But I wonder if you'd like to visit Sammy first? He'll be happy to see you, I imagine."

With a quick squeeze of my arm she led me toward the house. I felt a little foolish tensing my bicep in response. I wondered if it was not only Sammy who was happy to see me. It seemed a little lonely out here.

The inside of her house was just as maze-like as the outside, and as we entered I heard chirping and screeching. She had four birdcages; two contained species I didn't recognize, one was empty, and in the last was Sammy. I went over to it, and he peeped and flapped his way across his cage to greet me. I was delighted by his eager welcome.

"What are these other birds?"

"That's Chester," she said, pointing to a diminutive, brownish green bird with an orange breast. "He's a gold-breasted waxbill. And that one is Barbarossa, a ribbon finch, also known as a cut-throat." I could see why the latter name applied and why it had an alternate one. The bird was a light gray color with a striking red stripe across its throat.

"Barbarossa?"

"It means Red-beard."

"What was in this cage?"

"Oh, that's for my next acquisition."

"What are you getting?"

"That remains to be seen," she said with a mysterious smile as she walked into the kitchen.

"Can I take Sammy out?" I asked, ready to open the cage.

"I haven't let him out since he flew away that last time," she called.

I was crestfallen. I really wanted to hold him again, and it seemed nothing short of cruel to me that a bird, that had had a taste of freedom was now relegated to a small cage. Perhaps the reason for the closed feeling of the place was to not excite his anticipation.

"How did he get out?"

"My mistake. When I was cleaning his cage, I'd forgotten that I'd left the back door open and that was it." I thought her story plausible, but something told me there was more to it.

While she was speaking I stuck my index finger through the bars, and he pecked at it happily. His mirror dangled freely from the top of the cage, and I noticed as it swung around that a photograph of a man had been placed across the back of it. I was about to ask about it when she came and stood next to me at the cage. "Oh! What's happened there?"

"What?" I asked, in confusion.

"Your finger, look," she said, reaching out to my hand. I looked down and saw that my finger was bleeding. I hadn't noticed, but I never do. Working as a carpenter I often get cuts and bruises and never know how they happened. "Let me get you something," she said, moving away.

"I think Sammy got a little carried away."

"Sammy did that?" she asked, with some alarm.

"It's all right. It's my fault," I said. "I teased him, I think, by putting my finger into his cage." She looked over at him and a shadow of emotion fell across her face. I couldn't be sure what it was, but it seemed like more than just concern. For a split second, I had the image of two lovers involved in a quarrel. I examined my finger. It was just a superficial cut, a tissue would have done to stop the bleeding, but she came back with a box of bandages. I let her take my hand in hers and very gently swab it and put some kind of salve on it before wrapping a Band-Aid around it. She did this gently and with tremendous care and I watched her face and hands while she worked, finding her more and more beautiful. Her touch was exquisite.

"There," she said, and maybe it was my imagination but she seemed to purse her lips slightly to kiss . . . my finger?

I looked into her eyes for a long, slow moment. The image of kissing her came to me and I very nearly did, but restrained myself. Something about her look bothered me. It was calculating; sizing me up. "Thank you," I said, and changing the subject asked how long she had been keeping birds.

"Pretty much my whole life. My first bird was a canary when I was seven. My grandmother got it for me right after my father left me."

"Left you?"

"Died. He traveled abroad in his job and they think he picked up some kind of parasite. By the time they'd gotten him to an American hospital, he was gone. I never even got to say good-bye. But he was always leaving and it finally came to an end. It was just my father and me, you see." As her mood shifted, she fell into a kind of reverie and her eyes took on a stony quality. I felt uncomfortable with the tenor of her tale and stayed silent. But when she recomposed herself, she brightened and looked at me warmly. "Well, should we look at the shed while there's still some daylight?"

As we went outside, I noticed an eerie calm to her dwelling. Despite the number of birds, both inside and out, it was dead silent. She led me through the shed door, which was falling off its hinges. The chicken wire cage I had seen earlier was still without its dove and the adjacent wall was beginning to rot away. I examined it more closely.

"It looks as though you need to have the studs replaced and the siding, as well. It's very damp on this side, but it's not terrible. And there's this door, of course. I can relocate the hinges. The door itself seems sound."

"So, you'll do this for me?"

"Yes, I'd be happy to."

I made a plan to start work the following week. As I started to leave, she reached out and lightly stroked my arm with her nails. Her touch was oddly reminiscent of Sammy's small claws. "Thank you so much." I had a strong urge to take her in my arms.

As I drove home, I was flooded with images of her. By the end of the weekend I was obsessed.

I've had good luck with women, generally speaking. I'm used to working alone with only the woman of the house present, and often they start out a little curious about me and wind up sitting on the counter, swinging their legs and chatting away. They know I'm in charge, capable, and professional and not about to take advantage of the situation. That is, unless the offer is too delicious to resist. But there was something different about Ani. A little menacing, perhaps? Seductive yet removed. Like this was a game she played often.

Monday was a picture-perfect autumn day; clear blue sky, moderate temperatures, and a slight breeze. I loaded my truck with my tools and materials and headed to Wilmont Cove. As I pulled into the driveway, Ani came out of the house to greet me. Seeing her again was like taking a long, cold drink of water on a hot beach. I could feel something stir inside of me, although I tried to maintain my cool the whole ride out there.

"I have to leave for a while today," she said, coldly I thought. "Is there anything you need before I go?"

I was disappointed, and while I would have liked to tell her I needed her, I replied, "No, I don't think so."

"I'll leave the house open. Please feel free to use it," she said, throwing a look over her shoulder.

I reluctantly got to work, but my full attention was not on it, and after a while I stopped. I was enormously curious about how she lived and after a few furtive glances around, I decided to scope out the house. It was completely still; even the dust motes seemed to hang motionless in the air. I walked gingerly through the circuitous house, aware that (despite her open invitation) the spirit of my mission was tantamount to trespassing. I carefully opened and closed every door, peering into each room. On the right-hand wall of the living room I found her bedroom. The curtains were pulled and it was dark; the only light came through the now open door. It had a strong smell of incense, and scattered throughout the room were candles, some burned down with drippings of dried wax. Her bed was covered with a dark patchwork quilt, and the walls were hung with fabric that draped over the bed like a tent. The room was so contrary to who Ani appeared to be. She seemed sophisticated, urban, but the room had an old and oppressive feel to it. I became uneasy and backed out of the room.

The birds were quiet in their cages. I went over to take a look at Barbarossa, who was asleep on his perch. Something shiny at the bottom of the cage caught my eye. It was his fallen bell, but it drew my attention to his mirror, which, like in Sammy's cage, had a photograph of a man taped across it. I looked at Chester's cage, and his mirror did as well. I wondered why Ani would do such a thing, and a chill ran through me. I felt the air to be very close, and with goose bumps forming on my skin, I exited the house with the sensation of something at my back.

I resumed my work and did as much as I could, but my attention was split and I just couldn't focus. The daylight was fading fast anyway, so I decided to quit and started packing up my things. The dove flew past me, startling me with its sudden appearance. It hadn't been around at all, no doubt disturbed by the commotion. Ani arrived as well.

"Hi," she said with a bright smile that pulled me in once again. "Are you finished?"

"For today," I said, the uneasiness I felt earlier disappearing. She looked lovely in a soft blouse and skirt, the evening sun giving a glow to her soft skin. She wrapped her arms around herself against the chill, and I could see the skin on her smooth legs turn to goose bumps. It was all I could do to not lift her up and carry her into the warm house. The house; how strangely different it was than she.

"I'll make you some tea before you leave."

I'm not normally a tea drinker, but I found myself saying yes. She went into the house and I continued to clean up. As I re-entered the house I had been so anxious to leave just minutes before, I was filled with a curious feeling of anticipation. She came out of the kitchen with two mugs of tea that smelled exotic. We sat together on an old couch that had seen better days; in fact, the house was filled with secondhand furniture (perhaps they were family bequests or she couldn't afford better?) and we looked at each other over our mugs.

"How did it go today?" she asked, with a smile.

"I still have a little work to do. Just a small area of clapboards." The tea went down easily. "What kind of tea is this?"

"It's my own concoction. A blend of assam, hibiscus, lavender, and a little special something." Her eyes twinkled at me over the brim of her mug.

I took another sip and looked at her looking at me. She was, without a doubt, the most stunningly beautiful creature I had ever seen. The tea flowed through me and made me feel heady and potent. She took the mug from my hand. It was so quiet I could hear her breath grow shallow. Her lips parted; she beckoned me with her eyes; I leaned toward her. I could smell the scent of her—flowers and sunshine. She put her hand on my face. Her lips touched mine, and then she pulled away as if contemplating me. I could barely stand it. I pressed her into the couch with my body, my lips tight against hers. Her hands moved lightly over me, then she caught me by the shoulders and pushed me gently away. "I hope this is okay," she said, without any question in her tone.

"Yes." I was too lost in her to have a conversation about the ethics of work and play.

She gave me a coy smile, put her arms around me, and pulled me into her. Everything inside me responded acutely. I wanted this woman more than any woman in my life. My hands searched out the curve of her back, her waist, her shoulders, her face. I felt her hands all over me in an ardent embrace. She pulled me to my feet and led me into her room. She lay down on the bed and I leaned over her. In the veiled light, she looked dark and different. I looked into her green eyes and felt myself getting lost in their depths. Her eyes called to me, beckoned me to join her somewhere. I felt compelled to go but was disoriented by the power of it. I felt my will to resist ebbing and began a precipitous descent into her. I buried my face in her neck and pressed my hips against her. She gasped. I wondered if she knew how much power a female could possess. Had she ever been with a woman before? I felt her pulling at my clothing and then her hands and nails ran along my sides and back. "You're strong for a . . ." she whispered, but I kissed her before she could finish. I was strong; that's all there was to it. I was filled with lust for this woman. I needed to taste her skin, feel her yield to my hands. Our lips locked and she moved against me rhythmically. I pulled up her shirt, took her hard nipple into my mouth and teased the other with my rough fingers. She moaned, and almost made me laugh by asking if the finger Sammy bit was okay. "Shhhh," I said, smiling at how undone she was. I was in control.

She kissed my Sammy-bitten finger. I let her grab at my flesh, but stopped her when she unbuttoned my fly. I needed to savor her first. I followed the line of her body with my tongue, while squeezing her soft, quivering thighs. She slid her skirt off in one swift move. She was eager for my mouth on her and lifted her hips to show me, while her pleading eyes looked into mine. I held her hips and let my tongue meander along the contours of her belly. I was in no rush. I felt her hands going down my pants and I took them in mine and kissed them. "Not yet," I said.

My fingers slid easily into her. She gasped and held my head, pulled my hair, dug her nails into my shoulders. With my fingers deep inside her I lifted her small body to my mouth. She murmured, "Oh yes . . ." I could taste her, inside and out, as I moved my fingers rhythmically, feeling the heat of her desire. I was bursting with need by now, and I guided her hand down my pants, pressing her fingers against me. Allowing her to touch me after several attempts aroused her even more, and she lifted her hips as she came hard against my mouth. I wanted to yell out, the pleasure she gave me was so intense, but instead I clenched my teeth and then kissed her deep and hard, feeling her pulsate against my now still fingers.

I looked at her and my eyes were playing tricks on me because she looked completely different. I pulled away, gasping for air. Suddenly, one of the birds began screeching at full volume. I snapped to and realized it was Sammy. I turned in his direction.

"Are you all right?" she asked, placing her hand on my shoulder. I looked at her again, but she was unchanged. My head throbbed and spun around, disorienting me.

"Yes, I think so. Did you . . . ?" I decided not to speak my thought, that she was really two women; it sounded crazy, even to me.

"Did I what?"

" . . . hear Sammy just then?"

"Yes, why?"

"I don't know."

"You sure you're okay?"

"Yes."

"That was incredible," she said, running her hand through my hair.

I still felt odd. Her face, the bird. I got up to use the bathroom.

When I came back, she was fully dressed and waiting for me by the bed. I told her I had to leave. She was disappointed.

"I understand," she said.

What she understood I didn't know, but she took my hand in hers, kissed it, and led me outside.

"It's so dark around here," I said, looking up for stars and seeing none.

"It's mostly summer cottages and they're closed for the season so there's not much light at night. There's only one other year-round resident. He lives behind me through the woods." She gave my hand a squeeze. "I want you to come back."

Thankfully I couldn't see her eyes, but her words pushed against my uncertainty and I yielded. "Of course, I'll be back. I have at least one job to finish," I said, trying to add levity to what was an increasingly odd situation.

"Tomorrow?"

I felt the push again. "Yes."

Still holding my hand, she kissed me lightly and I got into my truck. The sound of the engine was harsh against the stillness and as I backed out, my headlights swept across her, throwing a strange, elongated shadow of her against the house.

On the way home I tried but could make no sense of what happened, except to say that I'd lost myself utterly. My mind, body, and even my spirit, I suspected, had been perilously close to dissolution. I vowed to gain some control and yet, it had been an amazing sexual experience.

That night my sleep was restless and disturbed by dreams filled with tortured feelings and images. I dreamed that I was at the top of a tree, grasping at a flimsy branch, while gale-strength winds threatened to blow me off. A woman with long, black hair and red fingernails asked me to fix the dashboard of her car with roofing shingles. I tried, but somehow got locked inside. I was grateful for the arrival of morning.

I got to her house late the next day. There were only a few hours of work remaining, and when I pulled into her lane and parked, it was with a combination of dread and longing.

As I came around the side of the house, tool bag in hand, I heard loud voices inside. From their manner, it sounded like a heated discussion on the verge of an out-and-out argument. I put down my bag and quietly let myself in the back door. I saw Ani with a man. They were clearly having a disagreement. The man was shouting and gesturing aggressively. I felt immediately protective of Ani and said, "What's going on?" They both stopped, surprised by my presence.

No one spoke for a few seconds and then the man said, "We're just having a neighborly discussion."

"Yes, I can tell from your tone. The whole neighborhood can hear."

"Who the hell are you, anyway?"

"This is my friend. She's come to fix the shed," Ani said, more evenly.

"Well, she can stay the hell out of this."

I moved closer to Ani and asked, "Are you all right?"

"Yes. Come outside with me for a moment," she said. I followed her out the back door.

"What's going on?" I asked.

"He's . . . It's a long story."

I wasn't at all certain that I wanted to hear that story. I felt like I was, again, interrupting a lovers' quarrel; an image I was loath to engage. Her eyes were cold and had a faraway look to them, and for once were not focused on me.

"If there's any way I can help . . ."

"Thank you, but no. I have to handle this as I've done before," she said, walking back into the house and leaving me alone.

So, she'd had dealings with this man previously. I suspected he was the other year-round resident. I heard no more of them, and over the next two hours I replaced the remaining pieces of clapboard siding. When the job was done I went inside in search of her.

The house was dark and so still it seemed completely airless. I heard a faint sound and followed it to her closed bedroom door. It sounded like sobbing and just as I was about to turn the knob, I stopped. It was sobbing, but it was also something else, like a mantra. It was a strange sound, the peculiar words making no sense. But whatever they were, it sent chills up my spine. I heard a muffled cry and without a moment's hesitation, I burst through the door.

The room was ablaze with the light of a dozen or more candles. The same woman I'd seen driving up to the beach house, coming out of the shed, in my arms and in my tortured dreams, was standing at the foot of the bed; beside her was an empty birdcage. The shadows, cast by the candles, made it feel as though the room itself was a cage and we in it. On the bed, lying supine, was the man. His skin was stuck all over with feathers. My God, I thought, she's tarring and feathering him! Nothing could be worth that. The woman turned and looked at me. She had Ani's eyes and the same hypnotic quality. I felt myself being drawn into them. She continued her rhythmic and soporific litany. "Drepanididae, drepanis, oscines, passerines." I saw nothing but her eyes, compelling me and pulling me into her sphere. I moved toward her. "Drepanididae, drepanis, oscines, passerines." With each step I felt myself weakening. "Drepanididae, drepanis, oscines, passerines." The man screamed, and a searing pain shot through my body. My legs gave out and I fell to my knees. The droning of the unbroken chant continued and the man's ululations were hideous and pitiable; like an animal, being eaten alive. I saw her raise something shiny that looked like a knife and she held it over the man's body. I forced myself to rise and threw myself at her. "No!" I cried, as I crashed into her and we both fell to the floor.

I tried to focus and I saw that the shiny object wasn't a knife. It was a mirror. I looked from the woman to the man, and in an instant I realized the horrible truth. My stomach heaved with terror and disbelief. The man was not being tarred and feathered; through some impossible kind of witchery, he was being morphed into the bird version of himself.


I reached into my pocket, took out Sammy's feather, and placed it on the table before me I as read the newspaper account. Through an anonymous tip, the police found Samuel Erhard of New River, Chester Murray of Weston, and R. Thomas DeSilva of Long Point at a residence in an isolated section of Wilmont Cove on Tuesday. The men had been missing since June. Donald Marshfield of Wilmont Cove was also found at the scene. All are hospitalized with undisclosed injuries. Their alleged abductor, Ani Covington, and an unknown accomplice are still at large. In what the police believe to be a bizarre related incident, the family pet, a ringed-neck dove, was found dead in its cage, its neck broken.

# Cinnamon Toast
### Nancy Sahra

Several acres away from the house and barn, a family cemetery sits coldly alone, centered in a drove of old maple trees where the shadows are deepest. A line of low hills—the steps to the Berkshire Mountains—rise at the edge of the pastures.

Always hungry and oblivious to the cold, a lone red fox carefully hurries along an ancient rock fence, casting an enormous eerie silhouette across the damp grass as he occasionally stops, yowling at the silver and white celestial rays as if chasing away ghosts.

The last slice of autumn has fallen to the ground, a blaze of color in daylight, at night just a pile of pungent, frostbitten moldy leaves.

Although the exterior of the three-story white farmhouse shows the wear and tear of two hundred years of harsh New England winters, the interior is warm and well maintained, furnished with spectacular antiques.

"Atmosphere," Zoë is fond of saying, "is the foundation for nurturing friendship."

From the outside, the house is quiet. Inside, slices of the moon slither through the tiny openings at the corners of the stained glass windows, casting dancing prisms that disappear into the folds of the thick mauve drapes. Dark, nearly black polished wood runs along the edges of the ceiling and over the mantel, showing the wondrous craftsmanship of another era. Zoë Quinn's philosophic words seem correct; her house is a natural gathering place, a safe haven for a multitude of friends.

"I just stood there. Ten years of self-defense training. A black belt in karate, mind you, and I was as immobile as a scared kid on the playground." Concise as it was, Shawn's observation carried something more tangible, a sense of deep fear.

She tasted bile as her throat convulsed noticeably. Her voice rose in remembered panic. "And now, thirty-six hours later, I can still hear that poor man's screams. See his body twisting, trying to break free. In the half light, his face was hollow, white with terror, and his black eyes helpless. It was as if his attacker was a sorceress casting a spell that rendered him immobile." Shawn O'Conner drew in a deep breath, the impression forever etched in her mind. Her mouth formed words that would not come.

She is nearly forty-two, a large athletic woman, attractive, with thick blond hair, pale skin, Irish green eyes, and a sturdy build kept trim through dedicated exercise and a strict diet. She is visiting her oldest friend, a not-long-ago lover whose specialty is homemade chicken soup and sweet cinnamon toast. Shawn works in commodities on Wall Street, is used to taking charge of people, and is normally resilient. Now, overcome with fear, she sits hunched on a brocade Queen Anne chair, her memory rendering her weak, her words strangled.

"I never go to Central Park at night, but from the moment I left my apartment, it was as if someone, or something, was pushing me, urging me forward." She flinched visibly, her fear was so acute. She bit her lip. "I knew him." Her slender hands trembled in her lap. "Jonathan Swain. He came to my office last week. My firm represents the company he owned. As senior analyst, my name was on many of his statements and transactions. He lost a great deal of money in the stock market, and even though I wasn't directly responsible, he blamed me. It was my department. My staff."

For a moment, the haunting sounds of the wailing fox filled the room until it seemed to touch Shawn's soul. She could see Jonathan Swain's face. Feel his terror. Almost touch his horrific wounds.

Looking at Zoë, Shawn forced herself to recall the memory. She found her voice again. "Of course, Swain's accusations of mismanagement were ludicrous, but the whole situation was terribly embarrassing and disruptive. He wanted a scapegoat for his own mistakes and wasn't about to be satisfied until he had someone's blood. My supervisor was backed into a corner. He had a high-profile client crying foul. He had no choice but to put me on immediate administrative leave until a full investigation could be conducted, and to appease Swain further, suggested additional disciplinary action might be taken after the case is reviewed."

Shawn gave a thin smile. "Swain was a nasty, powerful man, Zoë. He made his money in the meat-packing business and had well over a million invested with my company. And although he called the shots on his brokerage account, one of my subordinates enacted the trades." She paused, then added, "Fairly and judiciously. But, in the end, it was my department and the customer is always right, so I take the bullet."

The heavy smell of sandalwood incense surrounded her. Edgy, Shawn pulled at the neck of her pale blue turtleneck, and her smooth forehead showed a sheen of perspiration. "Strange as it may seem, as I watched the attack unfold, I felt pleased. As if someone was protecting and vindicating me." For an unguarded moment, she closed her eyes. "He had claw marks on his face. Deep gashes. Something a bear might make. Only . . ."

"This wasn't a bear," Zoë interrupted. "It was a mysterious being. A sorceress you say, a witch. Probably not of this earth and one who rides a broom and attacks unarmed strangers in the Big Apple," she said with quiet humor, taking a sip of her raspberry martini and draping her long legs over the arm of a burgundy leather wing chair. She knows the gold caftan she wears drapes flatteringly over the curves of her body.

Zoë is ten years older than Shawn, a New Englander by birth, with short brown, spiky hair and mischievous blue eyes. The thick, round, red-framed glasses she wears give her an eccentric look. She is six feet tall and razor thin. She is extraordinarily loyal to her heart, where Shawn remains her one and only true love. Her high-pitched laughter is filled with simple joy, as is her life. Staring at Shawn, she feels her nipples harden and a warm feeling come over her. Remembrances of their former passion caress her like licks of fire. She squirms in her chair, noticing how she has become wet with desire.

Like most former lovers, Shawn viewed Zoë Quinn with a mixture of personal detachment and tiny amounts of skepticism. She had left three years earlier to find breathing space. There always seemed to be an undertone attached to Zoë's love, a smothering. Still, they had a bond that remained. In her simpleness, Zoë was honest, humorous, and, above all, loyal. Shawn had learned to trust her and had come to her tonight, knowing Zoë was the only one to whom she could tell her story.

Face pinched, Shawn stared at her friend for a moment, as if accepting Zoë's sarcastic humor as part of her overall nightmare.

"This isn't my mind run amuck. I'm telling you, I was drawn there. I had no control. And then she attacked him. A blur of blood, flesh, and terrified screams. At first I couldn't see her. Tree limbs blocked the light. Then, as my eyes adjusted to the darkness, I saw her more clearly. She was dressed in black. Pants, shirt, a wide-brimmed hat that dipped down over her forehead hiding her hair and face."

Shawn stared into the granite fireplace, the shadow of flames dancing on her cheeks. Terror reflected in her green eyes. She would not allow herself to feel her fear, she told herself. She merely wanted to state the facts. "Her hands were as delicate as porcelain. I remember thinking that if Swain struck back, she probably would shatter."

With amused blue eyes, Zoë took another sip of her martini and then set the long-stemmed glass on a Chippendale end table inherited from her great-grandmother. Her words came slowly, as if each one carried a different emotion. Sarcasm, humor, concern. "So, let me summarize. You were somehow lured to the pathways of Central Park in the wee hours of the night, where a female being of unknown origin clawed a poor innocent man to death. Did she go for the neck and suck blood, a.k.a. vampire modus operandi, or just claw the bastard?"

Shawn frowned.

Zoë's blue eyes narrowed, yet their expression remained detached, as if she was bored with her friend's theatrics. Her voice slowed. "A witch, you say? Tell me, was she hawk nosed and tooth-less with ominous dark eyes? Maybe a black mole with sprouting hairs on her chin? Or did she just wear a T-shirt silk screened *Witch of the Day?*" She studied her friend dubiously. "Really Shawn, it sounds like you're blowing things way out of proportion. I certainly attach importance to your trauma, but perhaps this was as simple as an aggrieved wife or girlfriend getting even with an unfaithful partner. You said, in so many words, the guy *was* a bas-tard."

She allowed the caftan to fall open. The whiteness of her thighs contrasted with the brown curls surrounding her pubis. She leaned back as warm excitement coursed through her. She could not help the moan that escaped her.

Averting her eyes and resisting the urge to stand, Shawn lifted the brandy snifter beside her and emptied the glass in one large gulp. How many times over the five years she and Zoë had lived together had she heard her former lover minimize her thoughts, discount her observations, look for answers in tomorrow? And how like her to try and distract Shawn with sex.

Undaunted, Shawn continued the conversation, all the while nervously twisting a strand of shoulder-length hair. "Okay, sup-pose I am hysterical. How do you explain my presence in Central Park at two o'clock in the morning? I don't have a death wish. And I don't sleepwalk."

Sighing in frustration, Zoë answered, "Part serendipity, part stress." She paused, signaling her transition to the logical. "You need to get in touch with yourself. Whenever you're upset or maxed out, you walk. How many times did I find you strolling *this* property in the middle of the night? There's nothing supernatural about that . . . it's your pattern, your way of coping with pressure. I suspect you went for a walk and, without realizing it, turned into the park. My God, you'd just been suspended from your mega job. A loss of two, three hundred K a year. If that's not stressful, I don't know what is." Zoë smiled, though her voice retained a trace of annoyance. "And what on earth ever gave you the idea this woman was a witch?"

Shawn did not smile back. "When Jonathan Swain fell to the ground, he grabbed her shirt. It ripped at the shoulder, exposing a tattoo. The symbol of the witch's coven."

"I thought you said it was dark."

"It was, but I know what I saw."

Frowning, Zoë Quinn pulled her caftan closed and pulled her legs from the arm of her chair, carefully crossing them in front of her. "You were what, ten feet away, in the shadows?" She paused for effect, then continued. "Even if you did see the sign of the coven, that doesn't make this woman a witch. Tattoos of any and all varieties are popular today. It probably was no different than some bigoted skinhead tattooing a swastika on his arm. Brutally insensitive and stupid, but it doesn't necessarily make him a Nazi or a killer. Or in this case, a witch."

Shawn slapped her thigh, pushing forward in her chair. "Stop discounting everything I say. Doesn't it disturb you that this man, anyone, would die under those circumstances?"

There was something in her tone that suddenly held the room silent.

Shawn closed her eyes. The strain in her voice was a plea. "I don't know how, but I knew he was dead the instant his body hit the ground." Underlying her words was total awe and confusion. "Then *she* looked at me. Her hat still shaded her face, but I got the overall sensation she was surprised by my presence."

A jolting crack from the fireplace sent a plume of yellow sparks up the chimney. Zoë got up and pushed at the logs with a long brass-handled poker. "Who wouldn't be surprised?" she added after a moment. "No one expects to be caught in a murderous and revengeful act."

Shawn forced herself to keep on thinking, talking. "She stopped, turned and faced me. Her body was rigid, and even though I couldn't see her face, I imagined a malevolent stare."

"Some things are meant not to be seen." Zoë's red-rimmed glasses reflected the swirling orange-yellow of the fire. "Perhaps you were somewhere you didn't belong. A miscalculated call to the park by the spirits. An error if you will. After all, even the supernatural are allowed a mistake now and then." The sentence died there.

Shawn slumped back in her seat, finding Zoë's tone disquieting. It was almost as if her words carried an unspoken warning.

Again she closed her eyes, nausea returning as she struggled to bring logic to what she had witnessed. "Without a word being spoken, the witch seemed to say justice had been served. That this violent act was *my* revenge for what he had done to me." Perplexed, Shawn added more quietly, "She then slowly walked across the grass and disappeared."

"And what did you do?"

"I ran, and I didn't stop until I got to a phone booth on the corner of Sixty-third and Central Park West. I anonymously called nine-one-one and then went to my apartment."

Zoë gave a quick, sharp glance at Shawn. "You must keep this under wraps. Any connection to a murder this bizarre can only hurt your credibility." Zoë's face was serious now. "Was the crime reported in any of the papers?"

Sitting straighter in her chair, Shawn looked squarely at Zoë. "Nothing in yesterday's or today's, for that matter."

"Even in New York, murder is front-page news." Zoë placed one hand on her hip. "If he's dead, why no story and where was the body taken?"

Shawn felt the first flicker of doubt. Her mouth opened, but no sound came out. She seemed hardly able to breathe. Then her head bent, hands covering her face. Even she wondered for a second if this nightmare was just that—a bad dream.

"Before I left for here, I called Homicide, identified myself as the woman who had witnessed the murder in the park. The detective on the phone sounded pretty irritated and accused me of wasting valuable police man-hours by making a false report. He said there was no murder. No body. No evidence of any violent act in the area as I had described." Her clouded expression emphasized her disorientation.

Zoë's eyes widened in sympathy and understanding. Standing, she refilled Shawn's snifter with a small amount of amber liquid and passed it to her. Slowly, Zoë took a seat on a small footstool just in front of her friend, her knees nearly grazing her chin as she wrapped her arms around her thin legs and pulled them close to her body. Her tone was practical, yet caring. "You have been without sleep and are totally spent. You need to stay here and rest. I'll take care of you."

She reached out and caressed Shawn's muscled leg with long porcelain-like fingers. She shivered, remembering how it felt to lie between those legs. Her low-scooped caftan slipped slightly off her left shoulder, revealing the outer edge of a tattoo. Any attempt at understanding faded from her face as she took total control. Her tone softened. "I'll bring you hot tea in the morning with ridiculously sugary cinnamon toast."

Shawn sipped her brandy, licking her lips. The alcohol's fire heated her veins. Though her deepest instincts told her she had witnessed a murder a day and a half ago, the whole scenario seemed to have taken place in some other, more irrational life. She sat back, her drink supported in both hands. The fire's warmth surrounded her, and the touch of Zoë's fingers soothed. For some reason, the excitement of a high-profile job no longer seemed important, and Jonathan Swain was quickly moving to the remote edges of her memory. She ran a fingertip along the rim of her glass as she gave Zoë a long, considering look.

Zoë felt the heat of desire again at Shawn's steady green gaze. Shaking her head, she killed the thought. There would be plenty of time for that later. "Chicken soup tonight, along with thick buttermilk biscuits smothered in my homemade strawberry jam." Zoë's voice became softer still. "And tomorrow we'll walk the fields looking for the few geese that have yet to fly south. It's time you came home. When you've fully recovered, we'll move your things back."

Outside, under the shadow of a maple tree at the back of the cemetery, the red fox dug hungrily and furiously in the freshly turned dirt, the tantalizing smell of rotting flesh just inches under the soil.

# Games of Love
Ariel Graham

Of all the games they'd played together over the years, the one where Darcy killed her was still her favorite. The one where Elizabeth lured and lusted and led someone to her, where she seduced and promised and flirted until her victim acquiesced and followed her, anywhere, a cheap hotel room, Elizabeth lean and glowing against the bedspread and when his lips came down on hers, Darcy would come through the window or through the door, the jealous lover, wronged and terrifying, her rage and will sending the victim into a tailspin of horror. Heart rate would double and triple, adrenaline rushed, chemicals spiked—it made for a lovely feast, the two of them gorged on blood and each other.

They had a variety of games, Darcy and Elizabeth. After a few centuries with the same partner, you either have new games or a new partner. Darcy had always wanted to tie Elizabeth up, but bondage doesn't work with someone who can become incorporeal at will. But they had other games to make up for it, sexual and otherwise, personal, private and public, indoors and out; and mostly it just mattered that they were together. Even a few centuries hadn't dimmed their passion; just every now and then they needed an extra kick.

A few centuries. Their anniversary was coming up; they should do something special.

"What are we doing tonight?" Elizabeth sat perched on the end of the bed, honey hair about her shoulders and feet splayed wide on the floor. She felt lazy, hadn't bothered getting dressed yet, languid cat muscles stretching as she lay back against the rumpled bedclothes.

"Oh no, you don't." Darcy, on her feet, caught Elizabeth's hand and pulled her upright again. "No luring me back there, no 'long week, let's stay in.'" Kohl-black eyes danced behind silver lining. Her lips were bee stung, blood red, shiny. Elizabeth wanted to pull her down and roll with her, come up covered in Darcy's colors and make her start over.

Darcy moved out of reach. "I know what you're thinking." She shook her head, thick black bob bouncing around her ears. "We're going out. New club, fliers up today, just opening and I want in, so you"—one finger in the middle of Elizabeth's chest, prodding, poking, pointing—"need to look your all-time best"—the finger shifted, found a nipple and squeezed—"your most sexy"—and flicked—"because we are getting in."


Beautiful night. Beautiful people on a beautiful night. The new club glowed in neon purple and green, blood red at the door and the sign—INFERNO. Clumsy and corny but it was new, and it was beautiful and the muscle at the door only glanced at the squirrelly little woman with the clipboard before nodding them in, like there wasn't any question but of course they were in.


Hot inside. Airless. Reeking of cloves and cigarettes and essential oils and body heat and, beyond it all, the smell of sex. The pounding heartbeat of the music drove everything onward, upward. The beautiful ones prowled, languid hands and arched backs, sinuous muscle, white flesh. This was a place of leather corsets and lace luxuries, a place where a couple of drinks could cost a day's rent and where you didn't take your eyes off your drink if you didn't want to wake up in someone's bed with no idea of your past or present and maybe no future.

The music was a heartbeat. Past the smell of sex was the thunder and rush of blood.

"So, what do you want to do tonight?" Darcy's mouth was against Elizabeth's ear and Liz grinned, her arms around Darcy, head against her shoulder, both of them moving slower than the music suggested. Elizabeth watched the club as they turned, drifted through the other dancers, motionless and allowing the flow to move them. She watched lean hamstrings and the fine sweep of quads, watched muscled abs above too-short shorts below crop tops. She watched the swell of pecs and breasts contained in leather and velvet, in lace, in body paint; watched tongues circle lips and ears and nipples and necks; watched a girl just barely out of her teens lick down a man's rock-hard stomach and lap at the waistband of his jeans. Elizabeth closed her eyes, tongue against her teeth, played her mouth against Darcy's neck and nipped until Darcy moved her head fractionally and Elizabeth looked up—Don't?—but Darcy gestured with her head.

She was there, by one of the many bars, this one lit in yellow and green strips of plastic. The bartender's face in the eerie glow was demonic. The girl on the stool just looked frightened and out of place. Big eyes, pensive mouth, and her hands kept playing with everything, her drink glass, the straw, the rind from a piece of fruit, a napkin, shredded and falling to her black velvet pants. She wore a complicated top of leather and O-rings, and every time she moved, the top moved in opposition and she realigned it. At her throat a strip of black leather with a red leather rose, and under the rose her pulse beat quick and hard.

"She's afraid," Elizabeth whispered. She didn't want to take her eyes off the girl. "Someone dared her to come here."

Darcy moved her, swayed Elizabeth's back to the girl, and watched over her shoulder. "She came here on her own. She's as excited as she is afraid."

Elizabeth tried to move around again but Darcy held her. She closed her eyes and imagined the girl's face. "Who is she watching?"

"It will be you."

"But who is she watching now?"

"Everyone," Darcy said, lips in Elizabeth's hair and then on her neck and her shoulders, hot line down between her breasts and then, "Take her back to the house."

"The house?" They always took a room.

"The house," Darcy said and she was gone, slipping out of Elizabeth's grip and moving across the floor in search of prey, a male perhaps, or a drink or even drugs—no telling. Elizabeth felt a chill as if Darcy had just left her and then the fear that when she turned, the girl would be gone.

The girl sat on the stool beside the bar, holding her drink, her black velvet covered in flayings of the cocktail napkin.


Her name was Christy and she was in college, of course. Up close she was tinier than Elizabeth had believed, barely five feet and small and delicate, with blue eyes like morning glories and fine pale hair. And lost, so very lost.

Elizabeth wooed her, tales of other clubs and other times, not enough to make Christy question her age, not enough to sound like a slut, just enough to be interesting and somehow safe, safe and yet sensuous and new and alluring. She wanted to do it the old-fashioned way, with attention and laughter and soft touches and dampened lips. She wanted to tease and lead and entice with eyes and lips and legs almost as long as Christy's whole body, and when she finally used her will—just a little, just a nudge—Christy slid from the bar stool and took Elizabeth's hand as if there'd never been any question. As if all along it had been fated.


The house was warm, plant-filled, and sprawling. Terra-cotta tile and white-washed walls, luxurious couches, and more stereo equipment than most people could conceive of needing; no wonder there were bars on the downstairs windows even in such a nice neighborhood, bars on the windows and deadbolts on every door. Darcy and Elizabeth had done well over the years, sometimes married well and widowed better, sometimes simply stood to collect inheritances one wouldn't have expected.

Then too, they were not above rolling a john between them if need be.

It didn't look like a house where one person lived alone, but if Christy had questions she kept them to herself. Her inhibitions fell away when they stepped through the doors, as did her leather top of such curious design. Underneath she wore only tiny silver rings through perfect pink nipples; a third pierced her navel, and Elizabeth took it as an invitation to find any other silver. The velvet pants clung and twisted. They battled them together, laughing as if drunk, teetering on the stairs up to the bedroom. Christy argued the living room was fine, the stairs, the hallway. Her mouth was hot on Elizabeth's neck, on Elizabeth's mouth, on her breasts through the clinging second skin shirt she still wore. Elizabeth found she was in no hurry for Darcy's return.

Into the bedroom, the framed illustrations of Elizabeth and Darcy stood in plain sight but Christy wasn't paying attention. The bed was still tumbled, sheets soft and warm. Christy was pale enough to seemingly glow against the black sheets. Mouths came together, hands clasped and released. Christy's hands on Liz's breasts and Elizabeth trying to sink, wanted silver in her mouth, lights still on and the curtains open—

Darcy exploded into the room. Upstairs bedroom, sheer walls outside and the windows blew inward, curtains danced, glass rained on the thick carpet. Darcy paused on the sill, crouched and leather-clad, a night demon of lust and fury. Blood on her lips where a stray piece of glass had caught her.

Christy's heartbeat doubled. Her pulse pounded, blood sped, her adrenaline raged and she trembled.

"Whorebitchslut—" Now was the time Darcy acted, her

moment to play the jealous lover wronged, but there was no need. Christy was already past surprise and well into terror, already aware she'd seen them together, already where they wanted her. She pressed back into Elizabeth, who laughed and caught her close, hands snarled in blonde hair, against breasts, offering her up. They'd feed together, high for hours on adrenaline spike, death trip terror and any lingering drugs in the girl's system. Liz played her tongue along Christy's neck as Darcy padded across the floor. The bed dipped as she knelt and leaned forward to take one nipple in her mouth, tonguing the silver ring and then leaned up to kiss Elizabeth over the head of the squirming girl.

Darcy pressed tight against Christy, reached for Lizzie, fingers pressing up inside. "You're so wet."

Christy lurched, off balance, a stumbling attempt at the door, a way off the bed, a way out from between them. Liz and Darcy pushed apart. The illusion of freedom upped the terror. They'd let her get just so far and then—

Christy's lips on Elizabeth's were hot and tasted of cinnamon. Her hands reached as they had before, drawing Elizabeth to her and then reached for Darcy, her mouth leaving Liz's for Darcy's and Elizabeth felt cold, suddenly deserted, reached out confused as Christy's pulse continued to rage and her blood flooded with lust and terror and excitement. She felt Darcy murmur something she didn't make out but understood; they could feed later.

Hands and mouths and breasts and tongues and tongues and tongues and Darcy slid down between Elizabeth's legs and bit and suckled, and finally her fangs on the inside of Elizabeth's thigh, biting into the major artery there, Elizabeth flying alongside her, the two of them orbiting. Elizabeth turned to nip and bite at Darcy's wrist until her fangs sank deep and together they felt Christy's terror abruptly return, full force, crippling fear, somehow she'd missed it before but suddenly awake to the fact this was the last night of her life.

She bucked against them and thrashed, made a desperate attempt to throw herself from the bed and Elizabeth caught her, threw her down, properly hungry now and the prey ready and perfect, hot, fast, panicked, life at its best. She turned to Darcy, the girl caught on her stomach, one of Elizabeth's hands fast in her hair arching her head back, the other between her shoulders, pressing her down, turned to Darcy, who said, "No."

"No?"

Hands, Darcy's, gentle as Lizzie rarely knew them. Darcy's hands smoothed across Christy's back, moved Liz's hands off her. Smoothed and gentled and soothed and enticed, dropped her down from panic and pain to pleasure and peace, stroked and smoothed and touched until Christy's eyelashes fluttered, a gentle press of will and Christy slept between them on the bed.

"Darcy?"

She leaned over the sleeping girl and kissed Elizabeth softly, eased down beside the blonde, her head just on the girl's shoulder. "Sleep," she whispered, but to Elizabeth or Christy Liz couldn't tell.

Elizabeth lay on her back, staring at the ceiling, listening to the soft breathing of the women next to her as her mind raged.


Over the next few days the pattern emerged. Darcy and Christy way too often, until Darcy wasn't touching Elizabeth at all and Elizabeth didn't want her to. She took to sleeping on the couch at dawn, too tired to be bothered going up to bed. "You go, I'm fine here." Her nights spent wondering what she would do. Darcy had been her everything for so long. The one she came home to, the one she told things to. The one she played with.

Christy attached herself to Darcy as if she'd found her true calling or true nature or true self. The frightened college girl fell away. This Christy was sexual and outgoing and there was no doubt it was Darcy she stalked, as surely as Darcy and Elizabeth had stalked her.

She brought gifts, fine cheeses, good wines, drugs neither of them had much interest in; drugs worked better when sampled through the blood of the user, and Darcy no longer intended to feed from Christy and Elizabeth didn't want to. Christy brought a co-worker she'd always hated, angry misogynist and mean; his eyes lit at the idea three women wanting him and his terror was pleasing and spicy when Darcy and Elizabeth made use of him. They disposed of the body themselves and Christy watched, content and pale and blonde, her eyes on Darcy and Darcy's attention on her. Elizabeth watched and seethed and planned for Christy's death, but with every night, Darcy grew closer to Christy and there was less opportunity to kill her.

Until the night Christy went too far. Home at sunset, she brought a child, too young to be a threat identifying them and too young to be a possibility no one would be looking for him.

"She'll get us caught," Elizabeth exploded, and watched as Darcy's eyes ran between the child and Christy and the child cried and Christy watched Elizabeth with angry eyes.

"You can't do this," Elizabeth said. "People look for children. This is crazy. We never take them this young."

All the while, the child's frenetic blood pounded against her and Elizabeth wanted to drink, wanted that bright frantic energy and the terror inside. When Darcy turned away from the child and held out her hand to Christy, Christy followed without looking back. Elizabeth watched them climb the stairs to the bedroom, stood watching, numb, turned and reached her hand out to the boy. She didn't have to exert her will; the child took her hand because it was the only thing so far that hadn't threatened him. It offered a way out. Elizabeth took his hand and walked with him through neighborhoods until he cried in exhaustion and then she pressed her will, just a little, drove them all from his mind and left him at a convenience store miles and miles from her home. She caught the wind and made her way back, silent in the house, but Darcy would hear her and know she was there. If she was paying attention. If she still cared.

Up the stairs, incorporeal and silent. She glided to the bedroom door, stood listening to the sound of murmured voices and low laughter until the rage grew too much. She kicked through the door and stood at the end of the bed, stared down at Darcy and Christy wrapped around each other.

"I have a surprise for you," Darcy said. Her eyes were lidded; her body moved in warm waves.

"I already know what it is," Elizabeth said.

Christy moved her head back and smiled up at Elizabeth, her mouth shiny with Darcy's wetness.

"I just don't understand. How could you . . . after so long—"

"What I don't understand is how you could believe such a thing after so long," Darcy said and Christy stared at her, a tiny frown between crystal blue eyes. "Oh, she's good enough. She's got a tireless little tongue." She pushed Christy's head back down between her legs and Elizabeth watched the girl struggle and then lie still, waiting to figure out what was going on. "And all the rings," Darcy continued. "I have enjoyed the idea of leading her around by them." She looked contemplative, stared down at Christy, who watched her with growing apprehension. "But really, Liz, my love, she's not you. She has nowhere near your lovely experience. And she really should get that energetic little tongue pierced." She pulled Christy up to her, her mouth over the girl's, and Elizabeth watched as Christy's eyes went wide and she began to thrash and scream. Darcy pulled back and laughed, her lips shiny with blood, her eyes half closed in pleasure. Her hands slipped on the girl's biceps, just enough to convince Christy she'd lost her grip and the girl bolted, all pink and blonde and terrified, off the bed and away from the side where Elizabeth stood. Elizabeth lunged and missed and the girl fled for the stairs, downstairs and away, making more noise than anyone her size should be able to make.

"Everything is locked," Elizabeth said and leaned over to kiss Darcy. Dinner would be ready soon, hot and spicy and played out. They could hear her now, sobbing as she fumbled from dead-bolted door to dead-bolted door and all along the downstairs windows with their bars.

Elizabeth looked away from the bedroom door and back at

Darcy. Her eyes were bright, her dark hair in disarray. She still had Christy's blood on her lips, still lay beautiful and naked and spread across the sheets. She licked her lips at Elizabeth and grinned, her eyes half closed and teasing. "What do you think of your anniversary present?" she asked and Elizabeth grinned and moved to the bed.

# That Which Alters
## Heather Osbourne

Rain fell outside the cafe, the first autumn rain. Late leaves scuttled along the gutters. Dead smells, mould and cut grass, gusted on the sulky wind, mixing with the exhaust and cigarette smoke from the stop-and-go traffic. Through the steam rising from her hot chocolate, Kathryn stared at the streetlights blurred by the weeping windows. The gabbling circle of her friends might have been any one of a thousand background conversations for all she appeared to be listening. Des knew better. The smile hiding behind Kathryn's eyes ebbed and flowed with their words.

Des imagined that she was still damp after walking from Kathryn's apartment, two blocks away. It emptied her to wait there while Kathryn stayed out. Des hadn't come to her here before, but it was past midnight. Perhaps Kathryn had learned to expect her. From behind, Des laid her hands on Kathryn's shoulders, then slid chilled fingertips down her arms. Des touched softly, and quickly enough to startle, but Kathryn only smiled at her drink and leaned her back into Des's breasts.

Kathryn's friends had pressed three tables into service, and their bags and coats hung on mismatched chairs stolen from around the cafe. They didn't see Des. Kathryn settled against her, dark eyes fixed on the middle distance. "You're here," she murmured.

Fresh coffee weighted the air, bitter-rich, and Des breathed it onto Kathryn's throat as she bent closer. "Hmm," she agreed. "You must have been thinking of me." She placed her first kiss in the hollow behind Kathryn's earlobe.

Kathryn shook her head, a too-small denial, then tilted her neck to give Des better access. She sighed, and if anyone heard, they probably believed she was sliding into new daydreams. Small hairs lifted under Des's lips, and she smiled so that Kathryn felt it against her skin.

Des had never come to her here, but Kathryn accepted her as she had the first night, when Des sloughed dreams and took form in Kathryn's moon-lit room. Des had blazed until Kathryn's eyes watered.

"What are you?" Kathryn had asked, her palms tracing Des's brilliant outline. She didn't wait for a reply before her hands were reaching out to pull Des down to the bed.

That night, Des buried her fingers deep inside Kathryn and rode her thigh, her other hand splayed over Kathryn's throat. Des had smiled then, too, as she squeezed away Kathryn's breath. It was supposed to be that easy, her death. Kathryn jerked beneath her, and Des gasped as Kathryn's thigh slammed into her. Struggling for air, gulping, Kathryn scrabbled at Des's hand on her throat. Tears prismed her eyes. She bared her teeth and tried to scream around Des's constricting hand. Des moved her fingers, twisting as she thrust. Kathryn's hips lifted, begging Des to reach deeper, touch harder. Des felt Kathryn's lust as though it was her own, sinking between her legs, past the memories of a thousand years of deaths just like this one.

Des had stared into Kathryn's bulging eyes as her face darkened with blood, her swollen tongue poking between her teeth. Her soul flowed through Des's hand, sweet-scalding, like milky tea gulped before it cooled. Kathryn fought her for it and Des writhed above her, taking her life, but slowly, tenderly. Kathryn's pleasure fed her, and her death came close to shattering Des's borrowed form. She could have finished it then. She held Kathryn's life inside her, Kathryn's soul shrieking as it filled her. She could have ended it, but at the last instant she released Kathryn and cried out when she came.

Caged in her assumed body, afterward, she lay beside Kathryn and watched her as she slept.

Remembering, Des allowed a hint of fire to bleed through her kiss. She could still burn, if she wanted. She could rip Kathryn's soul from its anchors any instant she chose, in a single incendiary climax. Not here, though. Not in front of Kathryn's friends, when her attention was elsewhere. Des wanted them to be alone. She had come here to convince Kathryn to leave. Not to kill her, not yet.

Des mouthed Kathryn's throat, sensing her soul buzzing within her skin, like angry bees warming the walls of a hive. She tasted sweat-salt, smelling smoke in Kathryn's collar and chocolate on her breath. She felt, more than heard, Kathryn's hum of encouragement. Her friends were forgotten.

Des moved her hands lower, fingers searching below the hem of Kathryn's sweater. She was warm, and her breathing quickened as Des stroked the line of her ribs beneath the raspy wool. Kathryn stretched like a lazy cat, slow and seeming indifferent to Des's attention. Inside, she was dreaming of a long, slow seduction, of crackling wood stoves, crisp roses, and the far off hiss of rain.

It had been strange to return to Kathryn a second night. Des couldn't remember a time when she had failed to make her kill. Kathryn's soul had poured through her assumed body as though she was a sieve. The traces left behind, like lover's tokens, had urged Des back. She would not be free of the sylph-girl body Kathryn's dreams had chosen until Kathryn lay dead beneath her. Each time Des brought Kathryn, tense and quaking, to orgasm, more of Kathryn's soul seeped into her. Each time, Des's need to be with her climbed higher. And the months passed. Des could barely remember what it was to slide into a new body at a lover's whim, to drink a new soul each night.

Kathryn cradled her mug in her hands, making no move to leave. Des frowned, lifting Kathryn's thick hair away from her throat, exploring the exposed skin with her mouth. Waiting for her had been intolerable, but this—being ignored—was worse. Kathryn's idle lust should have inspired her. She knew it was in her to fan the flames, to tease and burn until Kathryn couldn't hide her arousal from her friends, and had to excuse herself, red-faced and panting. Des should have wanted to watch Kathryn run back to her apartment, pleading for her to appear, fully physical and ready to finish what she'd started. Right now, there was something untouchable in Kathryn's acceptance, a sense of safety. Des wanted to defy it.

She took form.

The body Des wore had small breasts, generous hips, a soft stomach that was almost flat. Her face was marked by a wide, peasant prettiness. Hair, red-brown like autumn leaves, rippled to her shoulders. In its broad strokes, the body owed much to Kathryn's first imagining. The details were Des's. Kathryn's soul leached through her hand the first night, showing her the small imperfections Kathryn needed in order to believe in Des's human disguise. Faded blue eyes. Tiny freckles spattered across a too-short nose. Pointed chin. Lips sketched in hazy curves. Clothing was something new, but Des chose tight jeans and a low-zipped hoodie from the minds around her, adding a tangle of necklaces and small hoop earrings.

Craig, sitting across from them, noticed first. He glanced at Kathryn, but his eyes widened when he saw Des. Her arms were draped around Kathryn's waist, lips teasing the side of her throat. Des shared a smile with him and stopped. Kathryn's head moved, protesting the end of the kiss.

"A new friend, Kathryn?" Craig asked, pitching the smirking question loud enough to interrupt the conversation.

The others looked over, grins and raised eyebrows meeting the sight. Kathryn twisted in her seat, narrowing her eyes at Des's manifestation. Des shrugged and smiled across the table at Craig. She rested her chin on Kathryn's shoulder, waiting comfortably for her answer.

"Not so new," Kathryn said, turning back to Craig with a smile, dropping her hands to cover Des's and hold her close. "This is Des." The words were dismissive, as if she expected everyone to forget Des the moment she spoke. Des's stomach tightened.

Impulsively, Des reached her hand across the table to Craig. He blinked when their palms met, his mouth opening with unasked questions. Des rifled through his lusts out of habit. Her form flickered in his mind's eye and settled on a body of his choosing. Tall, with black hair falling soft as silk, dark skin, full breasts. No clothes. His soul leapt to the surface of his skin, answering the black fire of her eyes. The handshake lasted only seconds, but the new form resonated inside her like a bell. Craig flushed, staring at her. Des wrenched away from his mind and fell back into her body. She shivered inside its familiar limits, licking her lips. Craig's soul was thick on her tongue, like caramelized onions and butter.

No one else had noticed the exchange. They were too far down the tables to offer their hands, and settled for joking with Kathryn instead. Des turned her shoulder on Craig and focused on them. She wrapped her arms around Kathryn.

"So then why haven't we met her before? Don't you trust us, Kath?" Tanya asked, leaning forward.

Nicole smiled at Des. "Kathryn's afraid we'll scare you off."

"Nah, it's the other way round," Martin said. "She's worried we'll spend the night telling embarrassing stories. Like the time she made pudding while we were camping, remember?"

"I remember you ate two bowls before you realized it had gone bad," Kathryn said. Her thumb moved over the back of Des's hand, rubbing warmth into her skin. Des sighed, cautiously relaxing inside her form, ignoring the memory of Craig's touch. Kathryn hadn't cared, anyway.

"Not my best night." Martin grinned at Des. "It's one of those stories that ends, 'And that's the most I ever hurled.'"

"See?" Nicole tapped the table with her index finger. "You're scaring her."

"More like *warning* . . ."

Des listened as the conversation drifted away from her appearance among them. She blurred herself in their minds, turning their questions aside. Only Craig watched her, his eyes flickering over her at odd moments, expecting her to revert to the woman she could be for him. Des clung to Kathryn and the form details she had built around this body.

She shouldn't have touched Craig. She felt how easily his body would surrender to her, his soul tumbling into her hands and setting her free and formless once more. She shivered. While Kathryn lived, Des was bound to her. She didn't want freedom at that price. Kathryn's passion satisfied her.

Still, Craig's gaze pushed at the edges of her form, reminding her of what could be, might be. Her body vibrated like a plucked string: red hair or dark, blue eyes or black, cinnamon skin or cream. Des itched to be alone with Kathryn, to confirm herself in Kathryn's mind. She should have waited at the apartment. Now that she had appeared, she had to follow the conventions, and wait until Kathryn made their excuses.

"So, you two . . ." Tanya drew out her question. Her barely restrained smile conspired with everyone around the table. "Is it, like, serious?"

"Tanya," Kathryn protested. Des blushed. She tensed at the sensation—it was so human. "We haven't exactly talked about it . . ."

"But it's been going on a while, right?" Tanya's eyes sparkled. "Come on, Des, you came out to meet *us*, didn't you?"

Martin groaned. "We're not that bad."

"If Kathryn doesn't want to say—"

"Nicole, you're no fun. It's a simple question."

"Maybe it's not." Nicole glared at Tanya when she opened her mouth again. She rolled her eyes and turned to Kathryn. "If it's none of our business, that's okay, guys."

Kathryn shook her head and looked down, picking Des's hands out of her lap. "It's not that." She stood up, unhooking her jacket from the chair's back. "Look, it's late . . ."

"Oh, now look what you've done." Nicole swatted Tanya.

"Sorry, jeez."

Martin hopped out of his seat. "Hey, don't go on account of us."

Kathryn grinned at him. "Don't worry, it's not just you." She grabbed Des's hand and held it up as evidence. Des nudged closer, sliding into her place under Kathryn's arm. She was just short enough to fit, and even knowing it was no accident, it felt good.

Martin laughed. Tanya stage-whispered to Nicole, "See? That's serious. Like you didn't want to know."

Des let Kathryn lead her out of the cafe, a few well-meaning catcalls following them. On her back, she felt the heat of Craig's stare, and the careless pressure of his mind. He asked her to give him death like a gift. She was grateful for the rain pelting them as they left, and the touch of Kathryn's hand in hers.

Kathryn threw her jacket over her shoulders, hunching under the rain. She shoved wet strands of hair off her face and laughed, a harsh, incredulous sound. "What the hell was that?"

Des smiled, and shrugged. She let the rain soak her. "I wanted to meet your friends."

"Oh, of *course*." Kathryn shook her head. "How very human of you. Do they meet your approval?"

"I still like you best." They were halfway home, the neighbourhood quiet around them. The asphalt shone beneath the streetlights. Des shivered and hugged herself. "Aren't you getting chilly?"

"No."

Des turned her face up. The rain fell like cold tears, running down her face. She could take form only where Kathryn was; it was her first time outside since she'd last taken a life. She pushed for the memory of it, through a veil of human thoughts. She'd found him in a park, his soul murky and sharp as wine.

"You're not cheating, are you?" Kathryn prodded her in the ribs with one finger. "Going all non-corporeal on me?"

"Hey!" Des jumped and slapped at Kathryn's hand.

"Nope, you're still really there." She grabbed Des's wrist and pulled her close. "Des . . ."

Des's smile widened. "Bearskin rugs? Roaring fireplaces?" She lifted her hands to cup Kathryn's face, drawing her down for a kiss. Her lips were cold and wet, but the kiss was warm.

"You read my mind," Kathryn murmured into her mouth, then turned aside, her voice becoming bitter. "Do you have to do that?"

"I want what you want." Des thumbed the droplets away from Kathryn's cheeks, unleashing her fire to heat the caress. "So I look." She pressed upward. Kathryn sighed and tilted her head, taking advantage of her height to press Des back. Des enticed her with small nibbling kisses that promised more than they delivered. Kathryn's hands clutched her shoulders. The rain dashed away the sleepy warmth of the cafe, and Kathryn kissed her harder, sucking on Des's tongue.

Des's assumed body came alive under the force, as if it was truly human. Her pulse crashed into a faster rhythm, and she gasped. Kathryn kissed along her jaw, and all her senses were focused on the trailing warm wetness. Des slanted her head up and caught raindrops, her mouth open and panting. "Kathryn."

"Yeah," Kathryn muttered, paying more attention to kissing her than to listening.

"We're still outside . . . and it's raining . . ."

"I know."

Des laughed, baring her throat. "You'll catch your death."

Kathryn twitched back, dropping her arms. Her eyes glittered black. "I'm dying anyway, aren't I?"

Des lifted a hand to Kathryn's neck. Soul and blood and breath, all vulnerable, in that one spot. Hers to take. But she hadn't even tried, since—when?

Why?

"What do you mean?" she asked.

"I know what you are," Kathryn said. "I've heard of succubi, Des. I can feel what you're doing. There's less of *me*, every single time."

"No." Des thought of Craig, his life offered to her with a touch. She didn't want it. She traced the line of Kathryn's throat. Her soul leapt easily beneath Des's fingers, mingling with the pieces she had already leached away. What she had kept for herself was not enough to kill Kathryn. It was only enough to make Des sick at the thought of a different lover and another death.

"You're going to want to meet my family next, I suppose. It's a strange way to haunt people." Kathryn pushed Des's hand aside. Her skin was heated, feverish, even in the rain. "Why the hell did you come?"

Des fumbled to explain. "I was lonely, waiting for you."

Kathryn sneered. "The demon is lonely."

Des shook her head. "Kathryn—"

"You can't *be* lonely. You don't have a soul, you know, no matter how many you steal."

"I don't want to kill you!"

Kathryn stood still, the patterned shadows of spruce branches dappling her, hiding her eyes. Des's body, so close to human, trembled in the wind. Rain pattered around them, and Des blinked the water away. "I don't want to kill you," she repeated, softly, testing the truth of her words.

Kathryn opened her mouth but said nothing. She turned on her heel and walked away. Her breath was a white mist around her head.

Des let her form crumble. The shuddering cold of her body followed her even as she faded.

The apartment was warm and dry. Des wanted to feel it, but she couldn't manifest without Kathryn's presence. She waited.

She waited, and thought of Kathryn. The wild light in her dark eyes when she laughed. The sway of her breasts when she emerged from the shower, winking at herself in the fogged mirror because she knew Des was watching. The breathy sighs she made as she slept.

Until Kathryn, Des had never watched a lover sleep, had never cared about their laugh. She had never stayed the kill for months. The severed pieces of Kathryn's soul curled and twisted inside her. When Des took form, she could feel; when she was human, she knew she never wanted to fade.

Des watched when Kathryn finally opened the door, tossing her keys onto the counter and kicking her shoes off. Water sluiced from her hair and jacket. She sat on the couch and tipped her head back, closing her eyes. "You can't leave me like this. Half-dead." Her voice was flat. She expected Des to be there to hear.

Des took form as she drifted closer. She knelt in front of Kathryn, holding her hips and looking up into her face. "You're beautiful."

Kathryn opened her eyes. She let one finger trail down Des's cheek. "That's not enough."

"It's all I know." Des pushed the sodden denim jacket off Kathryn's shoulders. "Let me?" she asked.

Kathryn sighed an acceptance. Her sweater was water-heavy and smelled earthy. Underneath it, Kathryn's skin was pale and chilled. Kathryn arched off the couch, enough for Des to strip away her pants. Gooseflesh puckered her nipples under the lace of her bra. Des kneeled on the couch, perching on Kathryn's lap. She pressed her body into Kathryn's. Kathryn's skin was icy, and Des's breath hissed through her teeth at the contact.

"You're so warm." Kathryn rested her palms on Des's stomach, rubbing small circles.

"Mmm." Des leaned forward and kissed Kathryn's neck, sucking on her pulse point until the blood raced beneath her lips. Her fingers worked the clasp on Kathryn's bra. She removed it and tossed it aside. She reached for Kathryn's breasts, pinching and rolling her nipples between two fingers. Kathryn moaned. Des took a deep breath, heat and excitement flooding her body. She was amazed at the pleasure surging through her as she worked to make Kathryn squirm. Something so human, so unexpected.

"Des . . . please . . ." Kathryn clasped Des's hand between hers, pulling it up to her throat. "Take it."

Des jerked her hand out of Kathryn's grasp. "No—"

"Damn you, this is all you've left me. I can't live like this." Kathryn's eyes glittered in the darkness. She shoved forward and found Des's lips with her own. The kiss was harsh and searing, exploring too-familiar territory. Des whimpered, burying her hands in Kathryn's thick hair.

"I'm not going to—" she said, the words lost in Kathryn's mouth. She pulled back to breathe, tears choking her. "Kathryn, I love you."

Kathryn laughed.

Des remembered that sound; it came to her from her broken memory, a thousand years of deaths. The laugh that dripped from her lips as she filled herself with a lover's soul. The laugh that speeded them to their deaths.

The world sharpened in Des's senses. The rough upholstery on the couch as Kathryn rolled her over and held her down. The sudden feverish heat of Kathryn's skin pressed against hers. The thud of her heart, pounding in her chest and in her ears.

"I can't love anymore, Des." Kathryn's face was open, hungry, her features distorted. "You took that, too." She held Des's wrists as she kissed every inch of her, her mouth searing Des's body. Her human body. Involuntarily, Des's hips lifted off the bed, her flesh quivering under Kathryn's assault. Her soul—her stolen soul—parted from her body, sheared away by a cut as thin as the line of a razor. It was still forfeit.

It wasn't supposed to happen this way.

Kathryn licked across Des's stomach, dipping into her belly-button. Des moaned, clutching at the couch. Kathryn breathed over the wet trails and crawled lower. She was lit from within, bright as magnesium fire. Des closed her eyes and cried out the moment Kathryn's mouth reached her, sucking and nibbling. Heat flashed through her body, and Des screamed, her head thrashing back and forth.

Kathryn clamped her hand on Des's throat, forcing her to stillness. Pain fired Des's nerves, mixing with the pleasure of Kathryn's tongue. She needed to breathe. She had never needed it before, but now the room darkened as she fought for air. She was lost, falling into rapture. She felt her form vanishing into the emptiness of Kathryn's splayed fingers.

Kathryn was more beautiful than ever, too beautiful to be human. Gorgeous as only a demon can be. Des loved her, and gave up her life like a gift that was only Kathryn's due.

"Kathryn," she said, or tried to say, but there was no air left. She disappeared into sensation, into dying.

Kathryn took her soul and faded, formless, into the night.

# Jane Doe
## Maria V. Ciletti

I hear the faint scuff of tennis shoes and the squeaky rhythmic sound of a gurney being rolled down the hall of the morgue and into autopsy room two. This is my second year as deputy corner in this ghost of a steel town where the high homicide and suicide rates keep us here in the coroner's office quite busy. I guess living in a place where sometimes the only way to make a living is by doing it illegally comes with a high price. I've seen my share of gangsters blown up in shootouts, felons decapitated in car accidents, and supposedly innocent bystanders shot up during drug deals that went bad.

Tonight seemed kind of slow, especially with it being a full moon, because it was almost ten-thirty and our first case was just being wheeled in.

"Who do we have here?" I asked Jenny the morgue technician as she pushed the metal gurney into the center of the room under the high-intensity surgical light.

Jenny reached under the plastic-covered body and produced the decedent's paperwork. "Jane Doe; motorcycle accident . . . dead at the scene," Jenny said as she flipped though the pink-and-white papers. "Dr. Epstein scheduled the autopsy for ten tomorrow morning."

"Let's get her checked in and prepped so Epstein won't bitch in the morning and we can get out of here at a decent hour," I said, tying my hair into a ponytail and putting on a yellow paper gown and surgical gloves to begin the intake.

Motorcycle accidents are usually pretty gruesome. The victims were usually going at a high speed when they dumped the bike, snapping arms and legs like twigs and sustaining road rash so severe, sometimes it scraped all their facial features away. Other times they hit something and catapulted from the bike suffering a broken neck, snapped spine and smashed skull.

Jenny sat across the room on one of the stainless-steel exam stools filling out the rest of Jane Doe's paperwork while I prepped Jane. I unzipped the heavy black plastic body bag to reveal the handsome face of a butch dyke; a face miraculously untouched by pavement or gravel or roadside brush.

As I would soon find out, this wasn't your typical motorcycle accident.

Jane's chestnut hair was in disarray, tangled with debris and caked with dried blood, the source of the blood being a seven-inch gash in the back of Jane's head, which seemed to be her only injury.

I photographed the body full length then in sections, with special attention on the head wound. After taking the photographs, I clipped a sample of hair from the head injury area and four other places and placed them in clear plastic evidence bags, labeling them accordingly.

Jenny finished her paperwork, tucked the papers into a manila envelope and hopped off the stool. "I'm going for coffee, do you want any, Dr. Caselli?"

"Yes, that would be great."

"How do you take it?"

"Black with four sugars, please."

"Four sugars? Jesus, Doc."

"I like my coffee like I like my women . . . strong, hot and sweet."

Jenny laughed and smacked the metal wall plate that opened

the pneumatic doors. They opened with a swoosh and she slipped through them and down the hall.

Jane Doe was dressed in motorcycle leather from head to toe. As she lay on the stainless-steel gurney I couldn't help but notice the bulge straining at the crotch of her leather pants that told me she was packin'.

I pulled down the overhead microphone and flipped the recorder on to begin the intake procedure. "This is case number 04-9338, Jane Doe Female, well nourished, well developed, approximately twenty-nine to thirty-one years in age, five-feet-six inches, weight one hundred and twenty-five pounds, DOA from motorcycle accident. Time of death undetermined this October 26, 2004." I rolled Jane Doe over and tried to remove the body bag from underneath her.

Jenny returned with our coffee as I was struggling to free Jane from the black rubber body bag. "Want some help?" Jenny asked as she set down the giant economy size Styrofoam cups of steaming coffee on the stainless-steel counter.

"Yes, thanks," I said. "Hey, get a load of this." I nodded my head in the direction of the bulge.

"Wow, looks like our girl was out cruisin' for a good time," Jenny said as we eased Jane onto her back again.

We freed Jane from the bag and started to undress her for more photographs and the preliminary examination. I tugged off Jane's heavy motorcycle boots. Jenny grabbed one leather pant leg as I grabbed the other. We yanked and pulled with all our might and were finally able to peel the leather pants from Jane's narrow hips and muscular legs. Jenny shook out the leather pants but was unable to take her eyes off the pink rubber dildo the size of a baby's arm that lay nestled in Jane's crotch.

"You into that kind of thing?" I asked, teasing Jenny about the dildo.

"No . . ." she said, but her flushed face and nervous giggle told me otherwise. She folded Jane Doe's pants and shoved them into a clear plastic evidence bag. She unbuckled one side of the leather strap-on as I unbuckled the other side. She removed the sex toy from Jane's clean-shaven nether regions and dropped it into an evidence bag.

I pulled a green surgical sheet from the linen closet and covered Jane's lower body. I unzipped her leather vest to reveal a torn and bloodstained T-shirt underneath. I used a pair of surgical scissors to cut a straight line up the middle of it to expose Jane's slender torso, well-defined abs and small firm breasts.

I continued with the head-to-toe assessment looking for injuries and clues to the actual cause of death while Jenny inventoried the rest of Jane's personal effects. A black leather saddlebag was the only other belonging Jane came with other than the clothes on her back. Jenny opened the bag and slowly removed each item: a pair of metal handcuffs, a red bandanna and a leather wallet that was so worn, the leather was as soft as a woman's inner thighs.

Jenny bagged the handcuffs and the bandanna, then flipped open the wallet. It contained thirteen dollars in bills, a condom and a cache of folded slips of paper with phone numbers scribbled on them. Each slip had a name on it: Lindsay, Jessica, Danielle and Marisa. No driver's license, no credit cards, nothing to help identify this woman.

"She's a very handsome woman," Jenny said, now sitting at the head of the exam table sipping her coffee.

I looked up from Jane's left shoulder, which I was examining for bruises, cuts and debris fragments. "Yes, she is. I bet she's left quite a trail of broken hearts."

I continued my exam and plucked three glass fragments from Jane's left anterior shoulder. I noted a tattoo of two women's symbols bound together with spiky barbed wire covering most of her firm upper bicep. I couldn't believe I was noticing the desirability of a corpse like this. It was starting to spook me—making me feel like a necrophiliac.

"I'm sure these women will miss her," Jenny said with a sigh as she spread the slips of paper with the women's phone numbers out in front of her. "I bet she has a woman in every city."

I finished examining Jane's shoulders and arms and moved down to her hands. She had exquisite hands. Large with long, thick fingers. Jenny may be into dildos but give me a strong pair of hands any day. Jane Doe had the kind of hands that held you so you knew you were being held. The kind of hands that just looking at made you swoon, knowing what they could do to you.

I scraped under Jane's short manicured fingernails, and thoughts of where these fingers had been intruded on my mind. Why was this dead woman affecting me so?

I shook my head to clear it. *I'm supposed to be a professional* . . . I tried to block out any more sexual thoughts and resume my exam.

Jenny held Jane as I examined her back and inserted a rectal thermometer to take her temperature, another way of pinpointing the time of death. Multiple contusions covered her neck, back and buttocks. Jane's skin blanched to touch. That, along with her 96.2 body temperature, indicated she had been dead for less than three hours. I noted my findings and then Jenny and I wrapped Jane up in the surgical sheet, zipped her back into the black plastic body bag and wheeled her over to the cooler where she'd keep until the morning for the real autopsy.

"That's it for tonight," I said as I slipped out of my paper exam gown and gloves and washed my hands in the sink. Jenny did the same. I shut out the lights in the autopsy room and headed home. It was already past midnight and we had to be back early in the morning to assist Dr. Epstein with the autopsy.

"Thanks for your help tonight," I told Jenny as we walked to our cars, the only two remaining in the parking lot.

"You're welcome. I'll see you in the morning."

I waved good-bye and waited until Jenny was safe in her car before I went home myself.

Once inside my apartment, I stripped out of my work clothes and headed for the shower. Streams of hot water beat on my flesh, easing away the tension and fatigue of the day. I dried off and climbed into bed. The cool cotton sheets felt good against my hot skin. The street light outside my window cast linear shadows along the wall and ceiling as it shone through the slats of the mini blinds.

I lay awake looking at the patterns on the ceiling and thinking about Jane Doe.

As I reached that place between consciousness and sleep I thought I heard a woman's voice. My body felt weighted, like I was drugged, as I listened to the woman's voice get closer and closer. I felt someone . . . or some*thing* . . . brush against me. My eyes flew open and my heart raced in a panic. I sat up in bed and flipped on the light but saw nothing out of the ordinary.

I lay back down and drifted off again but the strange presence returned. But this time pleasurable sensations radiated through my body as someone or something gently caressed my left breast. I felt like I was floating as my body responded to the loving touch. Lost in the sensation, I suddenly felt the shock of cold steel circle my wrists and clamp shut as my arms were tugged roughly over my head. Strong hands held me down, pinning me to the bed and rendering me helpless. Frantically, I struggled, trying to lift my head and look around the room to see who was there, but I couldn't see a thing. Even the slatted shadows created by the streetlight, were gone. The entire room was drenched in darkness. I trembled in fear.

"You know you like it this way," a woman's voice whispered. "I'll stop if you want me to, just say the word, but I don't think you want me to."

I didn't want it to stop. To my shame and embarrassment, I didn't want it to stop. The presence moved on top of me now, ravaging my body, kneading, pinching and squeezing my breasts to the point of tenderness. My insides throbbed and ached, wanting more, needing more. The sensation was exquisite and terrifying at the same time. What was going on? Did I inhale too much formaldehyde tonight? Was I dreaming or was this really happening?

Soft warm breath teased my swollen nipples followed by the warm wet feeling of them being engulfed in turn by an eager, soft mouth. I moaned out loud, unable to contain my ecstasy. My insides felt as if they were on fire as I squirmed on the bed, desperate for relief.

The warm mouth moved from my breasts down my belly. It lingered there for a short time, as if resting before it moved on, down my legs, deliberately bypassing the part of me that craved the most attention. I felt the hands on me again, caressing my calves, fingertips tickling the backs of my knees and then teasingly stroking my inner thighs, pushing my legs apart.

I shifted and squirmed, pleading with whomever or whatever was there, to please put me out of my misery. Wet heat overflowed onto my thighs as I writhed on the bed trying to get some relief from the searing need that was throbbing inside of me.

"You want me to touch you here?" the woman's voice came out of the darkness. Her soft breath fluttered across my swollen pussy. I moaned. The woman blew a continuous stream of air, now circling my furry mound, teasing my heightened senses by both promising and withholding pleasure.

The stranger's cool and impersonal tone broke the eerie silence again. "Lift your ass up and bring your beautiful pussy to me."

Immediately obeying the command, I arched my back, digging my heels into the mattress, straining my leg muscles as I lifted my butt off the bed, offering up my hot, wet sex.

Tongue met flesh and my throbbing clitoris nearly exploded with ecstasy upon contact. One finger, then two and then three slipped inside of me as wave after wave of orgasm ripped through my body until I collapsed on the bed in a damp heap in the tangled sheets.

My breath still came in gulps and my pounding heart hadn't yet recovered when I opened my eyes and discovered I could see again. Although the room was dim, I caught a glimpse of the women's symbol tattoo and suddenly the identity of my mysterious lover was shockingly clear. I bolted upright, my arms now free of their bindings, and switched on the bedside light to get a better look, but by the time the light flicked on, she was gone.

The Baby Ben alarm clock clanging away on my nightstand

startled me out of a deep dreamless sleep. I sat up and stretched. My memory of the dream was dull and faded. My arms and legs ached as if I was doing isometric exercises all night in my sleep. I never remember having a wet dream that vivid ever in all my thirty-six years. I stretched my hands out in front of me and noticed two circular bruises around each wrist; the kind of bruises that are usually created by handcuffs.

*What the . . .* I thought as I stood up on wobbly legs, rubbing my sore wrists. I felt like I was rode hard and put away wet as I hobbled into the bathroom to get cleaned up. Last night couldn't have been real, I thought as I showered and dressed for another full day at the morgue.

Jenny's car was already in the parking lot when I pulled in at nine-thirty. I parked next to her and noticed that she looked lost in thought still sitting behind the wheel of her car. I got out of my car and tapped on her window.

"Hey, you okay in there?"

Jenny jumped.

"Jenny, are you okay?"

She rolled down her window. "I don't know," she said.

"What's the matter? Did something happen? Did someone try and hurt you?"

Jenny shook her head. "No," she said looking up at me. "I had this really weird dream last night. It felt so real. That woman—you know, the Jane Doe from last night—she was in the dream and she was doing some incredible things to me . . . It felt so real . . . . I woke up in such a state . . . I felt like . . ."

"Like you'd been fucked all night long?" I interrupted.

Jenny's eyes went wide. "Yes . . . yes . . . it was unbelievable. It was like someone was there, in my room, but when I turned on the light, there was no one there."

"That's weird. I had the same dream." I was ashamed to tell her the sordid details. "Must have been all that sex talk last night. Maybe somehow it got caught in our subconscious and when we went to sleep, it caused us to dream like that."

We both laughed, feeling the absurdity of even the possibility of any of this being real.

"I guess you're right," Jenny said, sounding a little disappointed.

I opened her car door for her and we walked inside the morgue. Dr. Epstein hadn't arrived yet, so Jenny and I headed to autopsy room two to set up for Jane Doe's autopsy. After arranging all the steel instruments and cutting implements, Jenny pushed the gurney with the squeaky wheel over to the cooler as I unlocked the door and lifted the latch on the compartment where Jane Doe rested.

Jenny and I stood dumbfounded as we stared into the dank, vacant compartment. I knew this would entail a lot of paperwork and possibly cost me my job.

Jane Doe was gone.

Jenny remained leaning on the gurney when I saw her wrists. There, like mine were purple bruises circling each of them.

"Jenny . . ." I said, slowly rolling up my cuffs.

"Oh my God," Jenny said, seeing the purple bruises on my wrists that exactly matched those on hers.

# States of Grace

Joy Parks

*There was the time we kissed our way up the stairs, your lips never leaving my mouth for a moment. How kneeling on the floor beside the bed, you undressed me like a present, how you took me, your mouth so firm on my wetness, how quietly we made love, with no words, just sighs and cries of pleasure, and how it was different, deeper and sweeter than ever before. And how, after falling asleep in the gray afternoon, our bodies tangled in the sheets, I woke warm, your hand possessing me, stirring me again, fresh want of you, desire trembling in my gut, pinching my skin with light. I remember how you looked down at me, your face open with want, how you whispered "You're mine now." Your words unleashed so much want in me. I remember how I started to writhe on the sheets, to breathe so low, how I pulled you down to lie on top of me, wanting you to engulf me, take me with the sweet force of you, how I craved that possessiveness, and your hand inside me, reminding me that this is what we will be from now. That I am yours, for all your forevers and for mine, and nothing can change that. Nothing.*

The first thing I saw was the calla lilies.

I had planted them one spring, years ago, amazed that something so rare, something that cost a fortune at the florist shops back east, grew like weeds here. I was surprised that she had managed to keep them growing. That she had done that, made the effort. I had expected the house to look smaller, shabbier, like most places do after you've moved away, but it didn't. It didn't look any different than it might have if I'd only gone to the store and been back a half hour later. And there was something about that that made me feel sad.

It was late in the afternoon, probably about the same time of day that I'd first laid eyes on the house. Sunny, not much breeze at all, which was odd, being so close to the ocean. I shivered anyway. Just being here made me uneasy. I remembered Grace telling me that Oregon was the unofficial lesbian state. For me, it has been a state of despair, and not only because of what happened between us. From the very first night I spent here, listening to the low softness of Grace's whisper beside me, and the beat of the ocean just a few blocks away, there was a sense of loss I just couldn't shake. No matter how much I wanted to be with her. The feeling that I had made a terrible mistake, that something important was out of place, that I was out of place and time. And the longer I spent on the coast, the worse it became. I know you're supposed to feel free in all that wide-open space, but I felt trapped. Weighed down. There's something ominous and heavy in all that greenery, in how the mountains slide down against the coast, pushing you to the edge. Lots of people here are on the edge. A man killed his whole family in the backwoods the week I left. Shot his six children and stabbed his pregnant wife, said God told him to do it. Too many wild-eyed fanatics and born-agains and back-to-the-land types. Everything too extreme, too far to the edge. Plus the poor tourists and hikers who don't know any better, the tragic ones who get sucked up by the woods, swallowed by the ocean. It's the kind of place where you have to be careful.

*I shouldn't be here*, I thought. *I have trouble with careful*. It was too quiet. I missed the hiss of the subway beneath my feet and the safety of the crowd. I like my sky a little dirty and hanging like a curtain above the skyline. I like subtlety. I love the city and I always get a little crazy whenever I have to leave it. I missed Chris and my cell phone ringing every 20 minutes, and my office, and cabs, and my four cups of Starbucks. I missed who I had once been, and lost, then become again, and now protected so carefully. Here, this was the place where I got lost before. And I'd worked too hard to let it happen again. "Grace is gone," I whispered aloud. *And you shouldn't be here now.*

Grace. Gracie. Grace Ann. Professor Donnelly. G. A. Donnelly. GAD. GADzooks. I actually called her that once and still felt embarrassed about it. Love makes you stupid sometimes. This one had. Grace had been my first-year women's history professor, and I was desperately in love with her back then, but it was not fated to be, not for years anyway. I don't think she ever forgave me for not becoming a scholar, but instead listening to the beat of the other side of my brain and graduating as a marketing major. A capitalist. The enemy. But we did keep in touch, and it took a couple more decades, and my father's death for us to realize that school hadn't been our first connection. Turns out from the day I was born until I was three, when we moved away and she, then 18, left home for college, that we had lived about five blocks apart in Queens. We used to joke that, while a teenage Grace raced her bike past my house, infant me had recognized her and thrown my rattle, a sign that I would catch up later. It could have happened. Much more than mere coincidence, we both saw this as fate stringing us along, bringing us together at various junctures in our lives. And we liked it. We talked about past lives and how we might have been lovers, maybe married, and speculated on what horrible event might have made us lose each other. In our surest hours, we were each other's destiny, the one that had to be. One day she called me the love of her life. And I knew that I was hers, and she was mine, even if I wasn't really sure what that really meant. That kind of fate was comforting. And required no real decisions.

Finally, after thousands of dollars of phone calls, millions of e-mails and a couple of cross-country flights, I found myself jobless and homeless on purpose, racing toward Grace with only my books and my clothes. I was her second-to-last love affair, and far too young she'd finally concede, her last brave (my word), foolhardy (her word) defense against her own mortality. The gift she wouldn't let herself have. I was ready to love Grace forever, but it didn't last nearly that long. Somehow she managed to smother me at the same time as she pulled away, and pushed away, and ran from me. In the end, it was me who left. And there was no going back, no taking it back, no way to make anything right again. Aside from brief, polite notes at birthdays and holidays, there wasn't much between us but regret.

Then Grace died and left me her share of that.

When the shock went away, I felt nothing but anger at her for dying before we had a chance to make some sort of peace. And now I was sitting in the driveway of her house, our house for a while, there to oversee details that probably could have been dealt with by phone. I was there because that's what had been asked of me. The very last thing she could ask of me.

I wondered if my old key would still work. Or had Grace decided that 2,700 miles weren't enough of a boundary for her and changed the lock. Probably not. That would require phone calls and letting some man in the house, not worth the effort. I left my stuff in the car. It was a tourist town out of season; I could drive two blocks in any direction and get a hotel room.

My key fit smoothly and made an almost-familiar click. When I opened the door, the house smelled moldy and unused. There was that strong salt and ozone smell you notice only for the first day or so you're here, the one that sticks to your clothes after you leave. I remembered smelling it on my bathrobe, my heavier sweaters, especially my leather jacket, long after I had gone back east. At first it was a comfort, it smelled like Grace after she had gone out walking on the beach, her almost daily hunts for agate, her excuse to walk the dog and get away. For a time, I went with her, my city leather jacket standing out among a rainbow of Columbia raingear, my low-heeled suede boots sucking in salt and sand. I eventually got the coastal wardrobe thing worked out, but I still didn't fit in. I walked too fast; I didn't pay attention to the sneakers and swells, which made Grace scream at me for my own safety. And I couldn't understand what there was to see there every day. Grace stopped asking me to go, and on the rare occasion when she did, I turned her down, because I felt like she was doing it because she felt she had to, not because she wanted me with her. Charity. That had spoiled it. Even now, I didn't care if I ever saw the ocean again.

Grace had been dead a couple of months when I got the call from her lawyer asking me to come back to oversee the final details of the sale. I was just starting to get used to the idea that I would never have the chance to talk to her again, never get to make up for any of the things I had done, real or imagined, never tell her how well I had survived, and why there was no reason for her to feel bad or foolish or guilty anymore. The call couldn't have come at a worse time. I had been seeing someone for a while, someone who moved slow and didn't ask for more than I could give, and I had started thinking that I might even be ready to let myself feel. Commit. Really be with her, not just go out for dinner or movies, or to bed, but to be part of a couple again. Chris seemed to feel the same way but like a lot of women who fall in love with someone who has unfinished business, at times she felt like she was competing with a ghost. With Grace gone, that was actually true. She had understood my grief in the beginning, but its depth was greater than either of us had expected. She didn't understand why I had to do this, come here, and I couldn't explain it, and I seriously wondered what would happen with us when I got back. I promised to be gone only a week, but a lot can happen in one week.

*I love the warmth of your breath on my cheek, the softness of your flannel pajama top, the smoothness of your bare thigh against the back of my leg. You let your hand slide over my breast, my nipple firms against your fingers. I want you again and you know it, and I hear you sigh behind me, you kiss my neck. I roll back, filling the space you've created for me and you lie on your side, leaning your head on your arm. Your face is so close to mine, in the dim light, I search your face, your eyes. Without your glasses, your face is much younger, softer, smoother in the dark. When we make love, I forget about the years that divide us, what that means to you, all the things that have happened to you that I can never erase. But right now, at this moment, it doesn't matter. My nightgown is pushed up to my thighs, you push it up farther, I rise slightly so you pull it over my head, toss it on the end of the bed, which makes the cats snarl, jump down. You look down on me with such love that I want to cry out, throw my arms around you, beg you to let me stay with you, promise you that I won't make any demands that I know you can't handle, plead with you, like a child promising to be good. But I don't. Instead, I let desire roll over me, focus on the here and now, feel your fingers stroke the inside of my thigh. You kiss my shoulders, circle my nipple with your tongue, slide down my belly, further down, your tongue touches the lips of my cunt, you kiss me, one mouth to another. My legs open. My hands reach down, touch your cheeks, I can feel the muscles of your mouth, your tongue working, straining to please me and I open more, feeling the wetness of my cunt rushing out, such a gentle sweet ache, your mouth growing fiercer, tireless, your tongue now sliding inside me and out, my hips rolling with the same rhythm, in time with you, perfectly following you like I do when we dance in the kitchen, in the grocery store to the Muzak. Perfect, nothing has ever felt as perfect as this, you, your mouth hungry on me in the dark.*

The house was almost empty. Between the One Before Me and the One After Me, who both live within an hour's drive, just about everything decent has been carted off. Everything but a box of the things I had left behind, a garlic roaster, a high-tech measuring cup I'd bought Gracie as a gift, a chenille couch throw in a magnificent shade of lavender. A rainbow kite. Beautiful and unique and comforting things, but nothing essential. Nice to have, but not necessary. A lot like how Grace treated me.

The sun had come out stronger, which made the prospect of going up to the second-floor bedroom a little easier. The bedroom. Our bedroom. I crawled up the stairs slowly, trying to numb myself. Bed. Nightstands. The ruffled blue striped curtains that Grace had made on her own. I grinned to think they'd lasted that long. The bed was stripped down. That was that. I couldn't sleep here. No bedding. I turned to the closet. Most of Grace's things had been taken, but on the top shelf there was the quilt she had bought from a roadside stand, the Guilt Quilt I had called it, the one she refused to let me help pay for since it was already decided I would leave. The one she wouldn't let me help her put on the bed. I reached up to touch it and it fell to the floor. I bent down and saw something under the bed, under the side that Grace had favored. I dropped down and crawled across the room to fish it out. It was Ditto Bear. Finally, I felt the tears well up enough to fall. Ditto Bear, the rainbow stuffed bear I'd bought her when I couldn't tell her I loved her, so I said "Ditto" whenever she said it to me. I had bought her the bear and called it Ditto when I was still back east. And she had clung to it until I got here.

The One After Me must have missed it. And I was touched and rather surprised that Grace had kept it by her bed. I lay down on the bare mattress and pulled the quilt over me. It was oddly warm and comforting. I felt exhausted all of a sudden, the flight and the drive and the shock of being here hitting me all at once. The loss was settling in, not just Grace's death, but how I had lost her before when I was in school, and before that, as a child. Finding her and losing her over and over, and now there was no way to say good-bye anymore. The bare pillow smelled like salt and soap and I snuggled into it, turning my back to shut out the sun, and felt myself falling and spinning down into something dark and warm.

*Your eyes follow my fingers as they slowly caress my own breast. Your breathing grows louder as you watch my fingers stroking my belly and breasts, gently squeezing my nipples the way I want you to. You lie propped up on the bed, fully dressed. We've been to a party and you wore a tie, and now it's as undone as you are, whether you show it or not. I take your tie and pull it slowly between my legs. Now every time you wear it, you'll want to fuck me, just like you do now. Your eyes glass over as I slide down your legs, then straddle your ankles, too far for you to touch but close enough for you to see the shimmer of wetness on my legs. I touch myself, shiver, open my body to you . . . you're waiting, waiting until I'm too far gone, waiting until you know I can't take it a second longer. Then you'll be inside me, your need buried within the fabric of your pants and under-wear but undeniable and seeking contact with me.*

It was the smell of the coffee that woke me. My arms and legs felt like jelly and it took time to even get the strength together to stretch myself awake. It was late, I couldn't tell exactly how late because it was gray and rainy out, but I figured at least ten (one in the afternoon my time). I realized I had been asleep nearly sixteen hours and on an empty stomach. No wonder I thought I smelled coffee.

Grace's white terry robe was still in the closet, so I grabbed it. I must have fallen asleep in my clothes, but at some point in the night, had the presence of mind—or sense of discomfort—to take everything off so now I was cold.

I definitely smelled coffee. I tied the robe and started down the stairs.

"Abby?"

I couldn't move or make a sound.

"Abby . . . honey?"

More disbelief than fear, I think, but still, nothing would come.

"Abby? Is that you, Babycakes?"

That was Grace. No one else would dare call me Babycakes.

I rounded the sharp turn off the stairs that led into the kitchen. There she was, wearing her dark denim shirt, the one that made her eyes an even warmer, deeper blue, sitting on her stool against the kitchen cupboard, reading the paper and looking proud as hell that she'd managed to make me coffee. Lusting over the scent years after she gave up drinking it. Just as she'd done dozens of mornings when she let me sleep in.

Realizing you are in the presence of a spirit isn't at all as you would expect. It's not like in the movies where the poor victim sees an airy transparent specter, screams and takes off running. I wasn't frightened. In fact, I felt safer than I had in a long time, and something told me I had nothing to worry about. What I felt was more like confusion and, for some reason, I didn't want to look directly at her, so I looked around the room. Every bit of furniture, every piled book, every photograph and fridge magnet that was there when I lived with Grace was exactly where it should have been.

"Gracie . . . I . . . but you . . . how can this be?" Like I said. Confused.

"I've missed you, Abby. Haven't you missed me?" And she blew me a kiss.

Yep, that was Grace all right, in one of her cupcake moods, just like old times when she'd have to kiss me or squeeze my cheeks or some part of me every time she walked through the room I was in. And then she smiled, and it was one of her "love you" smiles, the kind that made you feel like the sun was coursing through you, you had gotten an A on your paper, you had won a lottery. It was that smile, that tone of voice that made me throw off a perfectly good life and come crashing into hers.

There was so much I wanted to say to her, but I was sobbing too hard to even spit out a whole sentence. But it didn't matter. I had a feeling she could understand.

She was warm, even warmer than she'd been in life because she'd had a problem with her circulation. For a moment, it flashed into my mind how I used to take her chilled hands and, sucking back my own shivers, hold them between my thighs to warm them. While at the same time, let her know that merely her presence has the power to make me wet with wanting her. A woman nearly twenty years older than me with cold hands and gray hair and the sexiest voice and most brilliant mind and greatest stories I'd ever heard. A flush of heat passed through me. And while I knew this, this moment, Grace, being in her arms, it was impossible . . . it sure felt real. Real enough for me.

"Let's go upstairs," she whispered. And she held my hand and led me up the staircase and I followed her, oddly at peace, like I had followed her up to our room so many times before.

*Your hand is between my legs, spreading my lips open. One finger enters me and I rise up to meet it, then another follows it, and another, you fill me up, you're breathing hard now, faster, you whisper my name again and again, the words bubble up wet, your own hips are moving, I know what this is doing to you, how fucking me is enough to make you come without me touching you, we've done that lots of times before. You get lost in me, forget yourself, forget that I am going, that there's only so many nights we'll get the chance to do this, you forget you don't want this, don't want me, you call me baby, whisper for me to come, press your cunt against my naked moving thigh to ease your need of me. And I come, and it's glorious and I scream your name and cry out loud, hold you to me, rocking hard against the solid strength of your hand. Then you hold me, wrap me up in the warmth of the sheets and your arms, and you fuss with the sheets while the aftershocks roll through me.*

The rain woke me up the next morning. The curtains were closed and I couldn't see out the window, but I could hear it hitting the ground with the kind of force you don't usually hear back east. Grace was gone, but there was a dent in the bed beside me and two silvery gray hairs on the pillowcase. I touched them with my finger. A souvenir. The kind of thing you come across all the time when you live with someone, a few strands of hair, the sound of their breathing at night just before you fall asleep, their scent on the sheets or on the phone receiver. The kind of things you don't pay attention to until it's too late and it's all gone away. This time, I was going to touch, to smell, to listen, I was going to drench myself in all those little things that nearly did me in, this time I was going to soak up Gracie, drink her in like the rain outside. There should not have been a "this time," I knew that and I had to follow it through to whatever the end might be.

I didn't hear her downstairs and I wondered where she was. Was she coming back? I hadn't really paid much attention to her schedule when she was alive, it would be strange to be so possessive of her now. I started nodding off again until I realized that I had to call Chris. I told her I would call her as soon as I was settled. And say what? That I'd slept with my former lover, who happened to be dead but came back because she loved me. To not make any plans for me, cause I might stay in Oregon.

No, I couldn't tell her any of that. New York was three hours ahead, and I knew she'd be at work, so I called her at home and left a message, saying simply that I'd made it to the house and was safe and would call again soon. Then I grabbed the real estate broker's card from my bag, realizing I had to get in touch, but I must have fallen asleep before I called, because when I woke, Grace was touching the card in my hand.

"You're not going to sell the house now, are you sweetie?" It was still raining hard, too hard to go out. The light was different and I couldn't tell if it was day or night. I wondered how long I'd been asleep. From the aroma wafting in from downstairs, Grace made me more coffee. I had actually forgotten about the house until she brought it up. I hadn't even had time to talk to the broker yet.

"If you sell, dear, where are you going to live?"

I didn't know how to tell her that I hadn't really had time to think about that. Or that I hadn't planned on staying in Oregon. I realized I didn't even know what day it was, and I was half expecting the rental car company to show up and get the car. I hadn't planned on any of this. And it was like she could read my mind.

"Abby, don't do it. This is my house. My home. And it was your home too. I asked that you be the one to deal with the sale because I figured you wouldn't be able to go through with it. That you wouldn't be able to sell it, that you'd want to keep it, stay on. That you'd come home and we could be together. You're not going to disappoint me this time, are you? Just like before?"

So I had disappointed her. I remembered it differently. But as usual, what counted was how she interpreted the event. I looked at Grace, trying to figure out what to do, how to deal with this. She wasn't easy to live with before, but now I was totally out of my league. I noticed she looked younger, more like I remembered her from school. And I had forgotten how she could cut you down with just a couple of words. It was her damn house. She could do with it what she wanted. I got up and went downstairs intending on going to the kitchen, but on the way, I stopped to lie down on the couch. I felt dizzy all of a sudden, weary, and knew I didn't have the strength to fight her about the house. I didn't have the strength to fight her at all. I closed my eyes and soon felt her arms wrap around me . . .

*I lie beneath you and raise my hips, meet your thrusts, stroke your hair while you slide your tongue inside my cunt, feel you taste my body as if you're starving. I whisper the things you most want to hear, cry out for you to fuck me, make your want of me so strong it will translate into the words neither of us can resist speaking. I wrap my legs around your hips, call you Daddy, and cry out how well you fuck me with your hands and your hips and your mouth, give you all the words you couldn't speak for so long, and everything that means. I hear you moan you're mine, mine,*

*mine, all mine, this fierce and gentle power that you've hidden finding its
voice between my legs.*

It's still raining and I can't remember the last time I ate. I call
Chris and leave another excuse as a message. I don't know what to
say to her. I've lost track of the number of days I've been here. I
finally got a look at myself in the bathroom mirror this morning
and what I saw scared the crap out of me. I looked terrible, pale
and my hair is going gray. Not just the few strands I had in front
but all of it. I haven't seen Grace in a while, but I can feel her presence and I don't know what to do. I want to go home, but I'm not
sure where that is anymore. And I don't have enough energy to get
off the couch. I just need to close my eyes for a little while.

When I open my eyes, Grace is there. It's Grace but not my
Grace. She's much younger now, younger than she was before I
met her, the young and wild and terribly scared version of her I
know from her photo album. And the stories she's told me. There's
a roughness to her, a sharpness age must have smoothed down. I
used to joke that I had wanted to know this Grace, but seeing her
like this makes me feel uneasy.

"Hey there, sweet stuff." She smiles. Runs her hands down my
body. Crawls on top of me and presses her thigh hard between my
legs. Kisses me. Sneers. "You still want to sell the house. You want
to make all this go away. It's all up to you?"

I push her back and try to sit up. I need some air. I need to say
something. Do something. I can't go on like this. Finally, I take her
hand. "Grace, you have to let me sell the house. I don't want to be
here. I couldn't live here with you . . . and now there'd be no way I
could stay. I have to move on. I have to let you go. It's nearly killed
me, but I do. I know that now. And you have to let me go too."

She laughs. "You're kidding me. All you went through. How
bad you wanted me back. How badly you wanted to come back. So
badly you couldn't even have a real life after me. Now you got me.
All you got to do is stay here and play nice and nothing's ever
going to change. We got what we always wanted, sweetie. You get
to be mine forever."

I slumped down onto the floor just to get away from her for a moment. I was so tired. I'd been tired since I got here. I thought it might have been all the time we spent in bed, but it was more than that. It was like something was pulling the life right out of me. And the truth is, part of me did want to stay. But this time I knew I'd be turning my back on my life again. "No, Grace," I said clearly and with more force than I thought I had in me. "I don't want this. Not now. I have to go. And so do you."

Then everything went dark again . . .

*We're in bed and you sigh and pull me closer. You tell me I'm the only woman you've been able to sleep with . . . really sleep with, fall asleep beside, feel safe with . . . in so long. Maybe ever. You say it's more intimate than having sex. Sleeping. You close your eyes and lay down your walls and guises, you let yourself be vulnerable. Your body can't lie in sleep, can't keep its secrets. You tell me this and then you're quiet for a long time. I hear your breathing change, slow down and fade.*

*Good night, Gracie. Sleep well.*

When I woke, the rain had stopped and the sun was up and high. I couldn't remember when I'd last seen the sun, it felt like weeks. Grace was gone, but I had expected that. I felt oddly relieved. Since I'd walked through the door, I'd almost lost myself over and over again and, this way, the temptation was gone. I had no idea how she had come back to me or made me come to her, all I knew was that I felt tired and weary and every bit as old and haggard as I looked in the mirror. And just a little foolish that I'd let her do it again. I lay there on the floor for a long time and stared at the ceiling and realized there was one thing I had to do. I had to get out of this house. And then, I had to talk to Chris. I didn't know how to tell her what had happened, and I certainly didn't expect her to understand. I just wanted to hear her voice and find out if she was still speaking to me. No more messages when I knew she'd be out. I'd call her at work this time.

Downstairs, the house was as bare as it was the day I'd put my key in the door. I had expected that. I picked up the phone, but there was no dial tone. I figured they must have finally shut it off. I didn't remember packing, but I could see my suitcases in the rental car outside. I could call Chris from the airport.

I floored it all the way to Portland and made it in less than three hours. Didn't even stop to go to the bathroom. The guy at Hertz didn't say anything when I showed up, so I just signed the credit card slip and figured I'd deal with the extra charges when the bill came. I couldn't remember what the original charges were going to be. In fact, aside from the time I'd spent with Grace, or Grace's ghost, or whatever, I didn't remember much about all the time I'd been there. In the shuttle to the airport, I tried to remember if I'd talked to anyone or even gone outside the house, but it was all a blank.

As soon as I got to the airport, I looked for a phone. First, I needed to call Grace's lawyer and tell him I wouldn't be able to make it. Then I had to call Chris. I didn't know what to say to her, but I wanted to hear her voice. I didn't expect her to understand. I just missed her. I passed a mirrored column on the way to a bank of phones and took a quick look. I didn't look so bad in this light. Maybe I just felt better being out of the house.

Chris answered on the second ring. I burst into tears the minute I heard her voice and started apologizing for not calling her and leaving so many messages. She was silent. I figured I had totally blown it.But she sounded more confused than angry.

"I miss you too. But when did you leave the messages? I didn't get any."

Maybe I had called the wrong number. I knew I had called at least once a day. But then, I didn't know anything for sure. I told her I meant to call earlier and hoped I hadn't worried her. She started to laugh.

"Are you always this considerate when you're away from home?"

"What do you mean?" I tried to sound relaxed. Normal. I had been expecting to be hung up on, so anything else was a bonus.

"I'm glad you called and I miss you too. But I wasn't worried. After all, you've only been gone one night."

# About the Authors

**Lynn Ames** is the best-selling author of *The Price of Fame* and *The Cost of Commitment* and a contributing author to *Infinite Pleasures: An Anthology of Lesbian Erotica*. An award-winning broadcast journalist, Ms. Ames is a nationally recognized speaker and CEO of her own public relations firm.

**Crystal Barela:** After working in the fashion design industry in New York for the past eleven years, I have left the insanity. I am trying on small-town life in Southern California. I've found the perfect setting for spending some quality time with my laptop and thinking dirty. If you liked this story, get out your vibrators gals, because there is more to be published in 2005. E-mail me for details or any comments you want to share. Erotikryter@yahoo.com.

**Victoria A. Brownworth** is the author of eleven books, including the award-wnning *Too Queer: Essays from a Radical Life* and editor of fourteen, including the award-winning *Night Bites* and *Coming Out of Cancer: Writings from the Lesbian Cancer Epidemic*. She writes for many mainstream, feminist and queer

301

publications including the *Baltimore Sun, Curve* and *Harrington Literary Quarterly*. She teaches writing and film at the University of the Arts, the nation's largest college for the creative and performing arts, in Philadelphia, where she lives with too many cats.

**Rachel Kramer Bussel** (www.rachelkramerbussel.com) is Senior Editor at *Penthouse Variations*, a Contributing Editor at *Penthouse*, and writes the Lusty Lady column in *The Village Voice*. She is the editor of *Naughty Spanking Stories from A to Z*, co-editor of the Lambda Literary Award–nominated *Up All Night: Adventures in Lesbian Sex*, with several more dirty books on the way. Her writing has been published in more than 60 erotic anthologies, including *Best American Erotica 2004* and *Best Lesbian Erotica 2001, 2004* and *2005*, as well as publications such as *AVN, Bust, Curve, Diva, Girlfriends, Gothamist.com, On Our Backs, Oxygen.com, Penthouse, Punk Planet, Rockrgrl*, the *San Francisco Chronicle* and *Velvetpark*.

**Maria V. Ciletti** is a medical administrator who writes medical articles and gay/lesbian fiction. Fiction credits include short-story anthologies: *Summer the First Time, 1985*, Alyson Publications; *Unexpected Pleasures*, Alyson Publications; and *The Things You Do for Love*, Alyson Publications. She lives in Niles, Ohio, with her partner, Rose.

**Amie M. Evans** is a white girl, confirmed femme-bottom who lives life like a spontaneously choreographed performance. She is a published literary erotica and creative nonfiction writer, experienced workshop provider, and a burlesque and high-femme drag performer. Her most recent published works have appeared in *Ultimate Lesbian Erotica 2005*; *I Do/I Don't: Queers on Marriage*; *The Best of On Our Backs 2*; *Back to Basics: A Butch/Femme Anthology*; and *Up All Night*. She also writes gaymale erotica under a pen name.

**Cynthia Glinick** was given an ultra-feminine name at birth without her mother ever realizing she was born a butch. Still, she likes the disconnect of being referred to, on a daily basis, as "sir" coupled with a decidedly un-butch-like name. This is Sir Cynthia's first published story but not the first ever written. She's been carting around boxes of lengthy epistles since graduating from a private girls' school in 1972 and is happy to see one of them make it to market. Her next story is about "that one" girl, at the private girls' school.

**Ariel Graham** writes speculative fiction and nonfiction articles under another name and is a graduate of Clarion Science Fiction and Fantasy Writers' Workshop. Ariel lives in Reno, Nevada, with her husband and more cats than is sensible. Her work can be found in *Sacred Exchange*, available through Amazon, in the erotic anthology *Monsters & Myths* from Torquere Press, and has appeared on Pink Flamingo.com.

**Patty G. Henderson** has been published since the early 1970s in magazines such as Paragon and Dale Donaldson's, Moonbroth. She is also the author of the Brenda Strange supernatural mystery novels. *The Burning of Her Sin* (Bella Books) was the first in the series, which is set in Tampa, Florida. *Tangled and Dark* (Bella Books) continues the Brenda Strange PI series, with a third, *The Missing Page*, due to follow soon in 2005 (Bella Books). *Blood Scent* (Justice House), an erotic vampire romance, was Henderson's first published book.

Patty has also sold short fiction to *Quantum Muse, New Camp Horror, The Murder Hole, T-Zero, Futures*, and nonfiction in *Mystery Reader's Journal*. She has a short story in the upcoming 2005 hardcover anthology *City Crime, Country Crimes* (Wildside), edited by Michael Bracken, and two short stories in another mystery anthology, *Short Attention Span Mysteries*.

Between writing novels and writing flash fiction, Patty still works full time at a photography studio. Patty G. Henderson is a Tampa native, born in Ybor City, and still lives in beautiful South Tampa.

**Peggy J. Herring** lives on seven acres of mesquite in south Texas with her cockatiel, hermit crabs and two wooden cats. When she isn't writing, Peggy enjoys fishing and traveling. She is the author of *Once More with Feeling, Love's Harvest, Hot Check, A Moment's Indiscretion, Those Who Wait, To Have and to Hold, Calm Before the Storm, The Comfort of Strangers, Beyond All Reason, Distant Thunder*, and *White Lace and Promises*. In addition, Peggy has contributed short stories to several Naiad Press anthologies, including *The First Time Ever, Dancing in the Dark, Lady Be Good, The Touch of Your Hand* and *The Very Thought of You*. Peggy's newest romance, titled *Midnight Rain*, will be released by Bella Books in the fall of 2005. She is currently working on something new and frantically searching for a title.

**Lynne Jamneck** is a writer/photographer from South Africa. Her fiction and nonfiction have appeared in various markets and anthologies in the United States, Great Britian, Canada and South Africa. Her first mystery, *Down the Rabbit Hole* (A Samantha Skellar Mystery) is available from Bella Books. She is the creator and Editor of *Simulacrum: The Magazine of Speculative Transformation* (www.specficworld.com/simulacrum.html). She likes vodka over ice and antiheroes and has a deadly thing for vampires.

**Barbara Johnson** lives in a Maryland suburb with her life partner and four rescued cats. Having never quite gotten over her childhood fear of the boogeyman under the bed, she always sleeps with her feet under the covers. Naiad Press published her four novels, *Stonehurst, The Beach Affair, Bad Moon Rising*, and *Strangers in the Night*. Barbara's adaptation of Cinderella appeared in Bella Books' Lammy finalist *Once Upon a Dyke: New Exploits of Fairy Tale*

*Lesbians,* and her next novella is due out in 2005 in *Bell, Book and Dyke: New Exploits of Magical Lesbians.*

**Karin Kallmaker** is best known for more than a dozen lesbian romance novels, from *In Every Port* to the award-winning *Maybe Next Time.* She recently plunged into the world of erotica with *All the Wrong Places* and numerous short stories. In addition, she has a half-dozen science fiction, fantasy and supernatural lesbian novels (*Seeds of Fire, Christabel,* etc.) under the pen name Laura Adams. Karin and her partner will celebrate their twenty-eighth anniversary in 2005, and are Mom and Moogie to two children. She is descended from Lady Godiva, a fact that pleases her and seems to surprise no one.

**Alison Laleche** was born in London of French descent in 1970. She publishes both poetry and fiction under a variety of pen names. Before becoming a writer, she worked as a circus juggler, a mortuary assistant and a pool hustler. She lives in England with her partner and their adopted daughter, Indigo.

**Heather Osborne** is a recent graduate of the University of Calgary. She is a member of the Imaginative Fiction Writers' Association. In 2003, she placed as an honorable mention in the Con-Version Short Story Contest, and her stories have been published in the *Calgary Herald* and the U of C *Gauntlet.*

**Joy Parks** writes articles, interviews, book reviews and recently short fiction, for many GLBT and mainstream publications. An award-winning advertising writer and strategist, Joy spends her days overseeing PR, communications and market development for a product and graphic design start-up in Ottawa, Canada. The scariest thing about her is her credit card balances.

**Radclyffe** writes love stories about women. Her romances include *Safe Harbor, Beyond the Breakwater, Innocent Hearts, Love's Melody Lost, Love's Tender Warriors, Tomorrow's Promise, Passion's Bright Fury, Love's Masquerade, shadowland, Fated Love*, and *Distant Shores, Silent Thunder* (2005); the Honor Series: *Above All, Honor, Honor Bound, Love & Honor, Honor Guards, Honor Reclaimed* (2005) and the Justice Series: *Shield of Justice, A Matter of Trust* (prequel), *In Pursuit of Justice, Justice in the Shadows*, and *Justice Served* (2005) from Bold Strokes Books. She also has selections in the Erotic Interludes collections: *Change of Pace* and *Stolen Moments* (2005). E-mail: radclyffe@radfic.com Web site: www.radfic.com

**Nancy Sanra** and her partner, Sherry, live in the beautiful Pioneer Valley at the foot of the Berkshire Mountains in western Massachusetts. Besides creating four Tally McGinnis mysteries, Nancy also writes children's books for kids with special needs and is in the process of completing a mystery series for young adults. A graduate of the University of California, Nancy is a retired regional sales director and now writes full time. Both Nancy and Sherry enjoy hiking with their wonderful dog, Snickers, and quiet evenings shared with good friends.

Nancy welcomes e-mail at NSanra@aol.com and reminds you to always follow your dreams.

**Therese Szymanski:** Oft accused of being a vampire due to her late-night habits and inclination toward wearing black, Reese uses copywriting and designing to keep herself apartmented. An award-winning playwright, she's the Lammy finalist author of the Brett Higgins Motor City Thrillers, editor of *Back to Basics*, part of the team that created *Once Upon a Dyke* and the upcoming *Bell, Book and Dyke*, and contributor to more than a dozen other anthologies. She enjoys backpacking, all forms of skiing and anything else she can hurt herself doing. Somehow, through the years and sometimes without her consent, she's started collecting swords, Zippos and bears.

You can e-mail Reese at tsszymanski@worldnet.att.net—preferably only when not trying to get her to buy a timeshare, join your religion, or spend money on weird new sexual devices or pyramid schemes.

**Jane Vollbrecht** is a recent newcomer to the Bella Books family. Her first novel, *Picture Perfect*, was published in March 2005. In September 2004, Jane retired from Federal Civil Service after thirty-one years with the same agency. She is now pursuing a new career as an author. She and her partner live in the foothills of the north Georgia mountains.

**Vicky "Dylan" Wagstaff**: A new gal to the world of writing, I only picked it up over the last eighteen months or so to stretch the limits of my dirty little mind. I live in England on my own, in a semi-reclusive state due to far too many hours spent attempting to hone any skill at writing I may have, by littering the world of fan fiction with my paltry attempts at erotica. This is my first published story, but hopefully not my last as I have plans for more, and am some way into my first book attempt.

**Julia Watts** is a fan of all things spooky, but "A Visitation" was her first attempt at actually writing a ghost story. Her other, more realistic works of fiction include the novels *Wildwood Flowers*, *Piece of My Heart*, and *Phases of the Moon*, all of which are available from Bella. Her young adult novel, *Finding H.F.* (Alyson, 2002) won the Lambda Literary Award in the Children's/Young Adult category. Julia is also a contributor to and co-editor (with Karin Kallmaker) of the Bella After Dark series of novella anthologies, which includes the fairy-tale-themed *Once Upon a Dyke* and the witch-themed *Bell, Book and Dyke*. Between the ghosts, fairy tales and witches featured in her recent work, Julia is clearly enjoying a second childhood.

**Kristina Wright's** fiction has appeared in over a dozen anthologies, including *Best Women's Erotica 2000*, *Best Lesbian Erotica* (2002, 2004 and 2005) and *Ultimate Lesbian Erotica 2005*. Kristina lives in Virginia and is currently pursuing a graduate degree in Humanities. She can be reached through her Web site www.kristinawright.com.

**Laura DeHart Young** was born in a small town in New Jersey—so small and obscure that she now lies and says she is a native Pennsylvanian (where she did live for more than twenty years). No wonder she moved to the metro Atlanta area of almost four million people seven years ago to enjoy a vastly different living experience. Now she yearns for vacations in the north Georgia mountains where there is no traffic and far fewer people.

When not writing and working for a technology company headquartered north of Atlanta, Laura collects famous autographs (Lucille Ball, Paul Newman, Elizabeth Taylor and Sally Field, just to name a very few) and dabbles in digital photography. She also loves travel, attending LPGA golf tournaments, reading, spending time with family, gardening, staring at her freshwater aquarium, and relaxing in the beautiful sunroom of her new home.

Laura's constant companion for thirteen years was her beloved pug, Dudley. Sadly, he passed away in 2004. Since that time, three pug ladies (Abby, Belle and Sherri) now live with Laura. Dudley would have loved them. And, oh yeah, Laura's partner of eight years, Jerri, also grabs a share of the spotlight whenever she can.